CLUB REVELATION

✡ ✝ CLUB ✝ ✡
ℛEVELATION

A Novel by Allan Appel

COFFEE HOUSE PRESS
MINNEAPOLIS

COFFEE HOUSE PRESS is an independent nonprofit literary publisher supported in part by a grant provided by the Minnesota State Arts Board, through an appropriation by the Minnesota State Legislature, and in part by a grant from the National Endowment for the Arts. Significant support for this project came from an anonymous donor. Support has also been provided by Athwin Foundation; Bush Foundation; Elmer L. & Eleanor J. Andersen Foundation; Honeywell Foundation; James R. Thorpe Foundation; Lila Wallace-Reader's Digest Fund; McKnight Foundation; Patrick and Aimee Butler Family Foundation; Pentair, Inc.; The St. Paul Companies Foundation, Inc.; the law firm of Schwegman, Lundberg, Woessner & Kluth, P.A.; Star Tribune Foundation; Target Foundation; West Group; and many individual donors. To you and our many readers across the country, we send our thanks for your continuing support.

COFFEE HOUSE PRESS books are available to the trade through our primary distributor, Consortium Book Sales & Distribution, 1045 Westgate Drive, Saint Paul, MN 55114. For personal orders, catalogs, or other information, write to: Coffee House Press, 27 North Fourth Street, Suite 400, Minneapolis, MN 55401.

LIBRARY OF CONGRESS CIP INFORMATION

Appel, Allan.
   Club Revelation : a novel / by Allan Appel.
   p. cm.
   ISBN 1-56689-118-3 (alk. paper)
   1. Jews—New York (State)—New York—Fiction. 2. Upper West Side (New York, N.Y.)—Fiction. 3. Brownstone buildings—Fiction. 4. Interfaith marriage—Fiction. 5. Evangelists—Fiction. 6. Restaurants—Fiction. 7. Christians—Fiction. I. Title.
  PS3551.P55 C58 2001
  813'.54--DC21
                               2001032483

10 9 8 7 6 5 4 3 2 1

I am grateful to the following people for their help, good cheer, and their very existence during the writing of this book: Janet Abramowicz, Joseph and Rosemary Appel, James Boorsch, Jean Boorsch, Stanley Cohen, Brian DeFiore, Dorothea Dietrich, Steve Fass, Chris Fischbach, Eileen Gillooly, J.Z. Grover, David Itchkawich, Marc Kaminsky, Allan and Cinda Kornblum, Michael Manekin, Leslie McNeil, Peter Minichiello, Lucy Oakley, Gerry and Anne Oppenheimer, Josh Perl, Belinda Plutz, Marly Rusoff, Nancy Shapiro, Layle Silbert, Peggy Sradnick, Nancy Stanhope, Elizabeth Vogler, Mary Louise Vogler, and Jo Ann Walthall. A deep bow of thankfulness goes to my wife Suzanne Boorsch and our children Sophia and Nathaniel.

I would like to salute Stuart Kramer and Dan Polin, who were founding members of the Christian Wives Club, an organization whose support has been instrumental in the writing of this book. I want to thank them for establishing the club and, even more, for disbanding it. Also particular thanks to Jane Mallison, Bill Zavatsky, Tom Sullivan, Nancy Elitzer, Cindylisa Muñiz, Margery Mandell, Keith Kachtick, Saul Isaacson, John Nichols, and my other inspiring colleagues and students at Trinity School.

I want to express my deepest gratitude to an indispensable editor and great presence, Sara Blackburn.

Had we but world enough, and time,
This coyness, lady, were no crime.
We would sit down, and think which way
To walk, and pass our long love's day.
Thou by the Indian Ganges' side
Should'st rubies find: I by the tide
Of Humber would complain. I would
Love you ten years before the Flood,
And you should, if you please, refuse
Till the conversion of the Jews . . .

—ANDREW MARVELL, FROM "TO HIS COY MISTRESS"

Let it not enter the mind that anything in the world's system
will cease to exist when the Messiah comes, or that any
novelty will be introduced into the scheme of the universe.
The world will go on as usual.

—MAIMONIDES

Don't worry. Relax.

Of course.

You're not relaxing.

You just can't see it.

Look, a yawn means simply that my body needs to take in more air, not that I am bored with you, Gerry. But if I have to yawn, I just do it. Jesus could be sitting right in front of me, honey, but if my blood is crying out for more oxygen, I just open up my mouth wide in front of the Lord too. He understands what a yawn means. It's not about you, Gerry. It's about the air I breathe.

Gerry Levine rolled down the window of the Toyota and inhaled deeply. The stream of air entered and expanded like a balloon at the base of his throat and then, he imagined, it changed into a tube and snaked down the narrow passages of the throat and lungs. The air was gasoline-tinged and chilly, but he let it blow on his face, and he was oddly comforted.

"Up with the window, please."

"Are you dozing, friend?"

"Wide awake," Gerry reassured Sam (back seat) and Michael (front seat). Michael, however, continued to be an unbeliever, and pulled his knees up in crash protection mode under his chin, with his frayed, malodorous sneakers pressing hard on the dented glove compartment door.

"Those two white lines, Gerry, are called *a lane,*" Michael said. "Traditionally, on our planet, the driver makes an effort to stay inside the lane."

"Well, whose planet are we on, then?" Gerry said, and with a flick of a glance over his shoulder, he floored the accelerator, weaved rapidly but skilfully through the crowded traffic, and was now coming fast on the cars ahead.

"Normal," said Michael, as much a whisper of reassurance to himself as it was a communication to Gerry, "just conduct yourself like the mature, normal human being that we know down deep you aspire one day to be."

But Gerry did not hear. *He understands what a yawn means.* Why had Marylee said that?

"Jezuz Christ, Gerry," Michael screeched as they drifted in front of a truck and its horn suddenly boomed like a six-teen-wheeled Titanic bearing down on them, "do you want to play tennis or end up in a baggy?"

It was a regular Tuesday night and Gerry Levine and his friends, Michael Klain and Sam Belkin (still dozing noisily, despite the honking, while one of his size-twelve-and-a-half shoes moved menacingly forward toward the gear shift) were bumping along the George Washington Bridge about four miles from the Caracas Health and Racquet Club in Caracas, New Jersey. Gerry continued to push his little ladybug of a Toyota to its mechanical limits, downshifting and lane-hopping around the huge trucks, even dashing diagonally to beat a motorcyclist. He was creating every driving challenge possible to distract himself, he realized, from these troubling thoughts about his wife, Marylee, because a new and still vague lament had entered their life together.

About a third of the way across the bridge, Gerry was about to bring it up with Sam and Michael, but he hesitated. He just didn't know well enough what was bothering him, although he was fairly certain now about one thing: it had begun just the other day, when Marylee met with the new renter of the restaurant space in their building. All Gerry really knew was that the renter was very young and very handsome, but perhaps that was enough.

It's too bad, Gerry thought as he veered around a blue and white delivery van, that a feeling is not a physical something like a tennis ball that you can see and strike. Or take on and off like the flesh-colored arm brace he had again forgotten to bring tonight. To pursue this, however, risked breaking the mood of mild male sports excitement of their Tuesday tennis nights together.

Tonight, like every Tuesday between Labor Day and Memorial Day, there was something simple and soothing, exciting yet almost inviolably ordinary about being in Gerry's rusting 1994 Toyota with its several mysterious squares of red light always blinking on the dashboard. Gerry and his friends, who had known each other nearly half their lives, joked sheepishly about the recent New Year's Eve—despite the oncoming millennium, they had all been asleep by twelve forty-five, having left Marylee, Judy, and Ellen on the roof of their building with kisses (between sexual and chaste) and a half bottle of champagne unconsumed.

Tonight, however, the men were sufficiently revived to resume their routine: to drive a little recklessly, to tell each other about fast cars they once had driven, and to assert with pride that they were about to enter the tennis purgatory between advanced beginner and intermediate at the Caracas Health and Racquet Club. In short, they did all they could to ignore the half-century mark rushing up toward them full of lights and warnings like the tollbooth that now loomed up ahead.

They left Manhattan and the great bridge's suspended lights behind them and slid in an instant into New Jersey, where Gerry took the twenty-mile-an-hour Caracas turnoff at forty. He downshifted hard and kept it at twenty-five to avoid the cop who usually waited in ambush behind the dazzling herds of reindeer that still grazed, illuminated, on Caracas's modest front lawns. Then in another eight minutes of banter about their jobs, sports, politics, and Christmas versus Hanukah, they turned into the club parking lot.

Here as the trunk popped open for them to get at their rumpled athletic bags and racquets, Gerry hesitated again over his worn sample books, a sheaf of overdue bills from his suppliers, a camera that he used to photograph each new installation, and a half gallon of antifreeze curled up beside the oily jumper cables. How, he wondered for an instant, can a man spend so many long years, decades now, buying and selling floor coverings? Yet he still liked the sound of these words that seemed to be always on his lips—linoleums and congoleums—all the *eum*s that reminded him of a long-ago Latin class in high school in which he had excelled and which had given him a fleeting sense of mastery. This thought rose quickly out of Gerry but expired in the brisk air of the parking lot, along with other thoughts associated with the implements and emblems of workaday concerns.

Yet tonight they lingered there longer than usual among the neon-lit Volvos, BMWs, and Subarus parked in their jaunty diagonal slots, as if the men did not want to relinquish the moment. Sam Belkin too was trying to prepare his mind for tennis by taming his preoccupation: finding financing for his most recent documentary project, a film on the economic and social plight of the world's tiniest nations. The obvious funding sources—these various impoverished atolls and archipelagoes themselves, with a total population smaller than that of a good doorman building—collectively didn't have a plugged nickel to help him make his $1 million production budget. And Sam knew this because he had taken every ambassador out to lunch, some more than once. Unless he could come up with $300,000 in the next few months, he was beginning to think of dropping the project altogether.

Sam stretched his tall frame upwards and stared at a glittering splash of stars unusually bright tonight in the sky over Caracas. An intuition with the power of joy and release filled him and for an instant he knew with irreducible certainty that, should there be life on other planets, the extraterrestrials too would not have the slightest interest in funding his documentaries. He sighed extravagantly, extracted his two black-holstered cell phones from his pockets, and settled them into the trunk of Gerry's Toyota like a gunfighter hanging up his firearms before entering a tamer precinct.

"Shutting the trunk, Klain," Sam said.

"Shut away," Michael answered.

As Gerry and Sam peered above the lights of the parking lot to argue about which bright light above the radio tower was Venus, Michael, a librarian by day and hobbyist philosopher by night (if anyone would listen), tossed his dog-eared copy of *Being and Nothingness* (which he had been fondling on his lap throughout the drive) into the Toyota's back seat. He confirmed that Gerry had his keys (they had been locked out once), and clicked the door shut.

Together, the three men entered the club and quickly surveyed the dimly lit space for its inhabitants: the slouching tennis players, waiting nervously on dark blue chairs for their court time, always reminded them of the cabin of an airplane at thirty thousand feet at around four A.M. Their eyes traveled to a TV mounted high on the opposite wall playing the night's big game and then to the stocky, illuminated soda machine below it. Gerry, Sam, and Michael now began their search for an available player who might make a fourth.

This pursuit was always part of the Tuesday night ritual and could be even more enjoyable than their game. It was animated by the unspoken agreement that a well-preserved sixty- or even seventy-year-old was preferable to a player their own age because the former usually played even more slowly than this fiftyish trio. In this manner, despite mounting evidence of volleys that they could no longer handle and serves that meandered over the net to land with all the force of a snowflake, Gerry, Sam, and Michael could often create a game where they sustained for two precious hours of play the illusion that they were keeping the rampaging diminishments of midlife at bay.

An unabashed hypochondriac, Michael in particular craved playing with older and sometimes retired doctors, these days in particular a frequently recruited white-haired cardiologist from Iran named Ganesh, who often haunted the bar and had a surprisingly powerful backhand. Tonight, however, there was no Ganesh; indeed no one at all appropriate could be found, so they trooped onto the court, piled jackets, bags, and water bottles in a heap by the net posts, and prepared to play their usual game of Canadian doubles.

While Gerry and Michael jogged twice around the perimeter of the court to warm up, Sam dropped down on the baseline to do fifteen vocal, grunting push-ups before they started their practice hits and serves in the still promising fluorescent air. Perhaps tonight, Gerry thought, everyone will play like the heavy-hitting team from the nearby college that periodically practiced at Caracas but which was mercifully absent this evening.

Then the game began. Gerry's windmill serve looked as if it just might be on tonight, Michael thought, as it whooshed through and landed just millimeters from the centerline for an unheard-of first ace. On the next points, however, Michael, the existential rabbit among them, zigged and zagged for all balls no matter how hopeless, like a Sisyphus in short white pants. He continually adjusted his glasses and his carefully arranged headbands, one red and one white, to find the perfect position where he could see clearly and also dam up his profuse sweating before it streamed into his eyes. Gerry was amused by the cascades of perspiration that Michael, a skinny man of 138 pounds, was able to produce. As usual, Michael said it was nerves. This would have been a good opening for Gerry to mention Marylee's remote behavior and the considerable time she had been spending with the new tenant, but he let the opportunity pass again, with some regret.

For once the sets began in earnest, there were no more opportunities; the intense, if mediocre, tennis was too serious to leave room for discussing their wives. Anyway, their marriages were all long-standing and secure—or at least tonight they still believed this was the case; a fairly secure and happy conjugal condition was what they had in common and therefore could commonly ignore. So they played the by turns energetic, by turns lugubrious tennis of fairly contented men who were old friends and whose easygoing competitiveness was enough to make the games interesting yet agreeable. They exchanged jokes at the net and mimicked each other's awkwardness at the service line. They shouted "Good get!" or "Beautiful placement!" Yet they also meant: How in God's name have we become such old farts that we compliment each other on *that?*

Let it be, Gerry was thinking. Keep your eye on the ball and let it be. But tonight he whiffed his forehand and double-faulted with amazing regularity, and the ball seemed to pass right through, as if the gut of his racquet were a gaping window. On the way home, Gerry was so demoralized that Michael drove—an unusual occurrence. After ten minutes of silence, when they arrived at the tollbooth, Sam leaned over to him in the back seat and said, "Gerry, nobody in the history of the Caracas Health and Racquet Club—among whom have been nonagenarians hitting prone from iron lungs—no one, my good friend, has ever played as poorly as you did tonight. What the hell is on your mind?"

Gerry opened his mouth to answer, his lips even formed the first syllable of his wife's name, but nothing came out.

This night—and on all of what they called their Caracas Nights—Marylee Jeffers, Judy Klain, and Ellen Belkin were generally content to let the State of New Jersey, its health clubs, Toyota mechanics, police officers, toll-takers, and elected officials, deal with their husbands.

While Gerry, Michael, and Sam played tennis, or played *at* tennis, as Ellen had put it when she handed Sam an apple and sent him down to Gerry's waiting car, the old brownstone, which the three couples had bought together fifteen years before, reverted to the women, who, after all, had put in the most work restoring it. The 1882 structure was on a quiet ailanthus-lined street six buildings in from Broadway in the heart of the Upper West Side. It had stairs that creaked on all five flights, thick red and black carpeting, dark polished wooden banisters, elaborately framed hallway mirrors, two daguerrotypes of a sail-strewn New York Harbor (Michael's find), and an agreeably bracing nineteenth-century mustiness that no amount of Judy's Janitor-in-a-Drum could remove.

Above the restaurant space that stood two steps below street level and in the shade of the ailanthus, each couple had their own apartment: Judy and Michael's stark Buddhist retreat (hers, not his) on the parlor floor above the restaurant; upstairs, Ellen's media control center: books by the thousands, in Dewey Decimal order, in custom-built white cases on six walls, with three video monitors (this, the mark of Sam) above the mantel; and on the fourth floor, Marylee and Gerry's place, the sparest, most modern and minimalist living area, done in a style that Marylee had dubbed Scandinavian-Jewish dance studio.

Somehow, however, despite Marylee's best efforts, their floor had recently begun to seem cold and uninviting to her. She did not know why she no longer liked the half dozen items of smooth, light, veneered wooden furniture, or the large and immensely heavy glass table in the dining room that had given Gerry a slight hernia the one time he had tried to move it, or the abstract wire mobile that hung down between ceiling fans. Even the shining parquet Gerry had put down himself had begun to seem tacky. At least she still loved her kitchen, with its ceiling wine-glass rack and the inexpressible feeling it always gave her that the best meal was yet to be cooked. However, Marylee's eye would then alight on the several oil paintings on Jewish themes mounted on otherwise serenely empty white walls in the living room. These especially were getting on her nerves tonight.

They included Moses stumbling down Mount Sinai carrying tablets that reminded her precisely of the shape and color of 500-milligram Advil (Marylee did have a bad headache); then there was Jacob struggling with the Lord as His angels ascended a sinuous ladder of roped light to Heaven above. This composition had always struck Marylee as having the look of a Biblical construction site accident. However, her favorite among what she called her poor Jewish paintings collection was a three-by-four-foot scene on the wall that opened into the kitchen. This painting depicted the brazen serpent emerging from the rod Aaron flung down before Pharaoh and Moses as they lobbied to let the Jewish people go. It used to remind Marylee of the stories of snakehandlers she had heard about in Virginia when she was a little girl. Now she could no longer stand to look at it.

Gerry and Marylee had received these pictures as gifts from the Belkins (Ellen had disassociated herself from the selection), who had bought them from a struggling street artist in Haifa, when Sam was on location there taping interviews with Holocaust survivors years ago. Because of their association with this fraught subject and because Sam actually liked them—and still did—Gerry and Marylee had let the pictures remain on their walls for, now, eight long years. This evening, however, on her way to meet Judy and Ellen, as Marylee paused in front of Aaron and Moses, she stuck the nail of her pinkie into an egregious glob of green paint that for the past three weeks she had found particularly ugly. When Marylee deftly flicked it off Pharaoh's headdress, she exhaled with relief out of all proportion to the gesture, and continued upstairs to the Museum.

The Museum—or more accurately, the three couples' Museum of the 1960s—was the common space on the fifth floor of the brownstone: fifteen hundred square feet of 1960s nostalgia crammed with yellowing copies of the *East Village Rat* and other underground newspapers, books, LPs of the Beatles, Stones, Donovan, and Dylan, a poster of Che Guevara, a rucksack overflowing with assorted berets military and otherwise, a canteen allegedly dropped by a soldier of the 101st Airborne defending the Pentagon against anti-Vietnam War demonstrators (Judy and Michael had been among them), a *New York Times* clipping of the memorial to Alison Krause and the other students killed at Kent State, beanbags, encrusted tubes of body paint used at Woodstock, and various other memorabilia precious beyond words, such as a fret allegedly preserved from one of Jimi Hendrix's self-shattered guitars. No one could part with any of this junk—and certainly not Sam's reel-to-reel Wollensack tape recorder, which still could play (if he could find the reel) Barry Goldwater's acceptance speech at the 1964 San Francisco Republican Convention. The Museum—Ellen had come up with the name—was the capstone of the building, uniting the couples' apartments and giving the place a secret and creaky charm, a kind of grown-ups' history playhouse.

The nostalgia that pervaded the building was often sad and powerful—a nostalgia both for the real past (their old suitcases, Birkenstocks, engineer boots, backpacks, and duffel bags were everywhere) and also a past that never was, because the first plan for the Museum had been to outfit it as a nursery. However, there were no toys or tricycles or now-dusty stacking rings in sight, since none of the couples, despite some strenuous efforts, had any children, nor, given Marylee, Judy, and Ellen's age, did it seem likely they ever would.

Up and down the common stairway of their building, eating an apple or transporting a glass of white wine by its long stem, the women visited each other on tennis Tuesdays, much as they had done when they had met in the dormitories at Barnard College thirty blocks north. In jeans, thick socks, sweatpants, and T-shirts, they dropped in on each other, sipped half a glass of tea, left, skipped back down or up to their apartments to do an errand, or, like tonight, returned to the Museum.

Judy, who had put on far too much weight since school, tonight substituted for her usual sweats a large dress, snugly pinned under the breasts and then sailing down to her ankles. Ellen had her usual slew of student essays to correct; a selection from the week's papers almost always accompanied her, like the president's nuclear codes, tucked into a tattered, sturdy brown folder that lived beneath her armpit.

When they settled into the Museum's circle of broken beanbags, the chaise lounge with only one arm, and the hassock that proclaimed, in graffitiesque letters, DICK NIXON / KICK ME, Marylee said she had an announcement to make about a potential new tenant for the restaurant space, which had been empty far too long. The candidate, she said, was about twenty-five, with a Southern accent that reminded Marylee of home. The financials he submitted presented some difficulties, she went on, because the young man did not appear able to undertake the monthly payments all on his own. "Yet somehow," she said with a reassuring smile she directed at both her friends like a lighthouse beacon, "I just know it will be all right."

"Anyone feel like a joint?" Ellen abruptly asked as she looked up from the papers on her lap. "Why is it that, after all these years, freshmen themes still make me want to get a little high?"

"Not during the business part of the meeting," said Marylee.

"Since when did we ever have a business part of our meetings?" Judy asked. "We just sit around, get high, and ramble until what needs to get attention gets it. Then we bitch a little about the guys, hug, and go to bed."

"Well, maybe things are different tonight," Marylee said.

After the debacle of Curry by Murray, the last restaurant tenant, and the space having been idle these last four months, Marylee urged them to be content with this new tenant, even though he did seem, well, a little irregular. The nearly $4,000 monthly rental was needed to cover the brownstone's mortgage, and they all could use the financial relief. She hoped Judy and Ellen would not ask too many questions and instead rely on her usual good business judgment.

They drifted around the Museum as they always did—the place was like their own in-house flea market—had more tea, although Marylee switched to wine, and Ellen eventually had her Woodstock-era antique joint of Mexican grass, which hung from her lips like a smoking relic; it was not really worth the anticipation; it never was any more. They eventually reconvened for business on one of the Upper West Side's few extant and miraculously still functioning waterbeds, not only still afloat but also fitted out with pillows on several of which was crocheted Ho Ho Ho Chi Minh, the Viet Cong Are Gonna Win, provenance unknown. Ellen put on at low volume Roy Orbison's greatest hits, they began to sing along, and then, thanks to the wine, the stale weed, the watery undulations, and the cozy warmth of the Museum, and who knew what else, the world suddenly seemed a more perfect place.

Although a desire to be silent about the new tenant once again enveloped her, Marylee also knew she should say *more*, a lot, in fact. Yet what was the harm in just thinking about him herself for a bit longer, what was the rush to puncture the amiable anesthesia of the moment?

"So, okay, what's the tenant like?" Ellen finally asked. "Really."

"Physically?"

"Sure, why don't you start with the internal organs!"

Marylee paused. "I couldn't quite say. He's sort of all over just plain nice, a very nice and helpful young man, like people used to be."

"A non-New Yorker?" Judy asked.

"Oh absolutely. Like I told you. Very far away. I actually think the South. The most important thing is that he appears to love us," Marylee added quickly, "and he wants to begin renovations immediately."

"Well, that's reassuring. Is the paperwork covered?"

"It will be."

"More wine?"

"What's his name?

"William Harp."

"You're kidding."

"Why would I kid?"

"Because it sounds like an alias, a pseudonym," Ellen said. "Serial killer."

"Must be," said Judy.

"Kills with wire. Piano and harp," said Ellen.

Marylee stood and ran her fingers through a large jar of vermilion clay beads on the floor beside the waterbed. She stared at the three-foot face of Eugene McCarthy still campaigning at her from his New Hampshire primary poster, 1968. She rearranged a shelf with a tangle of hopelessly knotted lanyards and a broken-down hookah and rhetorically demanded, "When are we going to throw all this stuff away?"

"Never," answered Ellen. "What kind of restaurant are we going to have, ML?"

"I really don't know. He's peculiar, but he puts a smile on my face. Happy meals, I guess."

"What's gotten into you?" Ellen said to her. "Gerry make love to you this morning before work?"

"Must be," she answered vacantly.

"Sex has made her crazy," said Judy. "And not a bad way to go it is."

"Shall I proceed with the lease?" Marylee asked.

"I have no time for legal papers this week," said Ellen, "or to interview Harp. Whoever he is, we trust you completely."

"I don't know about completely," said Judy. "But you obviously have a good feeling for the guy. He's not a fly-by-night, is he?"

Marylee shook her head.

"He's not going to do something dumb like nine hundred varieties of bagels that will die instantly?"

Marylee assured Judy that though he was young, he did seem to know the business and to have lots of energy.

"Well, what is it?"

"What is what?"

"There is something on the tip of your tongue," Judy said to Marylee. "Spit it out. What is there about the place, or is it the kid?"

"Nothing, really," Marylee said, choosing her words carefully, "except that I think he is devout. Religious. Personally quite religious."

"That's excellent," said Ellen, "mainly because my impression is that such people usually have a sense of responsibility. They don't ever scoot out without paying the rent because they feel God is the ultimate landlord."

"I couldn't agree more," said Marylee, very much relieved. "I couldn't put it better myself. You know what else is a plus about him? He has a sense of humor. He told me he thinks God has a problem with the Upper West Side."

"That's because not even God can find an affordable studio here anymore. I say go right ahead. Rent to him. Just make sure he has insurance and that we are covered during the renovations and for three months on the deposit. Right?"

"Of course I'll make sure," she said.

Marylee finished her wine, set it on an old Muntz TV stool, and stepped through the ornate empty frame of a mirror that she remembered having brought up from Virginia twenty years ago. She unearthed a Cabbage Patch Kid from underneath a collection of doilies and handed it to Judy. She blew dust off a copy of *The Norton Anthology of English Literature,* one of whose black corners was turned up like a ski jump.

She handed the anthology to Ellen, who flipped through it and said, "Who remembers the difference between dramatic irony and verbal irony? Please write three succinct paragraphs. Who agrees that we really have got to jettison this shit?"

"I say throw it all out," said Marylee. "I'm attached to none of it."

"Since when?" asked Ellen. "You were always the biggest packrat of all."

"Not any more. Don't know. I just feel light all over."

Judy, who had begun meditating five years ago, said, "Even though the Buddha counsels in the Four Noble Truths on the dangers of clinging, I want to hold onto this stuff forever."

A brightly lit disk with the boy's handsome face emblazoned on it approached and then receded in Marylee's mind—she puzzled about what it reminded her of, and then realized: it was like a cameo in an old movie. She reached down into the box of books marked POLITICAL and lifted up a volume by Herbert Marcuse, then one by Frantz Fanon. The discontent among the classes was universal and inevitable. There was no arguing with that, although there was a time a few decades ago when she *would* have argued. She sighed and returned the well-thumbed paperbacks to the box.

"If we don't throw this stuff out, then someone," said Ellen, "has absolutely got to dust. Just because we love the Sixties doesn't mean we have to breathe them. Anyone know where the grass went?"

"Enough," said Judy, as her own eyes began to close. "I think we've all had enough."

Marylee looked up as Ellen withdrew an essay from her folder, shook it out noisily like the deli man popping open a bag, and began to correct it. She sensed Ellen was irritable tonight, and, sure enough, in an instant she looked up from the essay before her and said to Judy: "I really find it irritating when you drop off like that and start meditating right in front of us without any warning. It's very personal, and I frankly find it out of place, Judy. It's like flossing your teeth in public."

"I don't mind her doing it," said Marylee.

"You don't mind anything," Ellen snapped. "But, Judy, honestly, why do we always have to look at you meditating?

You never say, Excuse me! It's like looking at your stomach digesting, only it's your mind digesting itself."

"I like that," Judy said. Yet, eyes closed, she went on meditating, and Ellen went on correcting, and Marylee felt like a graduate student living in a dormitory that never was, with the world and every possibility and career still open before her.

"I don't care if you start cutting your nails, or flossing or whatever," Marylee said. "You're my friends, and I love you."

Ellen peered up skeptically over the tops of her glasses and scrutinized Marylee. "I think the winter and the end of the millennium and the end of the world have made you pale. Are you sure you are not coming down with a cold? La grippe? Postnasal drip?"

"No," said Marylee softly. Then she added, "Oh, maybe something." But she knew that this was false. She had never felt better in her life.

<hr>

JANUARY 4, 2000

New York City

Dear Daddy:

Things are going just fine for me here in the Big Apple. You've had a wonderful idea, planted in just the right place and at just the right time. Praise the Lord, I think it will be catching on fast. One day there will be franchises dotting every Jewish community in America. I think I already found some loving people—Marylee Jeffers and her husband Gerald Levine (she doesn't use his name) and

some of their friends—to help me to set
things up here. More on them later.

The most important thing for you to
know is that the Word of the Lord has made
a safe beachhead on the Upper West Side
and we are digging in. Jesus is alive and well
and in good hands with me, thanks to your
love, inspiration, and support. I want to
emphasize the support part, Daddy.

William put down his pen. He did not feel that he should go
on in quite this tone. He wanted to be encouraging without
lapsing into too much flattery. For one he would be found
out, and it also made him hate himself if he went on so. Yet it
was expected of him, and he continued.

How smart you were to suggest I arrive
here *after* the false hoopla of the new year,
the new century, the new millennium, the
new soda, new candy bar, new everything!
How right you were to teach me that only
fools believe the Lord keeps to an earthly calendar.

I told the barber who gave me my first
New York City haircut this morning that the
calculators and date-setters for the Endtimes
are destined to have it wrong. He agreed
with me. I told him that it wasn't a question
of a specific year, day, hour, and second. He
agreed once again. I told him our message
plain and simple—I was practicing on him,
of course—that it was a question of the
Conversion of the Jews and when they

would just stop deluding themselves. The barber agreed big-time.

Funny thing, William thought, but he was almost certain that the barber was Jewish. This, he decided, he would certainly not write to his father.

It was a good haircut, short around the ears and neat as the eighteenth green, so I gave him a big tip and blessed the fellow in the Lord's name. The weak may have given up on the Jews but not us. Not you and me.

Well, just as the world did not end, for a while there I didn't think the partying would either. For days the whole neighborhood has been pooped out and is just beginning to stir like a drunk slowly awakening. The streets still smell of alcohol, marijuana, and various other scents of dereliction. Everywhere you look you see furniture and appliances on the sidewalk, chairs and couches, tables, and right out the window from where I'm sitting, I see there is a microwave with a pile of books sitting inside as if just waiting to be warmed up. Shelves and strollers and forgotten lamps litter the sidewalks, as if the owners had fled in shame or confusion or been snatched away. Yesterday I dragged in a few pieces and I write you from one perfectly fine mahogany table I am proud to have rescued.

It all reminds me of Matthew 24, verses 40-42: *Then two will be in the field; one will be taken and one will be left. Two women will be*

grinding meal together; one will be taken and
one will be left. Keep awake, therefore, for you
do not know on what day your Lord is coming!

William sat down on the sill and parted the makeshift drape so he could see a few more squares of the sky through his gated window. This would be good material for the sermons, he told himself. And then in a whisper, he said, Come on in, sky. I'm waiting right here for you. Come on down here, you heaven of Jesus. William Harp awaits you. Then he sighed, but he did not allow himself to indulge in it, and returned quickly to his pad.

One day that will happen here, Daddy, thanks to the good work we are about to commence and make possible through the restaurant.

Within days, I found this place on the first floor of what they call here a brownstone building just in from the corner of Broadway, the busiest thoroughfare in the area. The address of the building across the street is Number 666! That's right. Well, actually it's 366 but with the paint chipped off the 3 looks exactly like a 6. If that isn't a sign, Daddy, I am a blind man; you know what it means better than anyone alive: that from this new establishment we will fight the great fight against the Devil and Antichrist and all things that cohabit at such a nefarious address.

The Lord works in mysterious ways because the restaurant space I have rented is in the ground floor of this five-story building, and who do you suppose lives on floors two, three, four, and five? Marylee Jeffers, Ellen Belkin, and Judy Klain, three fine Christian ladies. And here is the kicker, Daddy: All, I believe, are married to Jewish men—Gerald Levine, Sam Belkin, and Michael Klain, and the couples own the building together!

I am only beginning to learn what I need to know about them but here is what I've gathered so far: One of the ladies is from the South, that would be Marylee Jeffers with whom I am most friendly because she handles the renting. She hails from a small town at the other end of Virginia from us. When she heard my accent, she went on for a half hour about her glory days as a high school homecoming queen and Princess of the Peanut Festival. Marylee is a very handsome woman, with high cheekbones like Grandma's and a don't-tread-on-me look in her green eyes. The other two women are one large and one thin, the thin one being Ellen, a Catholic, I believe, from Arizona, who is always jogging, and the heavy-set woman— that would be Judy—happened to mention that her relatives came to Connecticut about 4,000 years ago with the Pilgrims. She was making a joke, of course, but she said there were definitely Mayflower descendants and good Episcopalian Colonial Dames in her heritage. Judy is now a Buddhist.

They are confused as all get-out, Daddy, just as you said they would be.

Just as I am too, sir, but I cannot tell you.

The three couples bought this building together in 1984—it was kind of a cooperative commune in which everybody argued about everything all the time, Marylee says, and they all lived together, arguing and fighting, and smoked marijuana, indulged in LSD, and briefly did, as adults, all the sinful 1960s things they used to do as students.

Praise the Lord, they have come through it all and remained great friends and all three are proper married couples now, although I haven't yet detected any sounds or signs of children. Perhaps the kids are grown up and gone on their way. Now the three couples still own the building together, as I say, including the restaurant on the first floor that I am writing you from; it is a fine space although much work needs to be done, especially in the kitchen. More on that later.

There is much I do not know about these people. Yet I am convinced they will help me and, as you always say, that the Lord had a purpose in directing me to rent this particular space. Marylee and Judy prepared all the papers and explained the terms and checked the references you gave me. At $3,900 a month, with free oil heat but not the electricity, it is a genuine New York City bargain.

They already have been very helpful giving me a full list of handymen, contractors, restaurant suppliers, and the like. They have done this kind of thing before, that's for sure, and they really want our restaurant to succeed. Because of what she does in her business, of the three women Marylee in particular knows about such things as product launches and buzz and she feels strongly our restaurant needs a real launch.

By the way, Daddy, do you know what "buzz" is when it does not pertain to bees? It is what happens when there is so much talk about a thing it becomes such a big deal, people will line up in the rain and, like turkeys in the barnyard, wait without umbrellas just to get in. Marylee says that in New York, which they call *the City,* just plain the City as if it's the one and only, buzz is everything.

Well, I took a long look at Marylee Jeffers Levine and said to her I thought Jesus was everything. She hesitated and then answered me with a question:

"Billy," she said, "do you think Jesus had buzz?"

"He had, he has, and he will have all the buzz. All the buzz in the world."

"In the beginning, God created the buzz," she said.

"Amen to that," I answered.

I'm writing all this in here just the way we spoke it to give you a flavor, Daddy, of these people. They speak very smart and very snappy with not very many pauses to let anything sink in, but they are God's children, as you have taught, like any others. I am His servant, the Lord is with me in every breath, and because of that I believe I am prevailing. I have secured Marylee's friendship, and the others will come along soon.

In fact, Marylee has already volunteered to help me with the buzz and to learn all the ropes, to get my permits and inspections from the City, which can be tricky. Marylee and the others, of course, need the rent money and want our restaurant especially to succeed because three previous restaurants in this very place all failed over the last five years.

"None of them had a single ounce of buzz," said Marylee. "You know why yours will work?" she asked me. I raised my eyes to heaven indicating you know Who when she said, "Yours will work because you have it."

"What?" I asked her.

"Buzz."

That's when she started calling me not William or Billy but Buzz. Do you like it, Daddy? Buzz Harp? I believe I will insist she stick with the name you gave me.

Then I told her my partner, meaning you, and I would like to know why the restaurants before ours failed, apart from deficiency of buzz. She wanted to know who my partner was. When I told her the ultimate partner was Jesus, she wanted to know if He was going to co-sign the lease and pay the rent because she thought I was a little young to have the necessary credit line myself. She was nice enough about it, but I had to tell her a little about you, Daddy, even though I know you told me to play that part down. We worked all the details out, as I said. Copies of the signed documents are enclosed, just as you asked.

Now, to get back to why the other places failed, I want to tell you what she said because, as Marylee remarked, it's instructive and the restaurant business in a place like the City, where there are so many establishments competing to satisfy all tastes and palates, well it is a low-margin affair allowing little room for error or miscalculation, especially in pricing. Those are her own businesslike words.

"The first failed restaurant in the space," she said, "was a health food establishment and it failed because it only attracted people who thought food was a form of medicine, not fun." The second place, called Curry by Murray, failed because no one believed curry could be cooked by someone named Murray. And the last, the Blue Snapper, an all-fish restaurant, failed because its pricing, she said, made no sense. In New York, she says, pricing is everything, along with the buzz.

An electrician is coming in just now, so will continue this later. With love to you and praise of the Lord on my lips, I am

Your Billy

Daddy:

A few days have gone by and here is some
more information to report. I am not the
only tenant in the building as I originally
thought. After smelling fumes like disinfec-
tant blowing up from the basement, I went
down two flights of steps and I discovered
there is a meditation teacher, a Buddhist
whose name is Nawang, living there. What
was floating up was not Lysol but sandalwood and pine incense. The Buddhist was
burning enough sticks of the stuff to purify
an airplane hangar—certainly enough for
the pit he inhabits down there in order to
prepare for his prayers, or what he calls his
meditations.

For some reason I lost my Christian
patience and gave him a piece of my mind
because the incense stunk so. The good news
is that a few days later Marylee introduced
me to him more formally and we now get
along okay because he's agreed to lighten up
on the bad-smelling sticks. He is a small
brown man about five foot two with smiling
eyes. He lives here and also has some mysterious business at the United Nations that no
one is sure about. (Don't worry, Daddy, I
know the Antichrist is likely to have a presence

at the UN. My guard is up, and nothing will catch me unawares.) The Buddhist holds classes in the basement, although Judy, the very large woman from the second floor, appears to be, so far as I have seen, his main and maybe even his only pupil.

Maybe, Billy thought, I should emphasize the Antichrist part a little more; it always made him feel strong and purposeful.

As you know, Buddhists sit on pillows and stare off into nowhere and they are no threat to us. I am now certain Nawang and yours truly are the only tenants of the Christian ladies and their Hebrew gentlemen. Well, just like you said, this is New York, Daddy. Antichrist's Grand Central Station.

Marylee Jeffers is in business, coming up with concepts and designs for something, what I don't yet know; maybe she works with her husband Gerald in his floor covering business. Apparently the Buddhist came to their attention on one of their business trips to the Philippines, and begged Marylee to take him to America. Marylee, so I heard Ellen describe her, is always collecting people. In their view I guess I am the newest addition!

Ellen is what they call an academic who teaches English and writing at the City College. She's fond of asking me questions. I think she is fond of her students, only she doesn't allow herself to show it much. That's how they seem to be here in New York: if

you like something, or someone, you're supposed to act the opposite, and, in any event,
to be nonchalant. Ellen's husband, Sam, has
rarely surfaced and I have barely had a
chance to talk to him.

The third of the women, Judy Klain,
dabbles in real estate when she is not spending time with the Buddhist. She likes to sell
clean empty spaces and she urges people to
have no furniture in them so that a room can
always look like the possibilities are endless.
I told her possibilities were endless in Jesus,
but she acted as if she didn't even hear me.
Day-to-day, Judy is the one who manages
the building and sees after things like the
exterminator (you must spray monthly in
the Big Apple, otherwise after the winter the
cockroaches begin to crawl out from the
nooks and crannies and are so big, she says,
they walk off with your shoe).

Judy's a real exaggerator and I wanted to
give you a taste of it. She's the one I will give
the rent check to, although the deposit you
sent (thank you so much) I gave to Marylee.

Now let me write this down again so I
can remember too: Their husbands are, in
order, Gerald, the floor covering man, who I
introduced to you already, that's Marylee's
husband; Sam, that's Ellen's man—he's the
one who makes film documentaries. Ellen
says Sam is always on: on shoots, on location, on conference calls, or online. I don't
see much of him but when I do, there's a lot

to see, as he is close to six and a half feet tall, I would say, with cell phones sticking out of his pockets. The Buddhist Judy's husband is Michael Klain, a librarian who has been trying to write his own book for years, but he won't tell even his closest friends the subject. It must be going very slow, which explains his tired squinty eyes, thick glasses, and his impatience—he is always rushing—as if he is wrestling with something inside all the time. I usually see him going in and out of the building with a pile of books under his arm and balanced at the bottom on his hip; it is a shaky construction that always seems ready to fall like a tilting roof.

Now, here's the brief report you asked about on the neighborhood. In a word, busy busy busy, people speaking a dozen languages I never heard before, and living mainly in apartments that go up like the Tower of Babel.

And of course lots and lots of Jews. There are so many synagogues in the neighborhood! Some are large like old bank buildings but with stained glass, and others so small they seem almost like private residences. Very old people appear to do most of the Jewish praying. Yesterday I heard some of these speaking their Jewish language, which sounded a lot like German with a big sigh in the middle of it.

So far as I can tell, my ladies and their husbands do not attend any of the synagogues or churches or other establishments.

In fact, so far as I can tell, religion doesn't mean much to Marylee or Ellen although Judy inclines toward the Buddhist in the Basement or at least meditates with him in the mornings. I get the sense that these women are at the very end of their child-bearing years and if there are no children around—that seems to be the case or I would have heard them or tripped over some toys—that may account for an atmosphere of, what shall I call it, something between sadness and resignation that sometimes seems to fill up the building.

Are we ever going to change that!

"There's more infertility under this roof than you can shake a stick at," Ellen said to me, a complete stranger. It was more than a little embarrassing. I think they talk that way precisely to see me blush! But that's okay if it's another way for the Lord to enter their hearts.

Whether the Jewish husbands are practicing Jews is still unknown to me, although I don't see the telltale signs of that either—they play rock and roll on their Sabbath (I particularly hear Roy Orbison coming down from Ellen and Sam's floor), they order in many meals that they often eat together including Chinese food that smells to me of pork, and they tip the deliverymen (I can hear all this from my room under the front stairs), which Jews are not supposed to do on their Lord's day. All this will make our job easier by far. As they say here, I am on the case.

Sometimes Marylee goes down to the Buddhist in the Basement too. She says it's mainly to keep her body stretched and occasionally she does what she calls pelvis work; she strikes me as a woman whose children are behind her or who never had any, as I said. Marylee, Ellen, and Judy are all in their late forties and know each other from a long time ago, just like the husbands. They are like one big squabbling family. They might have met in college; they are in pretty good shape for old folks, except Judy is what you call very heavy, and she looks even larger by contrast when she's with her husband who is skinny and sallow as a stick of the Buddhist's incense.

These first field reports home were always the hardest, Billy thought. Maybe because he was rallying himself as well but couldn't let on. Anyway, his father demanded one hundred per cent dedication, and he would get it. Wasn't that his due?

Well, my future letters won't be so long. But you are right indeed, Daddy. New York is a city with many hiding places for Antichrist and the Devil—across the street in that 666 building or in the crowds on the packed subway cars. I don't believe I will ever grow used to the pace but I am trying hard.

Yet this building and these people seem genuinely Heaven-sent, although the kitchen of the restaurant, which I have saved for last to tell you about, is more like Hell-sent, a complete disaster: appliances broken, wires severed and hanging from the ceiling, and Murray's five-year-old curry still speckling the walls like a thousand hardened freckles. We will remove the dried curry from every surface and cranny, do a complete rewiring, and many other renovations, and then, with great optimism in my heart and some great Christian recipes, the work can begin.

I am following your orders to the letter and not telling anyone the precise mission of the restaurant. Not quite yet, although it's difficult to keep all the details under the lid because Marylee, in particular, has been asking so many questions. They are, after all, the landlords. Please note my new telephone number, which I am writing in big numerals across the bottom of the page.

I close by reminding you to take your medicine and keep the money orders coming. Several thousand more will be necessary almost immediately for deposits on appliances, fixtures, booths, tables, and another hunk of cash next week for the second payment to the contractor.

Praise the Lord, I am fast, Daddy. Let the work begin.

He paused before signing his name. Billy? Baby Billy? Or should he deploy the more mature, the more independent William? At times the whole problem with his father seemed reducible to such distinctions. With love? Or in praise of the

Lord? Who knew anymore? He walked over and stood in front of the cracked mirror above the sink in the back of the restaurant. He removed his small oval glasses and studied his own face as if it were a road map, destination uncertain. Then he wrote "William, your son."

2

Marylee sat in the thick, high-backed leather chair behind her desk in midtown. She was trying to type. Despite the office's sound-muffling new windows, she could still hear the honking four floors below on Madison. She surveyed her oval desk, strewn with drawings, client folders, swatches of color, and photographs of wall designs from the ancient world. It was all familiar, but like so much else these days, also slightly disturbing in an invigorating way; it was as if somebody had put an elixir in the air she was breathing. How, for example, could she be recommending these Pompeii materials to her clients as she had done for years, without taking into account all the little penis designs, which she had just now noticed for the first time?

She dropped her eyes from the keyboard and glanced down at the starched lines of the pleats on her yellow skirt, spread beautifully out over her lap. She wished her whole life were more like the skirt—neat, decorous, orderly, a skirt inspiringly in charge of itself.

Marylee picked up the photograph from the corner of her desk and studied it: Hawaii, two decades ago. The snapshot had caught Gerry and herself tumbling out of a hammock in mid-swing. They were both smiling, handsome, confident, in love. Suddenly, from below, the pulsating alarm of an emergency vehicle shrieked as it neared and then receded, as if the sound had risen up not from the street but the photograph and the past. Marylee put it down and tried to resume her work.

So a young man arrives out of nowhere—the words pushed their way through the door she kept trying to close on them—and he has this most ridiculous idea in the world: a Christian-themed restaurant. He knows virtually nothing about the restaurant business and even less about the Jewish neighborhood he has decided to move into. This doesn't bother him at all. His optimism is like the sun rising in the morning, and he has this Tab Hunter smile and something else about him . . . He makes her feel uncomfortable, slightly off center, but not in a bad way. What way? She should have told him, Fine, good-bye, and good luck. She should definitely have told him that. Only she hadn't.

The work on her desk still beckoned—two apartment building lobbies and a hospital gift shop had all been promised deadlines. An assistant looked in through the opened door, but seeing Marylee's preoccupation, departed without asking a question that could not wait, but did.

She remained floating within herself and far away when Gerry's regular midafternoon phone call summoned her back. As always, he had not much pressing to report or to say. Perhaps it was precisely this absence of urgency in him that provoked the opposite in Marylee.

"Look at us, Gerry," the words tumbled out of her, "you in tiles and me here among these carpets, screens, and wallpaper samples. Gerry, why have we chosen to deal in *surfaces?* All our lives. For so many years! We are the most superficial couple I know."

She did not wait for his answer but hung up. What would have been the point of waiting for a response? The outburst was undeserved by Gerry, a good man, decency personified, generous and devoted.

She knew that in a short time she would feel awful. And soon enough it began to surface from the center of her, a plume of self-reproach rising from a zone between stomach and heart, where all the anxiety of Marylee's life pooled. She knew she would apologize to Gerry tonight, and Gerry as always would surely accept the apology and even take on blame himself for having called at the worst time possible. Then he would hug her, propose they drop in on Ellen and Sam to play bridge, and then, noticing her quietness, he might withdraw the suggestion. He would put on some Barry Manilow or perhaps the soundtrack to *The Way We Were,* which he had been listening to lately. They would probably have a glass of wine together—he might ask her if he should open a special bottle or stick with their usual; then they would curl up on the sofa. Perhaps, if she indicated an openness, he might try to make love to her. It was likely she would allow it.

Nothing will have changed.

JANUARY 16TH, 2000

Dear Daddy:

Things are going really great. Even as I write to you workmen are ripping out fixtures, dropping the ceiling, putting up a new Sheetrock wall. But all the money is spent and more will be needed than I thought. Isn't it always that way! I guess this doesn't surprise you.

The good news is that I couldn't hold back any longer because Marylee Jeffers has been insisting on helping and she said she couldn't be sure how to help us with the buzz and all if I didn't tell her the concept of the restaurant. You see her business is working on things like decor, designs, what she calls *ambiance* for well-to-do people's expensive offices, apartments, and launches. That's product launches. So I told Marylee our concept. She did not bat an eye, except to say that the ambiance I had in mind left something to be desired.

William knew he had to be careful with his father's feelings, yet he still had to say it.

I have promised to be truthful in my communications to you, Daddy, so let me rephrase: Marylee's first reaction was to *laugh* at me. Mind you, I understood that she didn't intend a hurtful or mocking laugh. It was the laugh of the unbeliever. Also she stopped by in the morning dressed up very fancy to go to her office and she was in a big rush as everyone here always is and she wanted to know if we had a name for the restaurant. "I am proud to tell you," I answered, "that you are the landlord of *Loaves and Fishes,* the first Christian-theme cafeteria in the United States of America."

She stared at me for what seemed like an hour. Then in a whispering voice she said, "You must be joking."

I pointed to all the workmen, the construction, and the many invoices rubber-banded around my clipboard.

She gave me that I-am-taking-the-measure-of-you look once more and said, "Now if I remember my teensy smattering of Church history, Buzz—William—Christians didn't eat all that much. They were ascetics. Didn't they just fast all the time? Night and day until the Romans fed *them* to the lions? Are you going to be serving thistles and locusts covered with honey? Are you going to invite people in here and then serve water and air? Bill, darling," she said to me, "there is no such thing as Christian cuisine."

"There is now," I answered her.

Then she said, "You better rethink your concept before you go the way of Curry by Murray. In case you hadn't noticed, this is the Upper West Side. It's all Jews out there. All Jews, all the time."

"You are beginning to understand."

"Excuse me?"

I said, "There will also be God's word on every table, along with the pepper and salt, to read from while you eat."

"While you eat the thistles?"

"No, Marylee. The loaves and the tasty little fishes," I said.

"Okay. Now," she answered, and I could see all the gears grinding away in her trying to figure us out, Daddy. It was getting exciting. "Explain your idea once again. Explain the concept, Bill, so my little Southern female brain can grasp it."

"If the way to a person's heart," I answered, "is through the stomach, why not take the same route to their soul? It must be nearby."

"The souls of Christians?"

"No, ma'am. Christian folks will not be turned down at the door. But to use the lingo of marketing you favor, Christians are not our main market."

"You're—"

"That's right," I said, straight and slow. "Attracting the Jews in through the food. Then teaching them and, God willing, baptizing them for the Lord."

My heart began to beat like a rabbit's when she said, "Do you know what renting this place to you means?" I waited. "It means our husbands are going to kill us! Guaranteed. Now you come right over here, young man, and explain yourself."

Sitting me down like a little kid on a sack of concrete, Marylee asked if I was really serious about Christian cuisine and Christian themes and a restaurant designed to reach out, to find, and to baptize Jews.

Here's what I said: "Through the power of the Good Book, Good News, and Good Food—that's the innovation here, because we know how Jews love to eat—we will bring them to the Lord. He's waiting for His people to return."

"You're certain about this?"

"It's just a matter of time."

"Well," she answered, "I think in that

case we definitely have a little problem. I would strongly advise you *not* to mention any of this to Gerry or to the others," she said, "until I've had time to think it through."

I hope you'll be proud of my answer. "Our aim is to love all people," I said, "but especially Jewish people, by showing them the way to the Lord—through food. That's the simple concept—not much to think through." Her eyes lingered on me, as if she couldn't make up her mind if what she was hearing was the thought of a genius or a fool. Probably fool.

You told me not to be shy, so on I went. "You said earlier, 'There is no Christian cuisine,' but of course there is. Jesus was a Jew, Marylee. A nice Jewish boy. He made the Passover *seder*, the Last Supper, and the Paschal Lamb. Jesus' cuisine was Jewish cuisine. Therefore we will win the hearts of Jewish folks through Jewish cuisine at *Loaves and Fishes, the Christian Cafeteria.*"

She repeated the name several times as if it was a dress she was trying on.

"That's our name. And we will do so without offending your wonderful husbands or the other Jewish people who patronize us."

"How can you not offend! You'll lure—"

"Attract—Jews in here—"

"—and try to convert them? Here?"

"You'll help me with the ambiance and the buzz and I will take care of the rest of the Lord's work."

Marylee began to explore the premises, picking her way around the leaning panels of Sheetrock, the coils of BX cable, wood, and concrete. I followed her at a distance to allow her thoughts to percolate. "Our husbands will definitely kill us," she said. "Several times over."

Because you are a literal man and also concerned with insurance, Daddy, I want to point out that Marylee was just using the exaggerated manner of talking that they have perfected here in New York when she said Gerry Levine is going to kill her when he finds out the plans. She does not really mean that. Although he will probably be upset, I do not think there will be any homicides to report (I am continuing her joke).

My days and nights are nothing but work work work and yet I am also full of a sense of the wonder of it all as the restaurant comes into being. I calculate our opening is perhaps three months away. I will keep you informed of all developments, Daddy. In the meantime, continue to send support.

Yours in Christ,

William

3

On the following Caracas Night, Judy and Ellen were so eager to talk to Marylee that they hurriedly dressed their husbands in their rotting tennis gear and practically drove them to Caracas themselves. Judy gave Michael 500 milligrams of vitamin E (good for the heart) in a pill the size of a bullet. Ellen reminded Sam that they needed a quart of milk, some soda, and coffee filters, which could be picked up cheaply in New Jersey. Then they pushed the men out the door and into Gerry's patiently idling Toyota. Moments later they appeared on Marylee's threshold.

"Hi, honey," said Ellen as she crossed the threshold with her white square of essays beneath her crossed arms. "We found out, Marylee. You can't keep hiding from us!"

"Who's hiding? Come in, and pardon my mess."

The mess consisted of Marylee's opened high school yearbook, class sweater, a dozen spread-out photographs, and an assortment of small plastic Confederate flags. "Stirring sticks for highballs," she explained. "Extraordinarily valuable relics."

"Up to the Museum with this stuff," said Ellen. "For public consumption."

Ellen knelt on the floor beside her, peered into the yearbook, found Marylee, and said, "You're just as cute now. Only the hairstyle, and your judgment, are different. Why have you let this go on so long without telling us?"

"I told you everything."

"You're being coy, ML," said Ellen. "You knew more than you let on."

"Not really," said Marylee. "But this interrogation calls for some tea first. Who wants what?"

"Don't move," said Judy and she reached out with her strong arm and restrained Marylee from going into the kitchen. "Just tell us how you plan to terminate the lease."

"Terminate it? He's just signed."

"Only because you let him."

"I don't do things unilaterally around here. You gave me your okay."

"Well, it's obvious we made a mistake. So let's fix it. All we need to do is break the lease, ML."

"I see the lawyers' fees already," Judy said. "The guys will kill us if we break the lease. And of course they'll kill us worse if we don't."

"We'll break it." Ellen said.

"On what basis?" Marylee spoke quite calmly.

"This is New York," Ellen said. "One basis, another basis. There is always a way."

"He'll sue," said Marylee, although she had no certainty at all that William Harp would.

"So we'll sue back," said Ellen. "That's why God invented attorneys."

"He is not an evil person. He is not a danger to society," Marylee found herself speaking slowly, deliberately. "I've thought a lot about it."

"Not quite enough," said Ellen.

Judy settled herself on Marylee's sofa, put her hands on her lap, and brought her thumbs together. But she did not close her eyes. "Would you calmly share your thoughts with us," Judy said, "about this tenant?"

"Could you," Ellen snapped at her before Marylee could answer, "please refrain from using the word *share* except in relation to stocks and other equities? I'll throw up if you don't."

"If you don't stop barking at me," Judy said, "I will meditate in front of you until you die."

Marylee was taking in all this genial and ironic sparring and she was thinking that it was no longer amusing: *This is precisely what appeals to me about William Harp. With him there is tranquility, and here . . .*

"Okay," said Ellen, producing a handful of student essays, "I will try to use my time well while you share your thoughts with each other about William Harp. Just tell us, Marylee, given who he is and what he's up to, why you went through with the signing."

How long, Marylee thought, had Ellen been seeing her as a kind of student? What right did she have to speak to her this way? Wasn't it as if she were saying, Honey, you will get a far better mark if you just pay less attention to William Harp and throw him out. I can't give you a good grade if you don't.

Marylee replied with simplicity: "We talked, we made a considered decision, we rented."

Ellen asked, "Didn't we know the full story?"

"There's no reason to be hostile to each other," Judy said to Ellen with lots of pauses, as if she hoped, Ellen thought, to make the whole problem disappear through a secret Buddhist word-spacing technique. "There is no reason not to believe Marylee acted in good faith. Now we go on. It's not the end of the world."

The words, unpremeditated, just floated out of Marylee: "Yes, but what if it is?"

"Run that by us again?" Judy said as she shifted on the sofa.

"That's precisely why the kid has to go," said Ellen. "He has placed an apocalyptic spell on Marylee. You know the rules," Ellen said. "We can outvote you now, and you have to tell young Jesus to go somewhere else."

"Just like that? I don't think so."

"Sweetheart," Judy put firmness into her voice, "you

know that Michael will have a stroke and for the rest of my life it will be like living with Doctor Strangelove. He's bizarre enough the way he is already without a missionary starting to live under our roof."

"Now take Sam's *bobbe,*" said Ellen, "and the *zayde* too, the grandparents and the seventeen dead relatives—"

"What about them?" Judy demanded. Like Marylee, she knew what was coming, and she felt the need to head it off. "When they die, people do not become bodies just waiting to irritate the living. They are motes, specks, photons, dust in the never-ending cycle of *samsara.*"

"Samsara shmamsara, *zayde* would say," Ellen went on. "The dead are definitely not motes. In Sam's mind—and that's the only mind that counts with regard to domestic violence on my floor—they are indeed bodies of his Jewish relatives. If we rent to a Christian missionary, they will physically all turn in their graves, simultaneously, like in a Busby Berkeley routine."

Whenever Ellen and Judy began to entertain each other with their pidgin Yiddish and then linked it to the dead European grandparents, it was almost a certainty that the Holocaust and the Nazis and the total disappearance of Jewish heritage would not be far behind.

"Well," said Judy, "there's no getting around it. This is a big problem."

"Listen to you about the *bobbes* and *zaydes,*" Marylee retorted, though her reproof was mitigated by an involuntary reappearance—she had begun to notice this too—of her Southern accent. "All the prophecies of doom and all the *alte cockers* that get invoked around here before *anything* has happened! You know the most pathetic part of it? What you're both saying is, word for word, sentiment for sentiment, exactly what Sam or Michael would say."

In a gesture of slowly-forming resolve, Ellen put her papers aside. She pushed her glasses back up to the reddened notch on the bridge of her nose. She raised her palms up in exasperation and declared, "We are married to them, in case you hadn't noticed."

"Have you checked your body recently? You exist apart from them. We are married, yes, but not joined at the head, or at any other anatomical structure! At least I'm not," Marylee said calmly. "And you know the worst part of it? For two bright women, you are unaware of this. Listen, I understand your reaction. After my first conversation with William Harp, my initial thought, like yours, was: If we don't kick this kid out, and fast, then divorce is imminent! But that is unadulterated nonsense! Are we parrots? Or, conversely, if it is true, if it upsets the guys so much that we've rented to this boy, then what does that say about the slavish condition of our marriages?"

"Thank you, Pericles," Ellen said.

"Your mockery only strengthens my resolve."

"To do what?" Judy asked.

"Resolve to honor the lease," she answered, "because I am fairly certain that at least Gerry will not flip. He loves me and he will understand. And if you just back off and encourage your guys not to give in to some irrational, circle-round-the-wagons Jewish reaction, then Gerry can serve as a model for your two lunatics."

"Ten dollars says Gerry will flip," said Judy. "And they will find one lawyer to represent them all."

"I see your ten and raise you ten," said Ellen.

"I repeat: Are we *married* to our husbands or have we *become* them? Are we married to the guys or to their religion? And, by the way, permit me to point out how much they practice their faith. Close to *nada.*"

There was a long hiatus in the grilling, during which Marylee went out of the room and returned bearing a tray of butter cookies and the tea service. The women grew silent, and the clock behind the hanging plants in her high kitchen could now be heard, its tick-tock competing with the scrape of the teacups and saucers. There was definitely a little crisis brewing, along with the oolong and Red Zinger.

Ellen resumed the inventive twirling of her pencil above the stack of essays. Judy rose from the table and sat herself on the sofa in a new and, in view of her size, potentially painful meditative posture that forced her feet to point toward her armpits; as always, her thumbs were touching just slightly above her cupped hands. If her thumbs separated, that meant that Judy was very agitated. Out her window Marylee noticed the thin bare branch of the ailanthus, which always made her think of the scythe of the Grim Reaper, gesturing out toward Broadway.

When they could ignore each other no longer, Marylee repeated, "Well, *have* we become our husbands? Has anyone in this group converted to Judaism even after all these years? Is there a Jewish bride at this table? If so, will she please stand up?"

"We're all honorary Jews, for chrissakes," said Judy. "Scratch the 'chrissakes,' please."

"Judy doesn't mean honorary," Ellen corrected. "She means unofficial Jews, and she's right about that. Ex officio. Common-law converts."

"Not me," said Marylee. "I never felt that way. I'm still good old *shiksa* me."

"What I feel," said Judy, "is that after twenty Passovers and Hanukahs and more bar and bat mitzvahs than you can count, you do imbibe some of it, it works its way into the bones, you don't think about it, and the next thing you know, you have adapted. You know some five Yiddish words . . . then after ten years or so you know a dozen or two. That practically makes you a native speaker here. You know what I mean? Kind of like osmosis."

"So," said Marylee, warming to the subject, "you're not Orthodox, Conservative, or Reform. Nor are you just women married to Jewish men. You're something different. Something in between that hasn't been identified, tagged, or named yet." Marylee looked at them. "Common-law? Ex officio? What shall we christen it, you'll pardon the expression? Something not seen before in the history of the Jewish people or the Upper West Side. You're a whole new denomination: you're Osmosed Jews."

"OJs. Yes," said Ellen, rising up at the table in a mock salute, "we're OJs standing tall and goddam proud of it."

Untwisting herself from her *zazen* posture, Judy said, "You don't have to be Jewish not to want a missionary under your roof."

"Well," Marylee replied, leaning over Judy and gently placing her thumbs back together, "if we don't want missionaries in the building, what in the world is the Buddhist doing in the basement? Knitting? Did anybody object when *he* showed up and asked to rent? And what have you been doing with him all these years?"

"Not the same thing, dear," Judy said. "Nawang keeps to himself. He stays in the basement."

"Buddhist in the basement," Marylee answered, "Christian on the street level. It all amounts to the same thing."

"She's right about that," Ellen said to Judy. "Marylee's got consistency on her side, if nothing else."

"Nawang's not proselytizing." Judy shifted her weight once again and rearranged her hands, formally, as if they were ritual instruments, from her lap to the tops of her knees. It was as if she hoped such gestures might be seen as arguments. But Marylee and Ellen were unmoved.

"Look at you," Ellen said. "Before Nawang showed up you didn't know a Buddhist from a baseball. Now you're the Dalai Lama's best friend."

"It's a technique, not a religion," Judy insisted. "Breathing and stress reduction. Nawang would never open a provocative restaurant."

"Nawang advertises his classes," said Marylee. "He's been putting those silly flyers on the lampposts up and down the street and all over Broadway, and have we objected? No. But he's marketing the way religion has always done. And he's certainly sold you."

"Nawang is not after my soul," Judy answered with conviction. "But this Baptist minister, or whoever he is, he is very much after souls."

"Please don't talk about souls . . . words whose meanings we can't agree on; it's just gibberish." This was Ellen. "If I see *soul* in an essay, I cross it out and tell the kid: Say what you mean. Do you mean personality? Do you mean spiritual *feeling?* But don't leave me hanging on nonsense."

"You know very well what she means," Marylee said to Ellen. "You know what a soul is."

"I know filet of sole. I know the sole of a shoe," Ellen shot back. "But if a human soul walks down the street on Halloween and bites me, even then I have my suspicions."

"Can we just have another interval of silence!" Judy pleaded. "We're not getting anywhere this way." Then she intoned *"sunyata,"* her favorite Sanskrit word. She pronounced it with relish. "Nothingness. *Sunyata."*

"I can go for some of that too," Ellen said, emitting a sigh accompanied by a D+ written with a flourish in large red marker across the top of a paper (its thesis sentence was "Things are always changing fast in the modern world of today"). Judy continued to meditate and Marylee began quietly, so as not to disturb her friends, to load the dishwasher.

She tried to concentrate on each cup, spoon, and saucer, just as Judy had described her joy at her own Buddhist dishwashing practice. But suddenly the moment was pierced by one of the recollections that had been emerging ever since William Harp had arrived: With an extraordinary clarity she remembered the message on the marquee in front of the small church in Peanut Valley, Virginia, where she had grown up. It was in the form of unevenly placed detachable white letters on a black felt background, a free-standing rectangle framed in stainless steel on the green church lawn. When a Laundromat opened next door to the church, someone in the congregation had put up the new message on the marquee: "God *still* washes whitest of all."

Ellen put her papers down decisively. "Here's the point, Marylee," she said: "Nawang's lease is residential. For five years he has been in violation because he conducts a business here, and we all know it. And don't forget that he also keeps that sheep. That sheep will get us in big trouble one day, mark my words. We always just look the other way about the sheep because you—you, Judy—are his patron. I don't like what she's doing, but now Marylee thinks this missionary deserves a chance, or she thinks he's cute—well, he *is* cute—but now, for whatever the reason, we're going to have to look the other way again. Either that or evict them both."

"Harp is completely legal, commercial lease and all," Marylee said. "Not residential. May I also point out that we very much need the rent to pay the mortgage? It is not a question of cuteness or proselytizing, but of finance."

"I don't find Nawang cute, by the way," said Judy. She was shading into a very un-Buddhist blush. "Enlightened is not cute. Enlightened has got nothing to do with physical properties."

"Sure," said Ellen, returning to her papers. "I think you're both acting like a couple of sophomores. Nothing lower on the food chain."

Marylee knew that William Harp had already spoken with Nawang about the incense and also about the sheep, which, while it appeared to be his pet, Nawang also considered far more: a kind of holy animal. For the last three years, ever since Nawang had requested it, they had allowed the sheep to graze in the small backyard garden. This, despite the violation of the lease, health code, administrative code, zip code, Napoleonic Code, and who knew what other regulations. William Harp knew his rights.

Ellen looked up from a particularly obtuse paper ("A winning sports team can definitely unite our troubled city") that had put a pained grimace of despair on her face. "Remember this too," she said, "the more renovations he makes, the more he invests, the less he is going to want to leave. And he has already put in a lot. If we're going to do something, we need to act fast."

"We could just do nothing," Judy said. "Inaction, you know, is a form of action."

"Will you just shut up with that already?" Ellen said wearily. "Nothing personal, but Jezuz . . ." She caught herself, and Marylee riveted her eyes on her now, as if Ellen had just revealed a strand of her own God-given, deep-seated Christian origin in reproving a Buddhist.

Judy brought her hands from knees to the thumbs-together *mudra* position. "Can we just have some sort of . . . understanding?" Judy was soliciting for a consensus—any consensus would do.

"Nothing is going to be neat and clear," Ellen replied, "just because you want it that way. Our life is messy, honey, and it's getting messier."

"Why do you pose it as *us* and *them?*" Judy asked. "False dichotomies, sources of clinging and suffering."

"Oh for godsake, Marylee," Ellen appealed to her, "help Judy out of her misery."

"You seem more miserable than either of us," Judy said quickly.

"I'll tell you what's going to happen," Ellen answered her as she recapped her pen and neatened the papers. "When the restaurant fails, Harp will become, just like your Nawang, another failed leftover religious curiosity in our building, a little more detritus of the new century and the new millennium. We will have a fringe Christian to join our fringe Buddhist. We'll have Nirvana and the Pearly Gates both being peddled out of our building. What defect in our collective character does this tendency reveal?"

"You're forgetting one small thing," Marylee said to her friends. "What if the restaurant *is* successful?"

"Never has, never will," Ellen pronounced.

"Unless God is really on his side," Marylee said. The words emerged quickly from her, as if they had been waiting to roll out for some time, like a phrase from a long-forgotten and suddenly remembered song.

"Does such a cliché really have meaning for you?" Ellen said, but immediately regretted.

A seam that Marylee—and to some extent all of them—had been trying to keep sutured together all evening was beginning to fray and to tear.

"Is it not within the realm of possibility," Marylee inquired carefully, "that this person you are looking at, me, actually still believes in God? Is it a sin to love Jesus on the Upper West Side? I mean the cynicism that floats through this building and throughout our lives is thick as the traffic on Broadway. You were not always this way, Ellen. I am one of the people who remember you when."

"The Jews have not made me a cynic, if that's what you're

suggesting. Jews didn't invent cynicism. I'm convinced I was born this way under the sign of Saturn in the great desert of Arizona, and I'm proud of it. Is cynicism genetic? Please write three exquisite paragraphs defending a position. Look, I repeat: the restaurant will likely fail, and our lives will return to what has passed for normal around here. End of story."

Judy brought her hands prayerfully together once again. "Vegetarian, yes, maybe that has a chance, maybe even dairy or fish again, if it's done right. But 'Christian cuisine'? You're the businesswoman among us, Marylee. What's happened to your judgment?"

"If there's Christian music, Christian bookstores, and a Christian lifestyle, why shouldn't cuisine follow?"

"They starved themselves, for chrissakes!" said Ellen. "And water was very big, as I remember from my Sunday school. I can see Christian mineral water. Also dates, figs, honey, pomegranates. Sam will laugh himself to the point of abdominal injury. And if he survives, he'll come downstairs and destroy every appliance and fixture in sight."

"May I suggest that we emphasize the positive?" Marylee responded. "First, William seems to be planning on selling *Jewish* food! Then when—if—Michael or Sam or even Gerry raises an objection, maybe we gently remind them of the stunningly terrible tenants we have had here in years gone by. At least this is a new idea. And check out this young man *not* as a missionary but as a tenant: He has put a full year's rent in escrow, just as requested, no questions asked. We also have a bond against damage to the building resulting from the work he is doing. He got his contractor to give us a full set of the drawings for the renovations. You've seen them. The kid got his contractor to provide insurance and workmen's compensation for everyone who sets foot in here. If the pizza delivery guy stumbles, we're covered. If an electrician crosses currents and we fry every wire in the building, we're totally covered. William Harp is doing it all by the book, with a smile, and then some."

"By the book, he wants to make Sam's cousins and our neighbors into Christians," Ellen said. "That's minor, I suppose."

"No one says it's minor," Marylee answered. "Just allowable. Why shouldn't William Harp have a shot? A person shouldn't be vilified or run out of town or have his lease arbitrarily canceled because he's in the converting business. So he believes souls must be saved. That is his compassionate conviction. Why is that not legitimate? Or, as we say on Passover at *bobbe* and *zayde*'s: How is the converting business different from all other businesses?"

"One of the very best things about the Jews, in addition to the loyal husbands their mothers seem to produce," said Ellen, "is that they *don't* proselytize. They leave other people alone. That's one of the main reasons I'm proud to be an Osmosed Jew."

"I request just one thing," Marylee said. "Hear me. One thing." The quiet conviction she heard in her voice for the first time gave her a small but powerful thrill. It was as if she had just taken her first bicycle ride or achieved some other mastery that opened worlds up to her. Where had this come from? "Give some thought," she continued, "to whether we really have been left alone, theologically, God-wise, all these years by our husbands. Of course they *want* us to think that's the case. They want us to think we don't care much, and maybe we haven't for twenty years! But what if something has changed? What if we do care now? Okay, not you, but me? What if *I* suddenly care? Right now. In this very instant. Okay, let's say it's even because of this boy's showing up at our door. Still, if something starts to matter to us . . . look at the attitude," she said to Judy.

"You're exaggerating, Marylee."

"Am I? It's terrible the way you let even Ellen mock your religion, your Buddhism, and that's nothing compared to what your husband thinks about it."

"That's not so."

"I don't think he—or any of them—feels very respectful about your new faith, Judy. I'm sorry to inform you."

"Not my faith. My practice, my techniques."

"Yes, yes, your techniques, whatever. But I tell you this: over the years I feel Gerry and Sam and Michael *have* been proselytizing us. Informally and quietly, yes, but also methodically. What's the unspoken main idea? Answer: That their Judaism is somehow, some way, superior—a longer lasting, better, more sensible, truer path than every other, and that through our brilliant marriages to these men we too will arrive at this conclusion, if not now, then next year, or the next—in any event, soon enough for us to take care of them in a Jewish sort of way when they're too old to sleep through the night without peeing. I think this goes through their minds all the time. At best they *indulge* your meditating, Judy, or any other contrary practice or idea that appears. Mice that we have been, we ignore it."

"ML, what did you have for dinner tonight?"

Marylee pressed on. "And why? Because we simply don't recognize what's been happening to us until the frame of reference changes a little. That's exactly what this boy's arrival has done. It's not just another restaurant; it's a paradigm shift for me. I feel I've allowed myself, over the years, to be brainwashed. That's the truth of it. That's why it's good for us to have William Harp in the building."

"All right! Amen," said Judy. "And do you have a closing statement, counselor?" she put the question to Ellen.

Ellen remained silent for a moment and then said, "I have

endless papers to correct—and then some—before I sleep."
After another pause, she added, "Still, I think the kid should go."

Now a strange impulse seized Marylee and propelled her over to the brightly polished baby grand on the far side of the room. The piano had been a fortieth birthday present from Ellen and Judy, and its infrequent use often troubled Marylee, but not tonight. As she brushed her fingers across the cool wood, she felt the piano had been waiting patiently there all these years just for this red-letter moment to arrive.

Theatrically she raised the lid, hit middle C, and sat down on the bench. "Anyone remember this?" she said, as the opening chords of "Onward, Christian Soldiers!" flowed triumphantly into the room. "Anyone want to sing along?"

4

The whole of the next melancholy and rainy day Marylee yearned to be not in her office or with clients but with William Harp. She visualized the two of them conferring as they toured the construction site, with its astringent and powdery odors of plaster, primer, and paint, his Christian restaurant in the making. She was not walking hand-in-hand with him, of course, but beside him, a silent partner, building something significant together.

Marylee grew slightly dizzy, and then she steadied her balance by grasping the ledge and staring out the window at the endless streaming of people on the avenue. One person at a time, she found herself saying aloud, one at a time, and then she focused on a yellow umbrella moving more rapidly than the others up Madison Avenue far below. Marylee wondered what William Harp was doing at this moment. She tried to communicate with him telepathically. She felt foolish in the midst of these sensations, which had all the trappings of attraction, even romance, but were something of a different order.

The next morning, on her way out of the building, she saw William in the restaurant, leaning over a set of blueprints spread across sawhorses. Apart from a hello, she avoided him. She gave herself tasks. She had an impulse to be especially considerate to Gerry. That night she wanted to prepare a good dinner for Gerry, and did: pasta with pesto, including pine nuts and brown sugar, a favorite. She wanted to please him because he was being especially, awkwardly, agonizingly solicitous of her; he was not interrogating her, he was holding the door for her, he waited for her to sit down at the table. He was so considerate that she felt as if she were stabbing him in the eyes.

They sat beneath their hanging plants and ate in loud silence. Politely they gave each other the salt, the pepper, the canola oil, please. They exchanged a few words about the fine new leafing on the begonias and the ivy, which were surviving the winter quite well. It was as if two decades of their congenial marriage were somehow being erased like lines on the blackboard by an unseen hand in the time it took to prepare and consume the pasta. Yet being propelled back in time was also not without its strained new excitement, this sudden experience of working so hard to know each other anew.

"I think I've been taking you for granted," Gerry finally said. "I won't any more."

"You've been staring off into space a lot lately," she said more harshly than she'd intended. "Is that how you express it?"

"Look, I've been aware of your . . . your sadness about certain things." He was thinking of the infertility, the endless tests, the feeling of failure and of being somehow tainted, the whole travail they had gone through for so many years. He thought all this was behind them. Perhaps it never would be. But maybe that wasn't it at all. You never knew with Marylee.

If some people listened to their own drummer, as the adage had it, then Marylee listened to her own entire percussion section. If she didn't tell him, or at least mercifully give him a clue, he would never know. So the best approach he had found, the way to keep from appearing too much of a sleepyhead in her eyes, was to keep it general. "I've been meaning to ask why you seemed so sad."

"I'm really not sad at all, Gerry! I've been feeling pretty good lately. Work and then the restaurant."

"The restaurant?"

"You know. New tenant. Big new responsibility, and I'm running with it this time. Very busy, you know. Like you."

"Everything all right then?"

"Uh-huh. Peachy."

"Now that makes *me* a little sad," he said. "Because I know I've somehow lost out already, haven't I? I mean I've lost an opportunity to be the reason whatever it was went away."

She noticed the hopeful expression on his face, a passionate hopefulness that always seemed to shine in his eyes. Gerry had the dutiful brown eyes of a young boy—eager, curious, and, above all, wanting to be helpful and to please. Marylee had never known what to do with so much helpfulness, so much service offered. If she chose, which she did not, she could have spent the entire marriage, nonstop, saying thank you, Gerry, thank you for all you do for us. She knew Ellen and Judy sometimes viewed her as the selfish one of the couple, but she knew Gerry didn't, and what else mattered? He was like a natural resource, a Niagara of unending generosity, and she an eternally ungrateful beneficiary.

She went up to him and kissed him softly behind the ear, a kiss neither chaste nor arousing. They finished the meal, cleared, and began washing dishes without exchanging another word.

Afterward, when they discovered that the skim milk in the refrigerator had turned, Gerry insisted on going out in the cold for another quart for Marylee's morning coffee. She felt he would have driven upstate, milked a cow, and skimmed off the fat himself with his freezing hands if she had so much as hinted.

When he returned from the store, Marylee saw that the cold air had energized him. He changed a washer in the bathroom faucet that she had mentioned needed fixing. He apologized to her for having ignored it for so long. They were inoculating each other with courtesy, like travelers making their preparations before entering dangerous territory.

They sat reading on the sofa for an hour until Gerry began to close his eyes. His chin dropped. The book, a collection of aerial views of Paris, fell from his fingers. Marylee watched these stages of his nodding with familiar fascination and relief. Asleep, at least he could not offer to do anything more for her tonight. As long as it slept, his love for her would not make her feel more inadequate.

She watched and listened to his snoring. Over the years, its pattern had become familiar enough, the way it dipped into a wet silence before erupting—you never knew when, that was the rub—into a full-blown catarrh. Then suddenly, as Marylee scrutinized him propped over the pillows, she remembered seeing him sitting precisely in this pose, his mouth and eyes both slightly open, the snore arising from the back of his throat like the engine drone of a small model airplane struggling to gain altitude. The moment flung itself back to her with disturbing clarity: She had been lying in the hospital two years ago waking from the anesthetic.

"Now I know," she said practically aloud and with vast relief—Gerry could have heard it had he been awake—"that this did not begin with William Harp. I absolutely know it."

As if the infertility treatments had not been enough to go through—who knew, perhaps *because* of them—two years ago Marylee had discovered a lump in her breast. After the doleful biopsy came the treatments, the hair loss, the whole cancer travail. She came through it well enough and Gerry was his wonderful self throughout.

Yet there also had been this postoperative incident: when she had awakened in the hospital, Gerry asleep opposite her, Marylee had felt an emptiness that she had never experienced before.

She hadn't been able to keep her fingers from feeling her body that night. It had been natural enough after such an operation, but her fingers kept moving across her skin, back and forth, and in the sluggish zone between waking and the anesthesia-produced sleep, she had imagined her fingers as a platoon of five, of ten, marching back and forth ceaselessly across the area of her wound. Their mission was to reconnoiter the border where the bandages ended and the unbandaged skin on her chest met and to report back to her about what they found. The problem was that they had kept marching, loudly and stupidly, and the report had never arrived.

It was possible, even likely, that she had still been under the strong lingering effects of the Demerol. In fact, she had told herself at first, this had to be the explanation of what happened next. For stirring under her fingers just at the point of the incision beneath the bandages, Marylee had suddenly felt a rush of warmth. At first she was concerned that something had torn or was broken or was oozing out; yet there had been no pain, no discomfort.

Quite the contrary, it was a warmth she associated with the cozy reassurance of hands wrapped around a newly brewed cup of tea. Then she closed her eyes and saw the image: An old wrinkled man, but with an infant's face. She saw him lying there across her chest in his swaddling, right at the edge of the bandages. Pulling himself out as if the bandages were the white stone wall of a garden and he an old anthropomorphic rabbit, a cartoon character, but also quite human, a homunculus, the figure stared up at her and gave her a familiar wink.

Vision or Demerol-induced hallucination? What did it matter? What was certain was that this had happened. The figure was, she was now certain, baby Jesus in his swaddling, the same Jesus who had meant so much to her when she was a child. Once again he had been insinuating himself back into her life, at the point of the incision, where the scar would soon begin to form at the line where her breast had been.

Marylee's body was saying to her, One day you are going to die. Maybe not all at once, not during this hospital stay, perhaps, which will last only a few more days. More likely your death will be caused by what has brought you here, one failing rotting piece of your body discarded at a time.

Yet the figure was communicating something far more to her: I only *seem* to you to be a scar. I am not. Don't believe the mere evidence of this world. I am warmth; I am not an end of something, but a new start. She realized then, with the knowledge of death that the cancer had brought, that her faith, in fits and starts, was also returning. Not until tonight had she remembered that vision in the hospital. Now, as she stared at her sleeping husband, she could not stop thinking about it.

Why was it she had chosen not to wake him that night in the hospital to tell him what she had seen? Why had she to this day never even told him? Was it because she really didn't believe it herself? Or was it because Gerry, as a Jew, might not have believed what she had seen and felt? Or, the greater fear: Would he have laughed and mocked her?

How is it possible to continue to love your husband as I do, she began to wonder, and yet still feel a deep emptiness? Is this a mark of a failed marriage that I am denying? That we remain starkly separate and different, holding hands out of dull convention, affection, and habit, even as we inch toward the void? I know I'm overdoing it, she rallied herself. I know I should try to go up to the Museum. If she could be by herself up there among the reassuringly musty old paperbacks, bell-bottomed pants, madras blouses, and tie-dyed skirts she occasionally still put on when she was alone, she would grow calmer, she knew, if she put something old on, even for an hour.

But tonight Marylee did not want to be anesthetized by easy nostalgia, so she stayed put. She went up to Gerry and laid a finger on his nose; his snoring dropped an octave. She did it again, his snoring ceased, and then returned, like the purr of a very contented cat.

She roused him—he was a champion sleeper and even an excellent walker in his sleep, and nothing short of a bomb could wake him—and brought him to their bedroom. There she helped him into his pajamas and into bed. Is it possible, she asked herself, that I have had a vision? She sat on the bed next to him, and as his snoring resumed, she slid to the floor, cupped her hands, and for the first time, she calculated, in nearly forty years, bent her head and devoutly recited the Lord's Prayer.

5

Next morning, feeling refreshed, Marylee put on her red suit and matching shoes and left for work very early—she hoped it was before anyone else would be up. Yet as she stepped out onto the sidewalk toward Broadway and into a circle of wide hard winter sunshine, Billy Harp was there too, at its edge. Dressed in an orange warm-up suit whose brightness rivaled hers, he was sweeping in front of the building and washing the outside of the big window. In white paint written across butcher paper and taped to its inside, she read: "Coming Soon to Serve the Lord and You, *Loaves and Fishes,* your Christian Cafeteria!"

When Billy saw Marylee, he turned and said, "Enjoying the new year?" Marylee told him she was, and he quoted (she looked it up later) Zechariah 9:17, "*Corn shall make the young men cheerful and the new wine the maids.*"

"Is this your clever way of asking me about the liquor license?"

"Indeed I am, Ms. Jeffers, about that and a dozen other things, though I don't want to make you late for your job."

"I'll leave work early and drop by here at three," she said. "I've got some time. May I give you some advice on that right now?" she pointed to the *Loaves and Fishes* sign. "Take it down. The public shouldn't see it until you're really ready to open. Especially if you change names. Is that name in stone?"

"Nothing's in stone, Ms. Jeffers."

"Marylee."

In an instant he went inside, pulled the paper off, and crumpled it into a ball, which he threw theatrically over his shoulder into the mess of construction debris behind him. Marylee peered inside the space and saw new walls already framed. She saw a knot of new electrical wires dangling down in the corner of the exposed ceiling, where two shiny new ducts met. He was working fast. She smelled new paint, or perhaps it was an astringency in the cologne Billy Harp was wearing.

"You're making progress," she said.

"Praise the Lord," he answered. "Because of you."

6

A few nights had passed since the recollection of her vision, when Gerry's sudden need to attend a trade show in Islip, Long Island, from which he would not return until well after midnight, provided Marylee the opportunity she was looking for. She would have preferred to meet in the Museum of the 1960s, but Judy had set off a roach bomb there, and, from the smell of it, the place would not be habitable for days.

"For a lover of all sentient beings," Marylee said to Judy when they ran into each other in the hallway, "you kill more cockroaches than the rest of us combined. How come you didn't tell us you were going to set that thing off?"

"I don't think of cockroaches as sentient."

"Well, I'm sure they don't share your opinion. Is Michael in?"

"For a change, no. He's visiting his father at the nursing home. We can chat in our place if you want, since Sam's home."

"No, Ellen's expecting us. She said Sam's researching movie music. You know how he gets. He'll be dead to the world."

When they entered, Sam, upon his back, acknowledged them only vaguely through half-closed, music-filled eyes. He was lying on the thick rug in front of the fireplace wearing yellow earphones the size of shoeboxes. Since funding for his film on the world's smallest nations remained as minuscule as the subjects, all he could do at this stage was listen to hours of humpback whales calling to each other and other oceanic sounds, searching for what might be appropriate to accompany the footage of atolls and tiny islands he would shoot, he hoped, if he ever got started. From what Marylee could see, he was still relatively unfazed by developments in the restaurant, the same old job-distracted Sam—an encouraging sign.

Ellen led them over and around her supine husband and out of the living room. In her kitchen they sat on stools, helped her grate carrots for a cake, and selected from her endless collection of leaves from around the world. From the jar Ellen offered, Marylee chose an orange-peppermint-flavored tea from sub-Saharan Africa called Serenity, and Judy picked what turned out to be a dark packet from Nepal called Awake; the name grabbed her, but the brew was unexpectedly sulfurous and harsh.

"So, for what grand occasion have you brought us together?" Ellen asked.

Marylee hesitated.

Speak, Marylee, said the homunculus.

"Well, we've known each other for thirty years and it shouldn't be, but it's still incredibly hard to say this, but I feel that we have been *oppressed* for approximately the last twenty. That's what I've been thinking about since we talked last. I hinted at it then, but now it's becoming absolutely clear. I'm sorry, but *oppressed* is the only word for it. Oppressed. Every time I read about the Chinese persecuting Christian groups and the underground churches there, I think maybe persecution, like charity, begins at home. We have to do something about it. Now."

"Come again? We're persecuted Christians?" Ellen was incredulous.

"The guys subtly insist on a Jewish environment, a Jewish style around the house, just like I said. Don't you feel we acquiesce all the time, every second? And that's only for starters."

"That's for starters," Ellen said to Judy. "What's for finishers, ML?"

"I can't bear it," said Judy.

"Don't you dare meditate!" Ellen nudged her elbow into Judy's big soft flank. "You stay fully awake for Marylee's litany of abuses that we've suffered. For goodness sake, Marylee, we're not even Christians here. You have one Buddhist and one whatever I am, secular humanist. What's to persecute?"

"That's the point. That's not how you began in life," Marylee said. "And it's not William Harp the man or the restaurant that's gotten me started. Don't you think that for a minute. It's all about what he represents. Equal time. Tolerance. A reminder of what we often forget. That's the issue. That's why we should not only let him stay, we should actively help and encourage him to make up for so much lost time. I was thinking about what we said the other day, and I'm appalled that we were considering trying to shut him down. We should do the opposite. We should nurture his idea and see to it that it grows."

"A Christian missionary represents tolerance?" said Judy.

"Yes, on its own terms, but also because his work will result in the decline of the preferential treatment for the Children of Israel that exists under this roof."

"Preferential treatment?"

"What I'm talking about is a feeling of . . . triumphalism, that's it. Sort of a JEWS RULE that goes on here. You're still anesthetized to it, the way I was. You think this is normal, but it's not. It doesn't have to be this way. Because it's enough already! I prayed the other night, and it felt terrific. The Lord's Prayer. I never slept so well. I finally felt those feelings of joy and belonging that have been buried all these years. I discovered that, after all, I am still a Christian woman. Why has it taken so long?"

"Praise God," said Ellen. "Amen."

"Just shut up," said Judy. "Can't you see she means it?"

Marylee's relief was palpable. She felt herself in the middle of a field of new energy. She was running free. "Praise the Lord is absolutely right. But who's been stopping me all these years? Certainly not Gerry. Not Sam or Michael, not specifically or directly. I would never contend that. But an atmosphere, a seriously constraining Jewish atmosphere, does exist here."

"Wait a second," said Ellen. "Constraining what? Who?"

"Nothing else religious, seriously religious, can flourish within it. And that's unfair, and that's why it's got to change. How? We need to let this restaurant open and to help it succeed. Its success is ours. You see that, don't you?"

"We see trouble," Ellen said. "Anyway, you're wrong. Judy's a Buddhist. No one constrained her."

"Where were you when Michael composed all Judy's incense?" Marylee challenged Ellen.

"That's right," Judy said. "It wasn't exactly easy. And it still isn't."

"Nevertheless," Ellen said, "in the end you have not been repressed, oppressed—let's not abuse the language here—or otherwise religiously persecuted by your husband, have you? Too many victims. You are not a victim, Judy. I rest my case."

"There is something about the Buddhism," Marylee replied, carefully, just as Judy always contended, "perhaps because it has little or nothing to do with Christianity, that does make it an exception. I guarantee you that if I draped a crucifix or a crescent around the Buddha's neck, so to speak, that is, if Judy took an interest in Muhammad instead of Gautama, Michael Klain would become apoplectic. And that's what's wrong."

Marylee let a portentous silence pass.

"Now listen to these words that I am about to utter: *Jesus Christ, Our Lord Jesus Christ.* I said, *Jesus. Jesus Christ.* You see, I said it. Words that have not been uttered under this roof except as expletives for two decades. Given who we are, who I am, or was, there's something very wrong with this situation."

"Look, Marylee," Ellen said, fixing her eyes on her. "I have a simple goal in life: I just want to get through the semester."

"Well, maybe Jesus can help you."

"Marylee, you're too smart to be talking this way. It's well known," Judy continued, "that some very smart people, especially when they are in therapy, do not do well. Why? Because they can be too smart for their own good. You are outsmarting yourself."

"Do I believe that every reference to Jesus derives from a lame mind?" Ellen asked rhetorically. "Absolutely."

"I don't have your advanced degrees, but I know what it takes for the heart to wake up to the Lord. I sound like a cliché to you, but I am not. To myself I sound inviting, fresh, reborn. And it will continue through the restaurant and William's ministry."

"His what?"

"Do you want me to spell it out, Ellen?"

"All right," she said. "I'm an English teacher. Spell if you want, but you get graded on content as well. Passion is important, and I see you have not been full of energy like this since we redid the lobby. That's good. That's praiseworthy. B-plus for that. But, for God's sake, you cannot leave your brain at the door either."

"What do you want us to do?" Judy asked wearily.

"When—*if*—the tirades start," said Marylee, "you have to promise me you'll resist them. That's all. Just don't be cowed. Promise that if the guys begin to act as if the world is about to end, just calmly wait and say to them: *See, the world is not ending just because we have this boy on the first floor.* Now go take a shower and go to bed."

"That's all you want of us?"

"For starters. And don't make me break the lease."

Ellen impatiently shuffled through her papers and set them down as if they marked an invisible line of resolve. She stared at Marylee across them. "Okay, I am trying to visualize this restaurant, Marylee. Help me. What do you think the place will really be like? Something like . . . a Planet Jesus?"

Ellen's sarcasm was not all bad. In it Marylee heard notes of interest and possibility. She was encouraged. "Anything is possible now. That's the beauty of believing, even of beginning to believe once again."

"Stick to the restaurant, Marylee," Ellen came back at her tartly. "You are asking for our permission to let this kid build an eatery, not the kingdom of heaven."

"All right. I believe William Harp has the potential to be the finest Christian entrepreneur on the Upper West Side." Marylee went on to describe William's plans for the restaurant as she had learned them in detail earlier in the day. She had intended to be organized and to present a convincing plan to Ellen and Judy—after all, Ellen was right, she had to make the sale on business grounds first and foremost—but the ideas tumbled out of her, as they had from William Harp, topsy-turvy from a cornucopia of enthusiasm.

"You see, one concept—okay, maybe this one is not the greatest, but we can work on it—one concept William has is to have eight-and-a-half-by-eleven glossy signed photographs of famous contemporary Christians—a kind of Christian Hall of Fame—lining the walls of the main dining area. I know what you're thinking, but be patient: Waiting on the tables will be done by young people with religious interest, maybe even seminarians. Where they can be recruited Billy hasn't figured out yet. Maybe you can help, Ellen, with kids up at the college. But in his vision—and he definitely has a vision—these clean-cut kids will take periodic breaks from serving the customers to gather in front of the dining area—you know, forming up into an impromptu choir. And they'll sing both classic hymns and songs that are familiar to the Jewish customers—"

"*I Have a Little Dreidel, O Hanukah, O Hanukah, Come Light the Menorah?* Stuff like that?" asked Judy.

"I don't know why not."

"I could put my hands on the song sheets right now," Judy said. "They're up in the Museum—you know the place—in a box with the world's largest collection of half-used Hanukah candles and roach clips. I frankly would love to get them out of the house."

"Okay," Marylee continued, "so the tables will have the music—maybe on laminated cards so the food dropped on the pages won't stain them—and so customers can sing along. The tables will have other features too—flash cards with questions on Biblical trivia that customers can entertain themselves with while waiting for their meals to arrive."

"Flash cards?" asked Ellen. "Very quaint."

"Okay, also a little old-fashioned, a little hokey. Maybe an electronic version of that too. See how your reactions are already helping to refine the product. You're already making a contribution to the evolution of the restaurant. Bravo."

"Are you with me on this, Judy?" Ellen had seen Judy's thumbs groping for each other on her lap, had seen how she was shifting her seat, straightening her spine, clearing her nasal passage—the telltale signs Judy always made when she was getting ready to drop off into a meditative state. "Don't you dare tune out on this now," Ellen said, and then, in a loud voice, "Judith! Terra firma to Judith! Do not leave me alone with Marylee and her Christian entrepreneur! Wake up!"

"Don't shriek at me! I've heard everything," Judy said calmly. "Flashcards, waiters. I'm here."

"Well stay here, dammit. Not even the Dalai Lama drops

off into a trance in the middle of a conversation. Jesus!" The word pinged back and forth among them. "Okay, okay," Ellen said, "Who's the target audience, then? Just Jews?"

Ellen's irritability and Judy's desire to flee did not surprise Marylee. She saw beyond these reactions. She willed herself to see beyond them because she felt her heart was full, and the bemused indulgence of her friends drove her on.

"He is serious," she assured them. "Very much so, if short on experience. That's where we—or at least I—pitch in. William says the target audience includes young college students (nobody has told him that college students don't have much money!) and older Jewish people. In the entryway of the restaurant he's also assembling a Christian library so guests can browse while they wait to be seated. No opportunity to hear the Good News lost! The customers will be encouraged to take the books and pamphlets to their tables. In general and because, he says, Jews as a group are both smart and overweight, he is planning to create a place that has some intellectual heft—the thought heavy while the food will be nutritious and light. I think you could almost send that directly to *Zagat*. That's the deal, so far."

"*Zagat?*" said Ellen. "I was thinking more *Mad Magazine* or the *National Enquirer.*"

Marylee knew she could have done a far better job of describing the restaurant's business plan, but she was not displeased.

Ellen said slowly, "Am I too late to reserve a table for two in the corner among the Christian luminaries? How about under the picture of Pat Boone? He's my favorite Christian singer of all! Who's yours, Judy?"

"I actually do like Donny Osmond," said Judy.

"There's no shame in that," said Marylee. "I happen to think he's very cute."

"Don't you think William Harp is . . . cute as well? Isn't

that a part of the business plan you've conveniently omitted?"

"Please don't go down that road, Ellen," Marylee said. "It's demeaning to me and it makes a mockery of every consciousness-raising group we've ever gone to."

"That's a very nice speech, Marylee," Judy said sleepily. "But we both find him cute too, so you can get off your high horse."

Keeping herself under control, Marylee said simply, "Can I count on you at least to agree to help with the launch? It's really in our own best interest, and you know how much I'd like you to join me. Okay, I can understand if you don't want to help. What I can't understand, what I can't accept, is if you obstruct. Let the guys obstruct if they must, but not you. Not my best friends in the world."

"Marylee," Ellen said without edge, "you sound as if you are running for student body president. Or, in any event, that you are running."

"Well, I do feel that way. I feel very young and—partisan—once again."

"That's fine," Ellen said. "But who are you running against? Not us. We're not your problem, honey. We never were."

"What's the worst thing that can happen?" Judy asked.

"Our husbands divorce us," said Ellen.

"I'm not sure *that* would be so bad," said Judy.

"Exactly," said Marylee. "This moment is completely full of God's love." She stood and embraced them. "I love you both very much."

7

Dear Father:

Or should it be "Dad"? William crossed out "Dad" and started with "Father" again but moved the writing pad away from him, then closer, scrutinizing it as if it were a picture. He didn't like the look or sound of "Father". It was as if he were writing to God. His father was, after all, only that, not his God. William was no longer small and helpless. Yet he knew he still had to convey not only the substance but also the sounds of what his father needed to hear. He went back to how he had begun.

Dear Daddy:

How I adore them—they're like my Christian sisters of the Upper West Side, Marylee, Judy, and Ellen. Of course it's still mainly Marylee for now but I have perfect faith the others will come along because Marylee is the natural leader among them and somehow, praise the Lord, she is hearing God's word these days and He is saying: Help Billy, help Billy! Because Marylee Jeffers and I get along so well, the restaurant is evolving, and fast. No need to worry.

Now, having said that, Daddy, it's just as you told me: Nobody ever promised that doing God's work is going to be a cakewalk.

There's good news to report and just a little bad. The bad is that the Christian ladies' husbands have learned about our concept just a little sooner than I wanted. I didn't have a chance to be there in the same room with them when the news broke and to represent it just right and to explain how they should not worry and not feel threatened and to express my love.

Frankly I think this bad news is sort of good news. Here's why: I was worried that Marylee was going to try to water down our concept. I was even worried we might have to be moving on. But something has really clicked between Marylee and yours truly early on, as I've said, and I saw she was going to be my defender. I worked her a little like you talked about, of course, Daddy, and I guess I could take credit for enlisting her as such a big ally. But I credit it all to your good training, and of course to God. I believe she pretty much on her own has heard the Word and she has brought the other ladies to come 'round. They don't love us yet, that's for sure, but I don't see them calling the lawyers either. Now it's off to restaurant supply stores.

As ever,

William

8

"I know Sam's ears grew. He heard, if not every word, then at least one out of three. They know very well what's going on."

Ellen was speaking with Marylee over the phone and waiting for Judy to come on from home to complete the conference call. Ellen was in her office—really not much more than a wood-paneled graduate student's cubicle—just beyond the rare book room of the college library. But apart from the Museum, it was her favorite place to be, especially if there were no students around. Several piles of books, eleven and twelve high, like accidental totems, stood on Ellen's small desk, balanced so precariously that a breeze from the small transom high above or a sudden vibration through the walls might knock one over.

Marylee was also in her office, with the door closed; her desk was completely clear, cleaned, polished, and lemon-scented. A single pencil, brilliantly sharpened, lay upon it at an expressive angle, as if to say: *Pick me up. I will write the story of the rest of your life. I am a new beginning.*

Soon Judy came on the phone from home and the conference call began.

"ML, this is all about cold feet," Ellen said. "Wait, are you there now, Judy? Are your feet cold too?"

"Ice."

"In the Museum or at home?" Ellen asked.

"Why do you ask?" Judy said, but answered immediately. "Portable phone in the Museum, on chair liberated from Columbia president's office."

"That's not authenticated," said Ellen. "Almost certainly apocryphal."

"Fine," she said. "I mean now holding Janis Joplin album and reading liner notes."

"Excellent," Marylee said. "Janis was a profoundly conflicted Christian woman waiting to be reborn. Go ahead."

"I actually dreamed last night," said Ellen, "that I was Joan of Arc. It was not conducive to restful sleep."

"Precisely," said Marylee, "things are churning up."

"That's not helpful," said Ellen. "Joan was a lunatic. She heard voices. I have nothing to do with that kind of stuff. What I heard was only Sam, asleep next to me."

"So?" said Judy.

"So something was different. Even in sleep, his whole sleeping language, if you will. And he's been spending a helluva lot of time in the Museum."

"Michael too."

"A shift is taking place," Ellen said. "I know it."

"After twenty years," said Marylee, "you'd think you'd welcome it. It's just as I predicted."

"What kind of shift?" Judy asked.

"I think he's giving me the Evil Eye."

"Hold it right there," said Marylee. "I never told you it would be easy. Second, the Evil Eye is a superstitious concept of Jewish origin, Eastern Europe. For a highly educated woman, Ellen, you're amazing! This was why we needed a conference call? There is no such thing as the Evil Eye. Third, how can you believe in the Evil Eye and think I'm a fool for believing again in the love of Jesus? Banish the Evil Eye. Pray to our Lord, then go have lunch. I have work to do."

"No you don't," said Judy. "You haven't worked a full day since that boy arrived."

"There's work and there's work," Marylee answered, with finality.

"Don't go," Ellen said. "Please. Sam is very pissed off, in

case you hadn't noticed, ML. I tried to present the restaurant to him as a kooky, off-center Christian comedy place, but he wasn't buying. He kept asking me which side am I on. I want you to know that theoretically, spiritually, I'm with you, Marylee. You have a right to your renewal or whatever it is. I want you to know this. But I don't have the energy to fight what's coming my way from Sam. I know it."

"You promised. Find it."

"I just heard about two former Salvadoran nuns," said Judy. "Political refugees who want to open a taco place. We could break Harp's lease and help the nuns instead. It could be a restaurant for tacos and liberation theology. Would you accept such a substitute?" Judy asked.

"I leave it to your own consciences," said Marylee. "But I am not going to break the lease, unless you tell me I have to. I'll wait thirty seconds."

Ellen and Marylee now heard Judy slip the Joplin album onto the creaky turntable . . . *My friends all have Porsches I must make amends . . .*

Ellen composed herself. She was resigned. "A little guidance requested, Marylee. Tell us again how precisely we coordinate this."

"How about just telling them the truth?" Marylee answered plainly. "I thought that was the point we made: No dancing around who William is and what the place is about. No comedy club nonsense."

"I'm not so sure about the truth anymore," said Judy. "I know Michael is putting his head in the ground a few more inches than usual every day. He's cultivating ignorance, but it won't last."

"What did we spend half the night talking about?" Marylee asked.

"Do you think Harp would really sue if we reneged on the

lease?" Ellen asked.

"I give you permission to withdraw that question. Let's just tell the truth, gingerly, with tact, but the truth."

"In situations like this," Ellen said, "Judy and I agree: The truth is never quite sufficient. Something additional is often required. Like a big fat lie."

"The men do live here," said Judy. "Although they are definitely myopic, they are not blind. They will get it all soon enough, and faster than slower. Michael knows already. He's just denying it."

"I still say *lie*," said Ellen.

"Look," Marylee spoke calmly, "it's *how* the guys are told as much as what they see themselves or think they see that will help most and keep the craziness to a minimum. You're far better at why than how, Ellen."

"Fortunately," said Judy, "Jews are not prone to violence."

"But you do have to watch the quiet skinny types like Michael," Ellen said. "When he goes, duck."

Lord, won't you buy me a Mercedes Benz. My friends all have . . .

"Just shut that off!" Ellen cried into her phone. "You have the world's worst set of bad habits, Judy."

"Look," said Marylee, "why don't we introduce them slowly, in gradations, to the concept that the whole world is not Jewish. Reassure them that life will go on as always—even though I am fairly certain the ground is shifting forever, at least for me. So I guess that will make *me* a liar. But, step by step, we will wean them from this . . . coercion. It will be good for them. We show them even greater love than we've been dishing out for twenty years, and then they'll see this great new freedom they can embrace for their souls to soar to heaven! What do you say, my sisters?"

"I'm screaming," Ellen said.

"I don't hear any screaming," Marylee put her hands on her cool desktop. "I hear love being born again."

"I don't know what to do with that remark," Judy said.

"The screaming is the silent kind," Ellen said. "The worst kind. It's the screaming of men . . ."

"You're exaggerating," Judy said. "As usual."

"Well, the truth is they're thinking that their wives have made them complicit in the potential diminution of the Jewish people. Accept my paraphrase because, believe me, that's exactly how Sam will see it," Ellen said. "No matter how you spin or manage the facts, quiet screaming or loud. I therefore vote, like Karl Marx, to abolish all religions."

"Karl is dead and traveling in photons through the cycles of *samsara*," said Judy. "We're alive here and now. What the hell are we going to do? Really?"

"You're having your fun, Marylee, but don't kid yourself," Ellen went on. "We are playing with some very basic fire here. Maybe we should really rethink. Maybe it's better if we just eat the legal penalties and urge William Harp to go elsewhere."

Marylee was not discouraged. She had anticipated this conversation. She had been thinking about her vision, how she had been coming around slowly, in stages. In the Bible a heart may be changed overnight, but on the Upper West Side, it perhaps took a little longer. Ellen and Judy were entitled; one step forward, one back. "Look, tell me your *specific* concerns once again. Maybe I can help," she said.

Judy spoke first: "My only condition is that Michael's father not find out any of this. Not a hint, not a rumor, nothing." Her father-in-law was nearing ninety-seven and living in a nursing home nearby, *and* he was a rabbi. "It will kill him instantly."

"How would he hear unless you or Michael tells him?"

"He'll hear if it gets in the Jewish papers. He lives for the Jewish papers. Do you understand?"

"I will handle this like Colin Powell handled the Persian Gulf War," Marylee said. "So relax. There will be a media blackout and the sea of reporters—I mean maybe one Orthodox, one Conservative, one Reform reporter, and the one half-time food writer—will know only what we want them to, and when we're ready."

"And in the name of everything holy, no Pat Boone," Ellen said. "I look at the man's shining, beatific face, and I want to puke."

"Consider it done. News blackout is in, and Pat Boone is out. What else?"

"Make it all go away," said Judy.

Marylee knew that what her mother used to call the Great Spirit—and what all too soon in her mother's life had degenerated into merely spirits—was finding its way into her friends' hearts. The spirit grabbed at you and you wrestled with it as Jacob had wrestled with God and the angels. She told this to Judy and Ellen, but the spirit, for now, only caused silence at their ends of the line.

Marylee adjusted the phone under her chin so that she could bring her hands prayerfully together. "You're going to think I'm crazy for doing this. I know you're going to say to each other soon—maybe as soon as we hang up and you call each other again—that Marylee has lost it. But I haven't." She exhaled a breath of pure relief and said, "The more apoplectic the men become, *if* they become apoplectic, the calmer we have to remain. This is essential."

"All right, all right," Judy said.

"I want to offer a little telephonic prayer," Marylee said. "Will you join me?"

"I feel like throwing up too," whispered Judy.

"She meditates or throws up," said Ellen. "What a life!"

"You can puke over Pat Boone, and I can't puke over

something else?" Judy groaned.

"Buddhists should not cling to puking," Ellen said.

"You're just wonderful, the both of you," Marylee intervened. "Whether you throw up or not, I just love you. And I want to thank God for giving me two such wonderful friends as you. And for bringing the Christian cafeteria, or whatever it'll be, Loaves and Fishes . . ."

"That's the worst name I ever heard," said Ellen.

"Consider it changed," said Marylee. "And I thank each of you, my wonderful sisters."

"All right, all right," Judy said.

"Maybe the Christian restaurant or whatever-it-is is genuinely *b'shert,*" said Ellen, "as they say in Yiddish. Predestined. But right now it only feels predestined to cause vast trouble."

"By the way," Marylee said, "it's just occurred to me that calmness, serenity, and grace under pressure are all fine Christian characteristics. You know: figuratively turning the other cheek in all its variety. But getting all exercised, worked up, confrontational, laying down demands and shrieking— does this sound familiar?—and flying off the handle may be Jewish characteristics.

"I think we've negotiated this like strong Christian women," Marylee said. "I think the conference call is concluded. Congratulations to us."

9

Sir:

You should have heard the racket here when Ellen and Judy told their husbands. You remember I described the brownstone to you, how each of the couples has their own floor that they live on, all separate but equal in size, so to speak. Well, when it comes to arguing and feuding, they get all commune-like again. They storm through the whole building, demonstrating up and down the steps with thuds and quakes and yelling. It's actually mainly Sam and Ellen who caused the ruckus. Ellen—that's the college professor—went about debating her husband, who was shouting at her things like "How could you do this! Why didn't you check with us!" and so forth. Marylee had warned me already that Ellen's man, Sam, loses his temper quite a bit and that I shouldn't be alarmed if one night it appears that Goliath is traipsing about spoiling for a fight.

When the shouting began I wanted to step out in the hallway to help, but between what you always taught me about never getting near a fight between a husband and wife until I am a married man myself and know a thing or two, what Marylee advised, and also because Sam is nearly six foot four, I decided just to stay in back of the restaurant and think my own good helpful Christian thoughts. Those thoughts ran mainly to what I'd say if he rushed in and threatened to kill me.

You remember the Buddhist fellow in the basement with the foul-smelling sheep and bad incense I wrote you about? Nawang? I must give him credit where it's due because he came up and reassured me that Sam and Ellen do this a lot but Sam never actually hurts his wife, or any sentient being—that's the way Buddhists talk—although there was some danger Sam might punch his hand through some of my new Sheetrock. The Buddhist offered to sit and meditate with me until the fracas blew over. He said living here is good practice for him to learn to be like a stone in the cold river stream, solid and immovable, centered while the roiling waters rush by. That's another sample of the Buddhist talk that I'm passing along to you for the flavor of it. Naturally, I declined to take lessons in how to become a rock.

So I decided that I could help if I just lay down on my cot and prayed, and that's exactly what I did. I stared out the back window at a fire escape and a laundry line attached to it and I reminded myself how wonderful our restaurant really will be, how it was planned by God that I had found a building to live in that had three strong Christian women married to Jewish men, and what a fine start I had made with the help of these folks and the Lord. Then a door slammed two flights up and shook the whole place like a tremor.

I picked up my Bible and I read from Ephesians 4:26, *Let not the sun go down upon your wrath.* Over and over again I read those lines about anger and tried to send the sentiments out to Ellen and Sam brawling up and down the floors and cornering each other in the stairwells and everyplace but the fire escapes.

A little later I sent my thoughts out toward Judy and Michael, because you'd be surprised the fearful noise that a small quiet librarian and a large Buddhist woman can generate, although their squabbling was not nearly as fierce as Ellen and Sam's, with a lot more silences between the outbursts and a lot less cussing.

Next morning, my prayers were answered and I am happy to report that we are still here, and in business! Michael Klain, who used to be *very* friendly, and always asked on the way to his job at the New York Public Library how the renovations were going, and if the City's paperwork was moving along and so forth, well, he still asked.

His manner was a bit colder but it was not the cold shoulder. I count this a victory.

And here's more good news: Marylee's husband Gerry came by this morning along with her, and for the first time they sat me down, these two smart business people, and they gave me a dozen pages that Marylee had typed out on what we need to do to make a restaurant a success in the City. She called this the business plan. It's a lot more detailed than anything we did, so changes are coming your way, Daddy.

First, the name you devised for the restaurant—*Loaves & Fishes*—has to go, they say. The name has to be snappy if customers, especially of the Jewish persuasion, are going to patronize us.

Gerry said a name like *Loaves and* Gefilte *Fishes* might even work with what Marylee calls my prime old-fashioned Jewish audience. I didn't know what *gefilte* meant and I asked. Which was when Marylee sent Gerry one of her green-eyed looks and he raised up his hands, as if to say, I beg of you, don't get started!

Anyway, it was a joke, because a *gefilte* is a type of fish laboriously mixed up from carp and other sea creatures Jews eat, but no shellfish because that is against their dietary regulations. Most Jews don't even like *gefilte* fish, Gerry told me. They fake liking it (and sometimes even *toss* the *gefilte* directly in the trash when the grandmothers aren't looking, making out as if they just love it) because the point is always to please their parents and grandparents. So I am learning many behind-the-scenes things about Jewish food culture that will be important for the restaurant to succeed and important in fulfilling our ultimate mission here, Daddy. We are working on many other things as well, including a new name. A name with buzz.

There is already some curiosity in the neighborhood, says Gerry, and we have to capitalize on it. That's the way he put it, *we.*

But did they ever nix our idea of the fork and knife in the shape of the cross that we had in mind to hang over the restaurant's front door! Marylee says I need to begin to see our Lord on the cross as Jews often see Him—He frightens them. She told me I could ask Gerry about it and I did, right away.

He thought for a long time and then said, "I never realized until this very moment that I *do* have a problem with large crucifixes fashioned out of immense neon utensils. I'm sorry, Mr. Harp," he said, "but I just do."

Of course I could hear the sarcasm in his voice, but I forgave him, Daddy. It was only the New York way again. "And Marylee is absolutely right," he went on, "that it would be a marketing mistake to display symbols outside. And one more thing, son," Gerry said. "Listen to my wife. Marylee is right about nearly everything."

By the way, Daddy, I have finally met a really religious Jewish person. His name is Isaac, like the son of Abraham, and he is an easygoing fellow, the electrician Marylee found to work on rewiring the kitchen. He comes dirt cheap and from Brooklyn, which is a different burrow or part of the City.

Yesterday I walked in when Isaac was taking his break to pray the afternoon service standing right there amidst all the BX cable, hanging wires, tools, and ducts. He takes out his small black prayer book and begins reciting and rocking back and forth and mumbling the Hebrew words to no one in particular. I guess to God. His sister works along with him sometimes. Her name is Rena but she doesn't do the praying part and she is very modest, hardly looks my way, which is, I have learned, part of the way Jewish girls are. I saw her reading the sports section of *The Daily News,* which is a New York paper, while Isaac was praying, which really irritated the brother. They both wear black overalls and cover their heads all the time, out of respect for God, Isaac said. Underneath his woolen cap, Isaac has on a separate skullcap that he keeps in place with pins both when he works and prays; also he's got his facial hair arranged in these long sideburns that the Jews call "peyote." They are commanded to do this in some part of the Bible, but it rang no bell for me. Do you know the section, Daddy?

"The sideburns, the 'peyote,' sounds like the drug that grows in the desert," Rena said, "except you don't pronounce the 'e.'" Her joking irritated her brother. Actually he didn't like her talking to me, period, because it goes against their strict rules of conduct for girls as I've said. Still I can tell they both like me and they know everything about electricity. So much still to do! Opening still a couple of months away. Praise the Lord!

William

IO

It was already becoming another night of intensely below-average tennis for Gerry, Sam, and Michael even before they began to play. Yanking too hard on a new can of balls, Sam doomed all his ground strokes; when the can popped, so did his elbow. Michael was struggling to pull a hooded green sweatshirt over his skinny shoulders, and in the process he bent one of the temples of his glasses. It took him another ten minutes to remove the assorted athletic bands that held his bifocals, however poorly, in place.

When the games began, the balls flew wildly and the perspiration flowed, but after an overhead slam that put the games at six-one, Michael and Sam had little to show for the apparent effort. They were standing now on their side of the net glaring at Gerry, who checked his watch and inquired calmly, "Another set, gentlemen?"

"Sure," Michael panted.

"We're going to kick the shit out of you and make you come to your senses."

Sam broke off his glaring, returned to the service line, and promptly netted two serves.

"As we say in the Museum, center yourselves, gentlemen," said Gerry. "He who serves in anger double-faults in abundance."

"Here's the idea," announced Michael as he bent to tie his sneakers, which, with their laces wrapped at the ankle, appeared like a pair of ancient Roman sandals. "We should bring the Harp kid here, and he can convert Ganesh. Let him go convert *all* the Muslims in New Jersey, and maybe then he'll forget about the Jews in our neighborhood."

"Let's beat both those guys," Sam hectored with his huge wagging racquet, as if Gerry's partner tonight were the invisible William Harp. Then they began to volley.

Tonight they were in their favorite court, Eight. While it had the poorest light, including two overhead bulbs that tended to flash brightly and to thwart all attempted lobs, as well as the dullest surface of all the courts, the great benefit of Eight was that here they were farthest away from the lounge; here they were out of range of nearly all critical and disapproving gazes. Deliberately mixing up his geography, Michael had dubbed Eight the Tierra del Fuego of Caracas, the isolated promontory where the threesome could be loud, klutzy, and obnoxious without paying a social price.

"Guys like Harp never forget, no matter what you do," Sam was lecturing Michael as they scrambled to hit the hard stuff Gerry was sending at them. "They need to convert Jews like they need to breathe. Like *you* need to read. Like the cavalry absolutely needed to subdue the Indians—whether it was good or bad. Like the atolls and islands need the oceans to surround them for their very identity. They pursue you and bribe you and charm you and cajole you, and when they think they've got you—this is the payoff for them—they count you, they add you up, they calculate all the extra days they get in heaven for each Jew they haul in.

"Are you following any of this, Gerry?" Sam shouted across the net.

"No."

"Then they hang your foreskin in their collection over the fire."

"That hurts even to think about," said Michael as he lunged at a high-bouncing ball with spin right in front of him so that he should have easily stroked it but found instead only air. "What the hell are you putting on it?" He arched his question to Gerry.

But before Gerry could respond, Sam did it for him. "That's his new Jesus Christ topspin lob. No Jewish player has ever been known to hit it back. Right, Gerry?"

Sam turned to Michael as they exchanged places on the court to receive Gerry's next celestially assisted serve. "I really am not joking. And they *always* go for the Jews first."

Back now at the net, Sam hacked at the tape once again. This time it was for Gerry's benefit, but Gerry was unperturbed and returned Michael's counterpunch with an effortless but hard backhand that even Sam had to acknowledge was smooth as silk tonight.

"Like it was in the Crusades," Sam continued to mount his harangue and to slug the net, and occasionally the ball, to illustrate his little tennis-inspired tour of Jewish history. "Whack! Bam! Voom! They are on their way to kick Muslim ass in the Holy Land, see—" All manner of sound effects of battle galore came out of Sam. Michael thought Sam might have had too much wine with his dinner earlier in the evening.

Still, they just kept coming, like Gerry's strokes. "And on their way they knock off the Jews and steal their property, you see, and off they ride, no accountability. Are you hearing me over there, Gerry? So off they go now into the Rhine Valley, into southern France. Everywhere Crusaders show up, you have dead Jews, or converted ones. But not in our backyard, pal."

"I think my partner's not focusing," Michael said.

Here Sam paused, kept his eye on Gerry's lob, which this time was within his range, and reached for it like a grizzly on skates, smashing the winner.

"Break time, guys," Michael said and sat down near their gear, rummaging through the pockets of his extra pair of shorts. Finding the object of his search, he offered Sam an unappetizing square of unwrapped, speckled chocolate, vintage and provenance unknown.

Sam sniffed at it as if he were checking for microbes and then threw it into the courtside trash bin. "All I can tell you," he said, "is that it ain't happening here!"

"We are all relieved," said Michael, "that you are personally going to defend the Caracas Health and Racquet Club from any drive-by Crusaders in the neighborhood."

Gerry, who had been stretching in place, now walked toward Sam and sat down beside him. "Take a deep breath, Sam, and just stop obsessing." There was an imploring tone in his voice. "He's a tenant. That's all. Not a Knight Templar. And he's got some rights."

"People out to convert Jews in my building do not have rights."

"*Your* building?"

"You have not played well," Gerry said, "because you are not calm. I meditated with the Buddhist before supper, and you can see the results."

"This is how calm I am." Sam proceeded to demonstrate for Michael, Gerry, and the four players three courts away—the only others remaining in the courts at the ungodly hour of eleven o'clock—how he intended to deal with William

Harp, missionary. They looked on as he blasted the three orange balls they had just begun to use high over the mesh curtain and off the light panels, pinging and rattling into the air-conditioning ducts thirty feet above.

"Get a grip," said Gerry. "A few lost souls, and then it'll be over with."

"Exactly," Michael said as he retrieved one of the balls.

"He's got Marylee fronting for him, and you're going along with it. That's the issue," Sam said. "That's my problem, not the Crusaders."

He stood and slammed the broad white tape at the top of the net with his racquet. Once, twice, one more time until it was even audible to the kid managing the desk in the lounge, who stuck his head out the door to find out what the problem was. It was definitely time to go.

They gathered their gear and wearily trooped toward the break in the green netting. They passed through it and then walked off the court and into the lounge, where they dropped their racquet cases and jackets. Sam motioned the lounge kid toward him and, with a twenty-dollar bill theatrically flourished, purchased his forgetfulness about the evening's net-whacking offenses.

Back out in the parking lot, Sam, who had been ransacking his vocabulary for words pointed enough to express his anger and frustration, lapsed into silence. Instead of getting into the car, he selected a slanted white parking line, straddled it, and looked up with exasperation toward the sparkling cosmos. Gerry slid in behind the wheel, with Michael still sweating beside him, and they listened to the basketball game and waited for a few minutes with fraying patience for Sam to settle down and to finish his communing. When he didn't respond to a second honk, Gerry backed the car out of its slot and began to do circles around him.

"Waiting for the Crusaders?" Michael said through the rolled-down window.

When Michael snapped the door open, Sam finally turned toward the Toyota and folded his long legs to fit himself into the back seat. The car sped back to Manhattan. Through the fogging window, Sam declared neither to Gerry nor to Michael but to apparently anyone in New Jersey, New York, or the Tri-state area who cared to listen, "I just cannot believe that in the year 2000 we are letting them do this."

II

Marylee was waiting up for Gerry when he got home from tennis. It surprised her that her mouth had gone a little dry in anticipation. As bold as she had been with Ellen and Judy, she felt the opposite now as she heard Gerry's key turn the bolt in the lock; perhaps she was not so different from Ellen and Judy after all.

She let him have time for a hot shower, she brought him the thick blue robe with the hood that she had bought for him on their Bahamas vacation three years ago, and asked if he wanted to watch *Nightline;* for a change he was in time for it. Gerry enjoyed this program because avuncular Ted Koppel reminded him of his Uncle Maxie, a bookie now long gone, whom he had loved and believed to be the only wise man he had ever known.

Gerry and Marylee always enjoyed this time of night together. Relaxed from the tennis to the point of exhaustion, Gerry was often still mentally not ready for sleep. He was often surprised how playing late-night tennis (this was one of the reasons he continued, season after season) seemed to inspire his physical passion for Marylee; this was especially so if he'd played at least one good set—even one memorably placed shot would set Gerry up quite nicely for love. And even if the games were so-so (which was usually the case), his body almost always felt well stretched and eager to place itself beside his pretty and supple wife.

During *Nightline* they touched each other gently, they sent each other the subtle signals of couples long married—yes, no, perhaps tomorrow, are you tired, dear, of course we can wait, you'll be missing a great thing, have we run out of that nice sandalwood soap? Okay? Why not? Then, yes, tonight.

Occasionally, if they couldn't make up their mind to make love or not, they turned to the only other person in the room—their wise pal, Ted Koppel—for his opinion. They carefully scrutinized Ted's sign-off: for he had this way, after his summation, of projecting an intimate glance, a nod of the head, and sometimes even a coy wink that said to Gerry and Marylee, Okay, kids, we've agonized together for twenty-five minutes about gangsterism in the Russian Politburo and you've done your sportsmanlike part to pay it some attention; now slip off those jammies, and have a good time—you deserve it.

Marylee pointedly turned Ted off before the end of the show tonight. She slid over on the bed and put her hand lovingly on Gerry's cheek. Yet before he could secure it there with his, she removed it. "Last night," she said, "I was remembering a Christmas season four years ago when we were taking one of our walks down Broadway. The air was cold but still comfortable. Do you remember?"

"Try me," Gerry said, certain he did not have a clue but eager for her to go on.

"We were just walking above Seventy-ninth Street when I noticed that the tree vendor there was not playing any

Christmas music to attract customers. He was not ringing a bell, or hawking, or approaching passersby."

"Okay," said Gerry, "these things happen. Maybe he had a sore throat or wasn't in the mood."

"You remember the time I'm talking about?"

"Of course I do," Gerry lied. "More or less."

"His pines and firs were facing a bagel shop, and the vendor was standing forlornly watching customers enter and leave it. You remember?"

Gerry nodded.

"Each time the door opened, there was a little tinkle of a bell followed by onion, raisin, and garlic aromas that floated out and hung like a kind of invisible Jewish cloud above the poor trees."

"A Jewish cloud?"

"Yes, I remember turning to you and saying, 'How come virtually *all* the people we know in the world are Jews, and most of them liberal Jews, to boot?' You heard me—I know you did—but you did not answer, Gerry. It was hard to tell if you were thinking something profound or merely deciding if you wanted a bagel. So I asked again, 'Gerry, where are all the conservatives and all the Christians who *used* to be in my life?'

"'I saved you from them,' you answered.

"'Where are all the small-town people and the football lovers, all the good old boys who used to be in my life! They were dumb, but amusing.'

"Do you remember what you answered me?"

"I wish I did," Gerry said. "I hope it was clever."

"You said, 'This is New York.' You said it matter-of-factly, without bravado. You may as well have been saying, 'The earth moves around the sun.'

"'I miss them,' I said to you back then. I really missed them, and I still do. Then I reached down and hit the play button on the tree vendor's tape recorder. 'Good King Wenceslas' boomed out, and the vendor was furious and he growled at me, 'Why'd the hell you do that!'

"'It's Christmas,' I screeched back at him.

"'But I'm Jewish,' he said. 'Don't tell anyone.'

"'You see!' I said to you, as you pulled me along and away from him. 'You see! Evidence. I rest my case.'

"You said, 'You're sweet, Marylee. You're very sweet.'

"I said, 'Maybe not. I also miss the caroling.'

"You said, 'We can find a church and you can carol there to your heart's content.'"

"That was smart of me."

"'I mean real caroling on the street, Gerry,' I said to you, and I still remembered being a little alarmed by the pleading in my voice. I was telling you this and you were calling me cute and sweet, but you simply weren't listening. You were hearing maybe, but not listening. I said, 'Gerry, I miss a lot more than the caroling—the crunching along in the snow, the friendliness, the smiling at rosy-cheeked neighbors, and singing from door to door with so much good cheer until everyone comes out to join you.'

"Do you remember what you said then, Gerry?"

He shook his head; he was good and nervous now.

"You said, 'That kind of activity could definitely get you killed in Manhattan.' That's what I mean, honey. I miss who I used to be."

"I know who you used to be," Gerry said. That's all that came to him to say. He prayed it would be enough. "And I love that too," he said as he enveloped Marylee in his arms. Not being able to think of anything else, he kissed her and kept kissing her until Marylee turned her face away.

Eventually they slept.

12

Dear Father:

I hope this letter finds you in good spirits, and preferably sitting down. For you know I am a believer in getting right to the point, which I learned at your knee. The point is: the ministry requires a big infusion of cash and fast. This is because I have so many new things to do to make the restaurant work. My friend Marylee has advised me that ours is a restaurant with a message, and who could disagree with that! For the message to have the desired effect, she says, we need the latest-style messenger.

That messenger is now electronic. That's why she is strongly advising us to have some new elements neither you nor I ever thought of: For example, a big screen hanging above the diners, on which we show videotapes, DVDs, and films on Christian themes and great religious moments. With this technology, I can also tape sermons that a solitary eater might listen to, with earphones provided at each and every table. Having a Bible at the table handy to reach like the Gideons do in hotels is one thing. And the Biblical flash cards we thought of, well that is all fine and good, Marylee says, but to be wired, hooked in, digitized, that is the way the Gospel is going to be spread, along with, of course, the good eats.

Marylee says we can double the projected number of patrons *if* we have the screens and other features because they will give our establishment genuine bigtime buzz.

You see, people come into restaurants these days in New York not just to eat but, for example, to watch all sports, all the time in sports bars, or to get hopped up on caffeine in coffee bars that dot the city like an epidemic. Our place is going to be God's bar, all God's word, all the time.

And, by the way, Daddy, we have come up with a new name. The restaurant is going to be called Club Revelation! That's thanks to Marylee Jeffers herself. I'll preach from many books of the Holy Bible, of course, but the last shall be first! That is, Revelation will be the main course, so to speak. Wait till I write you about our Seven Deadly Sins Chocolate Pie. But that name, Daddy! I hope you like it. Club Revelation. Does that name have buzz or what!

So please send the amount indicated on the attached sheet, Daddy, because the projection screen and new sound system are expensive, even at the good prices that Gerry Levine—that's Marylee's husband—helped to arrange. All the wiring Isaac and Rena put in will also have to be ripped out and be replaced by a new system with coaxial cable and whatnot. Sorry about that, but it's going to be a system that will last for the ages.

Yours in the Lord,

William

My Dear Father:

Yes, I do have your letter right here in front of me cautioning about additional expenses. I hope it hasn't shocked you—too much. I'm fairly certain it is the price of a successful ministry, and that is what we are striving for.

This approach is the right one for the future. I can feel it within me, and because of that I have never worked so hard or so many hours in my life. While I am supervising the construction work, I am also preparing my sermons night and day. Can't you visualize the results already? There I am, moving among the tables spreading the Gospel, a few well-chosen words at a time, to this absorbed customer. There I am, Daddy, sitting down with a customer eating our delicate fried chicken but who is also clearly already lit up with the light of the Lord. Then, there, high

above the room on the screen, you'll be able
to view a tape of me preaching to the whole
assembly of diners. All Gospel, all the time!

William lay down his pen. He was suddenly conscious
of his alarming tendency to exaggerate—he was *not* working night and day. Not on the restaurant, in any event. He
chided himself that the tone of exaggeration suffused all his
words, written and spoken. In the name of Jesus, he said to
himself, with faint laughter, at least temper it a little. For
here in this ministry to Jewish people, the uneasy feeling he
associated with the truth kept surfacing; it was hounding
him and telling him, Don't exaggerate. Not even to your
father. He now dismissed this feeling in an act of cowardice
he knew he would soon regret and he resumed, but with the
resolve at least to try to stick to facts.

And we haven't forgotten about the food
in the other improvements we are considering. High quality that's going to mix deli,
which we will call *charcuterie* like the French
people, with Middle Eastern fare such as
couscous, baba ganoush, tabouli, and you
name it. Because our Lord was from the
Middle East, as you well know. But how
things have changed, food-wise, Daddy, from
the holy days of the Last Supper! Or, more
probably, there are many things Jesus and His
early followers consumed that we don't even
know about or have yet to discover. For
example, when He took a break from healing
the sick and blind, Gerry said to me just this
morning, He likely enjoyed a good falafel

Himself, along with a glass of new vintage wine or perhaps a spritzer, first-century equivalent of. Why shouldn't we sell these? Gerry wanted to know. Why indeed? I answered. So you see how we are evolving. I hope you approve.

Which reminds me, Father, a liquor license in New York costs upwards of $75,000 down these days. Is that all right with you?

He knew his father was prepared to invest in him and in this ministry, big-time. He visualized his father's eyes—the small, intense pupils that were impassioned, brooding, and full of hope for heaven staring at him. He feared his father's grimacing in the astonished disbelief that Billy knew he often leveled at the other missionaries, but not at him. Never him. He was protected but paying a price in a balancing act, whether in person or through letters, that William knew very well. Yet there would be a limit to what his father would undertake.

I look up from this letter, Daddy, and I can already see the faces of future satisfied customers sitting in our booths. I see empty Jewish vessels (I mean in spirit terms, of course) waiting to be filled up with the Word as you taught me to preach it.

The Lord works in mysterious ways and the computers and projection screens, the listening systems at each table, and all the other top-of-the-line stuff this infusion of cash will pay for, are all surely part of His plan.

I echo you, Father, in saying we need to advance *right now,* for there are so many Jewish people so close to me now, so friendly and so close, like Marylee's Gerry, and I sense others will soon follow. As you well know, the Rapture can occur at any moment *"with a cry of command and with the archangel's call and with the sound of God's trumpet, He will descend from heaven, and the dead in Christ will rise first. Then we who are alive, who are left, will be caught up in the clouds together with them to meet the Lord in the air, and so we will be with the Lord forever."* I Thessalonians 4:16-18.

You taught me well, and I don't forget.

You don't forget the $40,000, per the itemized list enclosed for the screens, equipment, and labor, and please think about the liquor license too. There's no time to lose.

With love from your son, writing from the tables of the exciting and life-changing and soon-to-open Club Revelation!!!

P.S. To help in our ministry among the Jews, I have begun a course of personal biblical Hebrew study thirty minutes a day, starting from Genesis. The electrician's sister Rena is actually teaching me the language direct from their Bible during their lunch break. Isaac doesn't mind this as long as we are studying seriously and hard, which we are, and as long as I don't sit too close to Rena. No problem. I have already mastered letters *aleph* to *zayin* in the ancient Hebrew alphabet. After I learn all twenty-six letters, which appear with no vowel marks in the Jews' scrolls, Rena said she would teach me marks to aid in the pronouncing. Do you know, she said to me the other day, that all the early great American preachers like Cotton Mather could read Hebrew and they even wrote the Jews' language to draw closer to the knowledge of God's heart? I know you are proud of me. And it's not taking away from my conversion efforts at all. In the original is the way to get closest to God's Word.

P.P.S. No, Father, I am not using "peyote," the drug. It was just a joke.

Your son

13

Marylee took three days away from her office to expedite work on Club Revelation, which was now becoming her major design project. She drove Billy to a group of restaurant supply stores downtown, where he picked out fixtures; then to the antique stores and to the fabric outlets, where she advised him about booths and wall coverings. She asked Gerry to call a friend of his who supplied restaurants with rolls and breads and he did not say no.

Marylee's own business was beginning to suffer—she'd turned down several potential new clients, including another major hospital gift shop expansion she could have done a lot with and had been wooing for months. Why, she wondered, as she lied that her stable of clients was already too full to take on new work, why had she become so expert at designing environments in which offerings of candy, flowers, newspapers, and hand-held board games were purchased for the sick and the dying to while away their last precious hours? What did this say about the state of her own spiritual life?

Never mind that she was earning less and less money. Gerry was still by her side in it all, financially, at least—not a demur, not a peep from the man even when she told him she had decided to invest $10,000 of her own savings in Club Revelation. He did not even ask, In exchange for what?

"Very good," was all Gerry had said, as if she had been reporting on the weather.

Marylee thought to ask him if he wanted to invest any of his money, but she hesitated. Then it occurred to her that Sam and Ellen did not keep separate checking accounts, nor did Judy and Michael. Why, she wondered, did she and Gerry? Such questions, previously unexamined, now seemed to arrive like formally delivered legal documents in Marylee's mind, commanding a response.

Still, she directed herself not to concoct flaws in her husband. Compared to the others, particularly Sam, Gerry was behaving very well about the restaurant. Not an absolute dream, of course, but he continued to be extraordinarily helpful to William Harp. Gerry made himself available to assist in a way he never had for the other tenants. He himself took care of the floors (new parquet, wall to wall, at huge discount, a complete steal), and he was working not only on his friend in the bakery business but also on another fellow who was connected to the state commission in order to expedite the painstakingly slow liquor license process. Gerry followed up, he gave Billy encouraging words, and all without ever once repeating one of the minister-priest-rabbi jokes (origin, Sam) that had been making their way up and down the stairs. The cheap humor was not Gerry's way. He also did a little more meditation with Nawang—so the Buddhist wouldn't feel slighted, he reassured Marylee—and he found it calmed him and improved the backhand, although not the forehand. Life was all right.

The money for renovations kept flowing from Billy's father, the rent was being promptly hand-delivered by Billy to Judy, and the restaurant, revised and reconceived, was—although not yet ready to open—nevertheless making rapid progress. Yet even as the work on the restaurant forged ahead and the husbands seemed, when not deliberately oblivious, then at least determined still to hold fire, Marylee felt an unease in the heart of the way things were progressing. She had expected Gerry at least to attempt to mount a little genuine resistance to her. To say *something*. Yet that had not happened. Not at all.

So the restaurant remained within the three couples' confidential knowledge, its imminent opening barely known even on the block, to say nothing of the immediate neighborhood and the larger Jewish community of the Upper West Side. Marylee was mindful of the social pressures in the Jewish community, and she thought a lot about old Rabbi Klain, Michael's ailing father, a short walk away, and the promises she had made to control food reviewers, social critics, and gossip columnists. Because she knew the tranquility could not last, Marylee resolved to try to enjoy what she had helped make possible thus far.

Her resolution lasted, at most, six hours.

Dear Father:

Before you send additional funds for the ministry, you asked for a few more details about Club Revelation and I am happy to provide them.

Just this morning, Marylee and I inspected drawings for a two-screen projection board system, the very latest. It will be centrally located, hang above the restaurant, and be visible from all points in the main room, like a mini version of the system in Madison Square Garden. On it, digitized Biblical texts that I preach from will be projected and there is also a cute little bouncing ball that will move to the words I am explaining or keep time to music if we are singing a hymn. This is both old-fashioned and new. They call it *retro* and it is guaranteed to be a big draw, says Marylee, and she knows about such things. It will make us not just a restaurant but truly a club, and maybe even a phenomenon with much Christian buzz.

During "down" time, the screen can also be programmed with different kinds of footage—for example, an apocalyptic video collage, they call it, with disasters such as bridge collapses, earthquakes, rampaging forest fires, police chases, car crashes, terrorist bombings, wrangling in the United Nations while famines wipe out large populations, floods from melting of the ice caps, battlefields, Rwandan rivers clogged with bloated corpses, and the bodies piled up near the incinerators of the Holocaust. In short, all the signs of the approaching Endtime being close at hand, which, in the calmer post-2000 atmosphere, will be far more persuasive to get Jews to think about and to change their ways in order to get into heaven while there's still time.

Billy's heart was telling him to say less, yet his obligations overruled.

Now listen to this: At an antiques flea market Marylee and Ellen took me to last week, on 27th Street, we found a hundred-year-old bathtub, with feet that look like an elephant's, and which is big enough for immersion. My plan calls for this tub to be tastefully surrounded ("tastefully surrounded" is how Marylee talks business, of course; I am quoting her) by ficus, corn plants, palms, and several aquariums with fish, iguanas, lizards, scorpions, and other creatures that call to mind both the Garden of Eden and the Judean desert where our Lord went to wander, fast, and to come to his mission (I am taking this from our promotional literature). All this is going to be Club Revelation's Baptismal Alcove! I hope you are proud of me for coming up with this idea. Marylee said she thought it was "a hoot." Ellen almost outbid me with the vendor because she said she wanted one like it for her bathroom. Unsanctified of course!

You see, our Jewish diner, who is so moved by his meal and by the preaching that he can no longer resist the summons of our Lord, now will not have to leave Club Revelation or delay his conversion even for a minute. He can go right into the back of the restaurant and enter the Baptismal Alcove. A group of supportive brother and sister diners will join him in the alcove and there, in the tub, immersion will take place, ceremony to be performed by yours truly. By the way, Father, do you think videos of baptisms should be provided, if requested, at no extra charge?

His father, a video fanatic, who taped everything, would like that one.

Daddy, I know you are skeptical, even suspicious about a number of the ideas I have written you about. I know you feel that Marylee Jeffers's counsel is resulting "only in my spending a fortune" as you wrote, a sum that you did not anticipate. But I assure you she is not out to sabotage our work. Quite the contrary. Remember that she is now an investor herself and her impulses are pure as the driven snow. This is simply the way things are done in New York. Expensively! Well-appointed Jews need a well-appointed and very trendy place to attract them. If I just took the Good Book out on the street with a drum and tambourine and urged people to come in to have a sandwich and coffee, like Sergeant Abernathy does in *Guys and Dolls,* it would be cheap, that is, as we say, cost-effective, but totally self-defeating. What stockbroker, lawyer, doctor, or businessman will be attracted to such a display, Sir? And are these not the very Jews we want to enter the Kingdom with us? No, I am convinced we need to invest at the high-end level in order to reap a harvest of souls for the Lord.

Harvest of souls? Whose voice was this? Billy wondered. How many voices, how many tongues could he detect speaking through him? This choir within used to inspire him, but no longer; it was now often garbled and off-key. With so many voices there, he was confused. How could he choose? And which voice was authentically his own? That had always been the question.

So rest assured that I am serious as death about our work, Father, and I hope you know it. The Jews need to be converted for our Lord to return, and Club Revelation will be a powerful machine to make that happen. Send the funds without delay. With love and gratitude for your setting me on the Path.

William

14

Sam Belkin's words were muffled and difficult for Gerry to understand because the TV was also blaring in the lounge and Sam was speaking as he peeled his saturated tennis shirt up and over his head. It's just as well, Gerry was thinking, because he had heard an earful of Sam's complaint already during the drive to Caracas and throughout the sets they had just finished.

"Tonight's performance, or nonperformance, proves our game has really gone to hell ever since we rented out the space," said Sam. "I can't raise any money. I'm laying off people, I'm putting too many of my projects on hold. This Harp character is so concerned that we go to heaven in the next life that we are going to hell in this one. He's a curse."

"You haven't been able to raise enough money for years," Michael said.

"It's time for you to shut up," Sam said, "and start agreeing with me."

"For the umpteenth time," said Gerry, "the kid is only trying to make a go of something. A start in business is not easy. Didn't you once start out and get a helping hand?"

"I think your wife has drugged you," Sam answered him. "She has always had sorceress potential, and this just proves it. She's done some Christian voodoo on you for sure, pal, and that's no exaggeration."

Gerry dismissed this remark with a smile and a sip of soda and changed the channel to a tennis match: a young kid, the Australian with the bionic arm, was serving artillery shells at Pete Sampras and trying to depose him. Gerry found himself rooting for the endangered king, and he was in no rush to get back home tonight; he was prepared to watch sports programs for another hour or two, as they sometimes did. But Michael, who had a nine A.M. meeting tomorrow at the library, and Sam, who had promised to drive Ellen to her eight o'clock at the college, were not in the mood. They had had enough of tennis in the flesh. But they had conspired to stay as long as was necessary tonight to accomplish their goal.

"The only program we're interested in watching," said Sam as he reached up and flicked off the TV, "is *What's Happening to Gerry Levine?*"

"I was watching the tennis," Gerry said. He was surprised, even a little shocked, by Sam's gesture.

"You are really and truly helping this guy, aren't you?"

"Come on!"

"Well, it is getting just a little serious," said Michael, "so we thought we would corner you. You can't get away."

Gerry raised his arms in mock surrender. "I'm helping, sure. I'm his floor consultant. Yes. Here I am. *Ecce homo,* pal. Shoot me."

"You're way beyond the floor and the baked goods, and the . . . you're giving him money for the work."

"Marylee is."

"It's the same thing."

"It's her money."

"And your conscience isn't bothering you? Not at all?"

"My conscience is fine, gentlemen."

It was now Michael's turn. "At the library, yesterday," he said, "a guy was joking that he used the e-mail to check in on his conscience several times a day. Any conscience calls to return, Gerry?"

Gerry nodded indulgently toward Michael and gave Sam, who was pacing through the lounge and pausing in front of the soda machine, a little more of his back to see. Then Gerry turned the TV back on to the tennis match. The televised ball appeared to be greenish blue, and Gerry was amazed at how hard it was being hit.

Sam turned off the TV once more and planted himself in front of Gerry. "I called six organizations," he said belligerently. "Six, and not a one of the bastards—anti-defamation, anti-anti-defamation, and contra-defamation, you name it—not a one was willing to find a law or a loophole to close Harp down. You see, Gerry, the plan was to bring in one of the big guns of the Jewish institutions, and they close Harp down; not you, not us. It gives us cover and an out with the wives."

"Who told you I needed an out with my wife?"

"Well, anyway, we're just going to have to do it on our own."

"Don't give up yet, Sam," said Michael, absently. He was preoccupied because suddenly everything on him began to hurt from the tennis—elbow, knees, and a three-alarm headache because Sam had served one into his ear at the end of the first set. "You never run out of Jewish organizations. That is one of the immutable laws of the universe. Keep calling."

"I said we'll shut it down ourselves."

"Would it upset you if I pointed out that the restaurant is not yet open, Sam?" Gerry said.

"Beside the point. It's simple. I'm going to set Harp out on a rock beside Belvedere Castle in Central Park so the vultures can come at him for lunch."

"There are no vultures in Central Park."

"This is New York. It can be arranged."

Gerry and Michael were fairly used to Sam's tirades—they were part of his act—and yet the outbursts could hardly mask how upset he was really becoming. "They said it was a free speech issue. Can you believe it? They said it would be like closing down a pizzeria because you don't like Italians. That's what one guy actually said to me."

"Amen to that," said Gerry vacantly.

"But it's a lie, and you know it," Sam shot back at him. "An absolute lie. Food is not the issue. You know exactly what this guy is serving up to people: Real Devil's Food Cake, Revelation Rhubarb, or Beast Rising out of the Sea Bouillabaisse—or whatever the hell goofy dishes he's going to cook up . . . none of that is the point. He's a proselytizer."

"No one is forcing anything on anybody," Gerry said. "You enter, you eat, you listen to stuff, you pay, you go. If you don't like what you hear or eat, you never come back. If you like, you come back. Like my business or yours. The free speech guy was right. Period."

"If even one pathetic Jewish kid who had a horrible experience at his bar mitzvah gets snagged by this Christian predator, then I am responsible," Sam declared. "You are too. We all are! That's how you should see it."

"'Predator'? Horns or no horns? A little too much on the paranoia," Michael said. "Please remove the soap box."

Sam was becoming livid, and Michael regretted his put-down; he should have known better, because it just inflamed Sam all the more.

"Or maybe you're waiting for one of our wives to get seduced by him." Sam emphasized the word *seduced* and carefully watched Gerry for a reaction. "Then that's our fault as well."

Gerry remained impassive.

"I just feel responsible for what your wife is doing, Gerry. And I can't for the life of me understand why you don't."

"In case you haven't noticed, Sam, Marylee is already a Christian. So is Ellen. So is Judy. So nobody is being snagged or preyed upon, my friend." Gerry's tone could not have been farther from triumphant; he spoke in a voice that was patient, quiet, steady, conciliatory. "All any of this means is that it's time to leave the women alone, especially Marylee. It's time to back away from the pressure, and let's just see if the kid can make a go of it. If he fails, I don't want Marylee to blame it on me. No male wants Marylee Jeffers to be angry at him. No female either, for that matter. It's a business, after all. You can understand business, can't you, Sam?"

"If it's just another business, then I'm Pete Sampras."

"And you're no Pete Sampras," said Michael. "I suppose we can always cut off the hot water," Michael went on. He thought Sam was being ridiculous, and he felt peeved. Suddenly sarcasm, not regrettable enough to censor, filled him up and ran out of him. "Deny them heat, why don't we! Deny hot water! Freeze them out. No basic services to Club Revelation; then we'll make the newspapers for sure. 'Christian persecuted by paranoid Jewish landlords.' First-rate stuff, and excellent for the Jews, wouldn't you say, Sam?"

"You're another burned-out case!" Sam fired this volley right at Michael. "Your father is a rabbi, for chrissakes. If he knew what you're allowing yourself to be the landlord of, it would kill him. It will kill Gerry's mother too, if she finds out."

"She won't if you don't tell her," Gerry said. "And, Sam, don't enumerate for me what will kill our parents. Don't be such a walking cliché of an aggrieved Jewish man. Here's a wake-up call: You're both married to Christians."

"A Buddhist, not a Christian," Michael was at pains to emphasize Judy's distinction.

"Well, she wasn't a Buddhist when you married her," Sam said. "Is it possible that a few of your really choice attempts to make her interested in the Jews actually backfired? Didn't you two clean latrines on an Israeli military base one summer?

Maybe it's you who actually deserves the credit for driving Judy to the ashram, my friend? So don't be so proud of your situation. It's even more ridiculous than his."

"Ashrams are for the Hindus," Michael added wearily. "Zendos and monasteries are for the Buddhists. I've told you guys this four thousand times. And we did not clean latrines. It was a chicken coop."

Michael was surprised by his own vehemence in defending Gerry. "And as to being my father's son, goddamit, I don't need your advice, Sam. Believe me, I know what will kill my father, and this news won't. Anyway, I'm not telling."

"Exactly, you meathead," said Sam. "You're afraid! You're probably embarrassed to tell *anyone* what's going on."

There was a pause. Sam turned the TV on and then off again, and he knew that, like a kid, he was one microscopic irritation away from a tantrum. True, they were joking. They were casual, but they just didn't get it, and Sam felt a sudden fury within him like a big forehand that he now caught, turned, and slammed at Gerry.

"Look, you and Marylee have been bamboozled by a slick operator masquerading as some Jimmy Dean look-alike. You are not dealing with a hayseed here. That's just part of an act. I've checked this out. I don't need outside help, believe me. When the Jewish organizations bailed, I did a little research on my own. Harp's father is not just some eccentric Bible-Belter with a little cash to give for his Jesus. Oh no. I'm on his trail, believe me. The Internet will tell you a lot if you're willing to put in the time. He's a megarich guy. In the oil business, no less, in Virginia—actually he owns oil fields in the Tulsa area too; that's where the bucks are coming from. And I assure you the money for this operation in our modest little building will be bounteous. There!"

Sam exhaled. "What is he after, Gerry?"

Gerry did not respond.

"What is Marylee really after?"

When Gerry refused to be provoked and just turned the TV back on, Sam sat down beside him at the table and pushed himself so close that Gerry's view was obstructed. If it had been anyone but Sam, Gerry would have punched him. Instead he just sat there, nose to nose, while his friend looked him over as if he were a strange new species. Finally Sam touched the tip of his index finger, like a stethoscope, to Gerry's chest. "Beats there a Jewish heart?"

"Same as yours, Sam."

"It would be bleeding if it were mine. If it were the same as mine, it would be having a goddam attack. You're killing us with this, Gerry."

"Look, I'd support Marylee in anything she wanted to do. In any business, any endeavor she loved. It's important for a person to find something they believe in. Wouldn't you do the same for Ellen, or you for Judy? What is marriage about, gentlemen? I'm supporting my wife in something that matters a lot to her. Sure, I guess I would mind a little less if it were an Internet start-up. But it's this restaurant."

"Christian Cafeteria," Sam said derisively. "Club Revelation!"

"It is what it is! And can't we please get beyond *us* and *them?* I wish I could believe in something the way Marylee believes in this. I confess I'm just a little jealous. What do you guys believe in—apart from tennis?—and look at the way we play! What do we believe in? We're all just working all the time, and kicking around in the Museum and smoking dope up there, and remembering and remembering, as if our lives were over, but we're only fifty! Why do you begrudge Marylee—and me—so? Honestly, Sam, I don't really know why it's suddenly so life-and-death with you."

Sam studied Gerry for an instant and then said, "Marriage is for better and for worse. In your case, my friend, I believe this is the worse part, big-time. The worst of the worse is that you don't even know what's happening to you."

"You are acting toward me as if we are not friends, as if I have suddenly been transformed into some evil thing. We own a building together, we practically live in each other's laps, we have been part of each other's lives for decades. You discount all that just because I don't share your prejudice about this tenant."

"Who the hell is prejudiced?"

"Sam, you're the guy who's in a dream. A deep Jewish fantasy. You're the guy who is closing his eyes and just wanting it all to go away. What makes you think that God speaks only to the Jews? Because if he did, he would be one fucked-up guy."

Gerry had become angrier than he ever wanted to be. He and Sam now stood face-to-face. "You're the guy who has to wake up."

"No heart attacks, please, gentlemen! No apoplexy." Michael planted himself between his two much larger friends. "Just patience and acceptance, time and quiet, respect for each other and the ability to take a step back, and a few beers, shall we get a few beers?—come on, for chrissakes, you're both grown-ups—and everything will work out. Thus says *my* wife. Without the alcohol part."

If Michael really believed in any of these nostrums or in the efficacy of his humor, that ended quickly with what happened next. For he watched in astonishment as Sam whirled, stepped away from Gerry, and in two paces stood before the soda machine at the back of the lounge. He put his nose against the metal just to the left of the coin slot and then kicked the base three, four, five times—it seemed to go on forever, and so hard that the sample cans toppled in their display vitrines. When the racket stopped, Michael noticed the delivery bin had been bent under the force of Sam's foot, and a dark cola was fizzing and dripping onto the rug.

"Good job," Michael said. "Free soda for everyone."

In inarticulate rage Sam strode back across the lounge as if he were fleeing something awful; then he climbed the steps, three at a time, up to the bathroom on the second floor. When he disappeared, Michael fixed his gaze on Gerry, who had resumed watching the tennis. He wondered then whether, in all these years that they had lived under the same roof, he had ever truly known Gerry Levine or Sam Belkin at all.

15

In March, three mid-sixty-degree days bathed Broadway in such concentrated sunlight that the new spring birds, which William had noticed in branches hanging over the lampposts, all began to sing as if they had discovered their voices for the first time.

To please Marylee, but also simply to *be* with his wife, Gerry also began to spend—to the dismay of Michael and the disdain of Sam—even more of his time, and also some of his money now, to make the restaurant ready for its scheduled opening. That event was set for—when else?—just after Easter.

If Marylee was frequently downstairs with Billy in the evenings, then Gerry would be too. He did not have a problem sharing Marylee in this way. Her energy was great, and Gerry was in this manner also expressing his own deep need to serve by serving her and this project. While he had become aware, over the years, of a kind of personal void that he filled by being enthusiastic and helpful about other people's enthusiasms, why should he feel this as a flaw? It was simply his way:

to place a dozen or so calls a week from his car on behalf of the restaurant, or to follow up from exhibition halls where he was showing his products, or from the offices of his many friends among customers and suppliers, who for Gerry's sake gladly turned over a desk for an hour and even brought him a cup of coffee while he wrangled on behalf of Club Revelation's liquor license.

Marylee had sensed from the day they met that Gerry had a generosity about him of a kind that she had never seen in anyone else. Seemingly limitless, pure, expecting little if anything in return, the generous spirit in Gerry was quite nearly defining. How could this be a deficiency now, especially if drawing on it always made Gerry so happy? Where was the harm? Where the loss? Nothing emptied out of him in the process. Didn't people, in fact, love Gerry for it? All these years she had loved him for it. What should be different now?

It did not escape Gerry that his service was also a way of avoiding words with Marylee. He never had fared well in explaining himself to her and, anyway, what was there to explain? You're busy, you're doing this, and I will help. It gives me joy and pleasure. Enough, let's get going. He was, of course, not unaware that she liked to corner him, but he had also grown adept, when this happened, at finding a chore to do, a task to perform, a call to make. In this manner, dishes and silverware were purchased for the restaurant, and Gerry had just finished getting quotes for liability insurance, but there had as yet been no discussion of God, Jesus, or his immortal soul.

Yet he could escape her for only so long.

Two weeks before the opening, they lay in bed together. They had not made love in some time. Marylee propped herself on her elbow and turned to Gerry, who was stretched out on his back with his hands cupped behind his head, looking steadfastly at the unmoving white blades of the ceiling fan. The blades reminded him of paddles, and he suddenly wanted to go kayaking on a quiet lake far from the City, a pristine lake, hidden, labyrinthine, miles of perfect limpid surface that would never be covered by parquet.

"I've been studying with Billy while we work, Gerry," Marylee started. He knew she was circling him. She often chose the bed for this purpose, and Gerry was happy to provide her with the pleasurable illusion of thinking he didn't know; yet he did. In his imagination he set down his paddle and drew the kayak onto the shore of his lake. He waited, but not for long. "We've been studying, you know, New Testament books and also some doctrine. Nicene Creed. Doctrine is what it really means to be Christian."

"I know," he said. "You've mentioned that. That's good. I can see you're into it."

"No, Gerry, it's not okay. I'm moving, and you're not."

"I'm happy where I am."

"Where are you, Gerry?"

"I'm in bed with my beautiful wife, whom I love."

"That's precisely it. Your love for me."

"What's wrong with it?"

"Not enough."

"Isn't that for me to say? If it's sufficient for me, it's enough."

"Please, Gerry. Try to understand. Until we began with this, with the restaurant, I felt lost, unanchored, unmoored, un-everythinged. I felt like you."

"Maybe that's the secret to why we got along so well."

"I don't feel that way anymore, Gerry. I don't feel lost."

"I don't feel lost either."

"Then how come you seem lost to me? That's what I find most troubling, Gerry. That my husband is so lost and so content at being lost at the same time. There's more to life than work, Gerry. There's even more to life than me."

"I worship you, Marylee. I idolize you. You have deep green eyes. They remind me of a lake only I know. There's only you. I have no other gods before you."

She listened to his irony with slowly developing tears and quiet incomprehension. Then she said, "If you believe only in me, Gerry, then you believe in nothing. Because I am very temporary, my love. You could blink and I could be gone. *One in the field and one in the house.* Raptured. Gone."

"I don't think about any of that, Marylee. I can't make a call that will affect it, can I?"

"But what about Heaven, Gerry? I have never heard you talk about it. The World to Come. I don't have a clue what you think. Or even what most Jews think on the subject. Help me with Jewish heaven, Gerry. Trees or clouds? Deli and kasha? Water? Frolicking Jewish souls in flowing white robes? Hanukah and Passover are not about heaven."

"Heaven," he began to sing phrases of a half-recollected song, "I'm in heaven . . . I'm in heaven . . . dancing cheek to cheek . . ."

"What is Heaven, Gerry? A real place with tables and chairs and a happy meal?" He continued to hum. "Please, Gerry."

"If I could get you in, I would," he finally said. "Who's scalping tickets?"

"I don't find it frivolous."

"I don't mean to be, but I'm no theologian. Is that what that kid is offering you? Heaven and divinity school once a week? I don't know. If you want me to take a course of study with you, I'll take it, Marylee. But I already know this: all I have is you and this world that I can touch. The rest is a crapshoot."

She reached over and put her hand on his chest and languidly rubbed the tufts of his chest hair—the shirt of his pajamas was unbuttoned—as she might a German shepherd or a large cocker spaniel lying eagerly on his back on their bed. Is this thought, she wondered, this way of looking at my husband, my thought, or a thought in the mind of God that He is sharing with me? And to what end?

She was twisting at his chest hair, curling and pulling at it, and he saw she was unaware that it was beginning to hurt him. Or was she? Gerry wanted to push Marylee's hand away, but he also wanted to tolerate the pain as long as he could. He wished she would instead lean over and kiss him on the lips or at least put her ear on his heart as she used to do when they were first married. "Hello, heart," she used to say, "Good to know you. Hello, lungs. Hello, pancreas," and so she had acquainted herself with the parts of her new husband.

"Are you listening to me, Gerry? When we are dead and gone, what will we have left? When we're moldering in the ground, where then is our love, and your devotion? When our mouths are full of dirt and our skin has fallen away from our bones, our skeletons . . ."

She felt as isolated and alone now as she had ever felt in her life.

He reached around and clasped her hand, held it in his grip for an instant, and then pushed it away. He wanted no more of her anatomical reverie, but he saw she was also locked into this perception like a car of a roller coaster going down the first steep drop. Yes, there they were: his hand, his fingers, his digits, his opposable thumb—my God, she really saw it this way, it was his *paw*—it all made her feel that here was one future skeleton reaching over to touch another.

"When you're a pile of dry bones, Gerry, what does it

matter that you were once married to the bones decomposing beside you, unless you rise together into eternal life?"

"That's a very nice thought. I would like to be with you eternally too."

"You know what I'm talking about, Gerry. Please don't belittle it and reduce it to Sonny and Cher." (God help him, he *did* love Sonny and Cher too.) "Don't force me always to censor myself and to speak in a kind of de-Christianized code acceptable to you. To suppress what I feel deeply because it's unacceptable to you."

"Not unacceptable," he said. "Only unbelievable."

Feeling mocked by him, she turned away, yet she still let him touch her arm; she felt he was desperate just to have his skin alongside hers.

For Gerry, her turning away was worse than her anger and her exasperation with him. He would have much preferred her to keep up her quiet complaint, he would have preferred her even to be overcome by tears, because at least he could then bring her the tissues, give her the big red handkerchief that was on the bedside table, get her *something*. But this averting of her face left him unmoored. He saw the lake and the beached kayak again. He read the clouds and smelled a squall coming, and he reached for the paddle, but it was gone. They were stranded beside each other in a place of deep wordlessness.

Finally, Marylee said, "I wish we had had children."

"Yes. I wish we did too, sometimes."

"But we chose not to. It was a real choice, wasn't it?"

"We tried, we talked a lot about it," Gerry said. "Then we stopped trying. You know all that. It was a choice, if that's what you mean. We thought we would be lousy parents. Workaholics, the both of us. We thought we would be enough for each other."

"Maybe we thought wrong, Gerry."

"I don't know," he said.

"Even God had children, Gerry."

"Children?"

"You know what I'm talking about. Please don't be cute."

"Yes, Jesus."

"Perhaps because we don't have our own, I think I am freer to think of myself, of you, Sam, Ellen, Michael, Judy, all of us, as children of God. And all children of God also have the same hope for eternal life, Gerry."

"I respect that," he said.

"But don't you agree?"

"I didn't say that."

"No, you would think of yourself as a pile of shit rather than a child of God!"

"Please, Marylee. I'm your partner in life. On the journey together we need to comfort and solace each other. We are not piles of shit."

"We are if this is all there is."

"Our love endures," he said. He instantly regretted it.

"Where?"

He was silent for a long time.

Then she spoke. "You call this solace, Gerry?"

"I am doing what I can. It's better to be desperate and lost together than desperate and lost alone."

"We don't have to be lost at all unless you continue to insist that's the only way. There's another way. Can't you just be open to it? Is that asking too much?"

"I don't think so."

"You've relinquished so much already, Gerry. You've given up on fundamentals. You lack even interest in fundamentals. You flee from them and have a head full of clichés, and little sayings, jokes and bromides, tennis and small comforts, and then on the day you don't wake up, there's death. And there are none of your solutions for that, Gerry. There's got to be more. I want more. That's why I'm doing this, Gerry. That's what I've been trying to tell you."

"What is it you want from me?"

"I want you to study with me. Learn what Christianity really is. Learn what you can rise up to. Not the clichés, not the preconceived ideas, but let Jesus speak to you."

"I have fewer clichés than you think, Marylee."

"All right but you're still . . . so stuck that it hurts me! I mean Billy is learning Hebrew and Judaism, and from the electricians, of all people. He's a kid, but he's curious about the sources of Jesus. You're not old and dead yet. You're not beyond change. Study a little. The early Christians were, after all, Jews."

"That seems fair. A little study never hurt anybody."

"That's what this has become for me, Gerry. It's not the restaurant alone, or the business for its own sake, but what it symbolizes. A new beginning on a journey. Is that so hard to understand?"

"New beginnings are good," Gerry spoke deliberately. "Of course I understand."

"No you don't."

"All right, if you insist, I don't. I don't, but I'm also willing to learn."

"It won't bite you, I promise," she said, "although I might."

She turned and anchored herself next to him. He was intensely relieved to be able finally to put his arm around her again and to look her full in her eyes. As they fell asleep, Marylee felt a lightening, as if she, untethered, had lifted off from the bed and might float away into the sky.

16

The imminent opening of Club Revelation cast a pall over Passover for all three couples. They talked briefly about having a *seder* together, a kind of private inaugural in the restaurant itself—they had managed three or four communal *seders* in the early years of owning the building, but in the past decade, they'd had only one, in the second year of Curry by Murray's tenancy. However, if you asked Sam Belkin, the ongoing construction and the very existence of Club Revelation in their building made a mockery of a communal *seder* in the restaurant, or anywhere, this year.

Marylee had already thrown the gauntlet down by urging Billy to open precisely *at* Passover, on Wednesday evening, the night of the first *seder,* with a free gala event for the whole Upper West Side. It would be a propitious time because most Jewish establishments would be closed—and an opportunity to have a terrific launch emphasizing the common origins of Judaism and Christianity. Marylee had even offered to subsidize the entire event. But when Michael and Sam got wind of the offer, they raised so many objections, and it hurt her to see how they piled on Gerry, who, as always, defended her. Since the construction suddenly slowed—she could not figure out why Billy was dragging his feet—a Passover opening soon became moot.

As it turned out, Sam and Ellen, who often went out to Queens to celebrate with his observant cousins, would have been out of town anyway. For Sam finally had located a potential funder for the tiniest-nations-of-the-world film—a Dutch pharmaceutical company that extracted kava, an organic Valium alternative, from a shrub that grew only on atolls off Papua New Guinea. The kava harvest coincided precisely with the eight days of Passover, and the company wanted Sam to be there to film it. Despite Sam's half-hearted effort—or perhaps because of it—the Papuans could not be persuaded to defer their harvest because of the Jewish Feast of Freedom. So Sam prepared to fly out of Kennedy, happy to bag the first big grant for the film—potentially $100,000—and even happier to get away from Club Revelation, which he viewed increasingly as a kind of religious cancer growing within his house, for which there was no cure except radical invasive surgery, which nobody except Sam appeared to want.

"I swear he's going to put little figurines of Jesus in the *afikomen*. I know it!" he declared before he dashed off to the airport with Michael. "It's your job," he said after Michael shook his hand at the luggage check-in and wished him good hunting, "not to let that missionary pollute the greatest holiday our civilization has produced."

"I'll take care of it, pal. No problem."

To Ellen, Michael said later, "Your husband hits, he criticizes, and then he runs three-quarters of the way around the world. Sometimes I wonder."

"At least he's taking a box of *matza* with him to New Guinea."

"That was probably your idea."

Each Passover, Michael had to decide between going to the nursing home's *seder* to be with his father, or going down to Florida (his parents were long divorced) to be with his mother at her compound, which was also not far from where Gerry's mother lived. Unlike Gerry, he didn't really relish either event, and Judy sometimes offered to throw a coin to help him decide. Last year Michael had made his decision after evaluating each parent's medical condition on the eve of the holiday. It made a kind of ethical sense to give his much sought-after filial company to whichever parent was, at the time the holiday fell, in worse shape and in greater danger of departing this life. This year the frailty of his father, no coin toss needed, kept Michael in New York.

Because he sensed an enormous pressure coming from Marylee, Gerry also remained in New York. His mother would be all right in Florida, and his sister was driving down from Atlanta to be with her. She also had a million friends at the compound, where the Passover table was as long as a Sebago palm is tall.

Gerry urged Marylee to go to the nursing home *seder* with him, Michael, Ellen, and Judy. It would be a hoot, Michael promised her, because Judy had concocted a special Viagrified version of the traditional *charoset,* the apple-raisin-walnut mélange for the *seder* plate, based on a thousand-year-old Tantric recipe for sexual virility; she had also diced it with a lot of Vitamin E, good for the heart and the blood pressure. The nursing home would become a lot peppier and Michael's ancient father, being a rabbi, would, God willing, preside once again over the nursing home's ritual meal.

Marylee politely declined. She announced that this would be the first year in the last twenty that she would definitely not be attending any *seder*—in part because the first two nights of Passover, the *seder* nights, immediately preceded Good Friday. "I'm going to stay home to prepare my body and my mind to contemplate Jesus' resurrection. I am going to pray. The *seder*s will only be a distraction. But thank you very much." With this declaration, she didn't leave much room for discussion.

"Isn't she being a little childish?" Judy said to Gerry.

"She's just being Marylee, that's all," he answered. But everyone could see how disappointed Gerry was, although he would never criticize her in so many words.

As they took a hiatus from the construction, Billy placed, at

Marylee's suggestion, a sign in the window that read, "Opening after the holidays. Have a very happy Passover and Easter."

When Billy confounded Marylee by abruptly announcing that he himself needed to go home to spend the Easter weekend with his father, Gerry volunteered to accompany her to Good Friday and Easter Sunday services, implying that she perhaps might relent, change her mind, and *quid-pro-quo* him with her beautiful company at *seder*s on the preceding days.

If the others hoped that Billy's departure ("I hope he never comes back," said Michael) would result in a change of heart in Marylee, they did not know her. She told Gerry she would be happy if he joined her at church, and that was that. On the night of the second *seder,* she saw him and the others off in front of their building and watched them walk toward the nursing home a few blocks away. "You all look very handsome and very pretty," she said. She felt as if she were sending them off on a long trip and stood there staring after them.

After proceeding a short distance, Michael and Ellen stopped, walked back to the steps of the building, and pleaded with Marylee, "It's crazy for you not to come to join us."

"What are you going to do here by yourself?" said Ellen. "You're going to sit in the dark and make us worry about you. You're going to be a Jewish joke."

"You just go and have a good time and ask the Four Questions," she said to them. "Give a hug to your dad for me, Michael, and don't drink too much." She practically pushed them down the steps this time toward the nursing home.

"Please, Marylee," Judy said. "I don't like this."

"Go," she said to her husband and friends. "I may sit in the dark, but I assure you I will be stepping into the light."

Once they left, Marylee re-entered the darkening main dining area of Club Revelation. She sensed Billy's presence in absentia, but she enjoyed the human emptiness and the silence of the place, the about-to-be-born feeling, the astringent smell of paint and primer, and the promise of the half dozen partially opened boxes of glasses and plates that had been delivered yesterday and still awaited full unpacking. She walked among the tables and finally selected the one where Billy usually sat to do his paperwork and write his long letters to his father. Here she found a copy of the Bible, of the type that would be on every table of the club when it opened.

She heard some of the new spring birds chirruping for their dinner, the hiss of some air brakes, the clunk of what she imagined to be those shiny pressurized metal kegs being dropped in front of pubs and restaurants, and the ebb and flow of white noise that drifted in from Broadway.

Slowly, she turned the pages of the Bible. She found that William had put his bookmark in Revelation 14:2-3, the section where, he had joked, his family was frequently mentioned in the holy text:

I heard a voice from heaven, as the voice of many waters, and as the voice of a great thunder: and I heard the voice of harpers harping with their harps. And they sung as it were a new song.

The quiet and solitude and separation that she had made between herself and the others was working; it was concentrating her mind. Using only the light filtering in from the street lamps, Marylee leafed through the Gospels, reading the several versions of Jesus' entry into Jerusalem, his upsetting the money changers' tables, the Passover meal with his disciples, his betrayal, arrest, trial, crucifixion, and resurrection on Easter. She had never realized how misunderstood Jesus was, as most people are misunderstood in life, as she herself was. Marylee's cheeks were wet with tears. She did not know how many hours she stayed in the restaurant, but when she recognized some notes of Gerry's voice drifting toward her and then heard them all approaching and coming down the steps, she got up quickly and, just before they entered, rushed up the stairs to their apartment.

17

The long-anticipated opening of Club Revelation took place on the last day of April. There was a splendid breeze and moderate temperature, the traffic was moving adequately for New York, no water mains had broken, no hazardous waste threatened the Bronx, the George Washington Bridge did not sway dangerously over the Hudson; not a hint of the apocalyptic sullied the early evening air as Billy and Marylee reviewed the bookings for dinner and found themselves encouraged.

Standing in the entryway in a white tuxedo (Marylee's idea) and fashionable French-style chef's hat (his own idea), and wearing no crucifix or other religious adornment (Gerry's suggestion), William Harp stood under the canopy of the ailanthus branches on the sidewalk in front of the brownstone and greeted people as they went down the two small steps and entered the club.

"You've had Easter, you've had Passover, and you've had Earth Day," he declared in a voice of evangelical sonority that surprised even Marylee, if only because she had not heard him project like this before. "Well, you haven't had anything until you've had Heaven Day, that is, opening day, at Club Revelation. Welcome, friends," he said, "we hope you'll find the food celestial, along with the message. Thank you for joining us."

In all, opening night drew a colorful crowd but neither the luminaries nor the heavily Jewish diners that Marylee and Billy had hoped for. Some of Marylee's and Gerry's business acquaintances were there, Michael had corralled two librarian friends, including a Russian Jewish immigrant from the Slavonic Division, and Ellen had invited a colleague intrigued with the place because, in addition to doing computer-based writing instruction, she was doing research for a book on the presence of angels in our everyday lives; she thought she might find a few at the Upper West Side's first Christian eatery.

Of course, the landlords, all three couples, were there, although Ellen had to browbeat Sam into attending. He took twenty minutes for his shower and showed up deliberately late. Nobody believed he was still jet-lagged from the flight home from New Guinea, and for the first time in their married lives (Ellen smiled broadly at everyone when he made his appearance), Sam wore a gold Star of David, actually a gift from his long-ago bar mitzvah, which he had rigged up to drape prominently over the knot of his tie. He was not enjoying himself. He made no secret that he still carried, folded up in his wallet, the phone numbers of several anti-defamation organizations as well as an anti-cult/anti-missionary hotline, and he regularly threatened to call them up. William treated his landlords with extraordinary courtesy, and Sam had to admit that no restaurateur had ever made their building exude better aromas.

Only two student waiters had been recruited, and these not from seminaries but art schools. Since Billy needed four, Nawang, the Buddhist in the Basement, was, to use Judy's term, "compassionate enough" to find and recruit at the last minute two young Tibetan novice monks, newly arrived in the United States and in need of some extra cash to tide them over. Their English was poor, so Nawang, beaming and bowing and enjoying himself thoroughly, accompanied them, navigating the young men in their saffron robes and translating for them as they took the diners' orders.

If the waiting staff signaled an amusing or even confusing religious message, there was no doubting the serious Christian ministry at the heart of Club Revelation when Billy's words began to be broadcast on the projection screen:

"Studying the Bible," he said, "we know that the time of redemption is near for the Jewish people, and we here at Club Revelation want to be part of helping them . . . of helping you. Besides Christians, the Jews are the only ones who worship the living and true God. Even though the Bible says that the messiah is Jesus—and Jewish people think it will be someone else—I want to assure all the Jewish people that it is okay."

On hearing this, Sam elbowed Gerry—they were all sitting at the same table, center but in back—and whispered, "It's very flaming nice of the missionary to tell us we're okay!"

"It's even more okay if you just shut up, honey, and let us listen," said Ellen.

"We all worship the same God," Billy was saying, "and God knows that Jews are very special in his sight."

William Harp sermonized on the need to prepare for the End, but he emphasized that it was critical not to get stuck in details, and he was adamant and straightforward in debunking the date setters and the calculators. "How many voices arose on December thirty-first, 1999, but a handful of months ago, and declared the recent turn of the millennium was to be the beginning of the end of the world? How many pilgrims sold their houses, their sport utility vehicles, and even as we speak are spending their last shekels waiting in hotels and staring up at the Mount of Olives in Jerusalem wondering: when will it happen? Well, that is, to put it mildly, very shortsighted," he said.

"St. Augustine had it right in *City of God*, a millennium and a half ago: *Some have said that four hundred, some five hundred, others a thousand years, may be completed from the ascen-*

sion of the Lord up to His final coming. But on this subject the Lord puts aside the figures of the calculators and orders silence."

Here Billy paused, and the tape had the attention of everybody in Club Revelation. *"For it is not for you to know the times, which the Father hath put in His own power.*

"But ladies and gentlemen, especially you of the Jewish persuasion, it IS going to happen. I quote you not Revelation or Elijah or Corinthians now, but your very own prophet, Bobby Dylan, born Robert Zimmerman to a good Jewish family of Minnesota: 'The world as we know it is being destroyed. Sorry, but it's the truth. In a short time—I don't know—in three years, maybe five years, could be ten years, I don't know'—Of course he doesn't know!" Billy interpolated— "'there's gonna be war. It's gonna be called the war of Armageddon, as sure as you are standing there, it's gonna happen.'

"And there's a special place for only 144,000 Jewish people to survive when the fire starts," Billy said. "How many will be in this elect from among the Jews of the Upper West Side? How many from Broadway? How many from West End Avenue? How many between Seventy-ninth and Ninety-sixth? Why, one of the big high-rises along the river probably has enough souls in it alone to make the requirement! There's not going to be room for everyone in the ark of redemption.

"So before the vaporization and the total destruction, while there is still a chance to enter the Lord's grace, do so. Start by visiting us at Club Revelation as often as you can. After tonight's gala there will be ample opportunity to meet with me individually and to talk about all matters of the heart. Until the End comes, of course, we have to eat. And although matters of salvation are weighty, the food will be light, and nutritious" (the opening evening's special dish was SOUL *meunière,* deliberately misspelled—Marylee again). "So come again, eat, drink, and be reborn!"

When the tape ended, there was applause, though sporadic, and right after it, strangely, a crash of shattered dishes as one of the Tibetans dropped a tray. Not missing a beat, the live and handsome Billy took the floor: "That is to remind you of the seven vials that were cracked in the vision of Saint John in Revelation: rest assured that pestilence, famine, death, and destruction have not been released here, although one of these waiters will be!" (Chuckles.)

The meal concluded with coffee and a choice of Seven Angels Cake or Tree of Life Fruit Salad (See Revelation 22:2), Bananas Foster (flambé, of course) while black-and-white Federal Emergency Management Administration footage rolled above on the monitor, featuring public service messages about nuclear attack and other disasters, circa 1949, which Gerry had located and downloaded (no help provided by Sam) after an arduous search.

18

With the launch of the restaurant and Sam's absence for a week while shooting a friend's film in the South, the men had to skip several Tuesdays before they all could go out again to play in Caracas.

On the night they finally were able to schedule, Gerry was so buoyant he let slip to Sam and Michael that he had begun to study basic Christianity with Marylee and Billy Harp. He knew that gave Sam more grist for his mill to ridicule him as a classic self-hating enemy of the Jewish people, but Gerry did not want to start lying to friends.

An agreeable easing in the tension among them had already set in and made Gerry's news easier to take—or so Gerry thought. This new atmosphere was triggered, ironically, by the opening of the restaurant and its early performance. Now that Club Revelation was up and running, they all could see that it was not going to take the world by storm. Not yet, anyway. It was not going to be Planet Jesus, but neither did it appear to be a potential blight on the neighborhood.

Despite Marylee's incessant phoning, no reviewers had been attracted yet from either the Jewish press or the world of food journalism. Only the Tibetan monk waiters seemed genuinely thrilled—in no small part because Judy had insisted that Billy pay a $12 per hour wage in addition to tips. In fact, for a potential threat to the survival of the Jewish people, Club Revelation was already being received, to the mitigation of Sam and Michael's anxieties, with considerable sleepiness; in truth, it was already struggling.

"It still might perk up and become a runaway success," Marylee said one afternoon to Billy, when she dropped by to cheer him up. Gerry had watched some of this conversation unfold from the stairway where he, uncharacteristically and for the first time, had concealed himself to listen to his wife comfort Billy Harp.

He had seen Harp sitting disconsolately at one of the front window tables looking over his weekly receipts. He heard him say, "I'm telling myself that very thing, Marylee."

"A business, especially a restaurant, is like a *pinot noir*," she said. "It needs time to breathe a little and to find its own flavor. Plus, lots of businesses succeed simply by lasting. That's what happened to Gerry's business. You have to last, Billy."

"I have to last," he repeated.

Marylee was neither surprised nor disappointed with the results at the restaurant. She appeared calm, slimmer, and even prettier in a gaunt sort of way, Gerry thought, as he watched her go over to William and give him an encouraging kiss on his cheek, right at the sideburn.

As he drove to Caracas, Gerry could not get this image out of his head. Ever since the opening, Gerry had also become aware of a certain note of desperation that had entered Billy's normally upbeat manner and voice. He had begun to call Marylee at odd hours and several times had come upstairs to solicit their advice on the thousand things he was worried about: how to get control over his menu (was he pushing it with Paschal Lamb Chops and the surprisingly popular Golden Calf's Liver?); how to keep waiters (they continued to come and go except for the Buddhists, but Billy tolerated them only because he did not want to offend Judy); he was also at a loss about advertising (there wasn't much of it); and he tried out on them all kinds of ideas for themed evenings—a Monday night open-microphone on the Jewish-Christian dialogue had already completely bombed.

The night Gerry secreted himself in the stairway, Marylee continued to advise William Harp, but no longer, Gerry noticed, with the energetic, hard-edged business savvy she had brought to the pre-launch. "Believe, Billy. Relax," she told him. "You are an evangelist, not a capitalist. Ultimately it's not about money. If you pray for customers hard enough, just like in the movies, I'm certain they will appear."

"I've been too good a teacher to you," he joked glumly. "You're really comfortable with this? You're okay with the results so far?"

"I am. Truly I am."

"There's an awful lot at stake in this," he said.

"I know, honey. The world hangs in the balance."

"Indeed it does," he said. "The big one and my little world as well."

That's where the kiss had come in again, Gerry now remembered—sideburn, or had she reached around to his neck? It gave little comfort to dwell on the kisses—sisterly, religious, chaste, or more—that Harp had received from Marylee over the last few fraught weeks. No matter their number or nature, the result was that she left William there, appearing, to Gerry, as forlorn as he himself often felt when she turned away from *him*.

Recalling this scene as he drove to Caracas caused Gerry to push the Toyota up to a maximum sixty-one miles an hour. Although he continued to floor the accelerator, there was simply no more power in the engine. Cowering in the back seat, Michael lamely questioned the necessity for the speed, while Sam, in the front seat, plucked stoically at the strings of his racquet, not looking up until they lurched, with screeching tires, into the parking lot and found a spot conveniently by the entryway door. After Sam remembered to make out a personal check to pay the $200 for repairs to the soda machine, they went out onto the court, warmed up quickly, and began.

Sam played a very strong set of singles against Gerry, while Michael, who had consumed three of Judy's tofu burgers (and, while she was out of the kitchen, a manly hunk from his private cache of hidden kielbasa), experienced a pain under his left armpit, which scared him and put him in mind of *ER* and the other medical shows on TV that he normally avoided; he decided to watch and to wait for Ganesh to arrive before he did anything more strenuous than fetch the errant balls and do the play-by-play on Sam and Gerry's singles games.

At 10:30, Ganesh appeared, listened to Michael's heart with the stethoscope he carried in his racquet bag (Michael was always asking), gave him cardiac clearance, and then teamed with Michael against Gerry and Sam. Reassured that he was not in immediate danger of dropping dead, Michael now played energetically, and they put on sustained pressure, with many deuce games going on, it seemed, forever. Nevertheless, Gerry and Sam were so strong they actually beat the Iranian, with a little help from Michael's habit of launching moon shots off his back foot and his flubs at the net toward the end of the second set.

On the ride home, they were not so exhausted that they could not remind themselves that thus far there had been no sold-out, waiting-list-only nights at Club Revelation, no trendy long line winding down the street, curling up Broadway, and requiring a burly clean-cut Christian bouncer, no huge buzz, and, all in all, absolutely no instant, successful appeal to scores of Upper West Side Jews. Nor had the newspapers gotten hold of the story yet—another considerable relief.

"I'm tremendously pleased with our failure," Sam said. "I want to compliment you on your excellent work, Gerry."

"As our prophet Bobby Zimmerman Dylan put it," Michael added, "'There ain't no success like failure, and failure's no success at all.'"

"Well, I'm pretty philosophical about it," Gerry answered. "A month or two is nothing. Wait. It could still take off. But even if it doesn't, even if it does stall and fail, it's been fun, tense but fun, and it's brought Marylee and me closer, as I've told you guys a million times. I'm even doing a little studying with her and Mr. Harp, thank you very much."

"Studying what?" Sam asked.

"We're reading Matthew and Mark now, and Revelation will come later. Not bad stuff, really. Parables, simple-minded stuff that sinks in for a guy like me. He's running a kind of class just for us."

"How cozy," Michael said. "Gospels for two."

"Well it's no secret. Thursday night late, in the kitchen, while we clean up, he tries to explain to a stubborn Jew like me—that's the way he puts it—what it means for Jesus to be indwelling in a human heart. Hey, don't be shy. You're both very welcome, I'm sure."

"Oh I'm sure we are," Michael said.

"For a Jew, Jesus indwelling in your heart, that's angina," said Sam.

Michael said, "Why are we doing this, Gerry?"

"'We'?" said Sam.

"Yes, 'We,'" Michael responded.

"Just pull over and let me out right here," Sam said. "Now."

Gerry ignored the request but accelerated and almost hit the bumper of the truck in front of them. He tailgated very dangerously, keeping no more than two feet between the Toyota and the vehicle in front, as if this reckless gesture were somehow an answer, or part of his answer, to their question. After two or three seat-gripping minutes, he abruptly dropped back—"Jezuz," Michael exhaled in relief—and said, calmly, "I asked Marylee nineteen years ago, just after we were married, to take a course on Basic Judaism. I'd completely forgotten about that until she reminded me of it the other day. I guess I wanted her to know about Judaism back then, even though I didn't know much myself. Some primordial instinct must have gotten to me."

"Just like now," Sam said in a voice hollowed by fear, "an instinct to become a statistic. What the hell is wrong with you, Gerry!"

"I think maybe *I* was the instinct," Michael said. "It was at the Y, right?"

"Exactly, and taught by the two-thousand-year-old rabbi."

"Rabbi Morton Fink, my father's friend. Dead now."

"He should rest in peace," said Sam, vacantly. There was something about Gerry's scary game of chicken with the truck in front of them and now the monumental bridge to Manhattan in the distance that, for the moment anyway, seemed to tame Sam's rage. He was penetrated suddenly by a feeling that many generations past, many dead people, especially dead Jews, were somehow, through the lights and clouds and the bridges of time, watching the way he behaved with Gerry and Michael tonight.

"Anyway," Gerry went on, "now Marylee's asked me in effect for equal time, equal treatment, tit for tat. So I accepted. What else could I do?"

"I have a novel idea," said Sam. "You could have refused. I'm sorry, Gerry, but sometimes I wonder if, with regards to Marylee, your mouth is even physically capable of forming the single-syllable word NO! It's a terrific little word. Try it sometime."

"May I suggest you find a tennis ball, Sam, and nibble on it a bit until we get home?" Michael said.

Then he turned back to Gerry, who in his usual enigmatic manner refused to respond, at least in words, to Sam's provocations. "As I begin to recall it now," Michael said, "Marylee didn't exactly rave about that Basic Judaism course, did she? Please keep the driving on the safe side of terror as you contemplate your answer."

"No," Gerry remembered it for them as he drove swiftly on, the highway lights on both sides like an illuminated gauntlet tonight. He squinted to keep his vision clear. He was remembering that the class Marylee took was deep in the heart of the feminist decades, and she had taken great exception to the way Rabbi Fink explicated the Garden of Eden stories. She was the first person to raise a feminist challenge to Rabbi Fink, Gerry remembered. She'd objected to Eve's being maligned, blamed, and criminalized for making Adam complicit in her dirty dealings with the snake.

"She told Rabbi Fink that if Adam and Eve were the first Jewish couple, she and her new husband, yours truly," Gerry said with a rush of pride, "were going to do a lot better! We were going to stick by each other and communicate and not rat on each other, not even to God. I was proud of her for speaking her mind to this revered guy with a two-foot beard. The only part she liked about the story was—I kid you not, she told Fink this—that Adam and Eve were naked all the time and always very cool. But that was ruined by having to watch out not to step on reptiles everywhere."

"There was only one goddam reptile," said Michael, but he was instantly worried that his exasperation had declared itself again—and fearful Gerry might respond with more automotive recklessness.

"Marylee was without doubt a contributing factor in the death of poor Rabbi Fink," said Sam. "She probably hexed him with the indwelling Jesus angina."

"Sorry," said Michael. "Ruptured intestine, sepsis. I remember Rabbi Fink's death well. My dad delivered a eulogy. It was one of the few times I ever saw him cry."

"Getting back to our Christian-in-training here," said Sam, "why the hell can't you leave well enough alone, Levine? The restaurant is dying. A stillborn. A Curry by Murray. Let it be. Don't study. Don't help. We'll say *kaddish* over it. That's it. Done. Hey, if you're desperate to take a course, may I recommend Driver Education!"

"If you had any kind of Jewish education," Michael pressed on, "you might have told Marylee that Adam and Eve should *not* be a model for Jewish couples because they were *not* Jewish. Regular normal people is who they were. Sorry."

"Get out!" said Sam.

"You think they spoke Yiddish, Sam? Do you really suppose they talked like your *bobbe* and *zayde?* In the Garden of Eden? I hate to break it to you, guys, but there were no Jews in Paradise. Period. God had not yet invented the Jews."

"But I know he was probably thinking about it already,"

Sam said, "because God likes the Jews, they are *His* people, gentlemen, and he doesn't like them becoming *goyim.*"

"Must you?" implored Michael.

"'Must you?'" Sam mimicked.

Gerry didn't want them to start up. Not again. Not in the Toyota—because he was not unaware of how stupidly he had been driving, and the impulse that made him do it continued to attract and to scare him. Ye he was also intrigued by this discussion and he even wished Marylee were there to hear it because he would surely botch it in the retelling. He leaned toward Michael to hear him, but he drifted out of the lane and had to jerk the wheel to avoid grazing against the sixteen-wheeler roaring past them on the right.

"Mercy!" shouted Michael.

"Sorry," said Gerry. "Okay. I'm focused now. Sorry, but who *were* the first Jews?" he prompted Michael.

"Abraham was the first Jew," Michael explained patiently. "Now stay in the lane and I'll tell you the rest. Deal? You see, he wasn't really a Jew until God went and made a covenant with him. Until then he was just Abram, without the *h* in his name. The *h* was added as a sign of God's secret name and because that is the Big Guy's letter, *H* as in the inHaling and exHaling of the breath of life. Likewise Sarai is the first Jewish woman, but only after she gets *h*-ed and becomes Sara*H*. These were the first Jews, my friends, not Adam, not Eve, not their kids, not even Noah."

"Not even *Noah?*" said Sam.

"There's no reason to be disappointed, Sam. Remember, Noah was a sloppy, naked drunk who had to be put to bed by his own children. And, therefore," Michael continued, "look to Abraham and Sarah as the model of a Jewish couple. They had plenty of sheep and land, quite upwardly mobile folks, they made themselves useful to the princes in their host countries, they lived to be a hundred and twenty, during which time Abraham never learned to boil a gourd of water, and they were cranky with each other most of their lives. Sound familiar?"

"Damn," said Sam, "and all this time I was thinking it was the naked duo."

"So let me understand this," Gerry said as he adjusted his EZ Pass device on the windshield and the Toyota slid through the tollbooth and onto the Upper Roadway. "God went out one day and found Abraham and Sarah—Abram and Sarai— and *converted* them to be Jews?"

"You might put it that way," Michael says, "although it's more accurate to say he made a covenant between himself and Abe and Sara."

"A deal," Sam said. "I remember this part. God the deal-maker. He decided to do a development deal with them—if you follow all these laws, then I will make you multiply like the stars in the heavens and you'll be like the fruit flies in the air."

"Where did you say you got your Jewish education, Sam?"

"I didn't."

"Maybe the back of a matchbook? It's be fruitful and multiply, dummy. That's part of the covenant, yes. God, however, did not promise that the Jewish people will be like the flaming Drosophila. Are we clear on this point?"

"Whatever," said Sam. "So you corrected me."

For Gerry, Michael summoned a little more patience. "You could have used a little more knowledge too, Gerry. You could have explained this stuff to Marylee twenty years ago, and then maybe we wouldn't have our hands full now."

"Well, it's never too late to learn," Gerry said, "and do you know what I've learned tonight, Michael? I've learned that God was a missionary out to convert people. I've learned that the first act in official Jewish history was for God to take a guy and convert him. In light of that, let's lay off my wife and Billy Harp."

In silence they drove the rest of the way to their street, and Gerry, unusually, found a parking spot right in front of the brownstone. As they piled out, they all saw Marylee and William Harp standing at the doorway of the restaurant chatting with and saying goodnight to the last diners of the evening.

19

Dear Father:

I am concerned about your health and would like to come home again soon—immediately even. But if I do, I know you'll accuse me of not trying hard enough and of using you as yet another excuse, so I . . .

He re-read this, crossed it all out, summoned the evangelist's voice, and began to transcribe effortlessly.

My letters have been pretty short lately, I know, but that is because the restaurant business is booming, and I mean that with a capital B. Praise the Lord. And have I been busy! Between meeting and greeting and preaching and going up to what they call Hunts Point Market in the Bronx early in the morning while it's still dark out to buy fresh vegetables, well, this should help explain why there seems to be less time for correspondence. It's something that happens in New York.

Still you'll be pleased, I am sure, to know that I still find time for personal prayer no matter where I am. I was stuck in New York City traffic the other day—Marylee and Gerry let me use their Toyota any time I need it except Tuesday nights—when everybody began honking and swearing and jumping out of the cabs of their trucks. I thought they were going to threaten each other with guns and knives in a very un-Christian way (actually this happened that I saw just once) . . . you don't have to worry about me, Daddy, then, or ever.

Under such circumstances I just remind myself of the purpose of our mission and I simply calm myself by repeating those sections of the Bible that you taught me as a child and I learned by heart and will remember until my dying day. You remember St. John in Revelation 1:3 tells us: *Blessed is the one who reads aloud the words of the prophecy, and blessed are those who hear and who keep what is written in it; for the time is near.*

Well, the time is indeed near, and the remodeled restaurant, with fancy video projection screen, is open and going great guns. I'm glad you read the little newspaper article I sent you about our launch. It was special and did we ever have a full house!

As to your asking why, after all the money you've spent, the article was only four lines long and didn't talk any about me personally or the work of the Lord, well, you know, Daddy, that is because space in these New York City newspapers is hard to come by since there's so much else going on in town. It's not like home.

The point is that we got in! We're on the map, Daddy. We have arrived and the Word, through the unique medium of food (another line from our little brochure) is definitely getting out among the Children of Israel of the Upper West Side.

What a wonderful idea you had, Daddy. You know how you can be certain the Word is getting out? Because the Jews who come in literally *eat* the Word, cooked with love by us, and conveyed in the daily specials. Yesterday, for example, was Short Ribs with Lake of Fire (See Revelation 19:20) Hot Sauce. "Guaranteed to make you suffer with delight" is how we wrote it on the menu, but it was not a big hit. Actually the Jewish patrons seem to favor chicken above all other animals. Our customers know, or soon will, from their taste buds to their intestines to their hearts, that the Day of the Lord's returning is nearing and the time is fast approaching when they have to lay aside all their stubbornness and accept Jesus as their Savior and Redeemer. (I'm giving you the flavor of some of my remarks in the videotaped sermon and the flavor of my individual preaching going on at Club Revelation.)

So don't you worry, Daddy. You take care of your health, don't forget those doctor's appointments, and know that your work is being carried on here among some of the world's toughest Jews. But they *will* come 'round because we are serving them up some of the sweetest food (I am becoming an excellent cook myself, says Marylee) and of course the sweet words of Jesus.

That's it for now, Daddy. With love to you and the community,

I am, as ever,

William

P.S. You might also consider sending Annabelle up. There's room for her, in the back of the restaurant, right near the Baptismal Alcove, and she would definitely be an attraction for these I've-seen-it-all City folks to come to the club in even greater numbers than they are attending already. Just let me know and I'll prepare a tank.

20

Here were some more signs centered on the hands and the eyes: Sam was stirring his coffee more rapidly than usual; his eyes lingering on Ellen, scanning her face (for what?) an extra second when she left for work; he was using a heavier, more impatient finger on the keypad of his phone so that the numeral seven broke, and the entire phone had to be replaced. Ellen may well have missed these small atmospheric changes in their lives altogether had they not somehow coalesced into the more notable alterations in Sam Belkin that began to register immediately after the opening of the restaurant.

On the opening night, Sam had spent hours making a mess in their closet in order to find his bar mitzvah-era Star of David. It finally surfaced, along with matching Star of David cufflinks and a "JFK for President" button in the Have-A-Tampa cigar box in the bottom drawer of their bureau. Ellen persuaded him to choose either the cufflinks or the tiepin Star of David, but not both. He had chosen the tiepin, which had less than the desired effect when Billy, noticing it, had said, "That is just beautiful, Sam. I hope you'll let me borrow it one day."

"Over my dead body, kid."

But this was only the beginning. Sam began to bring home Jewish takeout. This had not happened in years, maybe decades, and Ellen's rather delicate digestive tract suddenly had to confront nearly a foot of stuffed derma on Thursday and then, on Friday, the Sabbath, fried chicken from what was known in the neighborhood as the Kolesterol Kosher Kitchen. Then the following week there were kasha varnishkas with mushrooms from an outlet on the Lower East Side, which Sam obviously had made a special expedition to purchase. To his great pleasure, Ellen really liked the kasha.

She thought she understood his impulse and was only mildly surprised ("the shock of the inevitable" was how she described it to Judy) when Sam announced that he'd also decided all the rooms on their floor of the building should, after all these years, have *mezuzah*s affixed to the doorposts.

"Okay, here's a rhetorical question: why, after two decades of *mezuzah*-less life, which has not been half bad, why now, Sam?"

"You know why. I want to stake out what's the Jewish territory and what's not," he said to her. "It's going to be like the Green Line. The Christians better not cross it."

"I'm a Christian, Sam."

"You, I make an exception."

She even noticed, for example, in this locution and others, how certain idiosyncracies or inflections of Sam's speech were also changing ever so slightly. Not "I'll make an exception of you, or for you," but the more Yiddishized "You, I make an exception." As a writing and language teacher, Ellen found such variations interesting, even quaint, but also a little disturbing. She wanted to see where they would lead, so she chose not to battle him.

"Be my guest," she said. "*Mezuzah* away."

Nothing, however, prepared her for what Sam brought home from a Judaica shop the following day: six ceramic *mezuzah*s, not the modest pinky-sized items you saw everywhere on the West Side, but *mezuzah*s the size of an eggplant—and some larger—each bearing large black Hebrew letters.

"We're going to bump our heads on those things," Ellen said. Sam told her he would place them up high. She asked him what the Hebrew letters meant. He didn't know.

"Don't you think it would be nice to know? In case someone like a Con Ed meter reader with a bleeding head or a personal injury attorney saunters by to ask?"

"I'll find out from Michael"—he knew he wouldn't ask

because he didn't want to hear Michael's ridicule again about his Jewish illiteracy—"or, better yet, you can ask him yourself."

"Maybe I will."

Sam continued to work at mounting the *mezuzah* on the door of their bedroom. "What I can tell you, though, what I do remember, is that inside each are some of the holy texts of the Jews—the Ten Commandments and the Hear-Oh-Israel-the-Lord-our-God-the-Lord-is-one thing."

"The *Shema,*" Ellen said. "The profession of your faith. The creed."

"That's it! Good for you, kiddo. Creed. You must have learned that from me."

"I do somehow doubt it."

"The point is that this is the stuff you have to believe if you're a Jew. The Lord is one, one, one," Sam went on as he prepared the screw holes—such physical tasks, at which he was no good despite his large, strong hands, always put him in a foul mood. "The Jewish Big Guy is one. That's the point of the *mezuzah.* He's not split up into, you know, a committee."

"Father, Son, and Holy Ghost?" Ellen said. Sam didn't acknowledge this. "The Trinity. Not a dirty word, you know. Maybe *you* should sit in on Billy's class with Gerry!"

"I'd jump off the Brooklyn Bridge first."

"Be my guest," she said, but she continued to help him by locating screws he dropped and by steadying the ancient plastic stepladder that teetered under his weight.

When the job was nearly done, she surveyed one of the *mezuzah*s and said, "Isn't it really a little much? Especially the one on the outside of the front door, Sam? The one facing the hall? Couldn't that have been a bit more modest? It's the size of a shoebox."

"So?"

"Don't you think you should have asked the others?"

Sam didn't think so. He finished mounting the final *mezuzah* and, with sweat seeping into large circular stains on the belly of his gray T-shirt, climbed down to put the finishing touches on his work. He extracted not a rag, but a just-laundered handkerchief from his bureau, and, *mezuzah*-dusting and shining, he toured the apartment, radiating a sense of satisfaction and ownership that Ellen had not seen before.

21

Gerry had been joining them for an hour of New Testament study already for several weeks, but Marylee still felt that he remained, in spirit, somehow still barely more than her escort. His mind and heart were not in the class, and this distressed her. Of course she understood that Gerry had been working very hard. He had maintained a heavy schedule of appointments and travel to flooring trade shows. Marylee tried to convince herself that general fatigue must be the reason he seemed to have such little focus.

It was far more difficult for her to acknowledge that Gerry's ability or interest, rested or unrested, simply had its limits. This thought, that it was not fatigue or condescension but a vigorous blankness that continued to arise out of him, distressed her deeply. Marylee felt crazy to appear angry or ungrateful. Yet she needed to rouse him.

It was well past eleven. The refrigerators were humming in back of the restaurant and the streetlight was filtering in through the thickly leaved branches of the ailanthuses out front. All in all, it was a tranquil moment for Marylee and Gerry as they sat with two Bibles open before them at a table in the very center of the restaurant.

Billy was walking about spreading new linen, arranging

the empty white flower vases, and wiping down the plastic covers of his menus. Marylee had told him the little things counted. He wanted to please her and, of course, Gerry, in no small part because with so many tables going empty and his father pressuring him, he desperately needed them to agree to put in more money on advertising. To be successful, Billy felt he needed to be not only in the newspapers but also on the radio, television, the Internet (he didn't know what to do first)—Club Revelation and the Russian Tea Room in the same environment. They listened patiently to him, like the two parents they never were. "Calm down," Marylee finally said to him. She and Gerry promised to take all the issues under advisement.

"That's right," said Gerry, but there was hardly a trace of emotion in his voice.

"Remember, honey, what I've been telling you," Marylee went on—the "honey" she addressed was William—"that this is not the hour for capitalism but for Christ. Forget about the advertising and look at Gerry. You need to wake him up, this sleepyhead."

"Oh, I think you can do that better than I can!" William said.

Gerry was not so asleep that he did not hear her call William Harp "honey." Not that he hadn't heard it before, but in this weary state he felt as if the word this time were a wedge that quite nearly split his heart in two. When, he wondered, as he stirred in his chair, was the last time she had called *him* honey, my honey?

At the touch, affectionate yet still firm, of Marylee's hand, Gerry opened his eyes. She was speaking directly to him. "You see, what I got from Hanukah and Passover and all the weddings and bar mitzvahs galore that we've gone to—" Was he awake or dreaming? Gerry wondered—"What I got was that

Jehovah, the Jewish God, you see, never really *loved* the Jewish people. He was all right about being invoked at parties and celebrations. He was always there to remind you about the Exodus and splitting the Red Sea and the potato pancakes and all the things that he split and that he has done for you . . . Gerry?"

"Yes."

"Stay with this, please. God Jehovah was only on your case, Gerry, making all these laws you need to obey to stay on His good side. But does he never just plain love you? Just deep down and unconditionally? I mean why shouldn't He keep on loving you—if He ever did—even if you drive to the synagogue on *shabbos* or have a spinach salad with those tasty little bacon bits? Don't I go on loving you even if you crap up the bathroom! And who am I? Wouldn't you say that's the case, Reverend Harp?"

"I would say, yes," Billy answered, "and I am really impressed—although I don't want you to call me 'reverend,' Marylee. But no question, unconditional love is what Christianity brings to the theological equation. That's the invention, the new product, if you will. Love, because He gave His only begotten son for the sake of the world."

"I have nothing against love," Gerry said sleepily, and also because something seemed expected of him.

"But do you feel your Jewish God loves you?" Marylee prodded him again.

"My Jewish God, your Jesus, isn't it all the same thing?"

"Well, if it were, why would we be sitting here talking about it? Or why would people have been at each others' throats about the differences for thousands of years? Of course it's not the same thing. Is sole *meunière* the same as tuna fish? Is Club Revelation the same as Burger King? Sure, it's all food, it's all restaurants, it's all . . . Gerry, surely you can't be so lazy as not to think about the distinctions."

"But I see the similarities, Marylee. And anyway, it's not fair to say that God doesn't love the Jews. Didn't he choose them above other people?"

"To do His bidding maybe," she said, "but not because He loved them."

"There's a lot more about love in there than you think, Marylee," Gerry said, surprised by what seemed to be percolating up. "Doesn't it say somewhere in there that you should love your neighbor as yourself. The golden rule?"

"Very good," said Billy, who had returned to them and now joined them at the table, his hands folded on the freshly laundered cloth. "But Jesus takes it one step further, Gerry. It's not enough, He says, to love your friends, neighbors, your allies as you love yourself. That's the easy part. Read the Sermon on the Mount. You must love *all* equally, even your enemies. And when you do that, you become a true child of God. You see, love on this new level is the fulfillment of the Jewish law."

"That's beautifully put, Billy," Marylee said.

"Check out John 13:34: '*A new commandment I give unto you, That ye love one another.*'"

"The Jews had too many enemies to turn the other cheek," Gerry said. "And what proves it is look at what the Romans did to Jesus."

"But times are different now, Gerry," Marylee said. "There are no Romans anymore. Who is the enemy of the Jews today? A few anti-Semites and crackpots, of course. But there's a Jewish state with nuclear weapons. And in America? Here? My God, on the Upper West Side, Jews rule!"

"It is indeed a time for love," said Billy. Yet when he tried to look deeply and with great feeling at Gerry and to communicate this love, he felt only Gerry's weariness, like a big chasm that he was in danger of falling right into as well; beleaguered, he stood and embraced them both. "Rest in peace tonight," he said to them, "in the bosom of God's love."

The lesson was over—more suddenly than Marylee would have liked—and she slowly closed the Bible before her, raised it to her lips, and kissed the spine.

Gerry and Marylee left the restaurant through the side door, silently ascending the hallway stairs to their floor. Although married for twenty years and as connected as the top and bottom of a muffin, each seemed in a different realm tonight. As they climbed the steps to their floor, Gerry kept hearing the Beatles' refrain, "*Love, love me do, you know I love you,*" while Marylee sniffed the air for the source of the mildew that seemed to fill up the hallway. Halfway up the next flight, another odor assailed her. She turned on Gerry with a harshness she heard and instantly regretted. "Did you step in dog shit?"

He stopped, feeling, from the tone of her voice, quite clearly accused of a capital offense. As he carefully removed his loafers and inspected each sole, he said, "I'm not the culprit. Whatever you accuse me of, my darling, I plead innocent."

They continued climbing and now Marylee detected bacon, and then the odor of liver and onions drifting out from Michael and Judy's floor. It was, they knew, Michael's late-night macho carnivore dinner, which he prepared with secret relish only when Judy, whom no sound or smell could wake, had gone to bed.

"Last week," Gerry whispered, "it was kielbasa."

The meaty odor filled Marylee's nostrils with the pungency of blood, frying, and rot, and by the time they got to their own floor, a clinging swirl of such odors everywhere had enveloped her. She entered their apartment thoroughly nauseated, although she had little impulse to gag or throw up. It was a different nausea, of the spiritual kind.

In the bathroom, a fecal olfactory mote rose from the toilet and she experienced it like a bullet ricocheting about her brain. The flush was vigorous, but it also sent a spray, slightly urinary, back at Marylee, and she jumped quickly back from the bowl so as not to be hit; then the mildew seemed everywhere.

As she and Gerry got ready for bed, their own body odors mingled, and Marylee was aware of them as never before. During her shower, she saw pubic hairs streaked on the soap bar in the tub and on the drain. She felt her breast and her scar as she dried and wrapped herself in towels— one for her thick hair and one for her fifty-year-old body. She walked around the bedroom, approached the window, returned, stood on the threshold to the kitchen, and sniffed. Everywhere she turned she met with evidence of the body's leavings.

Since he knew they were not going to make love, Gerry decided to skip a full shower tonight. Still, a native fastidi-ousness impelled him to strip off his pajama tops and quickly to wash his armpits before he climbed into bed. While he soaped away, he forced himself to think about this talk of Christian love and to wonder why it put him in mind of songs for teenagers and romance and sex. Especially sex; he let his hand graze down to his crotch and he stroked himself, but just once. Perhaps there *was* something hardened about him— beyond his penis at the moment—something that was block-ing Marylee's message from entering.

In bed, she became aware of Gerry's talcum powder aroma—he had again used it liberally on his armpits instead of the deodorant she preferred. Marylee lay there on her back eagerly sniffing—the powdery sweetness of it, like confection-er's sugar, was not half bad, and the odor of talcum filled her nasal passages and sent messages up to her brain. There they mixed with fragments of what was said tonight—*There is no fear in love, but perfect love casteth out fear,* and *He that loveth not, knoweth not God; for God is love.*

"God is love, Gerry," she suddenly said.

"Love," Gerry repeated the word, rolling it like a lozenge on his tongue. "Love, lover, lovee, love."

"Yes. Love." With eyes closed, she rolled toward him and allowed herself to be swept into a cloud of talcum that somehow arrested and erased all the olfactory disgust of the previous hour. Within minutes, they were kissing passionately, and then they fell mercifully to sleep.

22

"You know, Marylee, I think I must have gotten you wrong."

Another few days had passed, and Michael was staring into Marylee's eyes, searching for a clue. For fifteen minutes he had been waiting for her on the sidewalk in front of the restaurant. They had had an appointment to be there, sort of, with Billy Harp.

It was a crystalline morning, spring brightly galloping in along the side streets of Manhattan, and Marylee had slept very well. For his part, Michael had slept terribly, and the difference was visible on their faces. His eyes were scrunched up as if trying to focus on the world through black-rimmed glasses not even put on quite straight this morning, so that his entire look was that of an unmade bed. By contrast, Marylee was, simply, fresh and beautiful. Michael stared at her, but what he was remembering was being up last night virtually every hour, suffering from a kind of metaphysical incontinence that allowed him no sleep. He had finally dozed off at about five and slept until seven, after having struggled in vain with the mind-body conundrum, from which he attained some relief when he got up to pee.

Michael had no intention of complimenting Marylee, although as unobservant as he usually was, even he noticed her radiance this morning. He tried to keep his mind from straying and his eyes from staring further. He had always found Marylee very attractive, but he did wonder if she and Gerry—who had left before dawn to meet with his sales representatives in Montreal—had made early morning love. Marylee hadn't seemed so absolutely sparkling in years, her skin clear, her eyes untroubled, as if a fever had broken or a crisis had passed.

They were talking while they watched Billy nail a *mezuzah* to the front door of Club Revelation. It was the identical item Sam had mounted. When Ellen mentioned Sam's "*mezuzah* event" to Marylee and Billy, Billy immediately asked if it would be a good idea to affix one to the front of the restaurant to attract more Jewish customers.

"Be my guest," Ellen had said, and she gave him the wrapping that contained the address of the store. Billy then called up the electricians, Isaac and Rena, who, he remembered, lived in the same part of Brooklyn. He had been looking for a pretext to call for weeks, and he now asked if they would meet him at the store. He had been missing them, he said, especially Rena, because the Hebrew lessons had been suspended after the restaurant opened. Rena, who answered the phone, asked him if he were really certain he wanted to buy a *mezuzah*. When Billy answered affirmatively, she hung up. But she had not said no, he told himself, and somehow he was convinced Rena would be there.

Billy had taken the subway to Williamsburg, where he climbed a flight of beaten concrete stairs up to the sidewalk, made two quick turns, and found himself standing conspicuous and nervous across the street from the book-crammed window of the Jewish Gift Barn. Here he took up his post waiting for his Orthodox, Jewish, female electrician and her brother to join him. He didn't mind the volley of split-second sidelong glances that came his way from mothers pushing multi-seat strollers and from their husbands shepherding along a toddler or two behind. He felt oddly drawn to these people—did they not feel themselves as much outsiders to this city as he did?—and Billy awkwardly waved hello to whoever seemed, by virtue of an extended stare, on the verge of greeting him.

The area was thronged with people and products, and the aromas of pickles, fish, and cheese, breads and cakes, and the restaurateur in him longed to step into the small stores and delis he noticed down the block to sample what they cooked. But he did not dare move; he had his orders from Rena. He saw signs using the Hebrew letters he had been learning, which were not Hebrew but Yiddish. He felt he was an anthropologist landed in a place where he had suddenly discovered this wholly new, black-hatted, long-skirted, large-familied species of Jews. It was so different from the Upper West Side. For a moment Billy wondered if he should have rented restaurant space in this neighborhood instead.

Rena finally arrived, alone. She told him Isaac had not been very happy about their shopping trip. She was being accused, she told William, of engaging in one euphemism after another, and their father was becoming inconsolable. She too had qualms about assisting a Christian minister to purchase a *mezuzah* for purposes of converting Jewish people.

"Still, you are here," he said to her.

Their eyes locked for a moment and she said, "I should not be."

"And I should not have put you in this position."

"It was wrong of you."

He wanted to reach out and touch her hand, but he knew that the slightest gesture of that kind would have doomed him. It was enough that he felt it, because Rena could sense it; she could sense everything about him. "It was very wrong," he said.

Then they entered the Jewish gift shop together.

In addition to the *mezuzah,* Rena helped Billy purchase some simple Hebrew primers ("Study these so you don't forget what I taught you") and a key to transliteration of the daily prayers, and even a box of yarmulkes. The entire efficient transaction took ten minutes, and Rena hurried it along, refusing to return the glances—and there were double the number he'd received alone—from other customers as well as from the gaunt young clerk.

Once they were out of the store, Rena barely allowed Billy to tell her what a good job she and Isaac had done on the wiring or to thank her or to ask when their next lesson might be. "Study," she said, "and good-bye."

Now the *mezuzah* was not only going up, but Billy had also asked Michael—who, he knew, was the most religiously knowledgeable of his landlords—to say the special blessing, or *brocha,* on the installation of a *mezuzah,* that Rena had said was required.

"We're going to have more of these than a synagogue," Billy said over his shoulder to Marylee and Michael as he tapped in his nail.

"Deceptive advertising," grumbled Michael.

"If it's good enough for every room on the third floor, why not the restaurant!" Marylee answered him. Billy decided to let her be his defender.

"To say nothing, and I will say it," Michael went on, "of exploitation of one religion's symbols by another."

"So sue for copyright infringement," she said. "Go sue God."

"Don't theologize everything," he said to her, "and don't be so coy. Coy, clever, and dishonest." Michael was impatient. He was late again for work—not that he was in a great rush to arrive and to sit on his stool in the main information room at the library, there, for yet another day, to master his irascibility and to answer the irritating questions of the poorly informed public. For he was indeed nearing the danger point, according to his supervisor, the intense and superstitious Phyllis Whatley—she checked, online and in print, no fewer than six horoscope writers per day—quite a peculiar avocation, Michael always thought, for the library's senior information systems specialist. Michael found it appalling that this woman, who tracked his absences and even knew the amount of time he daily spent in the bathroom (okay, admittedly, it did not really require fifteen minutes to urinate, and even after he explained, with full display of the desk copy of *Gray's Anatomy,* that he had a particularly convoluted urethra, she wasn't buying), still she was the individual who had his occupational future in her hands. *That* appalling fact was on his mind as he watched Billy Harp work, and Michael was therefore fast losing his conviction about the gravity of the numerous *mezuzah* violations unfolding before him.

"I am asking you, courteously, to please see to it that the *mezuzah* is taken down."

"Just stop it, Michael," Marylee said. "Stop it and get a life. A Jewish life or a Christian life, but just attach yourself to something and stop being such a policeman, naysayer, and put-downer. Look: the *mezuzah* looks lovely. I'm going to pick up a dozen for our place, but I like the smaller size."

"Marylee, I always had you pegged for being a real philo-Semite," Michael said.

"What greater philo-Semite," she answered, "than to love a Jew and to be married to him for twenty years! By that measure I'm a helluva more philo-Semite than you are, pal."

"Philo-Semites do not need to deceive Jews in order to try to convert them. The restaurant is one thing. A *mezuzah* belongs only on the doorways of a Jewish home, a Jewish establishment. This is neither. This is pushing the envelope, Marylee."

"Relax," she said. "Gerry's not bothered."

"No, he's not bothered by anything." Energy, source unknown, was oddly now flowing back into Michael. "Sam will rip it right off, take out the parchment for the *genizah,* and use the defiled item for firewood."

"Please, Michael."

"We will not be landlords for Jews for Jesus," Michael said loudly. "Even I won't stand for that."

"He is not Jews for Jesus," Marylee responded. Her voice was becoming more relaxed, and even charming, the opposite of Michael's strident tone. "He is Jesus for Jews, and we all know it."

"I love the Jews," Billy turned and said to them. "But if Jesus, who was a rabbi, had a *mezuzah* on his door, that's a good enough reason to put one on mine."

"So relax and go to work, Michael."

"The blessing first, though, Mr. Klain," said Billy as he stepped toward them and handed Michael a yarmulke. Michael hesitated. "You told me you'd take it under consideration."

"I'm still considering."

"Do us the honor, " Billy said.

Marylee put her hand out toward Michael, drew him to her, and then put her arm around his waist in a gesture of seduction, longtime friendship, and coercion that he may have been able to resist, but not this early and on such an exquisite morning.

"What is happening to us?" he said. Yet he opened the black skullcap, peered into it, read the label—a store in Williamsburg he did not recognize—and looked uncomprehendingly first at Marylee and then Billy.

"It's not going to do any damage, Mr. Klain."

While Michael just kept staring at them, Billy pulled out from the back of his pocket one of the cards from the packet he had purchased with Rena. "Please correct the words I know I'll get wrong." Then William began to read, in labored, English transliteration of the Hebrew, the special blessing for the installation of a *mezuzah:* "*Boruch atah Adonai Elohenu Melech haOlam, asher kidshanu b'mitzvotav, vtzivanu likboah mezuzah.*"

"Oh, man . . ." Michael declared. "Where did you learn that!" But he did not wait for an answer. He handed the yarmulke back to Billy and began to walk toward the corner to catch his bus down Broadway toward the library.

"Amen," said Marylee, who then signaled to Billy to go back in, which he did, while she pursued Michael, finally reaching him just before he turned onto the avenue. She tugged at his shoulder, which, she noticed, was covered with flecks of dandruff that she brushed off, grooming and deriding him in the same gesture. "Why do you and Sam act as if these little rituals are the end of the world? They're really not, Michael. Michael, are you listening?"

What was there to listen to? He only inhaled her perfume, felt an impatience rising with an irresistible intensity he did not want to yield to; in addition, two buses had already passed, were two blocks down Broadway, and none was coming now; he was all but certain to be late once more. Phyllis would look at him with those eyes that said, You are marching toward the occupational guillotine of a visit to the human resources office, and I will be happy enough to be your

Madame LaFarge. Between such an image and the *mezuzah* festival just conducted by an evangelist living in his home, he was suffering from what Judy said the Buddhists called split mind. That, and a genuinely splitting headache. Michael was ready only to walk quickly around the block, go home, sneak up the stairs, and go back to sleep.

"No more," he said to Marylee.

Then she disarmed him. "Judy asked me to remind you, by the way," she said, "that you're not supposed to forget to bring back some fish, some organic fish with a name I forget. Sounds like 'bizarre.'"

"Char," he said dimly, rolling the *r* as if it were part of an incantation, a soliloquy uttered by doomed Macbeth grimly stalking the heath. "Such little kindnesses will not redeem you, Marylee. But thanks. I won't forget the Alaskan char."

No, the world was not ending, but as he stood there, his glance shifting back and forth like a quick volley at the net from Marylee to the clogged frantic Broadway traffic and then back to her fetching smile, the world did indeed seem to be precariously shifting.

"I only want to say this," he finally stammered to her: "People who really like Jews, true philo-Semites, are not out to convert Jews. Are you with me on this, Marylee?"

"I'm listening," she said, and he could see she was.

"Philo-Semites simply leave Jews alone, because if they convert them, then what's left to philo?"

23

Dear Father:

Thank you very much for the suggestions and the encouraging words. We are continually trying many new items on the menu. My Bible Salad—dates, figs, olives, delicate pomegranate slices (no apples since the pomegranate was likely what Eve ate from in the Garden) and all the oldest foods mentioned in the Testaments—well, suffice it to say that the salad didn't quite have the oomph I was looking for, so we are back to the drawing board with it. However, chicken in all its varieties continues to be a big culinary draw with the Jews. (Is there a Biblical reference to chicken you can help me with?) Chicken soup, for example, remains tremendously popular. However, last week I made the mistake of preparing it with the little rib cages of the birds floating in the broth the way we enjoy it at home instead of with the little *matza* balls the Jews seem to expect.

When a diner, apparently enjoying the soup, turned his head suddenly (so I heard the waiter explaining to the Emergency

Medical technician), he began to choke. His face turned blue, the restaurant went wild, one of the Buddhists ran for me in back where I was cooking, and, although still knowing little English, he kept pointing to the Heimlich Maneuver poster which we have up on the wall of the corridor leading from the dining room to the kitchen.

I ran out and knew instantly what needed to be done. Not having studied the maneuver or practiced it, I nevertheless applied myself to the gentleman—I do not know if he was Jew or Gentile. What I do know, you will be happy to hear, is that he is not suing us. He had a huge barrel chest and abdomen and I pulled in on him several times, all the while praying to the Lord and making very sure the police had been called. I feared the worst because the man suddenly stopped struggling, and was turning limp in my arms.

But God did hear my prayer. Finally, help arrived, not in the person of the Emergency Medical Service staff (they came later) but Judy Klain—Michael's wife and a distinguished supporter of the Club and its outreach activities. Despite being a lapsed Christian and heathen meditator, she'd had good sense enough recently to take a Red Cross course, so she knew the maneuver. When she heard the ruckus (she was at the time downstairs meditating with the Buddhist I have written you about previously), she ran up and wrapped her strong arms around the diner.

Briskly pulling in at the solar plexus (I had not been forceful enough), one, two, three times she did this, uttering, I overheard, her Buddhist prayer or mantra, and all the while I was urging the other three diners (one of our unusually slow nights) to pray with me. So, while the victim of the chicken rib was turning a dangerous pale blue, we had all religions combined working away and empowering Judy. Finally the gentleman gagged and as he collapsed on the floor, a wishbone popped out of his mouth and fell at his feet.

I actually have it here before me, on my desk, wrapped in a baggy, as a sign of the fragility of life, of the necessity for God's help, and as a reminder that I need to take that Red Cross course myself as soon as possible.

No damage done. Of course, the buzz about our chicken soup is not really great in the community.

It has recently occurred to me that perhaps we should serve real Jewish food in the restaurant. I know this sounds outrageous, but, after all, to attract Jewish diners and through them Jewish converts, maybe we need to become kosher. I myself have recently sampled genuine kosher cuisine in Brooklyn in the company of Rena and Isaac, the electricians who have become my friends; I found it both spicy and satisfying. And, of course,

Our Lord kept strictly to the dietary laws as well. To be Him perhaps means we must first strive to eat like Him. Anyway, it seems to me to be a natural extension, Daddy, of our novel approach.

However, to do this at the restaurant is a very complicated matter requiring new kitchen appliances as well as rabbinical supervision that might be as difficult to come by as water on the moon. I have told you the incident of the chicken bone in detail so that you will not be too upset if there is a lawsuit and an increase for our liability insurance coverage. I trust you will agree that we cannot do without.

Finally, Father, I have been meaning to write to you that one of the great benefits for me, personally, in fulfilling God's ministry here on the Upper West Side is that in my spare time I am able to visit the many theological centers of all faiths in the metropolitan area. I am learning that there are many seas of spirituality flowing in Gotham and it is deepening my own faith. They are mainly in serious error, of course, but the people involved—for example Isaac and Rena's father, who runs, I have recently learned, one such theological seminary for rabbinical students in Brooklyn where I partook of the kosher meal—are deeply religious folks. If the Antichrist arrives here any time soon, he will have many strong people, of all persuasions, to oppose him.

This is all by way of saying my Hebrew, which I study on my own now, and occasionally with the Brooklyn people described above, comes along smartly.

Think of me here, Daddy, as St. Jerome—or perhaps it was St. Augustine. You remember the urges the monks used to write about? Human urges that came from the loneliness of being a monk. They used to beat their chests with sharp rocks, and under-nourished themselves too (they would have done a poor job of that had they worked in a restaurant!), and still they had those visions of dancing girls in Rome.

Then—and this is the part I want you to focus on—those monks began taking up the study of Hebrew. It was not easy. It was new and different, but it was so demanding it took their minds off the girls, because figuring out the Hebrew grammar problems simply drained them, and the urges disappeared so they could continue to work translating the Bible into Latin from God's original tongue.

The monks are my inspiration, my Hebrew progresses, work continues, and the restaurant evolves. (The insurance payment is due, Daddy, so please send the money. Remember the choking diner!)

With love to you and in the service of God, as ever.

William

P.S. Thank you for the news that Annabelle is on her way.

P.P.S. And don't you continue to worry about progress here—it is definitely not good for your health, Daddy. I realize I have not sent you any conversion documents yet. That's because the Jews of the Upper West Side are tough indeed. But between the Word and the Food, they are definitely coming along. When they see the power of Annabelle, that will also make a positive difference and a flood tide of converts will surely begin flowing to us.

24

At the Caracas Health and Racquet Club, Sam was stuffing himself into a too-snug and unflatteringly ragged Plant-a-Tree-in-Israel T-shirt, which he had last donned when he was fourteen and vice-president of his United Synagogue Youth group. His below-acceptable attire was not, however, affecting his play or that of his partner tonight, the imperturbable Ganesh. In his perfectly tailored blue polo shirt, Ganesh moved lithely about the court beside Sam, and they both in fact were playing very well; nevertheless, they found themselves standing a foot or two behind the baseline most of the night because Gerry and Michael were returning absolutely everything, and very hard. Gerry snapped a backhand at Ganesh, who bent low to get it but uncharacteristically netted the ball; Michael called out to Gerry, "Well done," and they talked for a moment about the placement and the troubling spin.

Such interludes of tennis talk, however, had become about the only form of communication between Gerry and his friends since he had begun the Christian lessons with Billy Harp and Marylee. Gerry knew he had grown more distant, although that consequence (if such it was) certainly had not been his intention. He knew how upset Sam and Michael were with him—it seemed he couldn't make them happy, or Marylee happy, no matter how he tried. What was he to do? Since every word out of his mouth appeared to offend someone, Gerry had decided simply to keep his mouth shut as much as possible. Still—what else was new!—Sam and Michael had misunderstood even his silences.

Tonight, Sam and Michael determined it was critical to go on the offensive in order to avoid losing their friend for sure, for Marylee had, they were fairly certain, profoundly accelerated the pressure on Gerry. Beyond pressuring him to accompany her on her journey, as she had described it to Michael, she had apparently upped the ante in a way none of them had foreseen: they feared she was maneuvering for Gerry to become Club Revelation's first convert.

If their wives had let them, Michael and Sam would have called the Jewish papers, they would have picketed their own building if necessary, they would . . . and so they had flailed and obsessed and threatened all week in the privacy of their apartments and in the presence only of Judy and Ellen. They had been told, however, in unambiguous terms ("It's you guys who are acting like jerks!" Ellen had snapped at them) that their horse had already fled from the barn. At heart they knew their wives were right, but more powerful impulses than good sense, rectitude, or even marital equanimity were driving Michael and Sam to do what they needed to do.

What Judy and Ellen reminded them about, of course, was that if Gerry was well on his way already, no amount of public embarrassment or guilt-inducing apoplexy on their part would convince him to remain a Jew. Their building and their lives would be splashed across the weekly religious newspapers, and who knew what other lunatics—or terrorists—might be attracted their way? And what would it all accomplish?

"Then what will work? What will stop him?" Sam implored Ellen to suggest some approach, some key, some simple insight that obviously had eluded him.

"Your genuine friendship might make a difference," she had answered. "And your example, maybe." Which is what had triggered Sam to undertake his *mezuzah* campaign. And he had done considerably more since.

Much to Ellen's consternation, Sam was, by increments, beginning to make their apartment kosher—not kosher style but genuinely kosher, in all the arcane complexity of the dietary laws. He had also turned the Museum of the 1960s upside down searching through the big steamer trunk full of their demilitarized military gear—backpacks, rucksacks, an Eisenhower jacket that smelled of fifty years of camphor, a duffel bag full of canteens, binoculars that no longer focused, cut-off chevron patches, an ancient West Point uniform, a U.S. Navy pea coat and bell-bottoms with all buttons amazingly still attached, until, almost despairing, Sam went back downstairs and retrieved his long-misplaced prayer shawl and *tefillin* in his old bar mitzvah bag; they had been buried in the bottom drawer of the dresser underneath the tangle of arm braces and athletic supporters. "What's the prayer," he had said to Ellen, "when you dust off your old religious gear?"

"I actually believe you think I might know such a thing."

She looked on with continuing surprise but less amusement, however, as Sam re-schooled himself in the use of this religious equipment and began to pray at home and to go to synagogue; occasionally he attended the *minyan* with Michael's father at the nursing home.

Michael also had not been unaffected by Gerry's nascent Christianity, nor had he been idle in offering a competitive and opposite example. He began again to light Sabbath candles—and to make sure Gerry knew that this glorious ritual was taking place right under his roof. Truth be told, Michael had always enjoyed this particular commandment, this *mitzvah*, which he loved to fulfill above all others. In particular, it gave Michael deep and inexpressible pleasure to watch Judy draw in a deep meditative breath, gather herself spiritually, and then obligingly spread her fingers above the magical flames of the candles and recite, along with him, the blessings that mark the sparks of light at the creation of the world:

"Blessed art Thou oh Lord Our God, King of the Universe, Who has commanded us to light the Sabbath candles."

"If my Buddhist can say the *brocha*," he told Gerry, "so can you. Go on, it won't kill you. It will change your whole perspective."

"My perspective is just fine, Michael."

"Go on," Michael persisted. "You'll see. It's the real thing, not mumbo jumbo." Michael knew he had made a mistake and tried to recover. "I know you're searching, pal. But why not search close to home? Light the candles."

"I'm not interested in the candles," Gerry answered, with an almost cynical finality that Michael was certain Gerry would not have been capable of before William Harp had arrived and before Marylee had come to influence him.

Michael then prevailed on Judy several times to invite Gerry—and certainly Marylee if she cared to join him, although that was not likely any more—to come down for Friday night supper.

"You really think the power of the Sabbath candles and

my vegan chicken are going to anchor Gerry to Judaism?" she asked him.

"Absolutely," he answered. "And don't forget the mushroom and chestnut risotto."

Although Gerry loved Judy's cooking and over the years had often eaten with them, thus far Gerry had declined. There was always an excuse, and behind every excuse, Michael was absolutely certain, stood Marylee.

Therefore Michael also began to prepare more drastic measures. He tracked down Gerry's mother's phone number at the Wayfarer Inn in Dolphin Tail, Florida, a compound of agreeably run-down bungalows with tall, bottle-washer palm trees fringed by a mangrove swamp, which he had once checked out as a possible retirement home for his own mother. Here, widowed Mrs. Levine was now managing the local Cancer Care thrift shop, playing cards, and attending senior mixers on the occasional lookout for a new man. A diabetic not in great circulatory or pulmonary shape, she would take the news of her only son's flirtation with a departure from the faith of his birth with, to put it mildly, a touch of myocardial horror. Michael had not called her yet, for to strike this low blow—tattling on a full-grown man to his mother—even he was still very hesitant to undertake. He was, however, preparing and assembling a full brief of justifications.

Some nights, like tonight at Caracas, Michael's and Sam's bewilderment and anxiety were such that they felt all they had left of their erstwhile great friend Gerry Levine was his windmill serve, his ground strokes, his competitiveness at the net, and good memories.

Between points Michael had vainly been trying to whisper key tenets of Judaism to Gerry. But the lessons were slow going, as he couldn't get much beyond the Ten Commandments during a six-game set. Nor did Michael fool himself.

He knew, of course, the project was laughable, yet he simply could not *not* try to use every opportunity to break through, and in the rescue effort he and Sam had coordinated as much as possible. Tonight Sam had even recruited Ganesh to throw some points, particularly off shots by Gerry, so that Gerry (as Michael jawed Jewish stuff at him) might begin to associate the glories of the Mosaic faith with cross-court volleys and winners down the alley. Lots of luck!

After the game, Ganesh had to leave quickly ("I have a lovely pacemaker to install early in the morning"), and, minutes later, Sam and Michael tailed Gerry into the club's bar, where they were determined to make their case if he let them, and even if he did not. They book ended him on bar stools and ordered a round of beers.

For his part, Gerry decided to skip a drink, declined Michael's offer to pay, and instead extracted a bill from his wristband for a soda, just to be sociable. He also wanted to be totally lucid in order to divert what he knew was going to be his friends' continuing interrogation. He wished the Toyota were not in the shop—Sam had driven tonight—so that he could dispense with the feigned sociability and leave Caracas right now.

"You know, Gerry," Sam began tentatively, "I really enjoyed playing against you tonight."

"Well, thank you."

"We love playing against you in tennis," said Michael, "but not in life. Life is different."

"Life certainly is different," Gerry agreed. "Delicious soda. Want a sip?"

"Our point is," Michael pressed nervously on, "religion is not tennis . . ."

"Well, Michael," Gerry responded with a sudden sobriety, "in that case would you mind telling me this: was it you on my side out there? Or was that the chief rabbi of Caracas I was playing with?"

Hearing his own uncharacteristically sarcastic tone, Gerry felt embarrassed and wanted to catapult himself out of the club immediately. Out and away, far away, or at least up to the Museum, maybe even for a good long toke on Ellen's stash of vintage Acapulco Gold. He had not done that in a decade, but he felt like it now.

"Gerry? Are you there?"

"Yes, pal?" But he was not prepared to listen, and he cut Michael off. "Look, if this is the price of playing tennis these days, maybe I don't need to play anymore. Next time I ask you to move into the alley on my serve," he said to Michael, "please don't turn around and talk to me about Maimonides' *Guide for the Perplexed,* or the Ten Commandments. The first commandment of tennis is: pay attention!

"I really don't want to talk tennis or to play it . . . under these circumstances. Not tonight again. Please, Michael. No more of the Inquisition."

"Okay, my friend. Sorry," Michael said. "I will just commune with the bubbles in this beer."

Sam, seeing Michael virtually capitulate when their joint presentation had barely begun, did what came naturally: he went congenially berserk, even though Michael, his signals and Sam's now hopelessly crossed, pleaded with him to be far more conciliatory. "You never make it easy on us," Sam began. "The old Gerry has disappeared, and you even make us jeopardize the tennis to get in two words with you these days."

"He's right, you know," said Michael.

"I mean, what should we do, Gerry?" Sam pressed on. "Should we open up a restaurant too—one for Jews on the edge like yourself? Then we can have you come in to *daven* with us over breakfast."

"From what Marylee tells me," said Gerry, "you're doing enough *davening* for the both of us."

"What I do in my apartment is my own business, but why don't you give it a shot yourself?"

"Is this the road we want to go down, gentlemen?" Michael reached around Gerry and grabbed at Sam's shirt.

Sam, who finally got the message, said, "No, I'm sorry. I'm sorry. I'm sorry for . . . for all of us."

They stopped talking then and silently sipped their drinks. Michael cast about for a new way to start. Sam stabbed ice cubes with his straw. "Look," Gerry finally helped them out, "this restaurant is what it is. How many customers per night? You tell me. Relax. It's a curiosity at best."

"We're not talking about the business, Gerry. But you. The restaurant is not a curiosity for *you*, Gerry. That's what's bothering us."

"We also happen to know," said Sam, "and contrary to what others around here might think, I am concerned about the so-called restaurant, that Jesus outpost in our midst. And we also know that you and Marylee are making up the difference between what he needs to make every week and what comes in."

"Sam, since when are we not permitted to spend our money the way we choose?"

Sam slapped the bar with his considerable palm; the glasses jumped. "Why don't you just let the place die! If people aren't coming, then it proves there's just no market in the neighborhood for this *matza*-ball missionary. Without you and Marylee, the place couldn't stay open for the time it takes to make a grilled cheese sandwich."

"Not true."

"True."

"Sam," Michael spoke with the weary intonation of a

teacher at the end of a long day of unruly classes, "I really don't think we should be focusing on the business aspect now."

"I know that," said Sam, "but what we have to talk about . . . I just can't get the words out of my mouth."

"Well, I can," Michael said deliberately. "Aren't you thinking about converting? Aren't you seriously thinking about it?"

"I wouldn't say I'm 'seriously' thinking about it," Gerry answered him vacantly, "but, yes, I am considering. To consider is still legal in the United States of America."

"But if Marylee were not on your case," said Sam, "go on, tell us honestly—"

"Would there be day if the sun did not rise?" Gerry said to him, and his response, unpremeditated, puzzled even himself.

"What's your point?"

"Aren't you being slightly, no, more than slightly disingenuous?" Michael said.

"This is making me very uncomfortable," Gerry said. "I am trying to say what is just obvious. You know, she *is* a Christian, and has been all her life."

"And Judy's a Buddhist. Has that made me one?"

"I just want to know," said Sam, "if it's something we did?"

"No, it's nothing you've done," Gerry reassured him.

"Then maybe it's something you ate!" cried Sam. "Maybe some crap Harp puts in his desert locust burgers! Look, would you discuss these things with a rabbi, Gerry?" Sam pleaded.

"Michael practically is a rabbi. Anyway, nobody said I *was* converting."

"Yet."

"You're just considering."

"Yes."

"If it happens," said Sam, "I couldn't live with myself knowing I didn't try to prevent it."

"Oh, you're trying," said Gerry. "I'll sign any document stating that you're getting in my way as much as possible. You'll get full credit, no, extra credit, for trying."

"Maybe I haven't even gotten started."

"Oh shut up, will you Sam!" Michael found himself suddenly far more exasperated with Sam than he was with Gerry. "You think doing what you've been up to really helps any? You think it's going to impress Gerry to check you out becoming a cliché—the superficial Jew? A *mezuzah*-and-kosher-hot-dog Jew?

"Well, fuck you too," said Sam. He slid off the stool and loped off through the bar. Gerry and Michael watched him turn to the right and then fling open the double-glassed doors of the lounge and step into the parking lot. They followed him out but stood off to the side, on the edge of the lot, like paralyzed observers. They watched Sam walk around his station wagon, kick its left tire, open the hatch, and rearrange a video camera, tripods, lights, a green milk carton full of tapes, and some other eminently purloinable equipment that he kept there as if tempting fate. In a kind of arrested amazement, as if they were witnesses to car theft or a crime so unanticipated they reacted with inaction, Gerry and Michael continued to watch the already heavy-laden vehicle drop down on its springs as Sam hurled himself in.

He backed the car out, gunned the engine so that the car was temporarily out of sight, and then it re-emerged into their view. He paused at the far end of the driveway to the consternation of Gerry and Michael, who until they saw the wagon actually bump over the curb and onto the road toward the bridge, did not believe Sam would ever abandon them.

"Did you guys choreograph this?" Gerry said to Michael as they walked back into the lounge. "There's no other explanation."

"Oh, absolutely," Michael answered. "Every flaming detail! Sam's waiting around the corner for you to give a press conference to renounce what you're doing. Then I give him the secret mirror signal and he comes galloping back to pick us up. Give me a break!"

"*You* pissed him off," Gerry said. "You drove him away. The credit is all yours."

"I did?"

"Yes, you made him feel shallow and superficial," Gerry said. "I've been there. I can understand superficial."

"He *is* superficial. So are you, so am I. We're all just idiots and fools in training."

"Not Marylee," Gerry said as they resumed their seats at the bar, waiting, hoping for Sam to blow off his steam and to return. "She's all seriousness, all the time. You would be impressed if you saw her, really up close. I mean the way I do."

"I think I've seen enough," said Michael. He decided to tread carefully now, and he wanted to change the subject, and, anyway, religion, philosophy, Michael's own heavy burden of doubts and wishes were, for the moment, somehow less pressing: the men simply needed a ride home.

After fifteen minutes of waiting for Sam to reappear, Michael borrowed Gerry's phone and then rummaged through the slips of paper in his wallet until, fortunately, he found Judy's cell phone number, because he could never remember it. He reached her in the Museum, where Nawang, who had come up to do a yoga class with Judy and Ellen (Marylee was downstairs with Harp), had been cajoled into a game of counterculture Monopoly, where every time you landed on a utility or railroad asset, you had to give it away and collected ten grateful dollars from Community Chest.

"We're having too much fun," she told Michael, "to come and get you."

"We're starting to walk now," he badgered her. "You know where we are?"

"Oh, yes, indeed, Michael," Judy answered. "I guess we'll be there."

While they waited, their rescue apparently assured, Michael could not restrain himself. "For godsake, Gerry, a conversion is such a serious matter."

"I can think of a lot more serious things," Gerry answered as he stood and began to walk to the door. "I need to get some air."

Outside, to kill the time, but also with a method to his circumambulation, Michael traipsed after Gerry as he walked briskly around the parking lot. It was like Gerry to distract himself from the chunk of sky that seemed to be falling on them by examining the BMWs, Bentleys, Volvos, Audis, and the few humble VWs and Subarus waiting patiently in their slots for their tennis-playing owners to reclaim them.

"You're going to set off an alarm if you get too close," Michael warned Gerry.

"It's exciting," Gerry said.

"You're going to set something off. Listen, friend," Michael was about to take the dreaded subject up once again, but Gerry interrupted.

"Some people care about cars," he said as he leaned over a black and silver Mercedes. "Look at this place. I mean some people are really serious about their vehicles. I'm amazed they don't charge us extra for parking the Toyota. But me, Michael, take me. I'm *not* serious about cars. I'm serious about Marylee Jeffers. I'd be dishonest if I told you what was happening is getting me very worked up because it really is not. You see, despite it all, I still have her. I don't care if it's the pre-Christian or post-Christian Marylee. I just want to be there for her. What she's doing doesn't seem like a big deal to me. Does that mean something is somehow flawed in me? A Jewish failure? An embarrassment to the rabbi who bar-mitzvahed me? Okay. What's new about that? Maybe I should go to a shrink. Sure, nothing new in that either."

"Stop it, Gerry."

"Oh shrinks, that's your department, Michael. You're waiting to give me a recommendation, no?"

"I'm not," Michael said as he followed him up to an unusual Hyundai hiding in the corner of the lot, where it had gotten Gerry's attention.

"Hey, Michael, maybe you should just assemble all the powers that be from every authority on everything that exists and just indict me. You know. Across the board, for everything. The whole package."

"I don't know, Gerry. I'm not a shrink. And you haven't committed any crime. But can you at least answer Sam's question: Is it *your* decision?"

"I haven't made any decision."

"Good. Keep it that way. Join the party. Keep being undecided for the rest of your life."

"It won't be that long," he said. And, to Michael's relief, Gerry laughed.

"Well, is it fair to say that if, hypothetically, you are *inclining* toward it, that such a decision would be based on your own thinking?"

"Is this Watergate? Are you my friend or are you Senator Ervin?"

"We just want to know if this is coming from *your* heart. It's a legitimate question. We love you, Gerry. We're your heart's specialists, so to speak."

"Heart attack specialists, you mean."

They kept circling the parking lot, glancing toward the corner to see if Judy had arrived yet. They were growing chilly, but they did not want to go back into the club lounge, as if it were the wrong direction when it was toward home they wanted to go. Then they grew uncomfortably quiet. Michael did his best to keep himself from being prosecutorial. But God help him if, in his mind, he had already pronounced Gerry guilty. "Just let me know if she's coercing you. Or if Harp is. You don't have to be in this alone, Gerry."

"I'm not alone."

The night was crisp, the stars bright, and Gerry thought he saw the Big Dipper low in the sky to the northwest. "Michael, do you ever know when a decision is truly your own decision, one hundred percent yours? Even when you're fairly certain your thoughts are your own, not borrowed, how can you really be sure, know beyond a doubt, that they aren't Judy's or your father's or somebody's on TV you listened to a month ago and now forgot the source?"

"I never knew you were such an epistemologist."

"I'm just a guy trying to get by."

"I think you're being coy, because we're not talking about if you like a TV program or not, or a candidate, or what your opinion is about the weather. We're talking about God, life and death, heaven and hell, order and chaos. Your soul and the whole religious ball of wax. Basic stuff."

"Look, Michael, most items in a product area are similar. Linoleum, congoleum. Is that Lexus so different from the BMW over there? It is, but it isn't. When you strip away the superficials—the shape, accessories, the lights, the stuff they have in common—they are both just expensive, fast cars with engines that will last. That's the way I see Christianity and Judaism. Two essentially similar products. It's really not God

or heaven and hell or salvation or its opposite that we're talking about. It's more like brand loyalty."

"That's clever, Gerry, but it doesn't cut it with me. It just
doesn't ring true."

"Can I help that? You see, that's exactly my problem. No
matter what I say or do. No matter how honest I try to be, I
am found wanting and I disappoint people, and I hate doing
that."

"Tell me something I can believe, Gerry. Tell me Marylee
is promising you oral sex every night, three times a night, on
demand, if you convert. *That* I can believe would be a reason
to become a Christian."

"Actually, we are getting along better than ever. We have
this . . . this whole thing, the restaurant, Harp, and more to
talk about. God, I mean, and death, and the afterlife. Is that
normal talk for you and Judy? What do you two talk about
when you're up in the Museum alone, or at dinner in your
place?"

"*You're* our table talk, Gerry. Judy and I talk about you
and William Harp and Marylee, and we laugh until our sides
split about Revelation Pie and St. John's Bread Pudding and
the whole stupid menu. We laugh, Gerry, and then we cry. We
cry about you. That's all we ever do anymore."

"Well done, Michael. Now tell me what Judy really
thinks."

"She says she loves ML. She says, Let's cut her some slack
and if she wants to torture Gerry, let her do it. Then I say, as
your friend and as a fellow husband, I say I want it to stop.
But she won't let me call the cops until there's blood on the
floor. Any spillage there yet, my friend?"

"This really does matter to Marylee, Michael. She's so
passionate about it. And you know something, it's exciting
when your wife gets passionate about something. That gives

hope that she can still get passionate about you again—you know what we've been through about kids, what we've all been through. Well, this is something. I see this new thing in her, and I understand and I don't, and I know it makes you guys miserable, but, bottom line, it makes me happy that she's got a drive and energy she didn't have before."

"Her energy, as you call it, is turning you against yourself."

"Where's the turning? I'm not hiding it. I'm not ashamed. I don't conceal that I'm Jewish like some people in business still do. I'm a Levine, for chrissakes! But, no, I don't flaunt it. I don't wear it on the lapel. I'm sorry, Michael, I can see your face is so fallen you better put your hand under your chin to hold it up. Look, the religion is . . . just there like . . ."

"Like what, Gerry?"

"Like I don't know. Like being a man."

"That's precisely my point. It's pretty basic. So now you want to change? You want to become a woman?"

"You're smarter and cleverer than me, Michael. I don't presume to debate you. All I know is that I can be Jewish today and, let's say, a Buddhist like Judy tomorrow or a Hindu or a Christian, and won't I still be the same old Gerry?"

"To Sam you won't be."

"And how about to you? Would I become some sort of traitor in your eyes as well?"

Finally, through the trees that lined the parking lot where he was peering, Michael recognized the van stopped at the intersection. As she made the slow turn, Judy flashed her lights. Soon she would be making the quick sprint onto Caracas Road and then the left into the parking lot. Michael and Gerry gathered their gear.

"Talk to me some more, Gerry. Promise me you won't go through with it suddenly without talking to me some more. I feel we've just begun and made a pretty good start to discuss this. Don't jump into Harp's baptismal tub or whatever it is without talking to me some more. That's the least you can do."

"Absolutely."

"Remember, Gerry, that 'baptismal' rhymes with 'abysmal.'"

"I won't forget 'that.' Sort of rhymes with 'crap.'"

"And if you do jump in," Michael persisted, "at least promise me and Sam you'll keep a little piece of you above the water."

"If you convert, you know, it's supposed to be a total dunk."

"Cheat, like Achilles did with his heel. Keep your pinkie above. Keep your pinkie Jewish."

Gerry threw back his head and let out a laugh that reverberated across the parking lot. "You want me to keep one piece above the baptismal waters?"

"Yes, for old time's sake."

"How about my nose?"

"A nose will do, my friend, but I'm not particular."

"You crack me up, Michael. First, it's the end of the world and now it's a joke. My nose above the water so that magically the schnoz will remain Jewish. So which one of us is serious and which one is not?"

The van arrived and the door slid open, and they heard Judy's "Hello, boys." But she was not behind the wheel. Nawang was.

"My first time," the Buddhist said with evident pride.

"No wonder you took forever to get here," Michael said. "You meditated your way across the George Washington Bridge?"

"Blissful," said Nawang, "but a little rough in second gear."

They climbed into the back seat. Judy put on her most

recent tape, a low, grounded chanting of the Heart Sutra sung by a chorus of Buddhist monks in exile in Dharamsala, India.

"Just don't go through with it," Michael said to Gerry, as they put on their seat belts.

"Through with what?" Judy asked.

"Please drive," Gerry said to Nawang. "This will be an adventure."

"Just don't do it," Michael whispered to Gerry. Then he leaned forward and put his arm gratefully across Judy's broad, comfortable shoulders. "I'll explain later."

25

My Dear Father and Teacher:

You are one hundred per cent right that I am no Saint Jerome. I am not so prideful as to have intended such a comparison. But what does it matter, Daddy, that a girl is teaching me the Hebrew? Would the letters of the Hebrew alphabet be different if taught by a man? Anyway, I am on my own a lot with the Hebrew studies since the brother Isaac and the father are, like you, not pleased that Rena and I advance in our studies together.

I want to assure you that Annabelle has been uncrated, inspected by a vet I found in the neighborhood, and she is installed in her tank in the Baptismal Alcove. She looks well and I sense in her green eyes that she remembers me. I will begin to handle her immediately, at least once an evening at the Club as Aaron did before Pharaoh, to show the power of faith and to get through to some of our tough customers. Incidentally, they seem to be really enjoying the hummus, baba ganoush, and pomegranate spread. The Mount of Olives Special Salad we have recently introduced also seems a hit. But, no, Father, the customers have not yet been moved quite to the point where they are rising and asking in mid-meal to be accompanied to our little version of the Jordan.

But, it *will* happen, Daddy. I assure you again and again. You don't need to keep reminding me time is of the essence in order to convert the Jewish people. Yes, 144,000 will be saved, 144,000 Saints to rise above the flames of destruction on Judgment Day, a large number, but really only a drop in Redemption's bucket given the Jewish population of the metropolitan area, the New Jersey corridor, and the Northeast.

God help me, he thought. Have I not been waiting for You for the longest time? Hello there, Lord? Billy paused for a response. He waited. He resumed.

Now, to answer the travel question you posed: Frankly, it is not a good idea. I do not think your coming up here will move the conversions along, Daddy. Magnificent as you are as a preacher of the Gospel, your being in Manhattan, where you will have to be constantly on guard for the Antichrist, will only drain your precious energy, which you need to restore your health. How is your health? Why do I think you are hiding some new development from me? Isn't it enough that Annabelle is now here on your behalf, as it were? Let Annabelle do her magic and wordlessly declare the power and the glory.

With gratitude, as ever, for your patience, your son,

William

26

Michael had told Gerry it was the hottest synagogue in town. Still, Gerry might not have agreed to attend Sabbath services at the Reform congregation, B'nai Luria, located only a block or so away, had he not sensed Michael's eagerness to, in a sense, give him equal time. Housed in a striking building with two bulbous cupolas and other Moorish architectural elements, the congregation was noted in the neighborhood for its soaring participatory music, five hundred voices strong, and in particular, for the services of *kabbalat shabat,* the greeting of the Sabbath at sunset on Friday night.

Because Judy, Nawang, and a few other of his students were just starting a *sesshin,* a weekend-long meditation retreat, and would be away in the country, Judy did not attend—she really wanted no part of Michael's salesmanship in any case. Ellen, who had already seen plenty of praying since Sam began *davening* away in their apartment before every window that faced east (after having also kissed each *mezuzah*), had little interest in going along with the synagogue outing; of course, Ellen also had an oppressive folder of exams to correct.

So, when Gerry told him that Marylee would be joining them, Michael could hardly raise an objection, even though he had wanted Gerry all to himself in this endeavor. When Billy Harp, of all people, suddenly insinuated himself into the synagogue party (he insisted that he was becoming—for purposes of the ministry, of course—quite a student of Judaism), that made four.

A few hours before sunset, Michael tried to discourage Billy one more time. "Who's going to mind the store?" he asked Billy. "You are running a restaurant, aren't you?"

"Oh, the Tibetans can handle things just fine, Mr. Klain. Their English is improving, and everything's all prepared. And it's not a serious problem if you have only six bookings."

"That many? What if there is a sudden rush of reservations?"

"Trust me," said Billy. "I've been looking forward for weeks for a chance to practice my Hebrew."

Michael went upstairs, dressed, and, undaunted, met the others under the ailanthus at 6:30; to secure good seats they needed to arrive early.

During the short walk over, in the throes of a kind of pedagogical excitement he had not felt since he had taught Sunday school at a Unitarian church to earn extra money in college, Michael lectured Gerry—and Billy, who walked beside him (Marylee was on her minister's arm)—on the finer points of the synagogue service they were about to participate in. "Above all, this synagogue specializes, so I've heard, in bringing the spiritual quality of Judaism to the surface."

"Where is it normally that it has to be coaxed up?"

Gerry's question, which Michael had not expected, flummoxed him and he redirected it. "My advice is just to concentrate, as Judy always says, on a few things: on the melodies, or maybe, if you want something more visual, on the glow of the eternal light."

"The eternal light never did much for me," Gerry said, "I mean how can you be impressed that this or that illumination is eternal after you've seen the janitor changing the bulb?

"When was that?"

"When I was in junior congregation. Just about the last time I was in synagogue," Gerry said as they walked. "The light went out during the service. I won't forget that. A small red light the size of a refrigerator bulb flickered and went out."

"You're making this up."

"Absolutely not. And it happened in the middle of the service just when they were bringing the Torah out. It was not a good sign, but it didn't seem to bother anyone but me. I'm not even sure anyone else noticed. But for me, I guess, the timing was fateful."

"What do you mean?" Marylee asked—they were at the corner—"Since we seem to be stopped at another red light."

"I mean that little filament failure must have rocked the foundation of my—pardon the expression—faith."

"You mean your own light went out?" Billy said in a tone Michael thought contained a little too much eagerness.

"Without my noticing it until years later. Exactly."

"It was just a matter of bad timing. And you're making this up."

"Why should I do that?"

"Okay. Scratch the *ner tamid,* the eternal forty-watt light," Michael said. "Let's concede the light. So, instead, try focusing on the Hebrew letters . . ."

"I love the Hebrew letters," Billy interjected, and only Michael's glare kept him from reciting all twenty-six of them in the singsong Rena had taught him.

"Fabulous," Michael said, which was the equivalent of *Shut up.* "They are really classic. Each letter also happens to represent a number, and the rabbis have done all this magical numerology with them over the years. During the service, Gerry, you could try to imagine the letters floating up off the page, ascending, and then actually becoming, let's say, flying numbers and then black birds. If you're going to ask me how they get outside the closed windows of the synagogue, don't ask."

"I think we can handle that," Marylee said.

They arrived in front of the imposing and ornate wooden doors of the synagogue and joined a waiting throng of mostly young people in their twenties and thirties. They entered and found seats in the orchestra area of the cavernous sanctuary, larger by far than even the facade would have indicated. Here they waited for the spiritual proceedings to begin.

As the synagogue filled up, Michael continued Gerry's unsolicited refresher course in Judaism, beginning with the prayer book, then pointing out the various ritual fixtures in the synagogue—the closed ark with the Torah scrolls inside, the facsimile of the tablets with the Ten Commandments (he skipped the unreliable eternal light), the two tall candelabra on opposite sides of the reader's platform, the *bima,* and the circle of twelve stained-glass windows above, each with its symbol of the twelve tribes of Israel.

"You're a Levite," said William Harp, proudly, to Gerry.

"He knows," said Michael.

Marylee draped her arm around her husband's shoulders and said, "What's it feel like to be fought over, honey?"

"It's about time," he answered.

The place was buzzing with the earnest and animated

chatter of hundreds of people—mostly unmarried, Marylee thought. The crowd milled around the aisles and in front of the *bima,* and it was by now already nearly seven o'clock. Showing far more interest and concentration than Gerry, William Harp was bent forward in his seat poring over the prayer book. He was trying to link the letters in order to pronounce the Hebrew words, and Michael grudgingly provided some tutorial help. For his part, Gerry felt fidgety, as if he were waiting for a very long opera to begin. "Are people ever going to sit down?" he asked.

"I have never, in all my vast experience in attending events in the Jewish world," said Marylee, "not once have I been to a wedding, bar mitzvah, or other service of a Jewish anything that actually began on time. What is it with the Jews and punctuality?"

"They're the Jews," said Michael. Then with a glance toward William Harp, he added, "For Jews, the apocalypse is *not* happening this week or anytime soon. If you've got all the time in the world, why should punctuality be a virtue?"

"Oh but the world *will* end, sir," said William Harp. "There's no getting around that."

"Not likely tonight," said Michael.

"No," William said as he surveyed the agreeable throng behind him. "Not likely tonight."

"Are we aware of this difference?" Michael directed the question to Gerry. "That Christianity is absolutely committed to a rip-roaring, rock-melting, people-killing, violent, apocalyptic ending, but for the Jews . . ."

"For the Jews what?" This time the inquiry was Marylee's. She paused and then beat Michael to answer her own question. "Jews will give you no better than sixty-forty odds that tomorrow the world's staying pretty much the same as we see it today."

"Not so," said Michael.

"What will happen then?" asked William Harp as he looked up from the prayer book.

"I'm no expert, of course," answered Michael, "but according to the sages of old, as well as my horoscope, the Internet bubble will soon burst, Florida's coastline will sink beneath the sea, and the Yankees will four-peat and perhaps even have the first season in which a Major League team won't lose a single game."

"What is also obviously certain," Marylee quipped back, "is that Jews will never get serious about the end of the world until it's too late. Of course you're also right about the Yankees."

With every seat taken, the sanctuary was overflowing with people standing perfumed cheek by after-shaved jowl when, finally, the smiling young rabbi and cantor in swirling blue robes with red fringe emerged from the wings. They strode confidently across the *bima,* signaling as they walked for the congregants to stand, and, to the accompaniment of a great crescendo of music, the collected Jewish voices of the Upper West Side rose as one and filled the great space of the synagogue with a sonorous Sabbath greeting, and the service began.

"That's a powerful sound," William said to Marylee.

"Try letting the melodies wash over you," Michael whispered in Gerry's ear. "Let the beautiful songs of the greeting of the Sabbath speak to you."

"They would, Mr. Klain," said William, "if you'd just let us hear them."

"Yes, yes, I'll shut up in a second, but I want to make sure Gerry understands the context so he'll enjoy this even more. You see, the words are saying the Sabbath is the bride of God arriving to meet her husband. That's the concept here."

"Sort of an arranged marriage," said William.

"Arranged by who?" asked Marylee.

Michael ignored her. "This first tune is called '*Lecha Dodi.*' It means, 'Come, let us go, my love.'"

"The Sabbath is like the bride of God?" Marylee came right back at him. "The Virgin Mary, then?"

"He said 'bride,' Marylee," William Harp responded. "Wife and bride is not mother."

"Thank you for the correction," said Michael, who now felt launched into his material, like a professor on a field trip, whose student has just made the perfect remark that is like a can opener for everything else. "Yes, you see, there's this huge female aspect of the deity—they call her the *Shechina* and she, it, is sort of the Great Mother Force of life. It's all pretty complicated— the point being that *Shechina* has been marginalized for hundreds of years by the mainstream rabbis, all guys, of course. But in Israel, Palestine, the Ottoman Empire in the seventeenth century, the sky was full of comets and all kinds of fireworks, the tides were high, the signs were everywhere and Rabbi Isaac Luria, a mystic—this is around the year 1666, actually—"

"Those are the numbers of the Antichrist." William Harp leaned in toward the others. "Six, six, six."

"Well, sure," said Michael. "They were looking for the Christ, the pro-Christ, so to speak, in 1666, and whenever he is expected, you also have to guard against the anti-guy. They're always looking for him too. You're the expert on this."

"You know I am, Mr. Klain."

"Anyway, Luria—that's who the synagogue is named after by the way, B'nai Luria, children of Luria—he unearths all this stuff about *Shechina,* the Female Mystical Force. He sets the ideas to some great music. He teaches, for the first time, these sober yeshiva boys to dance on hilltops at night, to go into trances, to fast until they have visions, to rip their clothes off and swim naked like seventeenth-century Jewish

Huckleberry Finns, and, what do you know! Surprise! He attracts a great following. You know there are no monks or real priests anymore in Judaism, which I personally think is a great loss, no more high priests even, not since the destruction of the temple. So these Luria guys become very popular, mystical Jewish pilgrims, monks of the Kabbalah, and they create an incredible sensation because of what their mission is: unleashing the great, hot, female Jewish force. It's so big, it's so out of control, that the regular rabbis call the police, quell the riot, and write poor *Shechina* out of mainstream Jewish life for generations to come. Until, more or less, our own time. Out of deference to Marylee, I'm giving you the feminist take on the phenomenon. But it's close enough."

"Okay, Michael," Marylee whispered as the prayers continued, "we get the pitch."

But Michael was not yet done. "You see, they meet, they join in a kind of mystical union that frankly is every bit as sexy as anything Christianity has to offer."

"Oh yes?" said Marylee. "We'll see about that." Then she gave Gerry a decidedly sensual kiss.

The prayers, hymns, and responsive readings of the service followed one upon the other and Gerry's bar-mitzvah-preparation-level Hebrew was not so utterly shabby that he couldn't follow some selections with fleeting moments of recollection and remembered pleasure. He was even able occasionally to point out to Marylee where they were in the prayer book they shared. Despite years of absence from regular worship—many more years had been spent studying at the side of his rabbi father—Michael still knew the service quite nearly by heart. For his part, William Harp took it all in like an anthropologist who had arrived, with limited preparation, but high eagerness, on a long-anticipated Jewish shore.

Forty-five minutes later, services concluded, as they had begun, in a spirited crescendo of communal singing of the hymn *"Adon Olam,"* Lord of the World, and the party began to inch their way back through the festive crowd to the sanctuary exit. Everyone, it seemed, was in the Sabbath's thrall. People were responding enthusiastically to the rabbi's request that, as they exit, they hail at least three of their neighbors, total strangers though they may be, with the Sabbath greeting, *Shabbat Shalom,* Sabbath Peace.

It was no wonder that William Harp, greeted by a half dozen female congregants with not entirely unseductive *Shabbat Shalom*s, was thinking suddenly about Club Revelation. Clearly his tables were empty on Friday nights because everyone on the Upper West Side was here.

By the time Michael, Marylee, William, and Gerry emerged onto Broadway, the congregation had spilled down the steps of the synagogue and drifted across the sidewalk, over the curb, like an overflowing human cornucopia, even filling the spaces between the parked cars. They kissed each other, embraced, and wished each other a restful Sabbath. Like a big, extended, long-lost family at a reunion, they were talking and hugging and letting the burdens of the work week molt away like so many invisible skins. Of course there were always a few diehards only partially in the Sabbath spirit, Michael noticed, doing the dotcom talk right in front of him. Yet the couples forming into rhythmic concentric circles all around them soon swept away the entrepreneurs in a spontaneous tide of *hora*s and other more complex Israeli folk dances Michael had once stepped to but now could no longer even name.

"It's an outdoors singles bar!" Gerry declared.

"If this kind of thing had been around when we were twenty-five," Michael said to Marylee, "maybe we wouldn't have gone off and married Christian women. Maybe we would have found beautiful Jewish women carrying on right here on Broadway."

"How do you know any of them would have been interested in the likes of you?" Marylee answered. "Then or now?"

Marylee suddenly grew weary of jousting with Michael. She accelerated through the crowd, and the others, navigating the talkers and dancers, followed. As she moved through the throng, Marylee experienced herself falling through an emotional trap door into an unanticipated gloom; she felt increasingly conspicuous and cold.

She noticed young men and women boldly striking up first conversations and then pairing up. She wondered if any of the people who were meeting here clearly for the first time tonight might eventually marry, have children, build a life, then grow old and die together, and, perhaps, with just one turn of time's wheel, have their funeral service in these very same precincts? She tried to drive the bleak thoughts away, but they persisted. The attractive young synagogue-goers were roughly the age her own children might have been, had there been any. It was suddenly all too much, and Marylee pulled Gerry off the sidewalk onto the street and led him quickly away from the hubbub.

William Harp stayed within the energetic crowd longer and could only smile in amazement at the number, variety, and liveliness of the Jews all around him.

As if acknowledging this, Michael said, "You've got a lot of work to do with this crowd."

"Yes, but maybe not tonight," he answered. Then he flabbergasted Michael by adding, "Did you know, Mr. Klain, that to make love with your wife on the Sabbath is a double *mitzvah,* a double good deed?"

Before Michael could ascertain where in the world the missionary had picked up this amazing Jewish tidbit, William suddenly remembered his restaurant, excused himself, and hurried back. Standing on his toes, alone now, Michael scanned the crowd for Gerry's familiar bald oval or Marylee's red beret. When he finally located them at the margin of the huge group twenty-five yards away, he realized that without as much as saying *Shabbat Shalom* or even a plain secular good night to him, they had just taken off, and now were strolling hand-in-hand south down Broadway. It was not the outcome Michael had been hoping for.

27

William Harp had been putting off speaking with Marylee about the dilemma, and attending the synagogue service had not made his divulging it any easier. Nor had it shown him how he could ask for this new help that he now desperately needed. For welling up in him was not only the familiar anxiety and fear from previous posts but also trouble of a new order that pierced him to the heart, and drove him contrary to its newest promptings.

For William had been living in high anxiety that unless he produced a number of real, live, interested converts and proof of them soon, the Reverend William Harp Sr. would soon arrive unannounced at Club Revelation and ruin everything. The conversion process, of course, always took far longer than his father's impatience permitted, yet a few prospects for conversion should have surfaced already; a few was not an unreasonable expectation. But since the visit to the synagogue, William had begun utterly to despair of ever finding any in time to head off his father's arrival.

Thus far, however, for all his effort at the restaurant (he went nowhere in New York, quite literally, leaving the club only to go to Hunts Point Market early in the morning or on other restaurant business), William had only one or two even *possible* conversion leads. Both were so thin and insubstantial he had hesitated even to relate them to his father: One had been an elderly, homeless man begging for food, who had come back to the restaurant two or three times. When he saw the *mezuzah* on the door, he'd described himself as a Jewish hobo, the last in the world, and proud of it. He had operated heavy equipment in oil fields, he said; when the fields went bust, he began to hobo, and then traveling became what he called his profession; and thus sixty years had gone by. William served him a first-rate lunch—salmon croquettes with kasha—but the hobo, William remembered, had looked at the steaming plate of food as if it were inedible. In fact, his system was so accustomed to another far simpler diet, he asked for a cheese sandwich and a box of Entemann's dough-nuts—Jewish doughnuts, he called them—which William went out to buy, leaving the fellow in the restaurant alone. When he returned with the doughnuts, the old man had not budged, as if just being sedentary there at the central table beneath the projection screen in the club were the world's greatest pleasure. He ate eagerly, accepted two cups of the day's special coffee, Celestial Cappuccino, and indulged William a few words about Jesus. Then the old man disap-peared from the community around Club Revelation forever.

There was also a young man, who, in William's view, had been an even more distressing case. He could not have been much older than a teenager, twenty or twenty-one at most. He had appeared one day with a guitar, a frying pan, one cymbal, and drummer's sticks strung over his back, all somehow kept in place by an elaborate duct tape construction. There was so much tape, in fact—on the young man's ski cap, across his shoulders in a kind of homemade set of epaulettes, down the sides of his jeans, and all over his tattered sneakers—that William thought of this prospect as Duct Tape Boy. He had come down the steps one late afternoon when William was setting up for dinner.

It rapidly became clear that this longed-for young visitor, however, thought the restaurant was a music club, and at first he wanted to know if he might audition to play. Not wanting to raise unrealizable expectations, William told the truth but ushered him to a table and offered an audition if the fellow could play Jewish or Christian songs.

Incredulous, Duct Tape Boy stood up as soon as he had sat down, and turned to leave, saying, "Everything's fucked, it's always fucked." William tried desperately to engage him, but no matter what he said, the boy always responded with nothing but these "fuck" variations: "It's all fucked, man, it's completely fucked, the whole fuckin' fucker of a world is fucked." Of course, William agreed with these charges—on first meetings, you always agreed with whatever a potential convert said—whatever was meant by them. Yet it was agonizingly difficult for William to know where, theologically, to go with such a lead.

Eventually he said, with as much empathy as he could muster, that Jesus could be the answer to a messed-up world that always seemed to disappoint.

"Jesus?" the boy said. "You have got to be kidding."

William knew, instantly, even before the words flew from his mouth, that he had made a mistake. He should have left Jesus out, even though He was, of course, always in; by name, however, the Lord should definitely not have been invoked until the specific cause of the boy's sorrow was ascertained.

"You know who's even more fucked than I am?"

"Please don't say it," William pleaded, because he knew what was coming. "I beg you, because Jesus is love, and He could be your salvation, son."

"I need a gig, not salvation."

"Pray with me," William said, "and let Jesus speak directly to you in the stillness of your mind and heart."

Duct Tape Boy took the measure of William as he stood on the steps beneath the ailanthus to leave Club Revelation. It was a toss-up which of the two of them seemed more forlorn. "Jesus is even more fucked than I am, mister. I'm outta here."

One night not long after the outing to B'nai Luria, William, Marylee, and Gerry were finishing their Bible study earlier than usual—at least Gerry was making it so because he was nearly nodding off to sleep at the same table where Duct Tape Boy had sat, this despite the apocalyptic verses they were studying, Daniel, chapter 12, pertaining to the final weeks of history, after which the present era was slated to come to an end.

The text William was elaborating on was verse seven: *The man clothed in linen, who was above the stream, raised his right hand and his left hand toward heaven; and I heard him swear by him who lives forever that it would be for a time, two times, and half a time; and that when the shattering of the powers of the holy people comes to an end, all these things would be accomplished.*

"The holy people is you, Gerry," Marylee was saying.

William noticed how tired Gerry appeared to be, and he wanted to come up with something hopeful for both Gerry and himself. "And do you know that it is technically quite possible that a whole people can change their ways and repent en masse, like the Ninevites in Jonah, or be converted in a single day—it says so in Isaiah 66—but however long it takes, afterward there is the certain glory of the Lord's temple established on the tops of the mountains, raised above all hills and all nations, and a stream will run through it. The stream of the holy spirit."

Despite this stream of words, something deeper was missing, and William didn't feel he had made much headway. Marylee was frustrated too. She had urged William to choose this section, with its complex arithmetic calculations, because such material on the calculations of the Endtimes might, she had thought, intrigue Gerry, who was very quick at doing numbers.

Yet Gerry's eyes were now nearly closed.

"Don't take it too personally," Marylee said to William. "It happens like this with Gerry in the movies as well. And the opera and the Philharmonic, and at museums, where only Gerry can sleepwalk past Renaissance masters, and especially at the ballet. At some point, you just stop going places with people if all they do is fall asleep."

"Well, asleep or awake," William said, "doesn't alter one eternal fact: everything is subject to the prophecies. In the ballet or at the baseball game, it's always still right there in the text: The hope for Jews and all mankind is anchored in the acceptance of Jesus as Israel's Messiah. You're our hope, Gerry Levine."

Taking her cue from William, Marylee prompted her husband, "Doesn't it feel good, honey, to be genuinely, profoundly needed for a change?"

"You mean by someone other than you?" he said, with a tired smile.

Gerry stood, stretched, and shook out the front of his turtleneck so that a few shells from the sunflower seeds he had been eating trailed onto the floor. When he stooped to pick them up, Marylee gave him a mock kick to the behind.

"You *are* needed, Gerry, and by more than me. The world needs you."

"Jesus needs you, Gerry Levine. And I need you."

"Yes, yes," Gerry said. "That is abundantly clear. But tonight the bed needs me too, and tomorrow Long Island needs me, and then Connecticut needs me. Everywhere floors need me and beckon me to cover them."

"Before the floors, Gerry," Marylee said to him, "reassure us on some fundamentals. Tell us again what makes the Old Testament old and the New new."

Gerry saw no reason not to be obliging tonight, no reason to deny them the satisfaction of showing them he had indeed learned some things, that he had not always slept. "You need me because Jesus has fulfilled all that the prophets have predicted, so that it's time for the old to just accept the new. The new and improved, just like in business. Not a problem at all."

"Only it's the most important business—in this world, and the next, isn't it, Gerry?" said William.

"I suppose so, young man."

"Your grade is A-plus," said Marylee. "Now get yourself to bed."

Gerry turned to go but then stopped at the base of the stairs. Nawang was just then coming up and he suddenly bowed to Gerry—he was going up to Judy for her regular late night *zazen*—and Gerry bowed politely back, as the Buddhist quietly passed him and ascended.

"You'll excuse me," Gerry said as he paused and leaned over the banister toward William and Marylee, "but sometimes I just feel like bowing to everyone and everything in sight. Religion doesn't matter. It's the bowing that counts." They said nothing to him, so Gerry took a step up, sniffed the sandalwood aroma trailing back from the Buddhist's orange robes, and said, "Am I really still so stiff-necked and stubborn? Is it still hard for me to accept all this? The answer is Yes."

"But Gerry," Marylee arched her words toward him, "don't think Jews and Christians and Buddhists. Don't even think old versus new. Think love. Being loved or being unloved. Think a love that embraces and transcends all faiths.

That's the choice that really matters. Think only love and that without it, how could we be good to each other? Without it, why should I be decent to total disgusting strangers who rub against me in the subway? Without love, why should we send money to Nicaragua, Bangladesh, or Bosnia? Or to Nawang's monks and nuns, wherever they are? Without love, what is keeping all of us from becoming cold as stones, or turning on each other and ripping our throats out?"

"There is certainly a lot of throat ripping out there," Gerry replied wearily. "I can attest to that part."

"And there would be a whole lot more without Jesus." Something surprising, unexpected, important seemed to be happening between them. Marylee moved forward in her chair. "People would murder each other like the animals."

"Animals," said Gerry, "don't murder in any moral sense, do they? They kill to eat, and usually not their own kind."

"That is the point, Gerry. We are above the animals and yet there is still something potentially terrible in all of us. I've known this ever since I was a kid. My grandfather still talked about lynchings that he had attended as a boy. He was actually proud of it. Whatever keeps this thing within us at bay and keeps us sane, Gerry, that's Jesus. He reaches out with love and caring, with an impulse that the animals do not have. That is Jesus. That is where He dwells."

Softly, William Harp said, "Amen."

Gerry stared with longing and, he thought, some of that love she was speaking of, right into his wife's eyes. Even though she was his wife, he did not take her for granted. He wanted to say something like that. He wanted to express something deep and elegant and meaningful, he wanted to show his appreciation of Marylee. Yet the words that bore his thoughts uncoupled and then piled on top of each other in a wreckage of expression that made Gerry want to cry. All that came through was, "I know, I know," and he was ashamed of these sounds he uttered.

"I fear you don't know, Gerry," she said.

He took another hesitant step upstairs and was suddenly overwhelmed by such a sleepiness that he felt as if he might faint right there on the stairway. Get to bed, he urged himself on, and he blew Marylee and Harp a kiss. But not before William, mistaking the gesture and the fatigue for a fluttering of the holy spirit about Gerry's face, thought to himself, My Lord, my Lord, perhaps some of this is really taking root, after all?

Yet his thought also made Gerry feel so guilty he had to turn away. He took another step up, but then he came back down two, drawn by the memory of something he had learned by heart a long time ago. He raised his arm theatrically toward his wife, and, pleased that he had summoned it up, he slowly recited without a trace of irony:

> Had we but world enough and time
> This coyness, lady, were no crime . . .
> And you should, if you please, refuse
> Till the conversion of the Jews

Then the curtain fell on his performance and he said a simple "good night" and went up to the apartment.

When he was gone, Marylee looked down at the table on which her hands lay, with fingers outstretched. The glossy red polish on her nails was dramatic against the starched white of the tablecloth. She stared at her hands as if they were disembodied things. Not quite claws, but tools for grabbing and tearing and taking. She was visibly shaken, and William, to reassure her, placed his hands over hers. "You were positively inspiring."

"For whatever good it will do him," she answered.

"Do you think he will come around?"

"I honestly don't know."

"A little, even?"

"Is a little enough, William? Will a little be too late for you, too?"

28

Dear Father:

There is very good news to report on the conversion front: As I wrote you, I have been holding a weekly and extremely well-attended conversion class Thursday nights right after we close the restaurant. Some VERY SPECIFIC CANDIDATES—yes, real people, Daddy—are moving along through our learning process and you will hear about them soon. Praise the Lord. So, yes, please pray for me, but be sure to do so from home.

You certainly can tell—because I haven't asked you for money in a while— that the club must be, as we say in business, on a firmer financial footing. My Christian wives—well, specifically, Marylee and her husband Gerald Levine—have been giving much out of their own pockets and of their own free will to further our mission and advance Jesus' work in this part of the world. I have printed up a brochure with the reasons to expect the End, and a little description, also attached, of the demonstration with Annabelle. That brochure has been grabbed up all through the neighborhood, which, you know, is another excellent sign.

Here is an additional sign. Are you sitting down, Daddy? I know you sometimes have a little difficulty standing these days (I AM REALLY WORRIED ABOUT YOU), but I mean, are you sitting down in the emotional sense?

Okay. Annabelle not only has been quite a hit with the diners but has also increased our buzz in the neighborhood. Now don't worry about this, Daddy, when you read the words that follow . . . she did a marvelous thing: A day ago, when one of the waiters, who was feeding her, forgot to secure the top of her tank, Annabelle got loose. She is, after all, a snake, and a snake new to the City. She was curious, Daddy, and following her instincts, she made her way somehow—no one quite knows how she got through all those doors (there is a lot always going on, with deliveries and repair folks)—down to the basement. There, since the Buddhist was away on retreat with his students, including Judy, Annabelle found the Buddhist's small sheep alone and unsuspecting. Of course, Annabelle ate the sheep.

Now if the devouring of a heathen's sheep is not a sign of the triumph of the Lord, I do not know a sign, Daddy, and you taught me to find and decipher them at your knee. Although the sheep was not large, it was still a mouthful for Annabelle and even as I write, she is at the vet's getting the best of the best care that New York City can provide, and this is the medical capital of the world. I want to report to you that Annabelle is off the critical list and is no longer in any danger.

Of course, when the Buddhist, always so mild-mannered and a thoroughgoing pacifist, came home to discover what had happened, despite being juiced up on a whole weekend of mellow meditations, he was fit to kill Annabelle, and me. I can't say I blame him because he did love his sheep and the animal apparently had significance not only to the Buddhist as a personal pet but also to his countrymen—wherever they are. Oh well, to Annabelle, a sheep was a sheep.

Happy to report that the Buddhist eventually calmed down with the help of his most devoted follower, Judy Klain, who consoled him and also, I think, wrote out a big check. For a while there, however, he could have won the prize as the world's most violent Buddhist; now he is no longer a menace.

So there is no need to worry. Annabelle will more and more be doing her part, as you can see by the small article in the residential newspaper ("Snake Electrifies Local Diners"). This has brought some increased attention to the restaurant, despite the fact that both the Buddhist and I have had to pay a small fine. Actually it's not so small—$5,000 each from the health department, since both animals were in the building illegally, and an additional $5,000 for Annabelle, bringing her total to $10,000 because a reptile is considered a dangerous creature.

But Gerry and Marylee paid our share and Judy handled the sheep's fine, even though it's dead. It was their responsibility, Judy and Marylee said, for allowing animals in the building unapproved by the health department.

As I say, not to worry, Daddy. You know Annabelle has been as attached to me as she has been to you, and I can easily manage her convalescence. If a snake could talk, she would not be asking for you but me—and I am here, Sir, to minister to her. She will be coming home from the vet in a few days (Marylee has found me a lawyer and we are fast-tracking—another New York City word—a special-permit approval for Annabelle to remain on the premises of Club Revelation not as a pet but as a vehicle, so to speak, of free expression of religion protected under the clauses of our beloved Constitution). The resulting buzz from all of this (please see the other enclosed articles) is causing increased revenue at Club Revelation, and, of course, when the pool of diners grows, so grows the pool of potential converts.

Soon Annabelle will be healthy and back on the job showing God's mystery and power. Thus the fines and the vet bills will, I am certain, soon be offset.

With many thoughts of you and prayers for your good health to see you through to the coming glory,

I am, your son,

William the Liar

William crossed out "the Liar," so that it could not be read. Then he sealed and stamped the letter. He put on his sneakers and shorts—he had recently taken up jogging because Marylee said it would get him out of the doldrums—and on the way to Riverside Park, he mailed his letter home.

29

Not quite by accident, Sam and Michael had come upon Marylee in front of the brownstone the Wednesday night after the debacle with the snake and the sheep, and now they really meant to have it out with her. Nor was it about Nawang's sheep, for which the Buddhist and Judy (vicariously) were still bereft. They had for several days been waiting for an evening when Gerry would be traveling, and this was it. A calm urban evening with a light, persistent breeze—in short, a good night for an ambush.

Sam and Michael had selected the hour when they were fairly certain Marylee would be bringing the recycling down for the Thursday morning pickup. As they watched her deposit in front of the building two bags of tins, cartons, and cans, they noticed she was wearing a not insubstantial silver crucifix; reflecting light off the street lamps, it rested at the base of her neck just above the border of her white T-shirt and the bib of her overalls.

"Killing time?" she said when she noticed Michael and Sam lurking about. Then she saw the direction of their gaze. "Sorry, boys, I won't cover it up. It's not pornography or pollution. It doesn't bite or devour like that snake or send out evil rays."

"In twenty-five years I never saw you wear one of those," Sam said.

"You saw what you wanted to see."

"Never one of those," Sam mournfully repeated.

Marylee's fingers flew to Sam's neck, and she said, "But look at you!"

For Sam still had on his gold Star of David, and the matching *mezuzah* that he had taken to wearing especially around the restaurant; tonight there was also some other item of metal or bone jewelry that Marylee detected behind the traditional emblems lying in the deep and hairy fossa below his Adam's apple. Marylee boldly examined the jewelry. "Are shark's teeth Jewish these days, Sam Belkin?"

"It's a whale's tooth, honey," he said to her. "You're the only shark around here."

"Marylee," Michael spoke in the most conciliatory tone he could muster, "we are on a very slippery slope. We need your help."

Since the sheep-eating episode, their building had begun to attract not only very hefty fines but also unwanted attention from around the block as well as a growing number of curious people from around the neighborhood. Sheep? Snakes? A Christian restaurant for Jews? It was only a matter of time, Sam promised her, before a film crew from the five o'clock news would also arrive. "Only because you will arrange it," she retorted.

"Since it began with you, it has to end with you."

"You guys intend to break my legs. Is that what this is all about?"

"We're just trying to talk—" Sam's tone wavered between threat and assurance. "Look, I'm sorry. I shoot my mouth off a lot, I know, and I'm about as diplomatic as a car alarm, but, Marylee, for Gerry's sake you really must stop."

"He is a very big boy, Sam. What exactly is my sin? What is it I have to stop? Wanting him to live forever is a sin?"

"Forever is not my department. Nor are sins. But living here and now is. Now, here, today, you're killing him, you're torturing us."

"That's an awful accusation, and a lie."

"We're not blind or dumb. We see you and the preacher boy brainwashing him," Sam said. "It's as plain as day. And there's something very wrong with that in its own right—the way you take advantage of him. But look what it also leads to: you turn our home, not just your home, but ours as well, into a religious circus. What came over you, a nice liberal girl from the South?"

Marylee turned her face away. She could not bear to look at Sam when he grew so patronizing.

She took a step away from them, as if retreating, but then turned and kicked the blue-tinted bag with its dozen empty milk cartons and detergent containers and rectangular Chinese takeout trays, their silvery foil sparkling beneath the street lights. "I am not a witch, I am not a sorcerer," she said, "I am not a tormentor."

She kicked at the bags again, but all the light recycling failed to make the noise she'd hoped for. "And I am sick of all this treatment and all your intolerance."

"Calm down. I apologize," Sam said.

"You apologize like people say 'Have a Nice Day.' What are you two really doing? You hang out here until I come out with the garbage. You rehearse so that if one of you says something stupid, Sam, the other will take the high road and 'force' you to apologize. I know the routine. What is it that you want? Just say it and stop playing these games."

"What's bothering us is—we repeat—we just don't sense anything coming from Gerry himself," Michael spoke slowly, one point at a time, as he had planned. "No great or even modest but genuine religious impulse coming from the man at all. Absolutely nothing says I want to go down this road, I want to convert! If Gerry were even once to say to me, to Sam, to anyone, 'I love Jesus! I have seen the light! I want to give my heart to the shepherd from Nazareth' . . . you know, all that stuff—*any* of that stuff—then this conversation wouldn't be happening."

"This is not a conversation. It's a mugging."

"Marylee," Sam weighed in, "we love Gerry. We want him back."

"What kind of love are you talking about? A love that excludes me, his wife? A love that excludes eternal life? What's that kind of love worth? Tribal love?"

"I don't want to call you an anti-Semite," Sam said. He instantly regretted it.

"Then don't, you creep," she shouted at him.

Michael put his hand on Sam's arm, shook it, and then stared up at him with an I-can't-take-you-anywhere exasperation; he hoped Marylee would grant them both a reprieve.

Michael could see she was ready to run inside. She would

remain here only for a few seconds more, and Michael felt he had nearly squandered his opportunity. "He is our oldest friend," he said.

"He is my life's companion," she answered. "I want him to come with me, Michael."

"Even if he's not convinced about the destination?"

"On that, the jury's out, and he is only just beginning. He'll learn. Then he'll learn more. Do you really have such little respect for your oldest friend that you deny him his ability to choose his own path? What if he doesn't make declarations on hilltops? Why should he? Who does? And who are you to judge these matters? You can maybe judge his tennis, but lay off his internal life. Maybe he thinks it's none of your business. Maybe there is business between husband and wife that is none of yours. Do you think I want to know what you say to Ellen and Judy about heaven and hell, about the meaning of life, or maybe the meaninglessness? Do you ever talk about these things with your wives? No, I withdraw the question. But I assure you I do not administer secret Christian amulets or wafers to him under cover of night."

She walked away from them, but Sam and Michael followed after Marylee, and the three somehow negotiated a continuance on the stoop. Michael wished he had foreseen some of this. He felt somehow exposed and poorly prepared for a grand defense of Judaism, and he also was undermined by his regard for Marylee, for she struck him now as not only sincere but also very awake and alive.

"He can't be merely a bystander to all this." Michael heard his words decline into stammers. She was staring at him with hard eyes. "I mean, you tell me. I'm pleading with you, Marylee. Give me something to work with. You owe us at least this: just what is it that appeals to Gerry about Christianity?"

"Besides you, of course," said Sam.

"There's got to be something more. Even you would agree."

"You'll have to talk to Gerry."

"We have."

"I guess you'll have to do better, Michael. You gentlemen do talk to each other, don't you? At tennis perhaps?"

"All that comes up is you, Marylee. Sometimes the ball, but always you. You are the center of Christianity for him. Please don't delude yourself. I think you *are* his theology. His father, his son, and his holy ghost."

"Watch where you're going, Michael. Watch the tendency to mock, undermine, and ridicule."

"Is it perhaps the afterlife?" Michael pressed on. "Maybe the appeal of immortality? I can understand all that. I find the Jewish concept of the afterlife a little lacking myself. But it takes a bit of reading. Here." Michael withdrew a crumpled list from his pocket. "I've made suggestions to Gerry over the years." He now handed the list to Marylee as if it were an item of state's evidence. "I've even kept track of them. Here."

She glanced at it, and shook her head. "You see at least we agree on this. He hasn't read one of them."

"Somehow a bibliography is not what's called for here," said Sam.

"That's the first true thing you've come up with today," Marylee said to him. "It's not about books or courses, including what Gerry's learning with William. And it's not all the ideas in your great big library, Michael. It's really very simple. All I know is that I am going to heaven if I love Jesus. That's not subject to debate, and it's not on anybody's reading list except God's. I want Gerry to go with me."

Michael knew he was losing. He told Marylee she made him feel as he had on the school yard in junior high school, when no argument ever could be won, no matter how persuasive the teenage debaters, because the loser, shrugging, always said, "Hey, everything is relative."

"No, there does have to be some absolute truth about the world, Michael. And there is. I frankly don't know how a smart person like you endures without."

"With difficulty," he answered. "With difficulty and grievous doubt. Still, I have the consolation that I'm not will-fully," he measured his words, "deluding myself. I am a what-you-see-is-what-you-get kind of guy. Just like Gerry. He does not see afterlife. He sees what we all see: continuance in the thoughts of friends, children, and so forth."

"There are no children in the picture here," Marylee said. "In case you haven't noticed."

"Forgive me," Michael said. "That was stupid."

"There's a lot you gentlemen have simply not noticed. Judy's gone on a long journey and left you, Michael, way behind on the shore. And you don't even notice. At best, you're waving to her from far away as the distance between you grows."

"You're way out of line, Marylee," he said.

"Am I?"

"She sits on the pillow and I don't, at least not very much, but nobody has left anybody around here."

"On my journey, Gerry goes with me."

"Don't you think you're being a little unfair to drag him along just for the company?"

"'Drag'? You're using the language of coercion over and over again; it's insulting."

"If we see coercion, we'll call it that," Sam said.

"I refrain from arguing with you," she said, and took the first step up the stoop. Yes, she did wish Gerry had some of Michael's interests and background—he didn't even have Sam's superficial Jewish education—and this itch to debate things. "I refrain from engaging you because your viewpoint, the Jewish viewpoint, never holds for what is other than the conventional, the rational, the logical, the boring, the inherited . . ." She took another step up to the entranceway.

"You just 'refrain' away," Sam said, "and leave Gerry Levine alone. Do we have a deal?"

"I know that Jesus dwells within me," she said, "and I know that through him I will rise into eternal life," she repeated. "That's *my* deal, Sam. Those words are not just empty sounds. There has got to be more to life than just one day following the next. Grow, work, decay, and then just die? Disappear? That's it? No! I know Jesus dwells within, too. That means everything. It's like a life preserver tossed to me—and to anyone who will catch it."

"How did Harp get you to talk this way?" Sam was incredulous. He was weary from his traveling, morose about his endless fundraising turn-downs. His movie was nowhere, and he had no patience left for what he thought was a case of simple betrayal. "I really thought you loved Gerry."

"You're making me cry, Sam."

"Not as much as I'm crying, Marylee. It's as if you've stabbed him—"

"Call him off!" she shouted at Michael. "Call him off."

Marylee turned her back on them and in a short time regained her composure. "Look, Sam, I know that such phrases—rising to eternal life, the spirit made flesh—strike Jewish ears, your ears, as primitive and stupid, illogical and inane. You're thinking, Jews are too smart to believe such stuff. But it's possible you are wrong. Will you at least be open to the possibility you are wrong?"

"Sure, anybody can be wrong about heaven because no one's been back to do the documentary," Sam said.

"Precisely," she responded. But she knew she was exactly where she did not want to be now.

"So, tell us how it's done if you think the dead actually rise bodily?" Michael pursued her.

"Yes, I do, if you must know. They rise. Absolutely. Maybe not by busting the tops of the coffins like you see in the medieval sculptures, but, yes, up and out. North, south, east, and west, up and down are not the issue, are they? Anyway, time and space bend, which we know from science, from Jewish scientists, from Einstein. We all emerge into the new realm of our souls. So call it atoms, quarks, quirks. Call it anything you want. It's a new heaven and a new earth."

"What about male and female?" Michael asked. "Are there genders in heaven? And are the genders involved in sex?" Michael was suddenly filled with hopefulness as scraps of reading in college—was this something from St. Augustine's *Confessions?* From *City of God?*—rose mercifully to him in memory.

"Now this is getting interesting," Sam said. "How about breasts in heaven? If everything's made of air and clouds, neutrinos and mists, how can—?"

"Come on, Sam," Michael said. "Let's keep to the high road here, away from fairy tales and Christmas card sentiments."

"What's wrong with Christmas sentiments!" Marylee challenged them right back. "Who ordained you the chief rabbi of Christmas sentiments?"

"You know what he means, Marylee."

She spoke right into Sam's eyes. "What does Ellen say when a student tells her, 'You know what I mean'?"

Sam only shrugged.

"Where have you been all these years, Sam? She tells the student, 'The answer to your question—You know what I mean?—is simply, No. You didn't express it, so in fact I have no idea what in the hell you are talking about.' You know what I mean? What I mean is, precisely, this: try it again, or you flunk."

"We don't happen to be talking about expository composition or about Ellen—"

"Get the earphones off, Sam. Wake up.

"Okay, I'll tell you what I think. I don't shy away from this stuff. As to breasts, if I have them on earth, and, as you see, I do have them, then there's no reason I can't take them with me. You can take yours too, Michael. And you too, Sam. Now do you want to talk about bras? Will we need them?"

"Seriously, Marylee," Michael's voice had a conciliatory note in it, "will your body here be your same body there?"

"The martyrs of the early church were convinced, absolutely one hundred per cent convinced, that God, who is everything, has the power to do everything. That included reassembling the parts if the breasts and arms and legs and even cute little circumcised penises were ripped apart by wild boars in the arena. Did you know that, Michael?"

She had changed, Michael now saw. She had become someone else.

"The very *thought* hurts," Sam said.

"I'd like to get back to the afterlife," Michael pleaded.

"Sure," she answered, "if you think sparring about it is going to get you what you need."

"What *I* need is not the issue, Marylee."

"I'd like to get back to the breasts," said Sam.

Michael ostentatiously ignored him. "We're not playing games or being coy, Marylee. This does matter to us. What do the church fathers say, what do *you* say about your general condition when you are resurrected? Do you rise at the age you have died or when you are born? Like little cupids, little *putti?*" Michael and Sam exchanged a glance. "Okay, and those breasts, will they have a sexual function? Will they turn people on? Will they lactate? Or will they be just aesthetic things?"

"I don't know all the answers, Michael, but I don't feel I

need all the answers. I don't feel I need to analyze everything. Why do you need answers to questions that do not occur? Why do you focus on the details? And, by the way, how about getting out of my face!"

He stepped back now and apologized for crowding her, but a major point propelled him up the step and toward her again: "How about this very basic question, then: will you be married in heaven? And be together with your husband? With Gerry? Do you at least know beyond all doubt the answer to that one? Because if you're not one hundred per cent certain you're going to be together with Gerry in heaven, give us the courtesy of letting us be together with him for a few years more on this earth!"

"Touché," said Sam.

"Shut up and let her answer."

There were tears beginning to pool in Marylee's eyes now, and she knew they were being produced by Sam and Michael's love for her husband. She didn't feel she had much erudition left to match Michael's and, God help her, even her love for Gerry, at least at this moment, didn't seem to have their intensity.

"What is love?" Michael almost whispered, because, he realized, she was right. Arguing with her, being louder or brighter, didn't matter now. It was as if he were at the end of a very long pier and trying to be heard by someone in a ship that had already begun to clear the harbor. He also wondered if she was right about Judy.

"All I can tell you, Michael, is that I have faith, which I did not have before. And I experience this as a miracle. Just like in the song: I felt lost and now I feel found, or at least less lost. It might not be perfect, but it's an improvement, and it derives from faith. And do you know why I have it?"

"That's what we're here for, Marylee. That's what we want to know."

"I have faith, Michael, because I have had a vision."

They both heard Sam groan; they both ignored him.

"That's right. A vision. It's nothing I can debate you about, nothing that I can make you see. Or make you believe in. But I know as I live and breathe that Jesus came to me. That's what all this derives from. What else can I say?"

"A vision? Where?"

"You'll make fun of me."

"I swear we will not. What vision, Marylee?"

She took a deep breath and noticed, as she let her breathe go, how intently they watched her; she saw no reason now not to answer. "It was in the hospital. When I had the cancer surgery."

How could they have gone on about breasts, how could they have forgotten about her operation! "I'm sorry," Michael said. "I apologize for the both of us."

She felt another surge of tears but resented letting them be seen. Marylee had exposed herself enough, but there was no way she could not finish. "That's when Jesus came to me. I saw Him clearly as I see you now. Is such a vision allowed, Michael?"

"It's not for me to say what's allowed. I'm really very dumb sometimes."

"Do you know any Jewish people to whom God has spoken lately, Michael? Sam, do you know any? You've been praying up a storm. Ellen tells me you have turned your apartment into the Jewish quarter. With any results?"

"When a Jew prays, that's how he communicates to God," Sam said. "Visions are not part of the deal. Are they, Michael?"

"Not usually."

"But does God ever answer?" she asked Sam. "Have you had any direct answers ever, or is it just one-way? A busy signal all the time?"

"My prayer," Sam said, "would definitely be answered if you just left Gerry alone."

"William says that the last time God spoke directly to the Jewish people, that is, the very last time He *revealed* Himself to any Jewish person until Jesus, was to Moses on Mount Sinai. And not to any regular Jewish person since then. That's a long time between revelations. Aren't the Jewish people thirsty? That's what William asks me. That's what I've been asking my husband, and I pose the same question to you. When you have the answer, you know where to find us."

Marylee rose from the stoop and moved quickly toward the door of the brownstone, leaving Michael and Sam eyeing each other with a sense of their failure. Michael followed her briefly, hoping she would stop, but she did not. She entered the building, and he stood before the closed door as if a stranger in front of his own house. Sam began to rearrange the blue bags of recycling that Marylee had kicked about. A woman sitting on the stoop of the Antichrist's building across the street who had observed this utterly unnecessary work, as well as the sometimes loud *pas de deux* with Marylee, threatened to call the police. Sam waved her off, she should mind her own business.

He looked toward Michael, who was now sitting on the stoop, his face cupped disconsolately in his hand. Sam raised his palms to the sky as if to register an official complaint for them both: "She had a vision!"

30

"Just don't talk to me anymore!" Judy said to Michael later that night. She sat on her deep blue prayer rug, a gauzy stream of light from the street filtering through the beaded curtains and a stick of sandalwood incense sending up a plume of smoke from its ashen tip. Although she had been meditating earlier, Judy had been near the window so that enough of the shouted words and Sam's hectoring had drifted up, entered her dedicated space, and shattered the silence.

Now the culprit she held most responsible was just ten feet away from her in their own living room, rustling noisily through the newspaper; it was a rudeness he usually did not indulge in when he saw her at *zazen*. She was, after all, trying to make up for an hour he had made her lose. Trying to ignore Michael once again, Judy concentrated her gaze on the trail of smoke rising in front of her. Paler than usual, the smoke ascended through the white blades of the slowly turning fan toward the top of the open window. If Judy felt an impulse to berate and even shame Michael—which she did—it was a feeling rendered inactive by an equally forceful sense of its futility. In such a circumstance, there was only one step to take: breathe, she told herself. Breathe.

Ever since the holy sheep had been eaten, tensions in the building had skyrocketed, and Judy could no longer deny this was the case as well between Michael and herself. Nawang's protracted absence—Judy assumed he was ransacking his island and archipelago for a replacement sheep—was becoming too difficult to endure, and it wore particularly grievously at the hours of the day when she had practiced *zazen* with him.

Hard-won, Judy's equanimity grew shakier daily, and she did not want to admit that the tensions between Michael and Marylee were the most powerful eroding force. Michael at best dabbled in *zazen* and had little appreciation for how vigorous and demanding her practice had become—and absolutely no idea how fragile an evolving spiritual life could be. Nawang would have said to her—had he been there—that conflict and adversity must always be welcomed, as a test of the spirit.

Yet it was very difficult. Judy's spirit felt sapped, and to hear Michael continue his rustling and for her concentration to be so flaccid that she could not get beyond her husband's annoying ways simply made her feel now as if her own development were an utter failure. Why couldn't Michael get the picture for a change? Why couldn't he go somewhere, anywhere else: go work on his book or, failing that, watch a ballgame? Still, she only shrugged at him while she tried to calm herself by turning her emptiness into a canyon, a grand canyon for her to enter and to explore. For the longest time, neither of them spoke; yet Michael refused to leave her space.

He finally poked his head near her, broke the plane of the *zafu,* and said, "Marylee had a vision!" This Judy had not known, and she was instantly alert. "Anyway, she calls it a vision!"

"I can't help that, Michael. Marylee is always coming down with something. You know . . . her enthusiasms. It's part of her charm and what keeps their marriage going. And your interruption of my meditation time and time again will *not* keep ours going! Do you hear me, Michael?"

"A vision is not an enthusiasm."

"Let's just stay calm, Michael. I am working to keep it together, in case you hadn't noticed. I'm afraid Nawang may be gone forever. I'm worried that he can't endure the loss of the sheep. And if he can't, I—"

"Please, don't you become as dependent on the Buddhist as she is on Harp," Michael said.

Judy broke off, she tried to breathe deeply again, and to focus despite Michael's persistent, accusatory presence. Concentrate, she ordered herself, always a bad sign. All she saw in her mind's eye, however, was the sheep being slowly digested. "That hideous snake is back, Michael. If you're worried and need a focus, I have one for you. Here's the plan: help me kill William Harp's snake!"

"Happily," he said, "but Marylee won't like that. Plus doesn't Nawang harangue you not to cling to the ideas and especially the things of this world? Killing the snake is definitely in the thing category."

"Let me meditate, Michael. Please."

"Okay," he said. "Let's go kill it now. You open the tank, and I'll cut off its head. Where's the hatchet?"

When she refused to budge, he planted himself in front of the rug. "She had a vision!"

"Why do you keep saying that?"

"Because people who have visions cannot be treated as normal people. And they often go through with what they threaten."

"What's she threatened? You mean Gerry's conversion? Of course she's going to go through with it. What's wrong with you?"

"Did you hear what you just said? 'Of course she's going to go through with it.' But one person can't forcibly convert another! It's not *her* conversion; it's Gerry's. We can't allow that here. This isn't the Inquisition. This isn't baptism or death. Gerry doesn't want to convert. She's forcing him. You know it, Judy, as well as I do, and yet you just sit there on the pillow refusing to raise a finger to stop it."

"There are many other more pressing quality-of-life issues to address, very close to home, Michael. Why don't you see what you can do about the jungle conditions, with wild animals on the loose devouring each other in our own building? We have gawking tourists, we have another failed restaurant in the making, and visits from city inspectors will now be more frequent. Of course you're at the library, so you don't have to do anything except obsess and flap your gums. I deal with the real live nasty inspectors, and I live in fear of that reptile. Let Gerry become a Christian if he wants, as long as we eliminate the brazen serpent forever."

"Of course, what she calls a vision can be a hallucination."

"Michael! You have not heard a word I've said. I beg of you: sit and meditate with me."

"You know, I've had visions too."

"Take your shoes off, Michael. Loosen your belt. Take the *zafu,* take the other pillow from the cabinet. Count your breaths."

"You want to hear *my* vision, Judy? A year ago, I was at work, in the main reading room. I was sitting behind the reference desk as usual when a woman wearing a gray suit came up to me."

"Did I say I wanted to hear?"

"Her hair was gray, pulled back into a French braid, and a quite attractive one. She was, for a forty-five or fifty-year-old woman, quite beautiful."

"Silence would be better, Michael . . . you really thought she was beautiful?"

"She had this quality, a presence that commanded attention. She wore an exquisite perfume, green, verdant, that hovered around us, so I swear my senses were, well, heightened, and the greenness of it all took me somewhere—it's like I imagine the Garden of Eden on the first day the lawn was mowed."

"I didn't know you liked that kind of perfume. Continue, please."

"So she comes up to me and I wait there for her question. I think she's going to ask me, you know, the usual dumb stuff: my daughter is doing her third-grade term paper on photosynthesis. Where can we find the latest research on chlorophyll? Or where can I find a directory to eighteenth-century playwrights of Silesia? Or do you have a collection of the publications of the Import-Export Bank?

"No, not this person. She comes up to me and she just stares. The entire room, that hangar-sized space, goes suddenly silent as an empty palace, and it's as if this woman and I are alone inside. Now I notice she is also wearing a lapel pin. She leans toward me and I read what it says: LET'S GO METS. 'What's with the button?' I ask her.

"'I Am Who I Am. I therefore must be for the underdog.'

"'Excuse me, madam,' I begin to say to her, because I am irritated already. I think to myself, Okay, another crazy to deal with, part of the job. I also suddenly have to pee. So I say to her, 'Excuse me, how may I help you?' Do you know what she answers?"

"I can't wait to hear, Michael."

"She raises her arm toward me. Slowly, like a diva, and she says in a great, booming contralto, 'I am the Lord thy God who brought thee out of the Land of Egypt. Thou shalt have no other God before me.'

"The next thing I know I am staring out into empty space. The room is vibrating slightly but otherwise returning to normal; Phyllis is sitting on the stool beside me, her face in a catalog. All is as usual. A few people are scattered around the room. I give Phyllis a glance, and it is immediately clear to me that she has noticed nothing. She has not seen my visitor, although she now wrinkles up her nose, smells the faint remaining traces of the perfume, and asks me if I am wearing a new cologne.

"Clearly no one else has seen this woman. Only me. That was my vision, Judy."

"Congratulations, Michael."

"Now do I conclude from this that God is a beautiful middle-aged woman and a Mets fan? Should I found a religion on the basis of this . . . hallucination? And maybe it really did happen because the perfume was still in the air? What do I do with such a vision, Judy? Go convert myself and others?"

"Don't know."

"I'm going to tell Gerry, that's what I'm going to do. And I'm also going to call his mother."

"Don't you dare."

"I'm going to call Mrs. Levine in Florida." He pointed to the telephone across the room as if it were a secret weapon. "She has a right to try to keep her son from converting."

"Michael, please. She is old and sick."

"Well, we need some help here." He reached the telephone in two strides. "I don't care if I'm a walking cliché. That woman has a right to know."

"Gerry's a grown man."

"He's running, confused, and scared. He'll regret doing this. I'm going to call Mrs. Levine."

"You do that, and there will be consequences."

"I should hope so."

"I mean with me. Put the phone down. It's inappropriate. It's not your role to rat on your friend."

"The only way to counter a wife's religious vision is with a mother's guilt trip. Where's the number I put here?"

31

"You do realize how your husbands have been acting?" Marylee sent the words in, her emissaries, so she could herself stay outside.

She was leaning against the door leading to Nawang's basement *zendo,* his subterranean meditation hall, which, in all his years in the building, she had rarely entered, and never in these last few months. It was darker and more threatening than she had imagined. She stepped hesitatingly from the threshold and peered through the low light to see Judy, barefoot and in loose black sweatsuit, lowering herself gingerly onto a large meditation pillow like a cat settling into her usual spot.

"Well, come on," said Ellen, from her *zafu* beside Judy. "Let's get it over with."

"This place is creepy," Marylee said. "Forget the light of the Lord not being here. How about *any* light!"

"Clogs off, butt down," said Ellen.

"I think not," Marylee answered, now halfway back out the door.

"You'll soon sense Nawang's presence," Judy said. "Then you will relax."

"With cockroaches, I don't relax."

With its mandala wall hangings and the three basement support posts wrapped in striped orange and brown textiles, the *zendo,* Judy thought, seemed very welcoming indeed, and she was disappointed at Marylee's evident horror even at entering. It had a long rope of hanging gongs, drums, and mallets and a small shrine to the Buddha, whose potbellied teak statue was visible behind a line of votive candles in the corner. Judy had also lit several rice paper lanterns to speed Nawang's safe return; the lights of these cast cones of warm, buttery illumination about the basement. Above, through the ceiling, they could all hear William Harp moving tables and chairs across the floor of Club Revelation.

"Look," Marylee said as she walked quickly in and reached down to pull on Ellen's arm, "This just won't do. I'm taking you out of here. You too, Judy."

"Tackle her," said Ellen.

"Oh, for goodness sake," Judy said. "Take off your shoes, you're close to the earth here—"

"I'll explode if I stay a second longer."

"You agreed," Judy said, her composure breached. "You said, and I quote, 'a precinct neither Jewish nor Christian, a zone of peace and calm—to air out the problems that are gnawing at the friendship.' Well, this is the place, honey."

Marylee felt her throat go dry and narrow, and her heart began to beat rapidly. "I didn't realize I was going to have this reaction. How about the Museum? I'll go and open all the windows now. Come on up. Please."

"I'm grounded and I'm staying put," said Judy, but Marylee had literally fled the basement and had not even heard her. Ellen rose from her seat and waited for Judy to do the same. Judy did not budge.

"I'm no alarmist," Ellen said, "but you saw her."

"Not going," said Judy.

"And did you hear her talk about opening the windows? You did hear that, didn't you? Now pick up your pillow and let's go. I'm not waiting to debate it."

When Judy and Ellen arrived a few minutes later, the windows of the Museum were indeed all open wide and a lively breeze drifted through, churning the faint aromas of camphor, ancient clay beads, and incense. Marylee was sitting on the chair allegedly liberated from a classroom under siege in 1968 at Columbia. Her legs were crossed and she was bent over her Bible, which lay open on the wide part of the arm rest, reading it intently.

"You scared us, you know," Ellen said.

"Just sudden claustrophobia," Marylee answered. "I don't know how you tolerate that place. Here at least it seems there's air to breathe and sky to see. There it's the pit of hell."

"Christianity looks to heaven, Buddhism to the earth," Judy said, defensively. "I rest my case."

"What case?" Ellen said.

"I'm prepared to accept Marylee's apology. That's all I meant."

"Well, she hasn't apologized for anything," Ellen said as she sat on the floor near Marylee.

"No, and she's not one bit sorry either," said Judy. "Which is why she needs my help to apologize on her behalf. I'm good at apologizing these days, so I'd like to share my talent with her. She just wants to feel in control all the time. We know it and she knows it. And no amount of Bible reading is going to convince me otherwise.

"Well, you're not in control, Marylee, no matter where we have our little meeting. You're not in control and I'm not, and no one is, and the more you cling to the idea of controlling, the less in control you will feel. What heaven? What hell?" Judy had never erupted this way in front of Marylee, but she had not appreciated, until now, how offended she had been by Marylee's flight from the *zendo*. "Hell is acting this way with your friends who only want to help you—"

"Down," said Ellen, "down, girl."

Marylee closed her book and took the measure of her friends. "Your husbands are driving me away. That's bad enough. But now this. Now you. I'm not an ogre, you know. I'm not a witch, a brainwasher. If they were Christians, they'd think I'm the Antichrist. Am I?"

"Don't ask me that! I don't think in those terms. And you know that! Here's the point. You must get outside yourself, Marylee. Wake up."

"Oh, that's what's happened. I have awoken, and what I see is that you really think I'm terrible."

Ellen and Judy exchanged a long look.

"I've done nothing wrong. I am not an evil person. But they've turned on me, and I think they couldn't do this without your betraying me too."

"'Betraying'?" Ellen said. "'Betrayal' is a serious word, and an inappropriate one, and you know it, Marylee."

"I know I feel betrayed."

"That's because you're crazed with Jesus' story," Judy said. "You've got him and Judas Iscariot on the brain." While she spoke, she squatted down and rummaged through a box labeled NOVELS, ANTHOLOGIES, HOME REPAIR. "Look at this stuff! There's not a greatest story in the world, Marylee. There's no one story that deserves to be called the greatest story ever told. Why should it? There are as many as there are people. Every breath is a beginning, a middle, an end. You betray yourself when you deny this." Judy paused.

Marylee and Ellen both looked at her as if after all the months and years, she had finally found in an old box of books the reason she sat *zazen*. Now she went over to Marylee, took both her hands, raised her out of the chair, and hugged her.

"Since we're in the truth-telling mode, here's another," said Ellen. "You have thrown down the gauntlet, Marylee. Bigtime. We've talked about this. You knew they would eventually respond. You punch somebody in the nose, and they punch back. They're guys. Jewish guys, and you've gone after their best friend."

"'Gone after'? My God, he's my husband, in case *you* haven't noticed. I'm just trying to save him."

"And they're trying to save him from your attempts to save him," said Ellen.

"In my book, a salvation from a salvation is a damnation," Marylee answered. She was proud of her formulation. She was equal to Ellen and Judy's collective silent stare. "Okay then, what about you two? Do you approve of what's happening to your husbands? Their aggressiveness toward me is part of a pattern, isn't it?"

"Please, Marylee."

"I mean, are you proud of Sam, pleased with the praying and the jewelry? Let's just get this all out. With Michael and the sudden synagogue going? None of us is blind. We all see what's going on here. Do you feel this behavior is genuine? That's what they accuse me of—dragging Gerry to Jesus. Brainwashing him. I'm Torquemada in a red beret. Why? Because they feel there's nothing coming from his heart. Because he doesn't talk to his friends about Jesus when they play tennis, they are convinced it's all phony with him, all superficial. But Gerry is not a big talker. And when he plays tennis, he plays. Gerry is not much of a reader. He is not an intellectual. Gerry is a doer. And when a doer does, his action is equivalent to his belief. Is it the same with Sam and Michael?"

"They're Jews. They're allowed to be upset," said Ellen.

"But there's an eruption of Judaism in our midst. Is *it* real? Doesn't the Jewish practice that Sam and Michael are up to amount almost entirely to a kind of counter-Christianity, a stop-Marylee-at-all-costs Judaism? How much from the heart is *that*?"

"I won't deny," said Ellen, "that Sam is a bit of a laughingstock to me right now."

"Exactly," said Marylee. "I mean I want to keep myself from asking him if he's going to get a cute little Star of David earring to go with the neckwear."

"Then he can look like a pirate Jew," Judy said. "Did you know that Jean Lafitte, the New Orleans pirate and smuggler, who helped Andrew Jackson beat the British in 1812, was Jewish? Michael has been informing me lately."

"That's the point," Marylee said and then stood up abruptly and dragged an old blackboard out from behind the large framed Che Guevara poster. She found some orange chalk on the tray of the board and made an odd mark in the shape of a pot. "Here's Gerry's Christianity—newfound—and here are Sam and Michael"—she made two stick figures below. "Sam and Michael are down here, with their inherited and unquestioned Judaism, and maybe there they stay. But Gerry," she trailed a long chalk arrow, a trajectory to the top border of the board, "you see, Gerry is moving up to heaven, with a little help."

"Thank you for that lesson," said Ellen. "And wherever did that blackboard come from?"

"Look, how far will Gerry travel?" Marylee stayed up at the board while Ellen examined it. "I don't know. I only want the right—you owe it to me—to let my husband's faith be equal to your husbands'. If Gerry's faith is so far superficial, okay. But is it any more superficial than Sam's or Michael's Judaism, which is dragged strategically out from the nostalgic ancestral closet and then thrown back in when the service has been performed? I don't think so. I don't want to go to war with them. I like them. I even love the lunatics. All I'm asking is that, spiritually speaking, you permit my husband to be as superficial as yours."

"Seems like a consummation devoutly to be wished," said Ellen.

"Michael called Gerry's mother, didn't he?" Judy asked Marylee as she took the chalk from her hand and drew a big exclamation mark on the board.

"All right," Judy said. "I do apologize for that."

"And I accept it," Marylee said. "Grown men tattling on each other to their mothers. Do I laugh or cry? They were on the phone together from Florida," Marylee went on, "for half an hour. I had to get on too. Gerry tried but no way could he prevent Mrs. Levine from speaking to me. I mean, I love her despite what she said to me—"

"You love everybody, don't you?" Judy said.

"Here it comes," said Ellen.

"Speaking on behalf of her departed husband," Marylee quoted her mother-in-law. "As his representative from the grave, so to speak . . ."

"That hurts," said Judy. "I'm sorry he put you through—"

"No, listen," Marylee continued. "She said her husband would repeal his love for me if Gerry through my doing became a Christian. My *doing*. Then she said to me, 'I tell you the truth, darling. I always had a secret wish that you, eventually, over time, especially if there might be children, that you would consider, just consider, if only for the sake of the children, converting to Judaism. It was my dream that you would become for Gerry a nice Jewish wife.' Have I got the accent?"

"All too perfect," Ellen said.

"'And now I find out that he is thinking of becoming, for you, darling, a nice Christian husband, and I feel, suddenly, a lot of pressure.'

"'Pressure'? I said. And that was when Gerry, who did not want to see me tortured much more, pulled the phone back and said to her, 'Pressure, where, Ma?'"

"And she answered him, because he told me the whole conversation, blow by blow, when he hung up and we had a big long drink together. She said to him, 'I have pressure all over, son. From my Jewish head down to my Jewish toes. Bursting.'

"You get the picture?"

"A friend called the other day," Ellen said, "to tell me that Sam actually recessed a shoot so he could walk over to the corner of wherever they were to pray the afternoon service."

"Never happened before, right?"

"Praying on location did strike me as quite a departure from routine."

Marylee sat back down in the Columbia chair and carefully retrieved her Bible. They all stared at each other for a long moment. Then she added, "I am not being . . . triumphant here. But just *what* is going on in Michael and Sam's souls? Forgive me, but I do worry about the souls of my friends. That's how I try to understand why they tormented me—out of the tormented requirements of their souls. They do it because they can't help themselves yet. They have seen no light whatsoever. Or am I wrong? You're married to them. So I ask you, is there something changed *inside* Sam that he has to pray so much?"

"Haven't been inside him lately," Ellen answered, "so I can't be sure what's there these days. And that's the truth."

"Aren't you curious?"

"Well, yes and no. When I think about it—and I do have other things to think about!—I have no doubt his soul would present a terrifying vista, a ravaged soulscape, something out of a post-production studio with a wall of monitors that never ends, and maybe there are no remotes to use and the monitors have no dials either, no buttons, no way to control them. The kicker is that only one monitor carries Sam's genuine soul tape that must be distinguished from all the other footage. The others are false. Which is it? Who can pick the true one out. How's that?"

"Imaginative, but you beg the question. You don't actually think much about his soul, do you? Sorry, but that's what I get from your disquisition."

"I know this, Marylee. He would never wish you ill."

"I'm not so sure about that," Marylee said.

"Michael has definitely changed inside," Judy said. "Ulcers. We have milk of magnesia now the way we used to order wine. By the case. And he pours it down with some elixir—a brand of seltzer that you can only buy in Brooklyn and that has the magic approval of a secret board of rabbis. I have not been able to get him to meditate much, but you've sent him looking for a spiritual life. You're more powerful than you know."

"I certainly don't feel that way."

"Well, he had a hallucination at work. God appeared to him, and I think he tried to pick her up."

"Her?"

"That's right. A woman, at the library."

"He's making this up."

"I wish," Judy said, "but I don't think so." She looked into Marylee's eyes. "She was a Mets fan."

"Oh," said Ellen, "that makes it okay!"

Now, as Marylee withdrew into herself, Ellen began to rummage through one of the Museum's boxes of junk. Marylee walked over to the window that looked out toward Broadway, while Judy tried to stay as still as she could. A long, nervous interval filled up the Museum. Then Ellen said, "We used to have three garden-variety Jewish husbands. Not perfect, not rich, not particularly handsome, but funny and easy-going men who liked to come up here with us to read a little Dylan Thomas, and maybe smoke a little dope too. Life was all right with them. Okay, really. On the husband scale of one to ten, I would rate them a six."

"Five," said Judy.

"Five and a half," said Marylee.

"Anyway, not bad, especially after twenty years, but something has changed. I acknowledge that," Ellen said, "because now we've got, under the same roof, one convert-in-training, one returned Jew with a practice so ostentatious it verges on being bad for the Jews—you're right about that—and the third husband—"

"—he thinks of himself," Judy added, "as a mystic-in-training."

"I was going to say that he sees himself as being prepped for the gastroenterologist."

"I do believe," Marylee said to her friends, "that Jesus is the answer to all this."

"You're too smart to simplify that way," Ellen said. "Maybe Harp, but not you."

"My point is only that Judaism is like . . . like this place, a big, musty attic, this heavy course you enroll in, with a million books of required reading and endless boxes of stuff, and it's so complicated."

"But we like museums," said Judy.

"I'd say," added Ellen, "that it's more like living in Manhattan, tension and struggle all the time, and no place really ever to park."

"But Jesus, you see, He is like the weekend in the country on Sunday night, when you need to leave but don't want to because it's so beautiful, so tranquil, and finally stuff is all put away, there's order out of chaos, finally simplicity. That's my point to Gerry. With Christianity, that moment is preserved forever; you don't have to go back. You don't have to keep studying and worrying. You stay there in the country of never-ending love and you don't even have to work for it, or earn it, or study for it, or pass tests for it, or be challenged every day, every hour, by your husband's friends, because it is simply given. Given because you're you, because Jesus died for you, and that, my friends, is grace."

Ellen said, "Look, ML, some people find Jesus *not* a beautiful day at the country house at all but rather a loud and smoky afternoon at the trailer park. Your budget is low, the appliances and plumbing are broken and too expensive to repair, and you are desperate just for somebody to take care of everything for you. That's why you are willing to do anything, even to go to sleep in your head, in order to be taken care of. Nice try, but no sale."

"Is this the way you talk to Gerry?" Judy wanted to know.

"I told you, I am very gentle with him."

"If this is what you're saying, I'd call that pressure bigtime."

"I only share with him these feelings that have welled up in me. What's wrong with that? I am no inquisitor. I assure you Gerry is where he is through his own free will. How could it be otherwise?"

"Free will is not seltzer or bottled water," Ellen said. "It's never a hundred per cent pure or simple. And aren't you being just a tad self-deceiving? Gerry knows you'd leave him if he didn't follow you. Isn't that it, at the most basic level? Marylee, I think you might leave Gerry whether he converts or not! I've told you this before and I tell you now. Part of the reason I am not trying to restrain Sam the way you want us to, or trying very hard, is that, frankly, I think you might be getting ready to drop your husband." Here Ellen motioned down through the waterbed and the floor that they tiptoed over, strewn with junk, tie-dyed fabrics, old pillows with their political and druggie slogans. Her finger, pointing in the direction of

William Harp and the restaurant four floors below, was unmistakable. "Then you can land yourself right in that man's pulpit. Does *that* qualify as the truth?"

"It is not."

"We're not blind. We see the way you look at that boy. We've told you this a hundred times. And the money that's sustaining him. Please, Marylee, we're not fools here. We see the time you spend with him."

"With him, and with Gerry."

"Marylee, we love Gerry too. If you leave Gerry for Jesus or William or whomever, what will Gerry have left? He will have lost his wife and his new Christian God, whom he's not getting to know very well or very fast, despite you. And maybe that's why he should at least keep his friends, which he will also surely lose, or put at risk of losing, if he leaves what he's always known, however superficially. I don't know how Judy feels, but frankly that is why I don't mind letting the guys mug you now and then. They need to, and, pardon me for saying so, you deserve it. I also understand your need to retaliate."

Marylee was quite shaken; yet she was also oddly strengthened by Ellen's candor.

Judy listened to her breath whistling through her nose a few times, and then she said to Marylee: "Do you love Gerry? I mean really love him still?"

"Yes, I do," she said.

"Then that's enough for me."

"You just remember," Ellen said as she stood and walked around the Museum and carefully closed all of its five windows, "you please just remember that Gerry may never have had much of a God he believed in and maybe never will. But he did have a wife. And, as I recall, a very good one. A real companion for many years. You think hard about all of this, how far you push him. The man is devoted to you beyond all reason, beyond his own self-preservation. I couldn't care less if he loses his God, but I will never talk to you again if, as a result of what you're doing, he loses his wife."

32

JUNE I, 2000

Dear Father:

Let's be clear. I never promised you "thousands of converts." Our agreement, our understanding, has always been quality over quantity. So why, sir, and I say this with no disrespect, are you playing the numbers game with me now?

The point was to come to the Upper West Side, to use this unique new medium for conversion, food, and to show that we could win the hearts of some of the highest-quality Jews. A pilot project of the Lord's. And it goes well. But there is no reason whatsoever for you to be writing me that you look forward to a gathering at a venue like Madison Square Garden. That is not our plan or our way. Never has been. Are you all right, Daddy? Having read your recent letter with these statements, I worry that I should go home for a quick visit to see to the medications, although that would have a negative impact on the momentum of my work here.

Please, Daddy. I do not want you to be angry. I do not want you to, as you write, "pull the plug" on Club Revelation. Quality over quantity; that has always been our byword. And you know our research, you know what kind of area I am operating in. There has not been a single Jewish convert to Christianity from the Upper West Side in sixteen years. How can I be expected to do miracles in six months?

Yes, I remember very well what you said to me when I left. You said, Billy, through you, a great thing will be accomplished. Through you and your ministry, Jesus will penetrate this neighborhood. No new heaven and no new earth without first cracking the Upper West Side. No blessing, no Rapture, no ascent to the angelic realms without a handful of tough Jews there accepting the Lord. That's what we said: a handful.

As it says, Daddy, in Revelation, chapter fourteen: *Then I looked and there was the Lamb standing on Mount Zion. And with him were one hundred forty-four thousand who had his name and his Father's name written on their forehead . . . They have been redeemed from humankind.*

True. But where do you come by 144,000 being my responsibility? 144,000 is not a handful. 144,000 is the *total* number worldwide who will survive Armageddon precisely because they are Jews who, at the ultimate moment, accept Jesus as their Messiah, but they could ALL no more come from the Upper West Side than I could write a symphony. If I am responsible for all of them, then what are the other missionaries doing! Please, sir, it is a total number.

What we discussed was my share. I believe—no, I am certain—we said that if I brought home just about three for the Lord, three hard-to-crack Jews, that would be sufficient achievement. Your confusion is that when I said these three would be the equivalent of the 144,000 precisely because they are going to be so tough, coming from such a staunch Jewish neighborhood, and so forth, you forgot three and remembered 144,000.

If you make me argue with you, Daddy, I too can play the numbers game. I said three because, first, it is a magical number, the number of the Trinity. And if three are high-quality converts, the kind the Jewish community respects—doctors, lawyers, successful businesspeople—then their example will pave the way for others. The conversion of even one high profile Jew is like an assist on hundreds, thousands of others.

You argued for seven, you'll recall, because that number is even more magical and represents the seventh day, the Sabbath, holiest day of the Jewish week, but you eventually relented. You said that given the amount of time I would spend here, three

> would be fine . . . and I am well on my way
> to that goal. Three top Jews equals my con-
> tribution to the 144,000, and that will be it.

Billy stopped writing, and in so doing he became aware that he was breathing with a quick panting sensation. Next he noticed that his grip on the ballpoint was also terribly hard, and he consciously had to release the pressure in his hand. When he examined his fingers, they were stained with dark blue ink running in lines that reminded him of thunderbolts up to the first knuckle.

He stood up from his chair, looked over his hastily made bed, and rearranged the Hebrew primer and his Bible, which lay beside the rumpled throw pillow. He wanted to call Rena again, but her father had now forbidden all communication. Yet another father! Billy knew he would soon fall on his knees (first he had to finish the letter) and pray to Jesus to find where his soul was leading him.

> So, Daddy, I will not contend with you any
> more about it as Abraham did with Jehovah
> before the cities of Sodom and Gomorrah.
>
> So, please. If you upset me, then
> Annabelle will also sense it, and she will be
> upset, and she is skittish since eating the
> Buddhist's sheep. To succeed, I need your
> total, unconditional support, preferably
> communicated through letter, phone, and
> fax from home. I repeat. Do not come by
> suddenly, casually, by surprise. Do not fly
> up here. That would potentially undercut
> my authority, it would be a disaster for the
> ministry, plus I don't see how but you will

slow down the conversion process in my top prospects.

Since you insist I identify them—instead of keeping this as a surprise for you at the important baptismal ceremony—I will oblige: They include one of the Upper West Side's major Jewish businessmen, a tycoon of international trade between the US and Asia in floor products; I also have serious conversion negotiations ongoing with one of the Jewish world's most important documentary filmmakers, who is currently making a movie about the world's smallest nations. Finally, the third candidate is a distinguished writer, working on a major book about Jewish themes; he develops his complex works at the New York Public Library, where he is an esteemed member of the staff.

The challenge to overcome with this third fellow is that he has some familiarity with our missionaries' previous work. He knows how many times we have given up on the Upper West Side in generations gone by. And, Daddy, he knows all about the teaching of dual covenant theology. He thinks all Christians may as well become Jews because the Jews' special relationship with God is based on a covenant that existed thousands of years before Jesus Christ was born. I have had such conversations with this man. So you see, I am battling mightily for the Lord.

However, here is the silver lining, Daddy. Here is the kicker. This particular conversion prospect's father is an elderly rabbi who lives in a nursing home not too far from the restaurant. Incidentally, "rabbi" means "my teacher" in the Hebrew language. I am already imagining the impact his son's conversion may have on the hearts and minds of the entire area from Fifty-ninth to Ninety-sixth Street. The son of a rabbi!

Quality over quantity must continue to be our motto. So do not worry and do not harass. I will pray for you as you undergo the further procedures you mentioned and I will have these three Jews believing in Christ Jesus soon enough. I will keep you informed, as events are moving swiftly because the Lord is working in mysterious ways.

With love,

Billy and a healthy Annabelle

33

It is quite possible, Michael was thinking, as he sprinted about on the baseline and covered for Sam—Sam was wearing an ancient, peeling pair of Keds that were so tight, they made him flat-footed and slow—that if they did not have love of tennis in common, they might not be speaking with each other, period. To play effective doubles, however, required that you really communicate on the court. At minimum, you shouted "Switch" or "Cover the alley, you idiot" or "Forgive the decomposing frontal lobe neurons, what the hell is the score?" Michael and Sam, however, were not doing even much of that minimal talk. Fortunately Sam's serve was nearly unreturnable tonight, and at least Michael could compliment him on that.

For Michael, this was also one of his Buddhist nights on the court. As Judy had told him many times when, in his frustration, he talked about giving up the game, he needed to adopt a Buddhist approach: no conscious thought should precede the hitting of the ball. The action and the thought should be one and instantaneous.

For most of the evening, Michael was conscious of being in this Buddhist zone. "You don't hit the ball," so Judy's tennis advice went. "Let the ball release itself from your racquet." Indeed for a few games he had maintained an exceptional concentration. However, now the spell of good shots felt broken, and he expected to blow the one he was now engaged in: racing crosscourt, he caught up with Gerry's hard volley and returned it a millimeter over the net with so much angle and topspin that Gerry didn't even make a move for it. He just stared after it, declaring "Much too good," and then went back to serve the next one.

Michael and Sam, despite the communication breakdown, continued to do very well against Ganesh and Gerry, for whom the elusive chemistry was missing tonight. Perhaps Ganesh's game was just a little off because the amazing Iranian, still dressed in his cerulean blue hospital scrubs, had already performed two bypasses today, niftily finishing up the final suture just ten minutes before he was scheduled on the court.

If the crisp tennis were any measure, Michael, buoyed by self-satisfaction with his game, had at least forgiven Sam for his car trick of three weeks ago. Either that or the incident had altered their relationship in an indecipherable way (perhaps they took each other less for granted), with the result that their performance as a team against Gerry and Ganesh had rarely been better.

They had won two sets already and were screaming and jumping up and down as a third-set triumph, almost unheard of in the after-ten P.M. slot, seemed also to be materializing. But the games, especially the last three of the final set, continued to be hard fought, and the entire evening felt as if they had moved to a slightly new level—perhaps up to Ganesh's—with many points decided by all four combatants at the net, *bam bam*, very quick, like the professionals.

Of course, Gerry's imminent conversion to Christianity—a firm date had been set—and Michael and Sam's apparent failure to prevent this from occurring were never far from the tennis players' minds. After the first set, Sam had declared, "Jews one, Christian and Muslim nothing."

"And who might this Christian be?" Ganesh said as they all, having shaken hands, stood at the net and toweled off. "This is just an expression, your joke?"

"Nope," said Sam, "there is a Christian among us. Your teammate."

Gerry, with his back to this conversation, seemed to shrug.

Ganesh, who had sensed the presence of hard feelings, merely said with artful tact, "How fascinating."

He likely would have left it there had not Sam added, "The ceremony—the baptism—is coming up in a few weeks. Perhaps you want an invitation. Put it on your calendar. Sure to be a hot ticket."

"In the part of the world where I grew up, if you argue—or joke—about religion, you often end up regretting it, or dead."

"I'll be just fine," said Gerry.

"Well, you are launched on a new adventure then," said Ganesh, extending his hand for Gerry to shake.

"That's the way I look at it too. An adventure."

"It is funny," Ganesh spoke, as he turned to leave. "If I had to pick out the fellow most likely to change his religion, I would have not picked Gerry. I would have picked you." He collegially snapped his towel toward Michael. "Of the three of you, you strike me as a man the most—what shall I say?— spiritually restless."

"You're lucky you didn't put money on it." Michael attempted a joke, and wished he hadn't.

"I mean no disrespect to you," Ganesh turned to Gerry. "Only changing one's religion often has more consequences than changing one's wife."

"And how would you know?" Sam asked.

"Because I have done both. But I will tell you no details. We struggle in the dark toward the light, all of us. You see, that is an image from Zoroaster, the father of my current faith."

"You're not Muslim?"

"Of course not. I am a Zoroastrian."

"All these years," said Sam, "we had you wrong. Amazing."

"But it is truly nothing. You know it is my personal opinion that these baseball players"—he motioned toward the lounge and its set of elevated TVs with the baseball games visible from their court tonight—"who you see making the sign of the cross before the curveball comes at them, or the footballers thanking Jesus Christ for helping them throw a forward pass to victory in the Superbowl, this is very unseemly. You win because of your ability, not your faith. We will, I hope, continue to know each other as devotees of what we know is, however, the one true faith: worship of the little fuzzy eyeless green god Wilson. All hail the god Wilson. Gerry, I wish you only the best of luck."

At Gerry's unexpected urging, Michael and Sam left Caracas after the final set without even showering, having agreed to join him for late-night beer and burgers on Broadway near Seventy-ninth Street. Ganesh's graciousness was on their minds, though his name was not invoked, as they drove back to the City through a persistent drizzle that taxed the Toyota's brittle wiper blades. They ate as they had driven, quickly, because Gerry had an additional destination for them a few blocks west of the restaurant: a low-slung building of worn stone, with two sets of steps descending to a common entry-way guarded by an iron gate. At nearly midnight, as the trio stood beneath a ginkgo tree and observed it, the building appeared not only dark but also abandoned and foreboding, and a faint smell of bleach, ammonia, or the scent of a Laundromat drifted up from the basement level.

"It's the *mikveh,* men," Gerry said. "It's the headquarters of the Jewish baptismal font and alcove. And I did a little research too: it predates Christianity. It is very Jewish, gentle-men. Why have I brought you here? So that you can relax about baptism. It's like washing your hands and saying the blessing. Only it's your whole body that's getting washed. Nifty, huh, and right in the neighborhood."

"*Oy vey,*" said Michael.

"Now I understand why you are acting so screwed up," said Sam. "You're the only Jewish man on the West Side with a documented menstrual cycle. You come here often?"

"Gerry," Michael said—he aspired to Ganesh's patient tone and diplomatic style, but fell far short—"I don't want to shock you too much, but Jewish ablutions like washing your hands and saying the *brocha* before you sit down to a meal are not baptism. This is a place for traditional observant Jewish women, not for a businessman being driven out of his religion by his wife." Michael felt suddenly desperate to provoke a reaction. "How about finally grasping the gravity of what you're doing!" Gerry ignored the taunt. "It's not a joke."

"Gravity is in the eye of the beholder," Gerry said. "Come on down here and check this out." He led them, reluctantly, down the steps where they could peer in through the gated and mullioned windows. Not much was visible except a room with some kind of bench and closet area lit by what appeared to be a gloomy bulb.

"If you're so excited by this place," Sam said irritably—his white tennis shirt was hanging out, his hair was matted, and he was covered with sweat and beginning to feel itchy—"then why not cancel the ceremony at the kid's tub and get yourself baptized here? You can become a returning Jew, a what-do-you-call-it, Michael?"

"A *ba-al teshuva,* a repentant Jew."

"But gentlemen, I have already decided to allow myself to be baptized. Let this take the edge off for you. It's an ancient Jewish gesture, that's what it is."

"Gerry, Gerry," said Michael. "This is not a bubble bath. You know what Harp and Marylee are asking of you? By submerging, you relinquish all formal ties to Judaism. As you go under, you have to recite the catechism or whatever it is. The Nicene Creed. The articles of Christian faith."

"I know that."

"You have to say, 'I believe in the Holy Father and that Jesus Christ is the son of God . . .' the whole ballgame."

"I will say it."

"But will you mean it?" said Sam as he leaned against the entry gate. "Even if you go swimming in it, you cannot possibly believe it!"

"Look," said Gerry, "we've been over this territory a dozen times. It's words, words, words. The Christians said for two thousand years that the Jews were responsible for Jesus' death, and one morning they woke up and changed their minds and got it right, and so they changed the words. That the Romans were now, officially, the bad guys. For thousands of years Catholics couldn't eat meat on Friday, and now you don't go to hell if you do. Why? They changed the words. Every deal, every contract can have an amendment."

"So you're faking it, Gerry. You're goddam faking it for Marylee and Harp!" charged Sam.

"You're putting words into my mouth. What I'm doing is accommodating. That's all. I know I might not possess the greatest religious mind in the world, but at least I am keeping mine open. My mind can contain Jesus in it at the same time it can hold whatever you're supposed to hold if you're Jewish." He paused. "All that stuff."

"Try God," said Sam. "Try saying the word, the one God, dammit. As in 'Hear Oh Israel the Lord our God the Lord is One.'"

"Let me ask you a question," Gerry said. "How do you know that the Trinity isn't a unity? Again, magic with numbers. Three in one. Frankly, I think Marylee is right that the Jewish God in Genesis anyway mainly goes around checking up on people and dishing out the punishment; he's a little like you, Sam, or maybe Ellen when she's had a bad day with the freshmen. Things are not so simple."

"You can be both a Christian *and* a Jew?" Michael asked wearily. "That's news to me."

"And I'd appreciate your leaving my wife out of this," said Sam.

"And I'd appreciate it if you stop hounding Marylee. She should not feel persecuted in her own house."

"Calm down, boys," said Michael. "We're having a nice evening at the *mikveh*. Let's just keep it on a high intellectual level. The thing you have to understand, Gerry, I mean truly absorb, is that you, through the baptism, undergo a transformation. It is an official, external sign of what's supposed to be happening, or to have happened to you, internally. In a word, you are being reborn."

"Yeah," said Sam, "like that Swedish tennis player. He comes back from being down two sets, five-love to win the match. Björn Again Borg."

"Sam, please, for godsake!"

"The man doesn't believe in what he is doing," said Sam, groping for the steps from the *mikveh* back up to the sidewalk. "And yet he does it. I'm reaching the point where I'm out of ideas. Let's just go home."

"Not yet," said Michael. For a change, he felt only bad, not sorrowful and dejected, and still possessed of some spiritual energy. He could see Gerry's effusiveness beginning to fade. He could see in Sam's irritation his own. Yet he decided to try once again. "Have I asked you to read Franz Rosenzweig's *Star of Redemption?*"

"You have, but I haven't."

"Why don't you *read,* Gerry? A Jew reads."

"Well, by that measure, maybe I'm not one. For me, a review or a digest takes the place of the book; sometimes it's even better. We're not all like you, Michael. And I know all about Franz Rosenzweig. I am not a philosopher, nor will I ever be one. I'm in floor tiles. I'm the great philosopher of linoleum."

"Please, Gerry. You will be a terrible loss to me," Michael said, "if you go through with this."

"I'm telling you I will pop up unchanged. It will be like a car's changing registration from New York to New Jersey."

"You're not a vehicle, Gerry. You're a human being. And the idea of baptism is—to stoop to the fine level we have attained tonight—that you get dunked as Jackie Mason and somehow emerge as Pat Robertson."

"Incidentally," Sam said, "there's a helluva difference between New York and New Jersey."

"To the car," Gerry said, "it makes a difference? Does the mileage change? Does the engine? The car just goes on running, with a new sticker in the window. It just goes on being itself, and that is my intention."

Michael sighed. "You talk to your mother?"

"Yes, thank you, my friend. I don't take offense. You did what you felt you had to do. I spoke to her. She understands."

"Like hell she does," said Sam. "If she understands, then I'm Golda Meir."

"I told my own father, Gerry. I was visiting him after I heard that the date of your ceremony had been set, and I just started to cry. I had to tell him. I couldn't stop myself. I told him how bad I felt that we couldn't change your mind about it."

"You were appealing to him to appeal to me?"

"Maybe," Michael said. "He always liked you, but, truth be told, when I mentioned it, I thought he was actually asleep and didn't hear me. Probably the way I wanted it: to get it off my chest but without tormenting him. Why do I need to do this? Because you're making me feel like a lousy Jew myself. If I were any good, I could convince you that you're going down the wrong road. I could convince you, Gerry, that what you're doing isn't a name change, or a change of registration, or whatever you choose to dupe yourself with. I could convince you that you are washing away your memory—okay, not memory, but your formal connection—to all the Jews, and not only us, in the here and now, but also to those who were butchered, flayed, burned, garroted, had their tongues torn out, were shot, and gassed just because of their . . . registration. I'm sorry, Gerry."

Michael unshouldered his racquet case, and tried to give Gerry a hug; Gerry turned away slightly, and only half of him was embraced. Still, Michael was glad he had gotten this out.

It had to be said, those words that had seemed like troops, lined up at the back of his mouth, just waiting for the moment when they were ordered to march. Now they had come out. Would they do any good?

"You forgot drawing and quartering," said Sam despairingly. "You forgot drowning—"

"I will always be connected to all that," Gerry said.

"As a Christian, as a good Christian is connected to it," said Michael. "What a loss."

"Let's go, guys," said Sam. "We're getting nowhere."

"No, wait," Michael said. "Was it Marylee's vision? Is that what's gotten to you? Is that what she's holding over you?"

"What vision?" Gerry asked.

"You don't know? She saw Jesus in the bandages when she had her breast removed, man. She never told you this? That's when this all got started. That's what she told me. She said all this began with the operation. Oh, Gerry, back then, with the cancer, not with the preacher. She never told you?" Gerry did not answer. "What kind of marriage do you have?"

Gerry still did not answer, but his face grew vacant and disconsolate.

Michael was about to reach over and try that hug again when flashes filled their eyes, blue and red lights mingled alarmingly with the sounds of running feet and slamming doors. Large men brandishing sticks and now, Michael saw, guns were suddenly rushing down the steps toward them.

"Police officers! Put your hands high above your heads. Up, up. Now! Don't move!"

"Jesus Christ," said Michael. "Don't shoot."

"Keep your hands way up. Grown men pissing here again! What the hell is that? Holy shit, shotgun, shotgun!"

"No, no, no," Sam implored the cops. "Tennis racquets. We have only tennis racquets, cases . . . oh shit . . ."

"Drop 'em, motherfuckers! Drop the weapons or we fire!"

"Racquets," cried Sam. "Wilson, Prince, Head."

"Move, move," another voice yelled. And then, "Whoa, sergeant, it *is* a shitload of tennis stuff."

"Move, move," they shouted.

Two officers hustled Gerry, Sam, and Michael up the steps and into the light of the street lamp, which poured down on their tennis-weary, disheveled forms. "Who the hell are you guys? What are you doing here?"

"Don't shoot. Please, for godsake, don't shoot, officers," Michael begged. "We were only checking out the *mikveh*."

The police decided not to believe the midnight *mikveh* tour alibi, in no small part because neither Sam, Michael, nor Gerry was carrying even a shred of personal identification. Covered with sweat, and dressed suspiciously in some very unorthodox Bermuda shorts, gapingly torn T-shirts, and other highly unfashionable tennis togs, trying to explain their way through wild, matted hair, and the loud shouting (this was part of the reported complaint from the woman in the building adjacent to the *mikveh*), Gerry, Michael, and Sam looked simply awful, disorderly, suspect, and indeed as if they had just participated in a soccer riot or some other disturbance.

"Been drinking? Where's the I.D., gentlemen?"

For all these years, they explained to the officers, that they had been playing tennis in New Jersey, they had always left their wallets in their work clothes at home, pulled on tennis clothes, grabbed a few crumpled bills from the kitchen drawer and the car keys from the hooks by the front door, and off they went.

"You been driving to New Jersey tonight?" one officer asked.

"Sure," said Gerry. "Every Tuesday. Call up the club if you don't believe us. Caracas Health and Racquet. Please."

"Is that so? Caracas, as in drug capital of Venezuela? How many years you been doing this little trip?"

"Ten, twelve," Sam answered.

"Who does the driving?"

"Most of the time," Michael answered, "Gerry does. But we all do, yeah, now and then."

"So," the cop said, with a certain triumphant finality as he pulled out his pad and began to write: "Driving without a license or appropriate I.D. for twelve years, for each of you. A total of thirty-six years without licenses. Very good!"

"Oh for chrissakes," said Gerry.

"That's in addition to the criminal trespass," said another officer. "Are you boys not having a particularly good night?"

"See if Jesus can help you now," Sam said under his breath to Gerry.

"Let's go," said the officer, as he and his partner began to put handcuffs on them.

When it was Sam's turn to put his hands behind his back, the arresting officer, who was quite short, stood on his toes and whispered into Sam's ear, "If you say one more negative thing about Jesus Christ our Lord, I personally will kick your big fat ass all the way to Brooklyn."

The cop escorted them across the street, where they were ordered into a patrol car and driven to the One Hundredth Street station for further processing.

When none of them could locate their wives by telephone, they were taken down the precinct house steps and into a basement holding cell with a paint-stained, flickering bulb hanging from a wire above them. In the corner was a chipped toilet (no paper visible), so low to the floor that it was practically a hole, and against one wall of bars a bench big enough for three.

"Have we been arrested?" Gerry asked. He lay down on

his back, taking up the bench's entire length, and put his hands defensively across his forehead.

"Are we comfy?" asked Sam.

"You have to be fingerprinted and photographed first," said Michael, who was the only one among them ever to have been arrested—as a student during the occupation of the buildings at Columbia during the Vietnam War. "I think they are bored and they also don't like us on principle. I feel suddenly nauseous."

"Just keep it together," said Sam. "If you barf, or if I have to watch you take a shit, I'm asking for a cell change."

They lapsed into silence. Abrupt bursts of laughter drifted into the cell from a distant television or perhaps it was a radio. Then they heard someone calling out as if in pain. They hoped it was still the TV or radio and not coming to them live from another cell.

"Where the hell are the women?" Sam said. "When you want them out, they're in. When you need them to be in, they're out!" He had left a message on the machine, but somehow he knew Ellen would not be home for hours. Then he remembered. "She's taking some class. She's going to go out for drinks with the students. Forget her. Where's Judy?"

"Dunno," said Michael. "I think zoned out in a Tibetan restaurant downtown at a memorial service for the sheep."

"Which restaurant?"

"Something on Lexington—in one ear and out the other."

"Can't you at least call the Buddhist?"

"If he's back, he's not in the basement. He'd be with Judy. Anyway, no phone down there."

"No phone? In 2000 in the middle of Manhattan. Jesus Christ."

"He doesn't exist to please us, you know."

"Will you just shut the fuck up? Anyone know their lawyer's number by heart?

"If it weren't for you converting," Sam said to Gerry as he removed his legs from the end of the bench, "we'd be home in bed already instead of serving as the night's entertainment for the cops. I told you it was going to be a slippery slope. Didn't I tell you it would lead to nothing but heartache and trouble! Where the hell is Marylee, Gerry? Studying with her minister?" Their eyes met. "Well, interrupt the Jesus seminars, will you? What the hell are you waiting for! You want to spend the whole night here? Call the goddam restaurant."

Less than an hour later, Marylee, looking very attractive in a purple shirt, jeans, and high heels, was walking down the antiseptic corridor toward them. Sam, Michael, and Gerry all flattened themselves against the cool oily bars at the front of the cell, with their faces and the flesh of their bellies protruding between the bars.

They saw that she was not alone. William Harp, wearing a many-pocketed beige fisherman's vest, was walking behind her. The short cop who had bothered Sam about Jesus was also with them, and it was apparent that he and Harp had already struck up an acquaintance. When the cop walked away before they reached the cell, Sam shouted, "Hey, aren't you going to let us out of here!"

"Yes, yes," Marylee said. "He will eventually." She showed them a tolerant smile. "But not quite yet."

"Marylee, please." Gerry said. "It's been a very long night. What in the world is going on?"

"First this fisher of men here wants to say a little something to you. When else are you going to give William the time of day?"

"It's night, Marylee," Michael pleaded. "It's the middle of the night."

"Please, gentlemen," William began. "I don't want you to take this the wrong way."

"It's hard to imagine we won't," Michael said.

William turned to Marylee for reassurance, as if asking for permission to go on. Her nod seemed to dissolve a little of his reluctance, most of which remained in both his manner and in his voice. "Gerry, Michael, Sam, from the bottom of my heart," he began diplomatically, "I am grateful for all you've done for me and for the restaurant. But I must tell you about a problem we are having. Actually I'm having it."

"See a goddam shrink," Sam growled, "and let us out of here."

"This scene redefines captive audience," Michael groaned.

"He has a modest request," Marylee said. "Be decent enough to hear him out."

"Must you?" Gerry asked.

"Not a goddam sermon?" said Sam. "After all this, a sermon about Jesus Christ! This is the worst night of my life. Call the ACLU. Cruel and unusual punishment!"

"It'll only take five minutes," William promised. "I'll talk fast. It's not what you think."

"Mercy," said Michael.

"The cop gave his permission, so relax, boys," Marylee said. "He told me he'd seen lost souls like yourselves discover Jesus right in this very cell and then turn a new page in their heart."

"My heart," said Sam, "turns a new page, and it'll be major surgery. Please, Marylee."

"I feel compassion for you, Sam."

"I am not going to Jesus-talk you, gentlemen. Again, I want to thank you for renting to me and for helping me get the club started, and with humility, and with everlasting gratitude in advance, and with a growing appreciation of the Jewish religion, and with—"

"Send a card," said Sam, "and let us out."

"Just say it, William," Marylee said, placing her hand on his arm. "Just spit it out."

"I will. I will. I want, please, I am begging you—not just you, Gerry, because I know you are well on the road to accepting in your heart the joy and peace of Christ—but all three of you gentlemen—I am asking you *all* to consider undergoing baptism in the font in the restaurant."

Michael slowly backed away from the bars. Sam tightened his fists around them so that his knuckles began to turn white. Gerry could not believe what he had heard.

"It's not what you think, gentlemen," said William Harp. "Please hear me out."

"Fuck you," said Sam.

"A few more minutes, before you turn off and turn away," Marylee appealed to them, "or, frankly, we are in a position to tell the cop, who happens to be very friendly with Reverend Harp, to throw away the key." Her eyes were too bright, Gerry thought. She was talking much too fast.

"You see," said William, with an earnestness that—at least to Michael's ears—sounded sincere. "I really really . . . need you. I respect Jews as I never have before. How to explain this? In a new way. I have been studying with people in Brooklyn. I have read . . ." He broke off, glanced at Marylee, and then composed himself again. "You, Sam, remind me of the Apostle Paul. Before he became Paul, he was Saul of Tarsus, a very Orthodox Jew, like the electricians, like Isaac and Rena, and he was on his way to Damascus to preach *against* the Christians. Do you remember what happened to him on the road?"

"He got a flat." Sam started to scream for the other officers.

"Just shut up," said Michael, "please shut up." Michael felt dizzy and now only wanted silence. He wanted Judy to come into the cell and liberate him, squeeze him through the bars, and then envelop him in her big Buddhist arms.

"Go on," Marylee said firmly, "but get to the point."

"On the road, Jesus appeared to Paul in a vision."

"No, William," said Marylee. "It was not a vision, it was not an apparition of Jesus. It *was* Jesus!"

Gerry had never heard Marylee's voice quite so sharp, so harrowed, and with an urgency he could not identify.

"Fine," Harp said. "It was a powerful experience, and he realized that Jesus was our Lord and after that, he was transformed. Then and there he was converted, and as a sign he changed his name from Saul to Paul."

"Was that because it rhymed?" Sam said to no one in particular.

Marylee answered. "He converted and gave himself a new name because it was a new beginning." She waited for William to go on.

"Guard!" shouted Sam.

His cry and Michael's face of sullen disbelief and Gerry's desolation in the corner of the cell—the other two as far away from him as possible, as if he were a leper—were too much for William Harp. "Oh Jesus," he cried. "Oh my Lord Jesus! Help me in my hour of need." He dropped to the floor onto his knees, and he raised his hands in supplication toward the ceiling of the jail. "Oh Lord, I am nothing. I am less than nothing." He began to sob.

Marylee knelt down next to him, took him into her arms, and stroked his hair. He is like her child, Gerry thought. He is like her little boy.

William took the red bandanna Marylee offered him out of her back pocket and buried his face in it. Marylee raised his head, dabbed his eyes with the bandanna, and he eventually calmed himself (Gerry saw that it was *his* bandanna). Yet

William remained on his knees when he resumed addressing the prisoners. "I am a failure. Despite all you've done. Despite all your kindness and your efforts. Despite the *mezuzah*s, Sam, despite it all, the restaurant and I have failed."

"Good," said Sam. "That's the only true thing you've said so far."

"There's no getting away from it: I don't have it within me to be a fire-and-brimstone preacher like my Daddy and his before him. Yet I can't get away from it. I can't make the break. Look at me! Some families where I come from—Marylee can tell you—have long lines of generals, one generation after another. With me and my father, it's long lines of missionaries. Years ago, my father saw a peddler, a Hebrew gentleman whose name was Rosen, fall on his knees at a tent meeting in Tennessee and accept the Lord Jesus. A Jew in the South accepting the Lord as his messiah was a great thing to behold back then. My father saw this when he was a boy of nine and he was holding his father's hand, and his father—my granddaddy—was conducting the tent meeting. And from that day forth, my father has been totally committed to converting people, especially Jewish people, and bringing on the new heaven and the new earth.

"He's expected the same of me. But in one post after another, I have disappointed him. He knows this. He knows me. I came back from a year in Armenia—a year's work and not one new Christian converted from the Muslims. I spent another year knocking on doors in Romania, and not a single convert to our church.

"When I came home after that, I found Daddy different. 'You don't have the calling, okay,' he said to me. 'Not like we have had it before you.' He was calmer and had had a change of heart about me. Or so I thought. Was I wrong! He had just shifted tactics because then he said, 'Go try one last time, son.

Do one great thing for me in this life. Let me see it before I go.' Go where? I asked. 'To meet the Lord,' was his answer.

"You see, he had come down with cancer in an area of his pancreas where no operation was possible. And he said to me that he would provide any means and that he had a good idea and that I should go to New York City. His thinking was that I would meet lots of Jewish people here. He knew, of course, that it is far harder to convert a Jew to Christ than it is to shift a Christian in good standing out of his denomination and into our embrace in Armenia or Romania. Or to awaken a lapsed brother or sister. But since I had failed so miserably with Catholics and other gentiles, why not give the Jews a shot? Some, he said, might even be willing enough to listen to me. That is how this ministry began."

"Well, you've got one," Sam yelled angrily. "You're successful. You've got Gerry Levine. Levine, a Levite, one big Jew for Christ. So what's the problem? You're a success. Now let us out."

"No, sir," said William. "Our deal was a minimum of three. Don't ask me to crunch the numbers for you. But Daddy promised to set me up in business—I have always wanted to run a restaurant—if the restaurant was an instrument of the Lord. So we compromised, and the result is Club Revelation. But I'm a failure, a complete failure at that too.

"Because Gerry is simply not enough. Daddy's calculations are that one tough Jew from New York City counts as about 48,000 regular Jews in order to total the 144,000 Jews required to convert after Armageddon. So the minimum is three Jews from New York."

"Michael," Marylee said, "as the son of a rabbi, you might be worth 72,000 just by yourself."

"For godsake," said Sam.

"And the more religious you get," Harp went on, betraying

that he knew all the details of Sam's recent Jewish revival, "the greater is the power derived from your accepting Jesus. Your influence. The conversion of a person like you will be magnified. It's a question of quality converts over quantity. Three from the Upper West Side are better than, say, three hundred from Oklahoma. You know we study these things. My father has paid consultants, like a conversion think tank, and we know that to convert a Jew residing between Seventy-ninth and Eighty-sixth streets, between Broadway and West End, is rated significantly higher than converting a Jew in Jerusalem, Israel! I kid you not. That's why I'm here and why I was so thrilled to find you people when I came to New York.

"Then to discover that your wives are Christians, and then, even under these circumstances, still not to have made real headway . . ." William appeared to start to cry again but controlled himself. "For a while I even thought that I would convert dozens. But something has happened. You need to know that according to Daddy, you are the highest, the very highest-quality potential Jewish convert stock anywhere on God's earth. So when you do—"

"You mean when we don't!" Michael shouted. "This is really too much, Marylee!"

"I desperately need you, gentlemen. My father will be coming up to see a formal baptism in the restaurant. That's what I promised him. I've been delaying, but I can't keep him away forever, because for him forever is coming very soon. I'm running out of excuses and time, and, believe me, one of my strengths and special talents has been making excuses. Even though he can barely walk any more, he wants to see Club Revelation and your conversion there before he dies. He says he doesn't care if this is the last journey he makes. He wants to see my success. I've made this promise to a dying man and I ask you to help me fulfill it."

"Are you out of your mind?" Sam yelled. "You told him you had three lined up to convert?"

"Yes, sir."

"This is unbelievable," said Michael.

"I told you so!" Sam yelled. He began to pace the cell, across and back in two huge steps, like a big dog in a cramped kennel.

"But bear with me. Let me finish. I am making a proposal: after one more meal, sermon, and then the ceremony, I will be done. I will abandon the lease, and leave. I will take my father home, and, having seen his son be successful at converting three tough Jews of New York City, he will be able to die in peace. I will not have disappointed him, and Club Revelation will be history. It would be a *mitzvah*. What do you say?"

No one spoke.

Marylee approached the cell, put her hands through the bars, and eventually drew Gerry to her. "You of course have already heard the spirit, Gerry. You are different. You have always been different."

With her left hand, she held his face near and her fingers swept back his hair and she caressed him. Gerry thought: It's as if she is alone here with me.

His face in her hands was where he wanted to be, although not through the bars of a jail cell. Even though she was pressing on him until he hurt, he leaned forward through the bars to kiss her.

Sam shouted again, as he reached over to pull Gerry away. "Guard!"

34

They arrived home from the police station at nearly four in the morning. The smell of sandalwood incense, indicating that Nawang may have returned, suffused the front lobby and mixed with the lemon odor of the wood polish on the banisters. The three jailbirds and Marylee all went to their respective floors, and William down to his room under the steps.

Nobody went to work the following day.

The morning was warm enough to have coffee outside in the garden behind the brownstone, but none of the men was even close to being awake by the time Judy, in a never-worn green sweatsuit to greet the new weather, came outside. She carefully carried a pot of just-brewed coffee, two matching see-through flasks for the milk and sugar, and the day's *New York Times*. A few minutes later Ellen emerged swinging a plastic bag of *ruglach* and, in her other hand, clutching four mugs, one containing four spoons, in cloverleaf formation. Setting the coffee service on the stone ledge that framed the garden, they cleaned off the old wrought iron table, then placed the coffee and food on it.

They were soon reading and sipping in companionable silence when Marylee came out to join them. "I'm really sorry I didn't leave a note to tell where we were," she said. "You've heard about the adventure, I assume?"

"Yes," Judy answered, with a quick glance up, "I'm reading all about it in the metropolitan police blotter."

"And I feel so left out," said Ellen. "For years I've been yearning to see Sam behind bars. I think I missed my opportunity. Of course, the way things are going, he might commit an actual felony against William Harp, and then I'll have my chance."

"Marylee," said Judy, "you don't look very rested."

"Are we still friends?"

"Sit down, ML," said Ellen.

"You sprung our husbands from jail," Judy said. "What greater gift?"

"Did you hear the whole story? William's proposal?"

"It's the most extraordinary request I have ever heard," said Ellen.

"I knew it was coming," Marylee said.

"You didn't tell us," Judy said.

"You haven't seemed that interested. I knew William was losing confidence and beginning to lose his faith. And he was going for one grand gesture. If they hadn't been arrested for molesting the *mikveh,* William would not have had at them. But when I heard they were all in the cell . . . it did seem irresistible."

"Join the party," Ellen said as she shook the remaining coffee into her mug and seemed to study the pattern the liquid created. "Look, it does diminish Harp's credibility, doesn't it? I mean as a man of God." Ellen now leaned over toward Marylee and reassuringly touched her shoulder. "I don't know why the kid just doesn't tell his father where to get off. Because, you know, nothing will make Sam get baptized. Nothing on earth or under heaven. Not even an Emmy."

"Even to make the restaurant history?"

"It's fading fast in any event, Marylee. I know you know that; you just don't want to believe it."

"Oh, I acknowledge it, all right," she said.

"Here's what *I* acknowledge," Judy said. "I have a husband who believes God is a middle-aged Jewish woman who frequents the information desk at the public library and is a Mets fan. So I will not rule out Michael's capacity to participate in a show baptism. Never more in my life have I appreciated so much the peace and harmony of the Buddha."

"Is Nawang back?" Marylee asked. "The whole building smelled like it."

"That was me," Judy said. I was so worried when I had no idea where you were and I had called the club and the Caracas police, and then the Bridge and Tunnel Authority. At least they told me there had been no fatal accidents. I didn't know who else to call or what to do. So I lit some extra sticks. Shoot me."

"And did it help center you, dear," Ellen asked, "to stink up the premises?"

"Well, I visualized Michael's body bloodying the girders on the George Washington Bridge. So I went from there and was able to visualize his death in some detail—it was a way of preparing myself for the worst—and I tried to follow what the Tibetans do in their tantric meditations. I pictured him really splattered all over the roadway, chips and parts and flaps of him, hardly an organ left intact; there he was, organ by skinny organ, broken bone by bone, from the scalp to the brain case, to the—"

"We get the picture, Judy," said Ellen. "But enough already with the visualization."

"Well, it's screwy," Judy said, "but I did feel better."

"We're all touched," Ellen said absently.

Judy broke the next interlude of nervous silence with some big news: "Nawang called," she said, proudly. "He said he was still in his homeland, still searching for another sheep."

"Where the hell is that homeland?" asked Ellen.

"For security reasons," Judy answered matter-of-factly, "he couldn't tell me precisely where it is. He said he could only return when he found a suitable replacement animal. But since his homeland is a small island," Judy said with a nod to Ellen, "he was also looking for funding for Sam's film."

"What a sweet man," Marylee said.

"I know he is also waiting for me to tell him," Judy added, "that the snake is absolutely, one hundred per cent gone. Only then will he bring the replacement sheep back. So, in principle, I will do anything to get rid of the snake and bring serenity back to our home. If that means urging Michael to be baptized for an hour or two, then so be it. If it enables an old man to die happily, and this restaurant and its sheep-devouring Christian snake to disappear in the manner of Curry by Murray and to join the everlasting cycle of *satori,* creation / destruction, then that is just hunky-dory with me."

"You rhymed," said Ellen. "Unconsciously. Hunky-dory, *satori.*"

"The best things happen unconsciously," said Judy.

Marylee listened to her friends with gathering sadness. She was assailed by the feeling that she no longer recognized their lives as inhabiting the same domain as her own. "More and more I need to find my own way," she said. "I've known for a while that William's faith was flawed, that he could be a guide but only up to a certain point. The Bible study was my idea. Talking to Gerry about Jesus was also my idea. Billy's mind has wandered. His father's on the way to visit us. A real mess. Nevertheless, I am convinced this is all part of Jesus' path for us to follow to the light. We are all part of a greater plan, whether we acknowledge it today, tomorrow, or—and this would be very sad—never at all. The plan is not altered."

"Even if a little old part like me refuses to participate?" asked Ellen.

"Then your refusal," Marylee answered her, "must be seen as part of the plan. There's no escaping it."

"Well, that's a very reassuring picture," Ellen said, "or a horrible one, depending on how you feel in the morning. But tell me, is Gerry really going to convert?"

"I hope so," Marylee said. "Every morning and night I pray that he will. I want to live a holy life with Gerry Levine. But our guides, even our partners, can travel only so far with us. What is the one truth of life that we know and that no amount of avoidance, or meditation, can obscure? Do you know the answer, Judy?"

"Just sit tight, just meditate. That's the truth."

"Ellen, do you ever teach your students the most important lesson in the world?"

"No run-on sentences?"

"That we are alone, we are utterly and terribly alone. In our bodies and in our minds, we are stuck. We never can get outside of ourselves, so we are never sure there is anything else out there. I mean, how do I know I haven't just dreamed up two friends for my consolation? Invented two wonderful friends, this yard, this solid table and chair to comfort me in a dream that does not end?"

"Come now, ML," said Judy. "Pinch yourself. Pinch me. We are alive, we are grounded, we are not dreaming each other."

"We are stranded in the howling void and the meaninglessness of existence unless we surrender to Jesus. Then, when we do that, and only then, the fruit of the spirit will be love, endless love."

Marylee stood up. Judy breathed deeply and then reached out for her hand and pulled her back down onto her chair, where Marylee sat, erect as a dancer, but to Judy and Ellen's knowing eyes, with a rag-doll interior, so that a breeze blowing through the backyard could have knocked her right over.

"Holy shit," said Ellen. "Come here, Marylee. I want to give you a great big hug."

35

Another week and then another went by, and the restaurant continued to sputter along. It attracted at most six or seven customers for lunch—often curious tourists, many of them German (William did not know why)—who turned off Broadway to sample neighborhood life in New York and were perhaps both puzzled and drawn by Club Revelation's small sign, the aluminum knife and fork crossed to become a shining culinary crucifix (Marylee had returned to the idea). In the evening there were perhaps twice that many bookings, twelve to fifteen people at most, so that William had to reduce prices to attract more eaters; however, after an initial surge of new customers, this move seemed to make little difference.

With business declining alarmingly, William reluctantly fired the cook who was assisting him, so now he spent large blocks of time in the kitchen himself, where he also relocated Annabelle and her tank; the reptile seemed to thrive in the heat of the ovens and grill.

William was not a bad cook at all, but the ingredients of desperation that had entered his life were also finding their way onto his rapidly changing menu. The Seven Seals Soup went nowhere fast. Likewise, the Carpenter's Pie—William's Christian variant of shepherd's pie—apparently had the psychological effect of making customers think not of Jesus' family profession but of nails, or so one marketing executive on vacation in New York from New Mexico had informed him; few people ordered it. Chicken Wings with Armageddon Hot Sauce fared much better, but the most recent Jewish-style dish—a carrot pudding that William dubbed Ten Commandments *Tsimis* (Rena had made the suggestion), a very good accompaniment to the Red Sea Snapper—was getting lost in a kind of culinary no-man's land. And all the fidgeting with the menu and the pricing was doing little to establish the gastronomic signature Marylee had told him the restaurant required both to create the much-needed buzz and to ensure survival.

Then one of the dishwashers and a freezer began to have persistent and bizarre electrical problems, and Rena, the electrician, was seen coming in and out of the restaurant every few days, because no sooner would one problem be resolved than out would go the power once again. William could at least see Rena under these circumstances and ask her a Hebrew question or two. As she stood holding a fistful of wires or checking the freezer's grounding, she stole glances at his face, handsome yet also grown haggard with longing these past months, and she wondered what would become of them both.

William soon had to reduce the waiter staff too, so that as the date of Gerry's ceremony neared, he was down to only one regularly employed Buddhist monk, Nawang's student, who, like Judy, continued often to be focused less on work and more on his master's return. When it got crowded at Club Revelation, which could still occur on rare occasions, the young monk was assisted by the guitar player whom William had failed to convert. This young man—Duct Tape Boy—had remarkably returned, with his hair all shaven from his face and scalp, but with none of his former tattoos, rings, and other body-piercing paraphernalia in sight. With quiet resignation, he presented to William papers demonstrating that he was enrolled in a substance-abuse program downtown. There was a work requirement, and could Club Revelation help?

William was moved by the boy's return more than he could express, and he was only too happy to hire him to wait tables in the evening as the need arose. Nawang's acolyte and the recovering addict, in black pants and white shirt, looked remarkably like twins. The monitor above the tables was reprogrammed so that William's apocalyptic, end-of-the-world montages were replaced by CNN nightly news, but the images were often not all that different.

If Michael and Sam thought that William Harp's absurd request was going to slow Gerry's journey down the road to converting, they were far too optimistic. A week after what Sam kept referring to as the jailhouse sermon, the Toyota, which Gerry had finally taken to the shop, pulled up to the building right on time for their regular tennis Tuesday. Sam and Michael were shocked, to say the least, to see Reverend William Harp in the front seat.

Both thought that Gerry was giving Harp a lift back to the restaurant after an errand, and they expected the missionary to hop out. However, when William emerged from the Toyota clutching a Hammer 6.1 graphite racquet, with enlarged sweet spot, and wearing tennis shorts, sneakers, and a crisp white T-shirt that proclaimed FOOD IS LOVE across the front in large blue letters, they realized that he was to be their fourth for doubles.

Speechless, Michael slid in first, then Sam folded himself into a bundle of acute angles in order to fit into the backseat. Then Gerry floored it for Caracas.

Taking a new and uncomfortable tack with the missionary, Michael tried for small talk. "I'm happy it's you sitting up front," he said to William. "It helps to be certain about your eternal life when you ride shotgun in Gerry's trap."

"Truth be told," said Gerry, "tonight you are benefiting from $600 of repairs."

"That's about $400 more than this pile of tin and rivets is worth," said Sam. "Red light's still flashing."

"It defies automotive science," Gerry said proudly as he

gunned the car, which was undeniably swifter and steadier, around the smooth curve of the approach and onto the bridge's rough roadway. "The mechanic fiddled with it, failed, and then advised me to give the car two aspirins and to ignore the light."

"I can fix that, Gerry," William said. He leaned across the gear shift and then extended his hand under the dashboard. "Excuse me for reaching between your legs so to speak . . . Yes," he said. "Eureka. It's the loose fuse . . . there."

"Whoa," Gerry exclaimed, "the flashing light is no more!"

"A flaming automotive miracle," said Michael. "Praise the Lord."

"Amen," Sam grumbled and stared out the window.

"Back home," said William Harp, "we tear down and rebuild mainly American, but you learn a thing or two about these Japanese babies too. No one checks fuses anymore."

"What other remarkable talents do you have," Sam asked, "besides preaching, cooking, tormenting the wrongly accused in jail cells, doing one-minute car repairs, and wrecking our lives?"

"I've heard he also plays a helluva game of tennis," said Gerry.

"We shall see," said Sam. "We shall see."

When Sam got a better look at William Harp in the revealing neon light of the Caracas courts, he thought better of suggesting that he challenge him to one do-or-die game of singles for Gerry Levine's immortal soul. William's legs were slender but well-muscled, especially above the knee and at the calf. He hit through during warm-ups, the ball seemed to jump off his racquet with a youthful and exuberant *thwack* that made Michael's heart sink, and his feet were very quick as well.

Still, Sam couldn't resist: "If you weren't twenty years

younger than us, I'd play you the best of three sets for the rights to Gerry Levine."

William did not rise to Sam's bait. He said, soberly, "What gives you the impression Gerry is up for grabs?"

"How 'bout we just play the game?" Michael proposed. "Save the souls for the bar."

Tonight Michael had donned his across-the-brow intertwined two-headband-and-athletic-strap combo in order to soak up the sweat and to keep his slippery scratched plastic tennis glasses from flying off his face. For a change, he felt rested and was looking forward to playing. When they gathered at the net to decide on teams and to spin a racquet for the first serve, he said, with a nod to Sam, "Will you accept Gerry and young Reverend Harp against us? Christians against Jews?"

"Again?" said Gerry.

"Just play," Michael said to him. "Play the game."

The tennis began, and Sam and Michael won the first two points on Sam's low, curving serve. "Why'd you bring the kid?" Sam demanded of Gerry before he sent the next serve his way. "What's going on?"

"Can't it wait, Sam?" Michael said over his shoulder. "Let's play the game."

"No, it can't wait," Sam said. He dropped his racquet arm and stood challengingly at the baseline. "I mean we're not exactly one big happy family here."

"I propose we should be," said William.

"You still want to convert us?"

William said nothing.

"In that case, I'm serving this up your wazoo."

"Wazoo schmazoo," said William. "Please serve."

Sam did, netting it twice. Then it happened twice more. It was the first game he had ever in his life lost entirely on double faults. He and Michael went on to sixty minutes of embarrassment, tilting their racquets with increasing humorlessness at William Harp's lightning serves, which were consistently every bit as fast as Sam's at his best. They eked out, for the sake of pride, one or two games on Gerry's below-par play and actually came close to winning one set when Sam elevated his serve and did indeed match William's speed. But the outcome was as inevitable as the sun's rising. After the third set loss, Sam checked to see that the court was deserted; then he threw his racquet twenty feet in the air, scoring a direct hit on the air-conditioning duct.

"Ace," said Michael dolorously. "Finally a $275 ace." They assembled at the net and all shook hands; it escaped no one's notice that it was the first time Sam Belkin had shaken the hand of William Harp.

They walked through the lounge and saw on the mounted TV that the Israelis were removing an apocalyptic group that had arrived on the Temple Mount for the Second Coming on Christmas, 2000, but now, many months and false sightings later, remained undaunted and still refused to go home to Denver. "I won't go, He's coming, I won't go, He's on His way," one man with a shock of white hair was screaming at the camera as the guards dragged him away. "I don't want to be in Colorado when our Lord returns in glory to Jerusalem!"

"You see the kind of trouble you folks make," Sam said to William. "You should stick to tennis."

"I will, if you help me," William said. "I'll even throw in some lessons."

"Will you, now?"

"For example, you should come to the net every time you get your first serve in, because they're very strong; you do it only now and then, and that gives me a big advantage. I never have to worry about you. But when you come in, watch out!

You make us rethink everything because of your height so close up. Right?"

"Sam makes me rethink almost everything I do," said Michael. "All the time."

"And from the baseline," William finished his lesson, "your shot is also low and strong, but you always telegraph it with the position of your feet, so I know where it's going and I'm ready."

"All right," Sam said. "Praise the Lord. Where'd you learn to play?"

"At the Jewish country club."

"You're kidding!"

"I am," said William Harp, putting his racquet on Sam's back and guiding him through the passageway toward the bar. Gerry was already ordering beers.

They found one of the three booths free and slid in. "It was clever of you," Michael said to Gerry, "to bring him along."

"The best we've played in months," said Gerry.

"Thank you very much," William Harp said as he placed his hands prayerfully together on the table.

"We're not the kind of crowd," Michael said, "that says grace over the beer." But he was thinking that Harp's hands in this position reminded him of Judy's, only the thumbs were not touching; Michael had half a mind to reach over to the young man and make it so.

"Okay, the tennis was fun, it was even better than we've played when Ganesh was at his best, but bringing Björn-again here along," Sam chimed in, "alters absolutely nothing."

"There are some people," Gerry said, "maybe myself included these days, maybe William here also, and certainly Marylee, who would take offense at that kind of anti-Christian humor. For some people, to be born again, the concept, has validity and value and deep meaning. It means choosing dignity over desperation every day, in every decision. How's that?"

"Very good," said William.

"You do that anyway," said Michael. "In business, every day, for example, that you go to your job. With us, though, with your best friends, you don't have to be phony, you don't have to be reborn; there's nothing to begin with that's flawed or evil about you that has to be fixed or overhauled; you're pretty much there already. So, please . . ."

"Oh, I don't take any real offense at all," William said. "I understand how I've invaded your lives, how I've threatened you all. Without meaning to, of course, but I know I have. How could I not! I want to apologize for it all and ask your forgiveness."

"But you still want to convert us?" Michael said.

"I still need you to participate in the ceremony."

"Which amounts to the same thing," Sam interjected.

"So is it a real conversion or isn't it that you're asking of us?" Michael demanded.

"My father is failing fast, as I've told you. He needs me to convert three Jewish people. If I had any viable candidates, believe me, I'd go with them. But I don't. Empty. *Bupkes.* Nothing."

"*Bupkes,* is it?" said Sam.

"I need three, and I can't tell you I am going to fake it, because my father, sick as he is, will see through a sham right away. I'm telling you that my heart will not be in it any more than yours will be. With the exception of Gerry, of course. I nevertheless ask you to go through with this, as a magnificent favor."

"We already told you," Sam said. "No. Is *No* not clear enough?"

"*No* is never definitive. You were in jail, you were upset when I asked you before. You've had a chance to reflect and to think about it again. You are among the kindest people I have ever known. I throw myself on your kindness."

"Stop right there," said Sam. "I don't care if I enjoyed playing tennis with you. I don't care how many red lights you can fix, I don't care if you can raise a million dollars for my movie. The answer is the same. Absolutely not."

"Michael?" said Gerry. "You feel the same way?"

"'Do I feel the same way?' Is the Pope Catholic? We're like Martians and Venutians here. We're speaking different languages. Of course I couldn't do it."

"Even though it would be a *mitzvah?*" William Harp said.

The pale ale, whose foam matched the color of Michael's face as it continued to register William Harp's growing Hebrew and Yiddish vocabulary, sloshed from his nearly dropped mug.

"A *mitzvah* for my father, yes."

"What other secret talents does this boy have? *Mitzvah* indeed!"

"I've learned the Hebrew alphabet: *aleph, bet, gimel, dalet, hay, vav . . .*" said William. "Tell me what else I can do for you?"

"Who cares if he knows a Hebrew word or phrase," Michael said to Gerry. "Right, *bubeleh?*"

"If you had real regard for the Jews," Sam said, "and what they have achieved and endured for 3,000 years, you would cease and desist all conversion efforts, including putting the Jesus move on your landlords!"

"I am going to cease and desist immediately after my father comes up, sees the baptism, and goes home, a contented man."

"Contented, maybe. Duped, for sure," said Michael. "Is that the way you want it to be?"

"I've got to tell you," Sam said to William, "I thought what you did at the police station—falling on your knees and thanking God and begging us—I thought that whole thing was strictly a show. An act. And I think you're still acting. The tennis and the *mitzvahs*—look, I am very sorry your father is so sick, but what you did at the jail, and now this, all these desperate deathbed appeals! What are they except pages cut from the book of a sleazy televangelist? Is that who you really are?"

"If your father really is not well," Michael pressed his point with William Harp, "then he simply shouldn't come up here."

"And you should be home now nursing him instead of talking with us. Isn't that the Christian thing to do?"

"Impossible," William said. "What you can give me to give to him is better than a thousand nurses, than all medicine. I've been putting him off for months, Sam. He's been spending tens of thousands of dollars. I've been telling him great things. I've already told him all about each of you—"

"Who?" shrieked Sam.

"Us?" Michael said. "Me?"

"By name," William said softly. "My daddy knows all about you. Your jobs, what you look like, your families. I think he's really looking forward to meeting you. You—I mean your conversions—are the culmination of his career, that is, mine. He even knows Michael's father is a rabbi. He may even want to meet your dad, Michael, over at the nursing home. What a highlight that would be."

"I need another beer, fast," Michael said.

"You don't have to tell me how out of line I am. But your quality means everything to my father. He's probably telling the members of the church, 'Billy's got some really big, I mean really big Jews lined up to see the light of the Lord.' That's the way he talks. 'Really Big Jews.' You'll have to forgive the way he talks."

"This kid listens, but he doesn't hear," Sam said. "Your father is not going to meet *this* big Jew. Never."

William struggled not to let Sam derail him. "You see, he

rarely travels because—this is what I think—he's actually afraid of what he might discover. He gives money not only to me but also to these far-flung ministries, but he stays very close to home. And there aren't too many Jewish people nearby, as you can guess. So to him the Jews are very strange. You're exotic people to him. He has all kinds of notions."

"I'll bet," said Michael.

"Why in the world did you give him our names?" Sam asked angrily, "when you knew there was no chance in hell you were going to convert us?"

"Well, when Gerry started coming along, I thought to myself, who knows! You're best friends. You care about each other. I thought Gerry might begin doing some persuading on his own. It's not unknown."

"You thought wrong," Sam said.

"I'm at heart an optimist. That's the way things happen. I thought I might get lucky. Plus I just couldn't keep putting my father off anymore."

"What else did you tell Daddy?" Michael asked. "Did you send him our social security numbers? Mothers' maiden names?"

"No, sir."

"Our pictures?" Sam said. "Does Daddy like photo previews of those about to be dunked?"

"I haven't sent pictures, but I'd like to," William said matter-of-factly. "If you'll permit me, he's on a lot of medication. Weeks, maybe even days, are all he has left. Sometimes he spends the better part of the day, so his nurses tell me, sleeping in the bed, or, if they're lucky they can get him up into a chair. He has only periods of lucidity. And all he talks about is coming to New York to see the great work Billy has done for the Lord, and to fetch the snake he loves. That's what I want to provide for him. Then he will go home, and you all will be left in peace. Did I tell you he's also in a lot of pain?"

"I just don't know why you don't tell him the truth," Michael said.

"The truth is the very greatest *mitzvah*, kid," said Sam.

"The truth will kill him. I'd rather the cancer do it. That will be a lot more merciful. I'm begging you."

36

The date William had set for the baptism was only two weeks away, but Gerry was keeping his eye on another date as well; he was wondering—being able to do quick numerical calculations in his head was good for something—if a full two months had already gone by since he and Marylee had last made love.

In the past when she had argued with him and they had drifted apart, there was always this wordless way to recoup intimacy. But now it was not only the absence of sex, but the presence of celibacy, that amounted to an all-new challenge for Gerry to overcome. For celibacy was the ideal of Christian companionship; by now he had heard this drumbeat very often: sexual marriage was okay, she acknowledged, if that's the best you can aspire to. The early Christians, Marylee had told him, were allowed to have sex grandfathered into their relationships. However, celibate companionship within marriage was without question even more praiseworthy, much closer to the lives of the Christians of Jesus' time, much truer to the Lord's ideal.

"Virginity was, of course, *really* the top of the line," she had also informed him a week after William's appeal to convert Michael and Sam. Thank God, at least a small line of irony had moved across her face when she said it; Gerry hung on each such gesture as if it were a lifeline extended toward him.

Although Marylee's ability to joke had not entirely deserted her, it seemed to emerge only after a glass of wine. Since wine, however, was associated in Marylee's mind with the early Christians, her emergent asceticism somehow permitted her to drink a lot of it—at least three glasses, and often more, with dinner.

None of this escaped Gerry's notice, of course, but it was not in his nature to criticize her or to succumb to alarm. Instead, he would drink her wine even if he didn't care for it. He would say grace with her and make sure his mind did not wander. He wanted to make her comfortable, not out of altruism but because he needed to feel that way with her himself and because her evident suffering oddly aroused his desire for her even more. And of course there was nothing wrong with rituals that helped them marvel at the food and the drink that sustained their lives.

"We haven't made love for a while," he finally found the courage to broach the subject directly with her, "and if memory serves me, you are not a virgin, and abstinence will not remake you one. Or am I missing something here?"

"I could still sew myself back up," she said, without a trace of irony.

"I wouldn't want that," he said. "Never."

"You're a virgin yourself, Gerry."

"Oh?"

"A virgin of the spirit."

"I need help, I don't deny it," he answered. "But just make love with me, Marylee. Tonight. The unspiritual kind, which also is . . . for the greater glory. Both the Lord and I will be eternally grateful."

"According to Galatians, Gerry, *The fruit of the spirit is love, joy, patience.*"

He took this to mean he must be even more patient. He

was angry, he knew she would even permit him to show it, but Gerry chose not to. When had he? When had he ever had a choice except to follow Marylee's lead if he wanted her to be with him? His eyes lingered on her for a very long time. She placed her hands—palms and fingertips together—beneath her lips as if she were uttering a prayer. It was a gesture Gerry had never seen before. Then, from behind her hands she blew him a kiss whose meaning he could not decipher.

Four, then five more days went by, during which Gerry worked hard to convince himself there was nothing new in Marylee's religious obsession. Would it not pass, as others had, if he just outlasted her? Viewed objectively, was this all that different from going along with her year-long campaign to mount video cameras at the busiest Broadway intersections to document and then nab light-runners, especially cops? Or her anti-littering campaign? Or the way she single-handedly had tried to improve subway etiquette, standing arms akimbo, fearless, before large men with spread legs, declaring, "You're taking up two seats. Please close your knees." Or the way not long before William Harp had arrived (she had stopped soon after) she had lectured every unlucky if unmannerly after-six P.M. marketer who fell into her telephonic clutches?

Gerry had forgotten how many obsessions there had been. Remaking his spiritual life, he now told himself, was part of this pattern, and he visualized the next steps: There would be the ridiculous baptism, Club Revelation would disappear, and William Harp would depart. Then their normal life together could resume.

Yet there was something more, if he could only detect or define it. Despite the toll it took on him and the others, Marylee's path fascinated him. He continued to be the cooler person, living on the heat of the other (only, unfortunately, she was now celibate). All right, maybe Jesus was only her most disruptive obsession so far, but still Gerry sensed within the known pattern and the familiarity something that was not familiar. Perhaps he wasn't taking it seriously enough, but what more could he do? What greater demonstration of constancy in spite of the killing celibacy? What was the new element? he kept asking himself. And then one day at work he simply knew: for the first time in their married life, he felt he was somehow being punished.

Yet with Gerry's characteristic deference to Marylee's needs, as soon as this thought revealed itself, he put it out of his mind. One more day's patience—even one more month's (he was fairly certain he could handle that)—would reap its usual rewards, and then some. So be it, Gerry thought.

Then, however, he put together the meaning of the books. He noticed that Marylee had been collecting what amounted to a small library of Christian books, but only now did he see that they had a pattern and common theme: the early Christian heroes, especially women such as Blandina and Perpetua, who were martyred in the Roman arenas. Clawed flesh, dismemberments, saints' eyes cast ethereally toward their new home, defenseless women in bloodstained white gowns awaiting the final charge of the lion or the wild African boar . . . Gerry at first only glanced at these very gory stories, which Marylee was now keeping in the drawer of her night table, even under her bed. When she was out of the apartment, Gerry leafed through these books—they were well-marked and clearly well-studied. He read them and tried to imagine Marylee in the arena, waiting for the signal from the Roman emperor or the prefect to send in the leopard or—the new talk of Rome—the Asian tiger, mad with hunger. Even after all she had put him through or perhaps because of it, his regard for Marylee—or at least for her powers—was such that Gerry visualized her, a female Androcles, quite capable of taming nearly any beast with her glance and her affectionate touch.

Yet, he forced the thought on himself: You are a jerk if you don't examine these new facts, which, in addition to the books, included this evidence: She had not gone to work with regularity for two months, and she no longer took business calls at home. Over the last few weeks, Gerry had continued to cover for her: she was traveling abroad, she was very busy, she was consulting, she was considering selling the business— yes, indeed, it was successful—to a larger company. But then he dropped the sham of it all and simply told her callers, her suppliers, the dwindling few customers who still left messages, to seek their design solutions, their launch concepts, and their buzz requirements elsewhere.

There was more. Gerry saw on her bank statements that Marylee had given far more money to William Harp than he had realized. When he discovered she had also been paying much of William's rent to the building herself—it was like robbing Peter to pay Paul—he couldn't contain himself. "If Sam finds out, he'll . . ."

"He'll do precisely what?" She walked in, then calmly and under perfect control began to lecture him on the gospel of giving and money. "A true Christian, Gerry, cannot be a capitalist," she said. "A true Christian cannot be in the design business, the wallpaper, furniture, or the floor covering business, the exterior business. A Christian is always concerned with the deepest of deep interiors." Her tone was quiet, not abrasive or dismissing, but upsetting to him because it said, "I do not offer opinion but truth."

"Should a true Christian," he responded, "be in the restaurant business?"

She moved in her chair like a cat slightly bothered by a

noise, but with its settledness largely undisturbed. "It is mitigated by the saving of souls, although it would be better, I agree, to give all the food away," she said. "Perhaps we'll do that. Thanks, Gerry. I'm going to ask William."

When he looked through her checkbook (he regretted that he allowed himself to do it), he discovered that contributions in the amount of $54,000 had been sent away to various missionary organizations, from Syracuse to Sri Lanka. He asked her about it, but her only response was to say that she wanted to give more, and would. "I would divest myself, Gerry, of all worldly things. I want to be ready. I want to prepare."

"Please explain to me again," he said to her one night, overcome by it all, by all the changes that she always seemed to keep under control in front of Judy and Ellen and the others, but which, at home, surrounded them. "Its appeal is what again, my darling? Tell me why you are giving away our money, and even the mink coat I got you. You didn't consult me about the coat, you didn't give me the courtesy—"

"It was . . . mine to give away."

"Yes."

"I am sick of being a well-to-do woman, Gerry. I am sick of Zabars, I am sick of Prada and of Bloomingdales. So I will begin to give it away. Don't you want to give it all away, Gerry, my love? 'By austere living,'" she quoted one of the martyrs, "'we prepare ourselves for dying.'"

"The coat meant a lot to me. It meant that we were going to make it together, it was ten years, Marylee. It was your tenth anniversary present."

He had felt salty, warm tears well up when he said this, but her answer turned them cold.

"'Will the neck that wears a necklace bow before the executioner's ax?'"

There were other signs he should have picked up. Curled

up in their apartment, beneath the lamplight, in sweatpants and thick white socks, pale and thin, she looked as temporary and frail as a cut flower. She had lost weight. She was an errant beauty queen in search of a pageant. Yet her gaunt beauty mitigated his frustration and stifled the alarms that should have gone off.

Even so, the night after tennis with William Harp, the night after he had made yet another attempt to do the impossible for her sake, Gerry lost it:

"What I've done for you, tried to do for you with Michael and Sam, I think I may regret for the rest of my life. But I've done it. I've asked them. Please tell me why I have done it!"

She was reading, with a glass of dark red wine in hand. Gerry rose from his chair and literally sat on the floor at her feet.

"I am bound to you, Marylee. I serve you. What are you making me do? I have been trying! I can't tell you how bad I feel, but on I go. I'm going to lose them, just like I've lost you, Marylee. I'm not blind. I'm feeling guilty about everybody. I'm losing everybody."

"That's why it's time you find more than this life. You must find Jesus."

"But if you find Jesus and lose the rest, what is the point!"

"Eternal life."

"Oh Marylee," he said, "Marylee, Marylee."

"Maybe they will come round after all," she said softly. "God does his best sailing in uncharted waters, and they love you a lot, Gerry. I never knew how much. I think they would do anything for you. I think you might be surprised."

"Just send him home, Marylee," Gerry said. "Give Harp all the money he needs, pack him and his snake, and mercifully send him home to take care of his father."

"If we did that, what would become of you, my darling?"

"What do you mean?"

"Would you take the journey along with me? Would you still convert?"

"I don't know. I just don't know. What I do know is that you are racing away from me. You make me feel that something is very wrong with me the way I am, no matter what I do. Do you have any idea how much I have been showering? You give me these looks as if I am . . . dirty. As if something is repellent about me. What's the secret? What's so bad that has to be washed away? That I'm Jewish? Michael says even by Christian thinking, Jews are already special to God, and they are special to Jesus because Jews had a covenant with God long before there was a Jesus. In the time of Noah. Be fruitful and multiply. Think about that. I'm as much God's child as you are."

"You're a child of Israel," Marylee said languidly. "You are not an adult of Israel, but a child of Israel. Let us please take note of the behavioral difference."

"I don't think baptism will make you want to be any closer to me, Marylee. That's my big fear. If I do it for you—"

"You must do it for yourself."

"Even if I do it for myself, even if some halo suddenly goes on above me and inside me, I'm convinced that when I emerge from that tub, you'll be there to sniff around me as if I haven't showered. You are going to recoil from me. What is happening to us? What have I done that has to be cleansed and purified?"

37

"It is not a test of God, or gods," Ellen was saying to Sam, Judy, and Michael, a day later over dinner in the Museum. "It is a test first and foremost of their marriage. We have here salade Niçoise, with the anchovies removed, and pasta pesto chilled and cold as a false lover's heart. Don't knock the tray over, Sam. The honey mustard and pepper are with the utensils beside the beanbag."

"Lovely," said Judy. "I'm in a honey mustard mood."

"I'll tell you plain and simple," Ellen pressed on, "we're working up to our first divorce here. That's the word nobody is uttering. Not *Jesus Christ* but *divorce,* the latter being far more forbidden around here than the former. If I weren't so hungry and this dressing were not so tasty, I would cry."

The two couples had decided they needed a dinner together and away from both Gerry and Marylee. When Gerry unexpectedly cajoled Marylee into joining him in Philadelphia for the "New Directions in Parquetry" exhibition, the meal was hastily arranged. They were originally going to eat on the roof, but a dark and threatening sky had sent them back down to the Museum. Having closed the Museum's heavy, graffitied (BE REALISTIC / TRY THE IMPOSSIBLE) door behind him, Michael now sat down beside Judy and began to pick at the plate of food she had prepared for him. Sam too was poking at a square of olive-flecked tuna, directing the chunk, like a prop, down a chute of celery, over a little log of carrot, now down onto a plain of lettuce.

"Having fun?" Ellen said as she walked by, lifted the carrot off her husband's plate, and popped it into her mouth. "Divorce is what I said, and it can happen here."

Still more silence followed her declaration until Sam set his plate down and said, "It's like the flaming Middle Ages. She's set this task, this labor for her shining knight to perform, and then she continually ups the stakes. That's the way I see it, and—"

"Sir Gerald," Ellen said, "has outdone every labor of Hercules on her behalf—"

"Was I speaking or was I?" Sam said to his wife.

"You see," Ellen said to Judy, "first Gerry and ML divorce, and Sam and I will follow soon after—we're arguing so much. Unless, of course, you and Michael would like to precede us? But, no, us first, and since we'll have to find new places to live, there will be no more brownstone, no more nutty tenants, no more Museum of the 1960s for us. You two will remain here all alone in your awesome marital bliss."

"Will you just let your husband talk?" Judy said. "I know you do possess that particular skill when you want to employ it."

"What I was saying," Sam resumed stonily, "was that with Marylee it was, first, 'Let me open this restaurant.' Then it became 'Start reading about Jesus Christ with this missionary.' Next, it was 'At least be open and share my interest'; then it became 'Defend my interest in my Christian tradition against your persecuting friends under my roof.' Then the ante was really upped: 'Share that interest yourself, Gerry, and *prove* yourself by convincing your barbarian pals to convert. Do this, or get out of my life.' Where's this going to end?"

"Thank you, Sam," said Ellen. "White wine, anyone?"

"For putting up with all that, I vote Gerry . . . canonization on the spot," said Michael.

"He's a Jewish saint already, a battlefield commission— one of the world's most patient, great husbands," said Sam. "But that's obviously not enough for her either."

"Calm down, boys," Judy said. "The emotion will make us choke on the food."

"She wants to make him into a Christian saint as well as a Jewish one," said Michael.

"I'll tell you what kind of saint he is," Sam said. "I think Harp is *shtupping* Marylee. I think Gerry is aware of it and he is willing himself to ignore even that."

"Wash your mouth out with soap," Ellen said to her husband. "Of all the Yiddishisms in your vocabulary, that is the least appreciated. I think I liked your company a lot more before you were so concerned about Gerry's immortal soul. And kindly remove your big feet from my original San Francisco Mime Troupe puppet!"

"Or what's left of it," Sam said, as he lifted up the ragged stuffed doll and dropped it onto the floor.

"What I simply don't understand," said Michael, as he now began to pace the Museum, "is that even after Harp in effect has discredited himself, has promised to close up shop, and to stop trying to convert the Jews—whom he suddenly respects now like George Washington and the Dalai Lama combined—I mean how can Gerry continue to go through with this?"

"How can Gerry?" said Ellen. "It's no mystery."

"It never was about how. About what's logical," said Judy.

"But why isn't it obvious to Marylee that it's time to come to her senses, to cut the line and let Gerry go?" Michael demanded.

"Go down, Gerry," Sam mock-sang, "way down to Egypt's land, go down, Gerry, let my people go."

"It's the marriage, not the faith, I repeat for those not listening," Ellen said. "If you want to save the marriage, you know what you have to do."

"That's bullshit," said Sam.

"Okay," Ellen said, "I can throw the gauntlet down too. Go love Jesus for a day, or I'll divorce you for the rest of your life."

"Calm down, children," said Judy.

"To save Gerry's marriage?" Michael said. "You want me to take the dunk too?"

"That's right," Judy answered. "A worthy enough goal."

"It won't even work," said Michael. "There will be something else, just like Sam says, and then something more after that. There always is."

"I can't even fit in the tub," said Sam. "No sale."

"You'll be doing a favor for your best friend," Ellen pleaded. "You'll be performing a great service for him; that's a simple, pure, unimpeachable motive. You can just stop sniping at them, and analyzing what they're doing, and pointing out all their Aristotelian contradictions, Michael, because no one cares about that anymore. Just do what they ask of you. Set aside your abstract values and cut your real-life, flesh-and-blood friend some slack. Moses and Abraham and Leah Rabin will all forgive you. The future of the Jewish people is not hanging in the balance. You will not be vilified in the newspapers, because, apart from us, who will ever know about it? Please! Remove all religion from your thought and just perform a profound favor for dear friends. It's going to be Club Revelation's last hurrah. Are you with us on this?"

"If it's all one big, inauthentic joke," Sam protested, "why do it? Why go through with any of it? I know a dozen out-of-work actors. Why can't I hire three of them to play us and let *them* get dunked for Harp junior and senior?"

"He is expecting to see you three specific Jews," said Ellen. "That's been explained, boys. Not stand-ins. When they talk to him, he'll know."

"We can find really first-rate look-alikes. We can do up a crackerjack script. Michael and I can sit in the back of the room and look at ourselves being baptized."

"You cannot make a mockery of it. You have to go through with it in good faith—sort of—and as a deep favor to a friend," Judy said firmly. "A friend who—"

"No," said Sam, "you are dead wrong. No one, no matter how desperate, should ask his friends to violate themselves this way."

"Would you become a Buddhist, temporarily?" Judy asked Ellen, "if I told you my marriage depended on it?"

"Absolutely," said Ellen.

"I rest my case," Judy said.

"You're both full of it," said Sam, "and nobody's marriage depends on it. If Gerry's turns on an outrageous fake baptism, then maybe it doesn't deserve to continue."

"How am I going to get you back on your leash?" Ellen said to Sam. "You don't know anything about your own marriage, let alone your friends'! You go through with that stupid little ceremony—I don't care if you clutch your *Mogen David* collection in your closed fist—but you go through with it. Please, Sam."

"Conversion-for-a-day, or divorce?" Judy said. "Anybody want more salad?"

38

My Dear Father:

I am giving serious thought to coming down to see you for a few days and then accompanying you to our ceremony back here at the club. However, it is hard to know precisely when I can get away.

The waiting, cooking, and other auxiliary staff is being pared down, as I explained, because we are putting more and more of our precious resources into outreach, teaching, baptismal preparations, and the like, because there are so many folks interested. I am giving everything the personal touch you taught me is so important—mainly because I am doing just about everything around the restaurant by myself. Just like you said, Daddy, the love of food of this world has transformed many Jewish people into being interested in Jesus' divine food of love, forgiveness, and grace.

I appreciate your wanting me to visit the folks at home in your company. I am also honored and humbled by your request to deliver the sermon at church and to explain in glorious detail the inroads we have been making here among the Children of Israel of the Upper West Side.

Go ye therefore, and teach all nations, baptizing them in the name of the Father, and of the Son, and of the Holy Ghost.

You recognize, of course, the words of the resurrected Jesus, according to Matthew, 28:19, speaking to the disciples at Galilee. These would be the verses I sermonize on at home. Does that seem all right to you?

I am all but certain of saying a resounding "Yes" to your request and I will inform you soon about the tickets and when I will arrive.

Are you telling me the truth about your cancer, Daddy? I do not mind talking to you on the telephone; I always look forward to it. I want to talk to you and to hear your voice, my own father's voice. I don't care a hoot if you sound like a tractor on gravel or if your voice has gone scary like you write. I will not be scared. Are you having any visions of the Lord? One of my congregation, Marylee, of whom I've written you a lot, told me recently that when she had an operation for cancer—which she is fully recovered from, I want to point out—Jesus appeared to her then and there. I am going to ask her to speak about that vision at our baptismal ceremonies.

She hasn't said yes yet—actually I haven't asked her—but I am all but certain she will agree. I can't help but feel that the direct appearance of Jesus before her is responsible for her husband Gerry's eventually being ready to come to the Lord.

In addition to me, Marylee, Gerry, and others in our study circle around Club Revelation, our whole congregation and my other Jewish friends are all saying prayers for you. Rena, especially. I hope you remember her. She is continuing to help me advance in Hebrew. When I told her my father was ill, she showed me one of the Jews' most important prayers, the Eighteen Benedictions that religious Jews say three times daily. One of them goes, *Blessed Art Thou Oh Lord our God, King of the Universe, Who Heals the Sick.* I am writing that in the original Hebrew, with a special calligraphy, and I am enclosing it on parchment, for you to put beside your bed. I practice my Hebrew by saying this blessing three times a day for you, Daddy.

With love, your son

William

39

Once "New Directions in Parquetry" had concluded in Philadelphia, it was Gerry's intention carefully to fold his booth, crate his samples, put fresh batteries in his calculator, and send them all on to the next show, in St. Louis. Then the plan was to drive with Marylee down to Virginia. He had found and assembled some of her favorite CDs for driving music. What did it matter that she now told him the greatest hits of the Grateful Dead were prefigurations of the Resurrection? Couldn't they still enjoy the Dead, as well as thinking about the quick and the dead?

Gerry had even stocked up on those tangerine-colored, fifty-nine cent packages of peanut butter crackers Marylee used to crave on long drives. With the supplies prepared, Gerry imagined the hours of driving together as a kind of long-delayed new communion with her. For, although she often did not accompany him to the shows or work the booth with him, as he would have liked, they had always loved the car time of these trips together.

The plan was to take at least three days off—the business could fortunately well afford it—because he thought Marylee needed to get away from the City, from William Harp and Club Revelation, and especially from the hectoring of Sam and Michael. It would have been a good plan.

The last weeks she had also talked lovingly of her mother, who still displayed on the lowboy in her living room ashtrays and highball glasses festooned with a Confederate flag, a sabre, and the cross. Gerry was remembering how once or twice in recent weeks Marylee had also gotten started on how she missed standing in the circle of her fellow high school cheerleaders on perfect cool fall Friday afternoons. There, in her little red pleated skirt, she stood around the huddle of football players, including her boyfriend—who else but the quarterback?—as he led the team in prayer that they would be granted not only victory but also freedom from hamstring pulls, bone fractures, and the like, in the name of Jesus Christ.

Gerry felt he had no right to police or even to judge Marylee's nostalgia. He wanted not only to get her away but also to take her back to Virginia. He had been feeling guilty that he had not suggested it sooner.

Perhaps if he had really heard Marylee months ago, if he had truly listened to what she had been saying, and they had made the trip even half a year ago, none of this—no missionaries, no Christian cafeterias, no baptisms, no bitter fights between friends—would have occurred. If he had not been such a fool, so self-centered, he might have heard that she was less Jesus-sick than plain homesick.

Now, driving toward Philadelphia at a fairly steady seventy, which was far faster than he usually could coax out of the Toyota, he was hoping that later was better than never. Yet each glance he had of Marylee, curled up beside him in a black sweater with a silver brooch in the image of the Virgin Mary and a skirt, told him it might be otherwise. She acknowledged but did not open even one of the twelve packages of crackers he presented to her in a wrapped and ribboned package, his gift. As as to the Dead and other driving tunes, Marylee preferred silence.

"We're finally going south," Gerry said after an hour of wordless driving on the turnpike, "one step at a time, first Philadelphia, and then, as soon as the show's over, home."

Marylee only gave him a fleeting smile. Then, surprisingly, after a few more miles, she lowered her head onto his shoulder. She did it slowly, delicately, yet without hesitation, lowering first her ear and then her cheek, and then he felt the fall of her hair, and then the touch of her head. The elegant lightness of her head startled him. She had positioned herself on the front seat right beside him, out of the seat belt's range, with her knees tucked up under her, as if they were high school kids on an elm- and chestnut-lined road on the way to a rural drive-in. Never mind that they were hurtling past Trenton, with huge trucks hauling freight speeding at eighty-five miles an hour past them on both sides. Marylee's gesture, so unexpected, so old and yet so new, brought Gerry nearly to tears.

"I feel love all around me. Jesus' love is my seat belt, and yours too."

For the next fifty miles, she spoke not another word.

When he got back to their hotel room after the opening night of the exhibition, Marylee wasn't there. Her suitcase was on the bed, unopened. There was not a wrinkle on the bedspread, not a tissue removed from the box, nothing touched or disturbed in the room. There was no message written on the pad beside the phone, no pulsing call-the-main-desk light; in the bathroom, there was no note propped against the mirror, where she usually left him notes at home. The cleaning person in the corridor had not seen Marylee, and, no, the desk clerk had not seen her either.

Stay calm, he told himself as he waited for the elevator. Then, not able to absorb his own advice, he raced down the four flights of stairs to the lobby. Gerry's increasingly panicky circumnavigation of the leather chairs and loveseats and islands of ferns and corn plants brought him, finally, in front of a woman who bore a resemblance to Marylee. Although he was virtually certain she was not Marylee, he peered at her like a visual alchemist, hoping his gaze might turn this stranger into his wife. The result was that she raised her newspaper to cover her face. When a desk clerk eventually came up to him and asked if she could help, Gerry shook his head and quite nearly sprinted toward the revolving doors, and out of the lobby.

At once, outside, he began to jog, stop, and lurch along the street near the hotel, looking for a sighting or a clue. The colonial-style lampposts, the cobblestone streets of the square that fronted the hotel, with Independence Hall silhouetted against the sky and the horse-drawn carriages that moved in slow motion past him carrying their families of tourists—he had planned to suggest that he and Marylee take just such a sedate and restorative ride themselves tonight—all tormented him with evidence not only of another opportunity missed, but with the sense of a different life he might have lived with Marylee.

Gerry dashed into a florist's shop, where for an instant the scent of lilac and narcissus reminded him of her hair. But the shop was empty. The adjacent camera store, where he had followed the scent, had one customer, a middle-aged man dropping off film, and no Marylee in sight. Suddenly Gerry felt as if he must find her within the next five or ten minutes or lose his wife forever.

He raced to the hotel garage and found the car, like the room, untouched, exactly as he had left it. Disdaining another slow elevator, he jogged up the ramp and returned to the square. Sweating as much from anxiety as exertion, Gerry pulled up short in front of the hotel when he realized he had left *her* no note in case she had returned in his absence. He walked quickly back across the lobby and returned to their room. He found it precisely as he had left it, except the sense of Marylee's absence had begun to fill up the space like rising water.

Then Gerry was startled to find her purse, the small rectangular black one, lying against the side of the television. Had she, after all, returned while he was out looking for her, or had he missed it? He called her name. He opened the bathroom door. He flung open the shower stall. All dry as bone. He called her name down the hall. He returned to the room and opened the purse. Home keys still there, a compact with face powder, a small pad with pencil clasped at the border, nothing written on it. Remembering a scene from a TV movie, he lifted the first sheet to see if there was an impression, a clue on the second sheet, but this was no movie, there was no clue, it was all untouched. Inside the purse there was also a crumpled paper napkin with Club Revelation printed on it, and a small orange change purse with several Susan B. Anthony dollar coins. But her wallet was missing. Could there have been a robbery? Had Marylee resisted? Had she been harmed?

Gerry decided to give the situation an hour before he took any other action. He composed himself. He sat himself down on the bed, his hand on his knee next to the telephone ready to pick it up as soon as it rang. As he sat, he ransacked his memory for anything she had said that might give an indication of where she might be. She had said so little, however. They had simply agreed that he would return after the exhibition's opening reception—as always, she had no interest in attending—they would have a leisurely dinner, maybe that carriage ride. And then he had been hoping against hope to get to bed early and perhaps make long-delayed, long-missed love.

By the time the hotel detective arrived, Gerry was standing helplessly in the doorway reading and rereading the Do Not Disturb sign.

The detective, a short balding man in a blue suit, went through his litany of questions: Had anything unusual happened? Had there been a disagreement? A fight? Had they talked between the time they both checked in and when he returned to the room? No, he had been with customers nonstop. Did Marylee have any friends, relatives, even acquaintances in Philadelphia? Gerry was almost certain she did not; he shrugged and shook his head. Did Gerry mind if the detective looked around?

"Why would I mind?" Gerry said. "It's your hotel. Your hotel swallowed up my wife."

"That's not the way it happens, sir. I know you're distraught, so let me repeat the question: Do I have your permission to search the room?"

After he watched the man move methodically from the windows toward the center of the room and into the bathroom, he said, "What am I going to do?"

"Sit tight for now," the detective answered. "There are absolutely no signs of disturbance, the lock is intact, and all my favorite hotel thieves have taken the night off."

"Couldn't she have opened the door herself to someone other than—"

"Why would she open the door without asking who it was?"

Yes, even in her abstracted state, she would have asked, he was fairly certain of that.

"Mr. Levine?"

"Yes?"

"Try not to be too alarmed. She would have reported a robbery, wouldn't she? And even if she didn't, it's unlikely she was harmed. Hotel thieves—that is, *if* something happened here—rarely confront people. They're scared little burglars who like a well-dusted, pleasant environment in which to work and which we provide. They're basically antisocial creeps but not violent. They hear a noise, they don't do the deed. So even when you get robbed here, you're, so to speak, still nice and safe and in gentle thieving hands."

"I have no idea where she is."

"Well, I can assure you, Mr. Levine, that your wife is somewhere. It's not like you see on television. In Philadelphia people don't just disappear into thin air or a new dimension unless they're in the federal witness protection program. And even then they're usually in Idaho or Nevada or Arizona." As the detective spoke, he continued to lift pillows. He checked under the bed. "For some reason, the feds prefer states that end in vowels, except for Pennsylvania. Is your wife a federal witness?"

"Not to my knowledge."

"Just trying to lighten things up, Mr. Levine. Could she be out shopping?"

"She's not much of a shopper these days."

"What do you mean by 'these days'?"

Gerry shrugged, wanting to lapse into permanent silence like some of the martyrs Marylee had been reading about.

"The more you give me, Mr. Levine, the more I can help you. Maybe. Now tell me, are there things you can tell me about Mrs. Levine that I should know about?"

"She has not been interested in shopping in a while. She's been interested in . . . you know . . ."

"If I knew, would I ask, sir?"

"God."

"God?"

"Yes, religion. Bigtime."

"That's excellent. Now which God? I mean whose God?"

Gerry threw up his arms.

"If I may be so bold as to derive it from your name, you're Jewish. Synagogues? Could she have just gone off to one? They're usually closed at this hour, but maybe there is an evening cultural series somewhere. A concert? A lecture? Easy to check. Is that the kind of thing she might attend?"

"She's not Jewish. But you're right. I'm such an idiot. If she's anywhere, she'd be at some church."

"There are a lot of churches. Are you sure of your wife's religion, Mr. Levine? It's easier to find a missing Jew than a missing Christian. Far fewer of them."

Seized by an inspiration, Gerry went to the night table between the beds and pulled open the drawer. "You see! It's missing," he said.

"What?"

"Isn't there always a Bible, a Gideon's Bible, in every hotel room night table?"

"Usually."

"Well, this one is missing! Marylee took it."

"That's possible," the detective said. "It's also possible that the drawer might have been empty."

"I know she took it. She's at a church somewhere, clutching it in her hands and praying out on the front steps, even if the place is closed. Let's go."

In the lobby, the detective gave Gerry the option to call the police, but he preferred to get a list of nearby churches, which the detective provided, and to get a taxi to drive him around.

"I hope you find her," the detective said. "What do you think she's praying for?"

"Me," Gerry said. "You too. Probably all of us."

40

Gerry spent the rest of the day, half of the next, and $300 in taxi fare all around Philadelphia trying to find Marylee. Failing to locate her at any of the churches he went to (many were closed), he called Wiliam Harp, who gave him the address of one evangelical minister on the south side who had connections to his father. When Gerry went there, with Marylee's picture in hand, the minister, a gray-haired black man, did not recognize her. He said, however, that he would pray for them both, and he insisted on giving Gerry such a deeply felt hug that Gerry burst into tears.

Gerry returned to the hotel, found the detective, and asked him to advise the police to file a missing person report. Then, too unsure of his ability to concentrate, he garaged the Toyota and took a taxi to the train station.

During the ride back to New York, he sat staring out the window like a blind man. He would remember few details of this physical world that rushed before his eyes for an hour and a half—not the shabby trackside warehouses and machine shops or the forlorn empty billboards, not the occasional muddy suburban baseball field, not the streets with everyday houses, lawns, and cars. Gerry's eyes were desperately looking inward, ransacking the snapshots of their years together—a good life, with friends and comfort and travel, a life not without its unhappiness, but one to run from? He was looking for what he might have done differently and for where it all went wrong.

By the time he arrived at Penn Station, exhausted, full of foreboding, and feeling like an absolute stranger in the city where he had grown up, Gerry was certain that Marylee had left him.

"If she were leaving you," Ellen said to him in front of their building, where she had rushed out to embrace him when the taxi pulled up, "there would already be lawyers, papers, forms. You would have heard."

"Oh no! This is the way she would do it. She would leave first. Abruptly and dramatically. Without a word of warning. You know her. Suddenness is her style. The lawyers will come trooping by soon enough. The summons will arrive. She's left me."

"With your famous baptism looming? Would she leave you unconverted, Gerry?" Ellen asked. "Wouldn't she let you be converted first, and maybe *then* leave you? That way she'd have it all!"

Gerry was so consumed by a sense of grievous fault that he would not relent; she had left him, he was sure.

There had been no phone calls to Judy, Ellen, or to Marylee's few active business contacts; Gerry knew, because he went through her Rolodex and called each number. He called her mother in Virginia who, in a slurring voice, suggested that the minimum requirement of a husband was that he not lose track of the whereabouts of his wife. But, no, Marylee had not gone to Virginia, or even called.

With a week to go before the conversion ceremony, it was

becoming clear—no one had to say anything—that there could be no ceremony of any kind without Marylee.

Gerry lived in fear of the phone—everything it could do, its muteness and its shrieking ring, terrified him. Still, he forced himself to keep making the calls—what else could he do? The Philadelphia hotel detective and the New York City detectives returned his calls but kept on providing only a kind of canned reassurance that convinced Gerry they were reading from a script prepared for the families of all missing persons. In order to come up with something, the detectives all said, it would take time, a little more time.

That phrase kept going through Gerry's mind—a little time—as if time were a sausage that the detectives were thinly slicing up. *To the last syllable of recorded time.*

As the hours at home wore on, Gerry searched through Marylee's dresser, her Filofax, and especially the books in her Christian library, one by one, in case some lead might appear, a scrap of paper with an address perhaps of a secret lover between the pages. He fanned his hope with such searches, but they yielded absolutely nothing.

When there was nothing else to search and he found himself instead opening her closets and touching the blouses, skirts, and dresses hanging there, he gave in to Ellen, Sam, Judy, and Michael's insistence and stayed evenings with them. He took his meals most frequently with Ellen and Sam, except when Judy made him vegetarian chili and some other favorites. Yet these meals all felt like rituals of disappearance or the provision of favorite dishes before executions, or last suppers, and his appetite nearly disappeared.

He did not go to work, but spent his days waiting for news—what else was there to do? He gave in and sat *zazen* with Judy, but Gerry was so jumpy he could not remain on the pillow longer than five minutes, and his hands, instead of remaining still, one resting in the other, kept picking at each other, one finger pulling at the cuticle of another until it drew blood, as if the left hand were the enemy of the right.

Each night he paced up and down the common stairway of the brownstone, he walked the block hoping some clue might turn up, and then, one night when he returned to the building, he found himself not going up to the apartment but down the steps to Club Revelation. The forlorn restaurant, with its tables and chairs largely unused and full of thwarted expectancy, oddly comforted him. He cleaned, he swept, he went over William's accounts with him, and helped the young man to whom Marylee had been so close. He remembered *Wakefield,* and as he sat in the all-but-deserted restaurant, he wondered if Marylee were secretly observing him from the Antichrist's building across the street. From there might she not mark his devotion, and, beautiful as ever, with her heels and red beret and a shopping bag overflowing with new stuff from a store in Philadelphia, appear suddenly in the doorway, as Duct Tape Boy had, or the old Jewish hobo had, out of nowhere, seeking home?

"Do you think it at all possible," he asked William on the fourth night following Marylee's disappearance, "that she was, you know, elevatored up . . . swept up, swept away?"

"Raptured?"

"That's it. She talked about that a lot lately—thanks to you: *Two will be in the field; one will be taken and one will be left.* Well, maybe it's true after all. Maybe she was taken. Maybe she was just possessed of so much of this faith that she just evaporated into . . . I don't know what . . . heavenly vapors."

"She couldn't be raptured away, Mr. Levine, without a bunch of other believers. That's the theory. And anyway, it doesn't happen until the great Tribulation sets in, right before wars, famine, diseases, and disasters—the Four Horsemen of the Apocalypse arrive and herald the End of Days. That's when you get raptured away."

"Sounds like right now," Gerry said.

"I doubt it. I sure hope not." Then, spontaneously, in a voice both sweet and sad, which seemed to transport him back home and also very far away, William began to sing:

Jesus our Savior is a-coming to reign
And take you up to glory in His aeroplane.
There will be no punctures or muddy roads,
No broken axles from overloads,
No shocks to give trouble or cause delay
As we soon will rapture up the narrow way.

"Have faith," Billy said to him.

"Faith in what?" Gerry asked. "Which religion is best at locating missing persons?"

"I don't know. You might say Jesus is a kind of missing person."

"That's not very helpful."

"Story of my pastoral life. Can I tell you something? If it happened to her, if she got raptured away, then she somehow willed it. She did it *for* you. So you wouldn't have to go through with the baptism. She gave you your way out, Mr. Levine. So you could remain a Jew. I believe that. I truly do. She loves you, you know."

"She's left me because she loves me?" He just stared at William. "What am I not understanding here?"

"Marylee was overcome by the spirit. It's powerful. It does strange things, sometimes disturbing things that are difficult to understand, but there is a kind of inner logic to them, says my father, if we only can decipher it. It descended on her swiftly. I've never seen anything quite like it."

"So where is she? Where is my wife?"

"I don't know."

"If she's raptured," Ellen said to them on the fifth night after Marylee's disappearance, as they sat on the roof of the building on their old beanbags and rusting garden furniture hauled up from the Museum, "if that's what happened to her, then I am Harry Houdini." Both Sam's cell phones were back in his pockets, and Gerry had his portable with him in case anyone called.

The clarity of the sky over Manhattan and the lights from below somehow permitted half a dozen stars to peek through. "Keep heart, Gerry," Ellen said. "We've called everybody who is connected with anything in her life."

"And found nothing," Gerry said.

"That's good news; we've heard nothing bad either."

"I still have a bad feeling," said Gerry. "I can't get it out of my system. I let her get away from me. I let her down."

"We're ready to put up the pictures," Michael said. "I took care of all that. Five hundred of them."

"Not yet with the pictures," Judy said. "It's only been five days."

"Only," said Michael.

They sat and watched the stars, and then Ellen, who had some late papers to correct on her lap under a flashlight, read a few selections from those she was working away on in order to keep their minds off the grim possibilities. But none of the egregious student errors, not even that of the student who, in a paper on *Huckleberry Finn,* had described Jim as a "runway slave," could lighten the evening.

Ellen flicked off the flashlight, put her arm around Gerry, and tilted his chin up. "In the Greek myths, you know, the goddesses used to transform themselves into the heavens and become constellations. Andromeda, Cassiopeia. Can it be said that the goddesses are raptured?" Everyone was too despondent to reply. "Sorry," she said. "Bad taste. Something will turn up soon. I'm certain of it."

"I think we should go through with the baptism," Gerry said slowly.

"Come again?" Michael said.

"This is my theory. I think Marylee just took herself out of the scene. Deliberately. No one's taken her away. And she has not been raptured up, whatever that is. But she abducted herself from her own life. That's what she's done."

"Abducted from her own life? What on earth for?" Judy said.

"To see if we would go through with the conversion. Without her. To see if *I* will go through with the conversion on my own. We've all assumed she would be here, that she would practically preside with William. But now she's sending a message to me. A test."

"A test?" Sam said.

"Isn't that in character?" Gerry asked. "She didn't do this to excuse or liberate us, but to challenge us. Am I going to do it on my own? Are you guys going to do this on your own? If we go through with it, when she sees that, then she will reappear. That's the way to bring her back. Until then, she's . . ."

"Where? Precisely where is she?" Michael asked.

"Where the hell is she going to reappear *from?*" Sam wanted to know. "The Twilight Zone?"

"How do you know she's not right here, among us already?" Gerry said. They all looked at him patiently; they all knew he had been eating very little; they all were on their best behavior to encourage him. "I mean in the neighborhood. Maybe she's rented an apartment across the street like that guy in the story you're always talking about." He looked at Ellen as she spoke.

"*Wakefield*. Nathaniel Hawthorne. Puritan story."

"Yes," Gerry said. "He leaves his wife of ten years—"

"Twenty," Ellen said.

"—and nobody knows where he has gone. They look high and low for the guy, but nothing. No sign of death, but also no report, no word. But he was right across the street checking up on her virtue all the time."

"No one has to check up on your husbandly virtue," Judy said. "You're top of the line."

"You can let it go now," Michael said. "You don't have to become a Christian."

"Still, I feel—it's really odd—that she's far away but close, watching at the same time."

"Listen," said Sam, squatting down beside his friend. "Even *I* prefer the rapture stuff to this Puritan *bobbeh meisa* by Nathaniel Hawthorne. But if you really want us to walk across the street and knock on every door, we'll do it for you, Gerry. We'll start with the Antichrist's building and then hit every other building that looks in over us."

"She's sick, Gerry," said Michael. "I don't know if Jesus made her sick or we did or what, but she's wandered off somewhere. She's lost, and, God help us, we will soon find her. I can give you some Valium to help you sleep."

"She's testing me," Gerry said.

"Test's over," said Sam.

41

William Harp, in khakis, sneakers, a casual sweater, and large backpack, knocked on Gerry's door very early the following morning. He was sorry to disturb. Gerry told him there was nothing to disturb because he had not been able to sleep at all. He had not slept in forty-eight hours. There had been no word, not one ray of light in the darkness of what had happened to Marylee Jeffers Levine.

"Almost nothing could make me leave now with Marylee out there," William said, "but at six this morning, they called to tell me my father's going very fast."

"I'm sorry to hear that. You should have gone down there a long time ago."

"I think he's waiting for me."

"I've heard that sometimes happens. You seem to be a devoted son."

"I'm flawed. We're all flawed. So there will be no conversion, Mr. Levine. Not by me, anyway. And you must know I never wanted to do it. You will remain always and forever one of *Am Yisroel.*"

"Listen to you! I can always go someplace else to convert."

"I don't think you will."

"I would have. I would have done anything for her. I will still do anything. But look at me! There's nothing I can do. Where should I go? Tell me. You're her minister. What should I do? What happened to her, William? What really happened?"

"The spirit filled her up. That's all I know. And when that happens, a person's behavior can change. It becomes more than unpredictable; it's like a new internal guidance system. I've been ransacking my brain to guess where she might have gone or what might have happened. She was filled up with the spirit strong enough for six people. She didn't say a word to me for the last week, but she was radiating this light, Mr. Levine. Did you see it? She was following the light."

"What does that mean? How will that help me find her?"

"I don't know. Resist imagining the worst and maybe let her find you. When she's ready."

"And the restaurant?"

"Just close it down, Mr. Levine. Just like we talked about. I've been traveling on empty, on fumes in that department, for a very long time. You know that."

"I think I do."

"As soon as I'm through with my business at home, I'll come back to take care of the fixtures and all. I'll sell everything. But I'm going to see if we can't pay the rent through the end of the lease. It's only fair. I will not run off."

"Don't worry about any of that."

"Club Revelation's fit right in, hasn't it, with Curry by Murray? I'm sorry, Gerry—I hope you don't mind if I call you Gerry. I'm really sorry for all the trouble I've caused."

Gerry just stared at him; William felt himself as porous and insubstantial as an hourglass that Gerry was about to turn. "I've been calling everybody I can think of. I've been looking for a clue to give you. But there's nothing. I blame myself if anything happens to her."

"Don't rush away from your family if they need you. We're not going to throw anything out and we're not about to rent right away. You can imagine how far that is from my mind." Gerry calmly looked at the boy. He felt no rancor. He felt quite the opposite, a weary affection. "Take all the time you need."

William looked at his watch. He had little more than forty minutes to get to La Guardia, but he had the feeling that despite everything, Gerry wanted him to linger and to talk to him. "It's strange," Gerry said, "I've lost Marylee, and now somehow I feel that I'm losing you. Everything I touch I hurt, and then I lose. Eventually, I lose everybody."

"I will be coming back, Gerry. And not only because I want to see Marylee—I *know* I will see her again. I know it!" Here William reached out and grasped Gerry's forearm and tried to squeeze some of his own confidence into Gerry's bones. "I will see her." He squeezed hard. "You will too."

"You have to go now. The restaurant will wait. Sam will be only too happy to padlock it for you and keep the stuff safe for whatever you want to do next. Michael will write a big OUT OF BUSINESS sign for the window. You'll be giving them immense pleasure."

42

Judy and Ellen had done many odd jobs in their lives, but they never had been asked to ship a snake home before. Yet that's precisely what they were now engaged in doing on the sixth day after Marylee's disappearance. It was a relief to be distracted by this specific task; for the job kept at bay, if barely, the rising fear that something terrible had in fact happened to their friend.

They had found two young men from AirborneRep.com, a reptile transportation service—Ellen was always amazed that you could find absolutely anything in New York City—to send Annabelle home to Virginia. William had not wanted to ask them, but he had left so quickly—he actually had called from the plane, in flight over Delaware—when he realized how much it would mean to his father to have the snake by his sickbed.

They now watched as Annabelle, all seven-and-a-half cool, mottled green and brown feet of her, was carefully lifted from the glass tank near the baptismal tub in the back of the restaurant and delivered, with only one lunging wriggle of resistance, into the waiting crate.

"You get the feeling she's staring at us?" Ellen said.

"She can stare all she wants—I think that's the impression any animal gives when its eyes are at the sides of its head. I wouldn't take it personally."

"I'm absolutely certain she's staring at us."

"Yes? What does she seem to be trying to communicate to you, Ellen?"

"She's got this look that stretches back all the way through the generations, down through all the species—you know, 'male and female He created them'—back to the Garden of Eden. And she's saying, 'I came between the first husband and wife way back then, and I did the same thing right here in your brownstone.'"

"Don't cling to such a thought," Judy advised Ellen. "Forget about it and fill out this form."

"She's thinking about what she did to Gerry and Marylee: 'Whatever this woman was to this man for twenty long years may not have been perfect,' she's thinking, 'but I knew something about the woman that the husband did not know, and I planted a poison seed in there and I destroyed them. Right before your very eyes.'"

"Just shut up please, Ellen, and help me clean up this mess."

"And she's saying something else. The snake's turning that little cold pupil of hers on me and she is saying, 'You screwed up, bitch. You didn't take care of your best friend.'"

Having finished with the forms, Judy and Ellen watched as the men transported the crated reptile out of the restaurant and up the steps to their double-parked van. They followed, signed two more documents at the truck, and then Ellen, staring in through the side window until she caught the snake's eye, said to Annabelle, "I hope you enjoy the movie."

They re-entered the restaurant, empty now of both William and Annabelle, and began to push all the tables and chairs to the sides of the main room in preparation for a major sweeping and vacuuming. The women stood under the dark and mute projection screen, which hung down by its cable from the ceiling above them like some forlorn electronic tonsil waiting to be extracted. They looked at each other for a moment and then rolled up their sleeves and began to clean.

That evening they would join Michael and Sam to distribute the ten-by-twelve-inch posters with Marylee's photograph on them.

On the morning after the seventh day of his wife's disappearance, Gerry stood impatiently waiting for his old printer to finish the last lines of the e-mail message from Israel.

JULY 3, 2000

Dear Mr. Levine:

Per my conversation with you last night, I hope you will be comforted in the knowledge that your wife, Marylee, is well and here in our care at the clinic at Kfar Shmuel just outside Jerusalem.

As I explained to you over the phone, the police brought her to our attention four days ago under circumstances that it would perhaps be better to describe to you in more detail in person.

Suffice it to say that she had been wandering for two or three days throughout the holy sites of the Old City and was suffering from what has been termed Jerusalem Syndrome. She had temporarily lost a sense of her own identity and asserted to the police and then to us that she was Mary on her way to Nazareth to redeliver Jesus Christ. We are familiar with such temporary breaks from reality, which sometimes afflict pilgrims and first-time visitors to Jerusalem—this is the eponymous condition.

Speaking with Marylee in these terms, that is, not contradicting but endeavoring to understand the belief system she was entertaining at the moment, which our therapists are adept at, helped us eventually in identifying your wife and in suggesting pharmacological and psychotherapeutic interventions to make her well. Rest assured that we have treated her with both utmost respect for her religious convictions as well as for her physical condition.

We treated your wife with modest doses of anti-psychotic drugs, which, along with talking therapies, have proved their effectiveness in these situations.

While each case is unique and it is hard to know at this point how Mrs. Levine's will progress, we are happy to report that, after twelve hours, she awoke sufficiently to her sense of herself to provide enough information so that the police could trace your name, address, and phone number. This, as you know, permitted us to contact you.

In closing, permit me to restate the importance of your bringing not only a selection of her clothes, but also other personal items—books, some photographs, perhaps a memento or object of emotional resonance—that will help to re-anchor Mrs. Levine in her life.

I look forward to seeing you within a day or so.

Sincerely,

Dr. Ehud Ben Moshe
Director

A few days later, an e-mail arrived on Ellen's computer.

JULY 8, 2000

Dear Ellen, Sam, Judy, and Michael:

Jerusalem is beautiful, and so is Marylee. She improves daily but still doesn't seem to have any recollection of how, armed only with the clothes on her back, she got herself all the way from the Liberty Bell to the Mount of Olives. She has begun to ask about home, that is, our building and the neighborhood and New York.

She is talking a great deal about Virginia too, and she has spoken on the phone to her mother. She asks about the restaurant and William Harp and she seemed sad when I told her what had happened. But Dr. Ben Moshe (aka Dr. Milton Goldfarb, formerly of Pittsburgh, Pennsylvania) says never to shy away from giving a truthful answer to all her questions. She needs the truth, but to use Dr. Ben Moshe's phrase, one dollop at a time. So I don't go on and on about things but try to address specific answers to her specific questions.

We sit in the garden and read—I do the reading because she is still too weak to read herself—but she is eager to listen. So don't be shy about sending letters: you can e-mail care of the clinic's address, and they will give the messages to us.

Dr. Ben Moshe says Marylee will soon be remembering you all; that is, that memory returns often in levels, like an elevator ascending back up to the level from which it suddenly dropped.

I know she sends her love and she enjoyed the oatmeal cookies Michael baked. Ellen, the album of photographs from the Museum—especially the wild way we looked in the Sixties and the renovations of the brownstone over the years—was also a big hit.

Now here's the most momentous news of all: while there have been dozens of people over the years who come to Jerusalem and become afflicted with the idea that they are Mary, pregnant with Jesus, our Marylee—she is, after all, a Mary—is the very first one who is actually pregnant. I kid you not, my oldest and most wonderful friends. In capital letters: WE ARE PREGNANT. About three and a half months, according to Dr. Ben Moshe (he had to bring in a gynecologist to examine Marylee). Both mother- and child-to-be are doing fine. Due in the fall, around Christmas, or should I say, Hanukah? Or both. Due, in any event, when the winter arrives and the streets of the Upper West Side become beautiful in the snow.

Let me tell you her exact words when I told her she was pregnant. She was uncomprehending at first—you know that look she has of not wanting to be put on. It takes a long time to develop, like an eclipse, and then it just rises and her eyes transfix you like the face of the moon on a clear night. She turned her head toward me and she said, "It's a miracle, Gerry. It's really a miracle after all."

All I can say is, Keep up that good old Christian celibacy like we did and maybe it will happen to you as well.

Home in a couple of weeks.

With love,

Gerry and Marylee

Dear Gerry and Marylee,

We are writing one consolidated letter here
so you can read it to Marylee and be done
with all of us in one swoop.

Michael of course wants to know if you
are going to raise the kid Jewish. According
to catechisms or whatever they are of the
Reform Judaism folks, he begs me to
inform you, the child is already considered
Jewish if either of the parents is. So if you're
losing sleep in this department, don't;
you're covered.

However, according to the Conservatives,
for whom descent must be strictly matrilineal
for the child to be Jewish, a conversion ceremony will be necessary for the momma-to-be.
No need to even leave the comforts of home,
Michael says. We have our own baptismal
tub—haven't sold it, although we have an
antique dealer up in Hudson interested in
making an offer. The tub is easily convertible
into a *mikveh.*

But, seriously, dear friends, we miss you
and are looking forward to seeing you soon.

Some other news: Nawang is back and
has brought a new sheep. My highly observant husband—observant both in Jewish
practice (a lot less, thank God) but also in

the other ironic meaning intended, missing what's right under his own nose—has discovered that modest Nawang is not only a meditation teacher but also the cultural attaché of the island of Vuruda, a country so small, so poor, so beleaguered and riven by religious strife that he has had to live with us in secrecy and obscurity as to his identity. Thus the basement! No embassy, no nothing, and even Sam did not know about it. Many of the people he greeted, under the guise of teaching meditation, were his countrymen.

You see, Vuruda apparently worships the spirit as contained in one particular species of sheep, which is why his sheep's loss was so traumatic. This is also why, Judy found out, he had to spend so much time away on his island, where, with the help of other elders and teachers, he was able to identify the next sheep in whose body the previous holy animal's spirit is reincarnated.

The problem has been—and this is why he has been hiding with us—that another Buddhist sect from a nearby island hostile to the Vurudans worships another variety of sheep, and the holy animal was always in danger. You get the picture, I'm sure. And all that taking place right under our nose!

With Nawang's return, Judy is back to being herself again and Sam now has, literally, in our own backyard, such a great human interest story that more funding has already come through—thanks to Nawang—in addition to the pharmaceutical company. Nawang and the sheep will soon certainly be co-stars in *The World's Smallest Nations,* the documentary. Hallelujah.

Speaking of hallelujah, are you ready for this: William Harp has just written us that he will be returning to New York soon. His father died and he has a lot to do settling the estate. However, he is racing to return not only to deal with the restaurant. He has fallen head-over-heels in love with Rena, the Orthodox Jewish electrician—this explains why Club Revelation had to be rewired seventeen times! The girl's father, of course, is sending a Hasidic hit squad after William, but either they better hurry or it won't be necessary, because William is preparing to convert to Judaism. I kid you not, folks. The girl is meeting him halfway—no more Hasidism for her—the ceremony will be at that Reform congregation, B'nai Luria, where you greeted the Sabbath Bride what seems about a thousand years ago.

Michael continues to believe that God is truly a middle-aged woman with a braid who is a Mets fan. When the spirits have not descended on him, however, when he is in a plain old normal mood, he sends you his plain old normal love, and lots of it.

Inspired by you, he and Judy are going back to the fertility clinic to see what's what.

And I will settle for being godparent for any and all children crazy enough to come to live under this roof.

Hurry back, kids—that's a quote from Sam. He says his serve is rusty as an old can and he can't wait for Tuesday night tennis to begin once again.

With love,

Ellen

Good books are brewing
at coffeehousepress.org